D1025089

Praise for A.K. Wilder's

"An epic tale of intrigue, adventure, and romance.
I adored *Crown of Bones* with all my phantom-loving heart!"
—Pintip Dunn, *New York Times* bestselling author of *Malice*

"An imaginative, immersive journey to lift the spirits! There is nothing so engrossing as writing and characters with soul—*Crown of Bones* is abundant in both and will keep you enthralled to the end!"
—Traci Harding, bestselling author of The Ancient Future series

"If you like fast-paced action, a close-knit band of friends with powerful animistic magic, a smart, courageous heroine, and a superhero from the deeps of the sea—then do not wait!
Raise AK Wilder's *Crown of Bones* and read!"
—Gemmell Morningstar award winner Helen Lowe

"This book has it all—breathtaking adventure and compelling characters that weave into a rich fantasy world.
I dare you to put it down."
—Meg Kassel, author of *Black Bird of the Gallows*

"A magnificent tale of magic, villains, and heroes.
Highly recommend!"
—Merrie Destefano, award-winning author of *Valiant*

Crown of Bones

A.K. Wilder

Entangled Publishing, LLC
10940 S Parker Road
Suite 327
Parker, CO 80134
rights@entangledpublishing.com

Entangled Teen is an imprint of Entangled Publishing, LLC.

Visit our website at www.entangledpublishing.com.

Edited by Liz Pelletier and Heather Howland
Cover design by Covers by Juan
Background art designed by
L.J. Anderson/Cover Mayhem Creations and
Kevin Carden/AdobeStock,
camilkuo/shutterstock,
Susanitah/shutterstock,
Stanislav Spirin/Shutterstock,
ZaZa Studio/shutterstock,
Standret/Shutterstock
Map art by Kim Falconer
Chapter graphic art by Anna Campbell
Interior design by Toni Kerr

ISBN 978-1-64063-414-5
Ebook ISBN 978-1-64063-413-8

Manufactured in the United States of America

First Edition January 2021

10 9 8 7 6 5 4 3 2 1

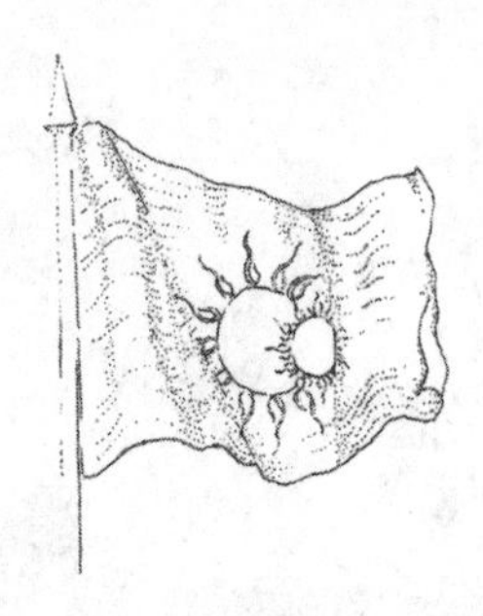

For all the fantasy readers, first-timers to die-hards,
who are willing to step out of their reality
and be lost in another world…

AVON EYRE
STEEPWATER
MORAB
TOKEN BAY
GOLLNAR
ASYLEEN
MANTA BAY
KUTOON
WHITEWING
TANGEEN

TUTAPA

LEPSEA
SIERRAK
ISLE OF AKU
MT BLADON
NORTHERN ATURNIA
NAVREN RIVER
FERUS RIVER
OTEB
CAPPER POINT
CLEARWATER
SOUTHERN ATURNIA
GLEEMARIE
PANDOM CITY
BLACK DART CHANNEL
PALRIO
TORETTA
SUNI RIVER
CABAZON
BAKTON
BAISEEN
NONNOVA

Hierarchy of the Robes

Black Robe
Red Robe
Orange Robe
Yellow Robe
Green Robe
Blue Robe
Brown Robe
Non-Savant

Si Er Rak Tablet - Fragment XI

Natsari, Natsari, where hides the crown?
The forests are burning, the children are drowned.
Natsari, Natsari, bring the dark sun,
Kiss us farewell, the Great Dying's begun…

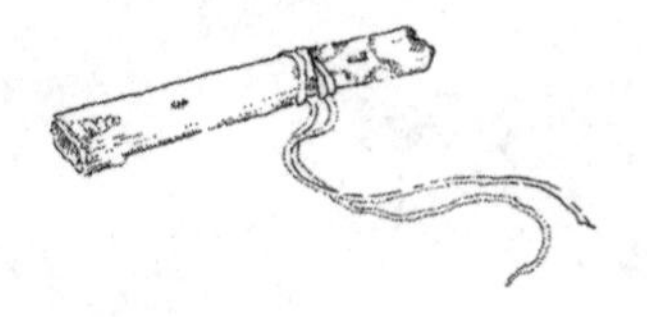

PROLOGUE

MASTER BROGAL

The Sanctuary bursts with children this time of year, untrained pups bounding through the halls, chasing their tails. They arrive full of hope, and why wouldn't they? 'Tis no small feat to be marked by the Bone Throwers as having potential. The question is, how many among them will actually succeed?

I look over the training ground and sigh, knowing it will be far too few.

My group, for example, not a *savant* among them. "Enough!" I clap. "Break for lunch."

They jump and cheer like a festival riot, and all I can do to remain calm is pinch the bridge of my nose. "Quiet. Midday silence will be observed."

I'm about to wave them to the dining hall when shouting rings out from the other end of the field. A flash of light shoots as high as the watchtower. Dirt pummels down like rain. The ground cleaves apart, fracturing in tremors that echo up through my feet. A brilliant, cresting form, ever shifting, pushes free, its mouth open in an earsplitting screech. I stumble and cover my ears as the sheer power of it hits me.

"Stay here!"

I drop one knee to the ground and raise my phantom before taking off toward the chaos. From the earth bursts my phantom, *C'sen*, red sparks trailing from blue wings as it soars overhead. *"Go!"*

From phantom's-eye view, I don't believe what I see. Huge. Writhing. A swarm of tendrils, claws, and limbs. But the mountainous phantom melts back into the ground before I can identify more, returning to its savant as quickly as it rose.

Left behind is a crater, deep as a man is tall and twice as wide. Around it, tiny red flowers bloom, spreading like spilled blood.

"Rune bands!" I call out to the black-robe Bone Thrower racing to meet me.

The hairs on the back of my neck rise. Never in all my years have I had to ask for them, but whatever has risen, it must be contained.

The child responsible sits at the far side of the crater, hunched. Cowl up. Unidentifiable. "Is it the Heir?" I whisper to the Bone Thrower. *Please, don't let it be the Heir.*

The black-robe shakes her head and hands me bone bracelets from her bag. "A girl from the harbor district. Raised it on the first try."

I trod over the fresh flowers to reach her, the scent of sweet lilac filling the air. "Show me your arms." She does and I cuff her thin wrists, my own hands trembling. "Where's her instructor?"

The Bone Thrower points at the crater, and I peer over the edge. There's a scrap of orange cloth at the bottom, all that's left of their savant robes.

"What is your name?" I ask the girl.

She doesn't answer. Just lifts tearstained eyes to mine. "Did I do it, Master? Did I raise my phantom?"

She's not even sure? "Stand up, child. Don't move." I wave to the savants converging on us. "Begin the guardian's chant." They form a semicircle behind her, robes swaying over the ground, voices rising in harmony.

I know what must be done, but still, I hesitate. The thought of what this might do to the girl—to all those around her—and by my own hand, no less…

"There's no alternative," the Bone Thrower says. "Bind it and *call* their memories. It must happen now."

My chest constricts. "What if the binding fails?"

The Bone Thrower wavers. "Then may the old gods have mercy on us all."

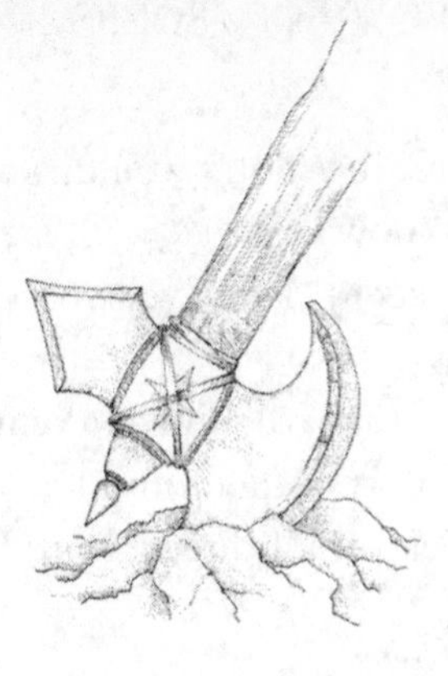

1

MARCUS

Nine years later…

Morning light blasts through the woods and I squint. "There! To the south."

I urge Echo, my black palfrey, on to greater speed, and the hunting dogs falling behind. We gallop hard, neck and neck with True, my brother's mount, careening around giant oaks and jumping over fallen logs. Autumn leaves scatter in our wake.

"They're headed for the meadow," Petén calls over the pounding hooves. His dark hair streams behind him, revealing his high forehead, an Adicio family trait. I've got it, too, but not quite as pronounced as his.

We're alike in other ways—same tall, broad build, brown eyes, and olive skin, though my hair is the color of brass, not black. Also, Petén's nineteen, two years older than me, and non-savant—he can't raise a phantom. It's a blow to him, for sure, because I am savant and therefore Heir to the Throne of Baiseen, a fact that turns everything between us sour.

"Head them off." I signal toward the upcoming sidetrack.

"So you can beat me there and win all the praise?"

I laugh at that. Father's not going to hand out praise for anything I do, even catching Aturnian spies, if that's what the trespassers really are. Besides, palace guards are coming from the south and will likely reach them first, so I don't know what Petén's talking about. He's right, though—I wouldn't mind being the one to stop them, just in case Father is watching. "Race you. Loser takes the sidetrack!"

He nods, and our mounts tear up the path for a short, breakneck sprint. Echo wins by half a length, and I stand up in my stirrups, victorious, waving Petén off to the right. On I gallop. It's a straight, downhill run toward the meadow. When I reach the open grass, there's a clear shot at the three men who race on foot.

"Halt in the name of the Magistrate!" I fit an arrow to my bow and fire it over their heads, a warning shot. I wouldn't actually shoot anyone in the back, but they don't know that.

"Halt in the name of Baiseen!" Petén yells, bursting into the meadow from the north.

The hunted men veer to the left and keep running. Petén lets loose his arrow, and it lands just short of them, another warning.

I'm close enough to pick off all three. "Halt!" I shout, hoping they do this time.

They don't.

My brother and I barrel down on them, and in moments, we've corralled the men, trotting our horses in a tight circle, arrows aimed at the captives in the center. The dogs catch up and bark savagely, ready to attack.

"Stay," I command the two wolfhounds, and they obey, crouching in the grass, their tongues hanging out to the side as they lick their chops and growl.

"Drop your weapons," Petén says just as Rowten and his contingent of palace guards, three men and two women, gallop into the field from the other end. Chills rush through me as Father appears behind them, riding his dark-red hunter. The captives unbuckle their sword belts and raise their hands as the guards join us, further hemming them in.

"Why are you here?" Father asks as he rocks back in the saddle. He turns to Petén. "Search their gear, if you are sober enough for the job." To me, he says, "If any move, kill them."

Sweat breaks out on my brow, and a tremor runs down my arms. My brother's not all that sober. In fact, he usually isn't. If he provokes them…

But Petén swings out of the saddle without falling on his face, and I keep my arrow aimed at each man in turn while he goes through their packs. They have a distance viewer and a map of Baiseen marking where our troops are quartered, the watchtowers, and the Sanctuary with numbers in the margin.

"Scouting our defenses?" Father asks. "Who sent you?"

Officially, we're not at war with the neighboring realms of Aturnia and Sierrak to the north or Gollnar to the northwest. But that doesn't mean one of their red-robe masters isn't behind this. Tann or even Atikis. Relations are strained to near breaking if the long council meeting I sat through yesterday was any indication, and Father suspects breaches on the border. Like this one.

The captives remain silent, which doesn't help their case.

"Answer." I try to sound authoritative. "Or do you not know who questions you? Bow to Jacas Adicio"—I nod to my father—"orange-robe savant to the wolf phantom, Magistrate of all Palrio, and lord of the Throne of Baiseen."

The middle one lifts his head. He's not dressed in the robes of a savant or an Aturnian scout. He wears traveler's garb: leggings, tunic, riding coat, and high boots without a hint of mud. Their horses can't be far away. "We're lost, Your Magistrate, sir. Meaning no harm or trespass. If you just set us straight, we'll be on our way."

It's a fair attempt at diplomacy, but unfortunately for this poor clod, his accent betrays him.

"All the way from Aturnia? You are *indeed* lost." My father turns to me. "Did you track them down, Marcus?"

My chest swells as I start to answer. "It was—"

"I led the chase," Petén cuts in as if I wasn't going to give him half the credit. Which I was…probably.

"Fine," Father says, though he doesn't seem particularly pleased. I can't remember the last time he was anything but frustrated with either of us. But then, it's no secret he's not been the same since my eldest brother was deemed marred. Losing his first son changed Father irrevocably.

While I blink sweat out of my eyes, the nearest captive makes to drop to one knee.

"Savant!" I shout.

"Shoot!" my father roars in command.

He means me.

I have the shot, ready and aimed, and I should have taken it by now. But the man is ten feet away. If I hit him at this range, with an arrow made to drop an elk, it'll stream his guts all over the meadow.

In the moment I hesitate, my father is out of his saddle and touching down to one knee. The second he does, the ground explodes, a rain of dirt and rock showering us. The horses' heads fly up, ears pinning back, but they hold position as Father's phantom lunges out of the earth. The size of a dire wolf, it opens its mouth, lips pulling back in a snarl. Still not clear of the ground, it begins to "*call*," a haunting, guttural sound that can draw weapons from a warrior, water from a sponge, flesh from bone. Before the phantom lands, the men's chests crack open in a spray of blood. Three hearts, still beating, tear out of their torsos and shoot straight into the phantom's mouth. It clamps its jaws and swallows them whole without bothering to chew.

Entranced by the brutality, my fingers spasm, and the arrow flies from the bow. Its distinct red fletches whistle as it arcs high and wide over one of the guard's heads, a woman who gives me an unpleasant look. The arrow falls, skipping through the grass to land harmlessly a distance away.

No one speaks as the horses settle and Rowten signals for the dogs to be leashed. I breathe heavily, staring at the corpses. Blood wells the cavities that were, moments ago, the bodies of three living men. Aturnian spies, most likely, but living men just the same.

By the bones, I feel sick. What if I got it wrong? What if the man had simply gone weak in the knees and wasn't dropping to raise his phantom at all? What if he really was non-savant, lost, virtually harmless to us? I cried out the warning that led to these deaths. What does that say about me?

"Peace be their paths," Rowten says, and we all echo the traditional saying for when someone dies. The path to An'awntia is the spiritual road everyone treads, though us savants are supposedly much further along.

I'm not so sure in my case.

When I look to Petén, I find him staring at the bodies as well, until he turns away and throws up in the grass. Somehow that makes me feel better, though I don't think it has the same effect on our father, judging by his expression.

Father examines the dead men's weapons. "Aturnian," he says and lowers gracefully to one knee. His phantom melts away as he brings it back in. It's a relief. Phantoms don't usually scare me, not those of our realm, but this one's different, more powerful, and so much better controlled than most. It's merciless. If Father had continued training at the Sanctuary, he'd be a red-robe by now, and not very many savants ever reach that high level. I shudder at the thought.

Before mounting up, he turns to Rowten. "Take the dogs and find their horses. Then call for the knacker to deal with this mess." In an easy motion, he's back on the hunter, shaking his head as he turns to me. "You raise a *warrior* phantom, Marcus. When will you start acting like it?"

Heat rushes to my face, and Petén, wiping his mouth on his sleeve, chuckles. Any warmth I felt for my brother moments ago vanishes.

"Ride with me, both of you," Father commands.

The road home is short and agonizing as we flank Father, one on either side.

"Petén, if I catch the reek of alcohol on your breath again, I'll take away your hunting privileges for so long, you'll forget how to ride."

"Yes, Father," he says quietly. "Sorry."

My lips curl until Father turns to me.

"Marcus," he says, his voice like a newly sharpened knife. "You know war is inevitable—if not now then certainly by the time you are meant to take the throne. Baiseen needs your *warrior!*"

It's a subtle reminder of my failings. "Yes, Father."

"If you can't master your phantom soon, you'll lose your vote on the Council as well as your right to succeed me." His eyes narrow. "You know this?"

"I do."

"Then why are you acting so bones-be-cursed *weak*?"

I couldn't choke out an answer if I had one. Even Petén looks away. My eyes drop to Echo's mane as it ripples down her neck. When I look up, Father's face turns to stone. He cracks his reins over the hunter's rump and gallops away.

Petén and I trot the horses back toward the palace. We crest a gentle rise to come out on the hill overlooking the expanse of Baiseen. The view takes in the high stone walls and gardens of the palace, the watchtowers and bright-green training field in the center of the Sanctuary, all the way down the terraced, tree-lined streets to the harbor and the white-capped emerald sea beyond. It's beautiful, but no matter where I look, those three dead men seep back into my mind.

"If they were spies, then war's coming sooner than we thought." I ease Echo to a halt. "But if they weren't, we'll have to—"

"We?" Petén cuts me off. "Keeping the peace when Father tempts war is your problem, little brother, not mine." He chuckles. "If you make it to Aku in time, that is." His face cracks wide with a smile. "This year's your last chance, isn't it?"

I open my mouth to answer, but he's already pushing past me, loping the rest of the way down to the stables.

Yes, it's my last chance, the last training season on Aku before I turn eighteen. That's when our High Savant, head of the Sanctuary, will hand me over to the black-robes if I haven't held my phantom to form. It would mean no initiate journey. No chance to gain the rank of yellow-robe or higher. No future voice at the council. No Heir to the Throne of Baiseen.

No trained *warrior* to help protect my realm.

The weight on my shoulders grows heavier. I know my father. He'll not let this incident with the spies go, and his actions may finally bring the northern realms down upon us. My thoughts lift back to those three nameless men. When I close my eyes, I can still see their shocked faces, hear bones cracking as their chests split open, smell the blood spattering the ground.

War draws near. And if our enemies are infiltrating our lands, I may already be too late.

2

ASH

The hall outside Master Brogal's chambers is dead quiet, except for my growling stomach. It wants breakfast, or maybe it's still queasy after the voyage back from Tangeen, but the High Savant's request came at first light, delivered by phantom, no less. *Come here, Ash. Do that, Ash*. Ahh, the glorious life of a lowly scribe. I'm not complaining, not really; I love my work. My days are spent poring over books, reading old tomes, studying the histories of the realms and logging the events of our Sanctuary. I've spent years becoming a recorder.

I look down at my feet, which are bare, and frown. Bad morning to forget my boots. Especially with who is walking toward me.

There's no way to avoid her, so I finger-comb my hair, trying to remember if I washed my face since docking before sunrise. At least I changed into a fresh dress, though nothing so plush as the girl's who stops in front of me.

"Ash?"

I want to groan, but instead I respond with what I hope passes for polite interest. "Good morning, Rhiannon." I lift my chin so I match her height.

Rhiannon, the treasurer's daughter, with her fine lace and pearl buttons peeking from the hem and cuffs of her robe, pushes a long, strawberry-blond curl back from her brow. If her attire didn't announce a high rank and standing, the attitude would.

She gives me an indulgent smile. "You're back."

Well, if we're going to state the obvious… "I am."

And just like that, we run out of things to say.

Even though we've attended classes together since we were little, there's a world between us, for a variety of reasons, one being because Rhiannon is savant and…

"You are not?" My inner voice finishes the sentence for me.

Thanks.

This voice is part of me, popping up at times like a sibling might—sometimes snarky, sometimes mean, but always supportive when I really need it. Almost always, anyway. I thought at first it meant I had a phantom, but Master Brogal straightened that out right away. Phantoms use no voice until well *after* they are raised, he said. Then he waved me off, claiming the voice in my head was my way of compensating for not having a phantom.

I couldn't look him in the eye for some time after that. It hurt so much.

Because I *could* have been savant. The Bone Thrower marked me as a potential and sent me to the Sanctuary to trial.

"Sometimes the Bone Throwers get it wrong," Master Brogal often says—too often, in my opinion. I think he means it to be comforting, but it's not. Nor does it help when he says savants are further along the path than ordinary folk. Most of the population is born non-savant, and happy enough, but to be honest, that's not me. I try to convince myself he just means I'm progressing at my own pace, but such lofty rationale doesn't always stick. Like now, for instance.

Rhiannon's phantom, a fluffy little meerkat with tawny fur and a black mask, comes out from behind her robe. It sits up on its haunches and chirrups at me.

I click my tongue and wave a little hello.

"Come here." Rhiannon pats her thigh, calling it back to her side. She doesn't seem fond of how her phantom behaves around me, and I have to admit, it *is* odd, considering no one would mistake us for friends. But the head chef has a theory. She says that in other realms, non-savants who attract phantoms are called pets. I've not gotten up the nerve to ask Master Brogal about it. He's not exactly welcoming of my questions.

"All phantoms delight in you," my inner voice says, confirming the idea.

I don't know about *all*, or even delight, exactly, but phantoms everywhere do seem to find me interesting. Still, it's not the same as raising one of my own.

"Why do you still long for what is beyond your path?"

I don't!

"I think you do..."

Rhiannon snaps her fingers in front of me, an irritated expression on her face. "Did you not hear what I said?"

Nope. Not a word. *You?* I wait a moment but all is silent. Leave it to my inner voice to choose this moment to go mute.

She huffs. "Ash, I wanted to ask—"

The heavy door to Master Brogal's chambers creaks open, interrupting whatever Rhiannon might've said next. She glances up, pursing her lips. "Goodbye, then."

With that, she spins and stalks away.

The tightness in my body relaxes as she disappears around the corner. I wonder what she wanted. Maybe she's hoping to get close to Marcus again? Last time she tried to set me and him at odds, it didn't work out so well for her. Later, she shamelessly pursued him, or was it the throne that attracted her so much? But when Marcus lost interest, Rhiannon blamed me. Of course, I wasn't exactly supportive of the match…

"Ash." Nun, Master Brogal's assistant, looms over me, his sculpted face as unreadable as ever. "He's waiting."

I duck under Nun's arm and he leaves, pulling the door shut behind me.

Inside, Master Brogal nods me toward a chair and keeps writing, his quill scratching the parchment in an elegant, unhurried script. He's bent behind his desk and seems to have shrunk since I left for Tangeen. There's more of his forehead revealed, golden tan contrasting his straight white hair that falls to his shoulders. Is it thinning? Surely, he hasn't aged so much, but it is a rare chance that I have to study him this closely.

I sit opposite him and wait until he puts down the quill and sets his parchment aside to dry. I'd planned to broach a difficult topic on return, one close to my heart. My apprenticeship is coming to an end, and I want to further my studies, so I might become a wordsmith and take my place as a valued member of the Sanctuary. I've rehearsed my request—many times. But doubt floods in at the last second. Maybe this conversation can wait.

"That's what you said last time…"

Um.

"And the time before that."

My inner voice is good at keeping track.

Fine. I'll do it!

Master Brogal temples his fingers and turns his expectant gaze to me. "You found something in the Pandom City archives?"

"Yes, Master." I pull my satchel into my lap, ready to retrieve the manuscript. "But first, can we discuss my advancement?" I have a whole speech memorized. "As an accomplished wordsmith—"

He cuts me off. "Yes, yes. We'll deal with that later. What did you find?"

I take a quick breath to recover. I'm disappointed—*very* disappointed—

but I know better than to argue. The High Savant is not a patient man. "I discovered a short children's poem. Or maybe lyrics."

He brightens. "Let's hear it."

I've no idea why Master Brogal has me collecting references to the Mar, the mythical race purported to dwell beneath the sea. He doesn't believe in them himself—most educated people don't—but still, he's instructed me to search for stories in every foreign archive I come across. Not that I mind. It's fascinating reading, though I'd rather be talking about my future right now, not a fictional past.

Master Brogal taps the desk, waiting.

I locate the manuscript in my satchel and smooth it out flat. "There are several references to the Mar and one to the sacrifices."

"Child sacrifices?"

"Yes." My hands go clammy at the thought. "And ships."

"Black-sailed?"

"Just ships, seen from below. It's all very oceanic. And something else. I've never heard of it before—a Crown of Bones. Shall I read?"

He leans back in his chair and waves for me to carry on, but his mouth dips into a frown.

I translate, getting lost in the rhythm of the words, my eyes dancing with visions of Mar rising from deep-sea grottos, mysterious ships with barnacle-covered hulls, sunlight streaming through kelp gardens, whales singing in the night… I shiver as I come to the last passage.

The persevering sea harbors all things,
Cast adrift beyond sunlight and stone,
While waves queue offshore in glittering strings,
Out on the ebb tide goes our Crown of Bones…

He sits up fast. "Don't stop."

"That's all there is."

"There must be more."

"I found notes in the margin of the last page." I lean in to show him, and he snatches the manuscript out of my hands. "I can't translate those. Do you recognize the language?"

He stares at the page, moving it closer and then farther away from his face. His eyes widen, but he says nothing.

"Master?"

Finally, he nods. "It's a Northern Tangeen dialect called Retreen."

"Never heard of it."

"It's a dead language."

"Someone's using it," my inner voice says, which I promptly repeat.

His frown deepens. "The notation is very old, the language no longer active."

"But what does it say?"

The High Savant runs his nail down the margin. "Nothing of importance."

"Please can I hear?"

"Very well." He huffs. "Short-horn cows, thirty-five. White-face steers, twenty, and one bull. Piebalds, ten heifers, two with calf…"

I blink. "A livestock list? In a storybook?"

"Not everyone treats records with respect." He stands, his shimmering red robes sweeping the floor, sleeves falling to his gnarled fingertips. "Anything else?"

"That's all I found, Master, but about my role in the Sanctuary—"

"I have a class to teach. Bring me the delegate report as soon as possible. That will be all." He's out the door in three strides, and I'm left staring at an empty desk.

My eyes start to well, and I exhale sharply, putting a stop to that. The chair scrapes the floor as I rise, shouldering my satchel. "I had a good trip to Tangeen, Master, save for the crossing," I say to nobody. "There's little chance of me becoming a seafaring scribe anytime soon. How have you been?" But it's a conversation we'll never have. Master Brogal may be my guardian, but he's no father. Not a warmhearted one, anyway. I've known this about him since I was eight years old, but still I yearn for… something more. It's foolish—I could kick myself—it's *so* foolish. I know better than to wish for what I can't have.

Taking a tie from my wrist, I secure my hair into a small puff of a ponytail. One side escapes and falls against my cheek as the High Savant's words drift back through my mind.

Short-horn cows, thirty-five. White-face steers…

I stop cold. That can't be right. Short-horn cattle are a newly recognized breed, crossed from Gollnar dairy stock and…something else? I don't remember, but the point is, the script in the margin can't be that old if he's translating correctly.

"And if he's not translating correctly?"

The chill deepens. Master Brogal wouldn't make that mistake unless he had something to hide. But what?

I reach across his desk to inch the manuscript toward me just as Nun comes through the door.

"You're still here, Ash?"

I jump at his voice and turn to face him. "Just leaving." The words come out too fast and with too hot a face.

"Well then, shall we both be about our day?" He tucks the manuscript into a drawer and shoos me from the room.

Back in the hallway, my thoughts spin. What could possibly be written in the margin of a children's poem that would make the High Savant lie?

"What indeed."

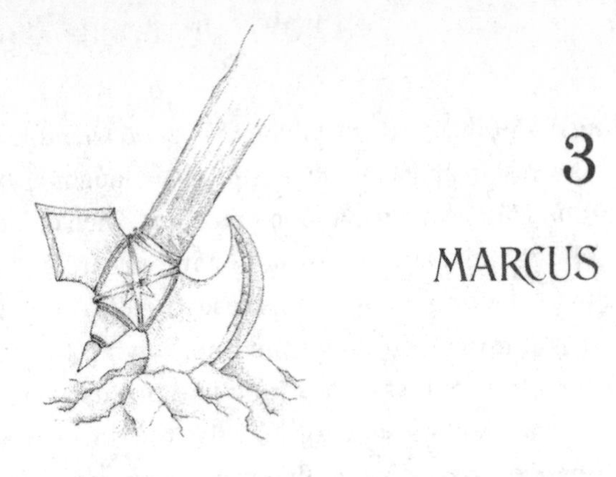

3

MARCUS

I'd rather be anywhere than here. I sit on my heels in the center of the training field, waiting for Master Brogal to call for *warrior* phantoms to rise. I need to stay focused, though my eyes drift to the sidelines, searching for Ash. She's my very best friend, home to me in ways impossible to explain. I crave her smiling approval and unwavering support, especially during these sessions on the field.

She's been there through all my years of instruction, sitting cross-legged in the bleachers or cheering in front of the colorful flags that line the entrance to the training field. Each banner represents a savant's robe color: brown like the earth, for the potentials who come in hopes of raising their phantoms. Then comes blue for young students who stay on and actually manage to raise their phantoms. Green, like me, for those graduating to the next level. Yellow for the successful initiates who've made the journey and returned from Aku. Orange for the upper echelons of mastery. And red for the High Savant who leads us all.

Actually, not all. The black-robed Bone Throwers are a clan unto themselves. They follow their own rules and traditions.

I keep scanning, but I can't spot Ash among the many savants jostling for a better view of the class. Where is she? Maybe not yet back from Tangeen? Did I get the days wrong?

Meanwhile, she hasn't missed much. Each training session comes and goes the same—with me failing. Soon the last one will arrive, and then it'll be too late. I'll have missed my chance to train at Aku and advance to yellow-robe. Everything hinges on that. Because if war is imminent…

I believe battles can be won with diplomacy. Father disagrees.

My head begins to ache.

"*Callers*, ready!" Master Brogal shouts. His red robes flare when he reaches the end of the line and turns to walk back. "Raise your phantoms!"

Up they come, the most numerous class of phantom in the realm, tearing out of the earth, dirt flying. My good friend Larseen, a yellow-robe with brown skin and a tangle of ropey hair, laughs as his jackal bursts from the ground alongside Rhiannon's meerkat. Then comes Cybil's cormorant, a *caller-alter* mix. Dual classes of phantoms are not uncommon, but one will always be dominant. In this case, Cybil's is mostly *caller*.

Brogal moves on down the line, waving for the students to raise their phantoms. Most *callers* look like ordinary creatures found in any of Amassia's realms, save for how some wisp away at the ears, tails, and wingtips, like sparks flying off a grinder or smoke from a chimney.

Farther along, more *callers* rise. A horse, mountain goat, even some human shapes, anything with a voice to *call*. Ash says they sound like a fine choir; I'm more interested in how well they perform, being our realm's main defense—especially given Father's proclivity to incite war. But none of these *callers* come close to the feats of the Magistrate and his heart-eating wolf. How did my father master it? I can't even hold mine to form.

"Someday, it will choose a form, and then we'll celebrate," Ash says to me all the time.

Well, that "someday" needs to arrive before the next new moon.

Today would be preferable.

Cold sweat runs down my temple. *"I can't be a black-robe,"* I plead to my phantom, mind to mind, but it's like talking to a stump. *"You think you'll be happier with the Bone Throwers?"*

Joining the ranks of the black-robed Bone Throwers is my only path if I can't hold my phantom to form. It's supposed to be a sign, but I know in my heart that's not what I'm meant to be. But still, better a black-robe than a non-savant with no phantom at all. Ash says that, too, and she's one to know. But then, she didn't have a black-robe sentence her brother to death like I did. The thought makes my stomach knot. If my relationship with my father is strained now, I can only imagine where we'll be if I become what he despises most.

My mind locks onto this worst possible outcome, trying to imagine what students go through in the Bone Throwers' caves. Carving and playing whistle bones, obviously, but they never talk about it. Black-robes keep to themselves unless asked to throw the bones. They predict the times for planting, harvest, hunting, or war. They determine the fate of the children in all the realms of Amassia. And if that sounds ominous, it's because it is.

The throw of the bones finds most children to be non-savant. They carry on, life as usual. If the cast says they *might* be savant and *could* raise a phantom, everyone applauds and, when they turn eight years old, it's off to the Sanctuary for them. But if the bones say they are marred, damaged in some way, the infant is sacrificed to the sea.

Chills wrap around me at the thought.

I couldn't even bring myself to shoot enemy spies—how could I possibly condemn an innocent baby to death?

Thankfully, Father's outlawed the practice in our realm of Palrio; it's the one mandate of his I support. But none of the other realms have followed his example. That's where I would start my campaign for change and cooperation among the realms. Discussions, more diplomacy.

"Marcus!" Brogal shouts, pointing at the ground cracking in front of me. "Focus."

"What are you doing? Stay put!" I command my phantom.

Of course, there is no answer, but the ground does smooth out.

Brogal works his way down the line, signaling each savant to "call" a chosen object—in this case, a baton. As I search again for Ash, objects fly through the air at a fair speed. The savants catch and throw again. Even the young blue-robes are close to mastering this game.

"Cybil!" Brogal shouts when the green-robe's phantom calls a teapot from the distant kitchen.

She must be thinking of refreshments more than the baton. Her chanting stops short and the teapot drops, shattering on the ground.

Watching the liquid soak into the grass pulls my mind back again to the meadow last week and what my father must have visualized for his phantom to have called those men's hearts. Death came so easily for him.

"Clean it up, Cybil, and go again," Brogal says as he moves down the line.

Next come the *alter* phantoms. Alters are capable of changing shape once held to solid form. There are two alter savants on the field today, Branden, an advanced orange-robe with a pure *alter,* and his younger brother, Samsen, yellow-robe and another of my close friends. Samsen raises a mixed *alter-caller*, emphasis on the *alter,* but strong with both abilities. Very handy.

The brothers' pale hair and even paler skin glint in the sun as they drop to their knees. Up from the ground their phantoms rise in the shape of hawks, morphing instantly into various other birds without losing a feather. When taking the perspective of their phantoms, they can see for miles and miles.

"*Healers*," Master Brogal calls as he strides farther down the line. These phantoms are devoted to the care and well-being of all Amassians no matter the realm or rank. Their phantoms rise, including Piper's double-headed black snake. She's an orange-robe instructor here to help with the less experienced students. Once her phantom drapes in its customary place around her neck, blending in with her dark-brown skin, it peeks both heads out from her curtain of braids. Samsen can't take his eyes off her. He never could.

Master Brogal doesn't call for *ousters* because there are none in Baiseen. Ousters are found mostly in the Aturnias. On the battlefield, well-trained *ousters* are devastating—blasting through defenses, throwing weapons out of hands with an invisible wind. It's said that the Sierrak realm's red-robe, Tann, raises the greatest *ouster* of them all, able to peel flesh from bone from half a mile away. Sounds farfetched to me. Maybe I'll find out when I get to Aku, though I hear Northern Aturnians aren't welcome there for training anymore.

That's saying a lot, because no one has ever been banned from Aku.

Brogal whistles sharply to grab my attention. "*Warriors*!"

I don't know why he uses the plural when mine's the only one. *Warrior* phantoms are virtually unheard of in Palrio, or Tangeen for that matter, making my phantom and me a boon—or would-be boon, if I could control the damn thing.

I'm the Heir to the throne of Baiseen and I raise the only *warrior* in a realm on the cusp of war. A *warrior* I can't use. The irony isn't lost on me.

I straighten my faded green robes, and the entire class moves back. They've learned from experience not to get too close.

To me. I call up my phantom. This is the easy part of the exercise, calling it up or back down. What happens in between, well, that's another matter entirely…

Instantly, it drops from my inner depths into the ground, where it gathers substance; then it explodes upward from the earth. I slam my eyes shut as a wall of dirt and grass hits my face, no doubt intentionally. I spit soil and squint, my eyes opening to a familiar sight. My phantom, huge and unformed, undulates like a sea of lights, better than thrice the height of a man, constantly shifting from various *warrior* shapes. One moment it's a bear with horrendous teeth and claws, the next a rhino that has everyone ducking for cover. Then it sprouts a giant's fist, swinging and pounding, and finally, it morphs into a lion, claws raking.

Useless, nebulous forms. *"Curse of the black-robes! Pick a shape."*

It does nothing of the sort. Each form bursts into the next until it's a blur of transparent, fragmenting figures, completely out of control.

"Marcus!" Piper shouts as she darts out of the way, her snake tightening its hold around her neck to keep from flying off. "Watch what you're doing!"

"I'm *trying*," I mutter.

"Smaller, Marcus," Brogal says in a quiet voice. He's beside me now. "Feel for the true shape it wants to take and steady your eye there."

It's like trying to track a speck of dust in a tornado. My fists tighten. "I can't do it!"

Brogal shakes his head. "Call it in."

I focus my mind and draw the phantom down into the ground, where it tucks back into the depths of my being, no doubt sulking.

Brogal motions the entire class in close, where we sit in a semicircle around him. "What happened there?"

Oh great, a public inventory of my shortcomings. Now *I* want to sulk. "I lost control, Master Brogal." No point hiding the fact.

"To lose control, one must have it in the first place, Marcus."

I keep my expression attentive, but inside, my guts twist.

Master Brogal looks over my head to address the others. "In the potentials' trials, Marcus showed great promise with his *warrior*, raising it on the first day. A blessing to the realm when fewer and fewer brown-robes succeed at all, let alone raise this class of phantom." The High Savant's cheek twitches when his dark gaze comes back to me. "But training cannot progress until the phantom is held to solid form."

"I know." I'm sure everyone else here does, too.

"Let's review." Brogal speaks to us all. "Who can tell me what the phantom is?"

Branden raises his hand. "The hidden power of the savant."

Brogal nods. "Anyone else?"

"What we are yet to become along the path," Larseen says.

"That which lies in the depths of being," Samsen adds.

"All true, and all the more reason why each savant must come to terms with their fears if they are to control their phantom, serve the Sanctuary, and protect the realm." He rests his gaze on my face, and I feel it heat.

The throb in my temples turns into a full-blown pounding headache.

"I know all this, Master Brogal."

"Do you? Then pay attention as I demonstrate."

We rise and take a respectful step back. Master Brogal kneels in the close-cropped grass, adjusts his red robes, and closes his eyes. In moments, the ground in front of him rumbles, and up shoots his phantom, a vivid blue flurry of feathers with crimson-tipped wings.

"Notice there is no dirt spraying the High Savant's face," I say to my phantom. I know it hears me, not that it will answer.

Like a magnificent bird of paradise, Brogal's *caller* flies to his shoulder, tail feathers flowing to the backs of his knees. The small bird puffs out its chest and trills.

"See what I've done here, Marcus?" Brogal walks toward me. His phantom extends its long neck and trills again. He speaks quietly now, just to me. "I've not concerned myself with making a phantom taller than the bell tower. There is no forcing. No trying. I simply allow. I *accept*."

The phantom bird cocks its head at me.

Brogal stares into the distance. "I thought I knew it all as well when I was a green-robe, but still I had difficulties."

This I hadn't heard before.

"I was the son of a Gollnar miner and a Tangeen wordsmith. They were hoping I would raise a *healer*. My father thought…" Brogal presses his lips together. "Suffice it to say that when my delicate and sweet-voiced *caller* rose, it was not what anyone expected, least of all me. I…resisted it for some time. But know this: we cannot fight who we are—who we are meant to be."

I look away.

Brogal turns back to the field and sweeps his hand out at the audience of savants. "Neither size nor shape determines the power of a phantom."

I nod. Everyone knows the strength of Master Brogal's little bird.

"Observe."

"He's going to use it!" Rhiannon latches onto Larseen's arm, pulling him toward her. I glance back at the sidelines. Still no sign of Ash. Brogal doesn't demonstrate often, and when he does, everyone rushes to see. As it is, the spectators—younger students and courtiers—press closer, excitement rising.

The phantom opens its mouth, and a clear melody arises. Thunderheads gather, blotting out the sun. The wind whips through the trees lining the field. As thunder rumbles in the distance, the High Savant paces about. We fall back, away from the center of the field, all eyes fixed on the red-robe master and his brilliant phantom. Brogal throws an invisible spear into the air. At the same moment, his phantom *calls* down a bolt of lightning. It rips through the sky and hits the field with blinding light. I cover my ears, the sound deafening. People cower, but the precision is exact. Only a single blackened spot in the center of the field is scorched and smoking. Everyone cheers.

Brogal drops to his knees and calls his phantom to ground. The sky begins to clear, smoke dissipating on the breeze. The High Savant ignores the applause. "Now then, Marcus." He steps back and commands, "Raise your phantom."

My breath escapes in a rush. *Think small. Think contained. Don't resist.* On the exhale, I drop to my knee and let the chant reverberate through my mind. Moments later, the ground rips open, dirt and grass spray my face—of course—and the phantom is up. I open one eye. "Dead bones and throwers…" It's larger than ever and lashing about madly. People scatter in all directions. The more mental focus I use, trying to "see" it take a contained form, the larger it grows. My head is about to burst with the effort.

"You're resisting!" Brogal's lost his calm. "It's going over the roof, Marcus. Too much! Bring it in!"

I bow my head, defeated. *"I can't fight you anymore."* My fists open, palms up and resting on my knees. In that moment, I understand that in all these years, that's all I've done—fought my phantom. Out of fear. Out of obligation. Out of the desire to be some great warrior they'd prophesied I would be.

Maybe a black-robe *is* the path for me…

Bile burns the back of my throat, and I swallow it down. *"If it must, then so be it."* With the thought, all tension flows away.

"Marcus." Brogal taps my shoulder. "Open your eyes."

What's it doing now? Torching the Sanctuary tower? Darting out to sea? I pop my lids, ready for charred grass and felled trees, but instead, I stare. At a fully formed *warrior* phantom.

And the *warrior*, huge but unwavering, stares back at me. It has its hands—human hands—braced on huge thighs to bend low so it—he—can meet me eye to eye. His expression is intense, penetrating. A *warrior* holding to solid form. I lick my lips. He's waiting. For me.

"*Hello?*"

I am De'ral. His deep voice reverberates in my head.

He finally speaks! *"Thank you."* It's the only thing I can think to say.

"Take phantom perspective," Brogal commands.

This is it. No more theory now. Everyone is watching, and I can sense their hopes rising right along with mine. I push my thoughts forward as I've practiced a thousand times in meditation. I shove my arms in first, and for a moment, they slide down the length of the phantom's limbs, like putting on a snug winter coat. I open and close my hands and feel De'ral doing the same. I make two fists and raise them over my head. When I look up, I see they are my phantom's fists, raised to the sky.

Cheers explode around me. Every student, courtier, and savant in the field is on their feet, jumping and clapping. I think I've just made history—the first and only *warrior* phantom in the realm…and the longest anyone's ever taken to contain it. Together, De'ral and I let loose a war cry.

Brogal, of course, has been waiting for this day for as long as I have. "Stand up," he urges as he ventures a little nearer. "Steady. No sudden moves." His voice stays soft, but the ferocity is unmistakable. I've no doubt he'll strike me down if necessary. "Now. Show them you can walk."

I climb to my feet. It takes all my strength and focus to move and keep a presence of mind in sync with De'ral. I knew it took energy to keep a phantom up, but I had no idea it would be this much. How do they make it look so easy?

I reach out to my phantom, but it's like staring in the mirror. My vision fluctuates between our perspectives. One moment I'm studying a massive *warrior* with burly arms and legs and long, golden hair woven into a single braid that hangs over his shoulder like a copper snake. The next, I *am* the *warrior*, staring down at Marcus Adicio, a green-robe who stands with effort, watching my every move. De'ral lets loose another war cry before turning to stand beside me. We march forward, the ground shaking with each of his giant footfalls. Everyone gives us plenty of space. I don't blame them. My control could slip at any moment.

"Call it in," Brogal commands.

"To ground, De'ral."

He returns like a wave rushing back to the sea.

I collapse face-first into the grass. I have held my phantom to form. There'll be no black robes for me.

Larseen slaps my back with a cheer and takes off toward the palace, no doubt to spread the news. There is so much relief in the crowd's hoots and hollers. I take a deep breath and sit back up, my strength returning.

Samsen and Piper haul me to my feet, hugging me and pumping my hand. They lift my arms over my head and shout with everyone else, "Hail Marcus Adicio, Heir to the Throne of Baiseen! Good speed to the Isle of Aku."

And, praise the lost gods, it's not a moment too soon.

Still, I feel a wisp of joy fade as I scan the crowd one last time.

My biggest moment to date, Ash, and you missed it.

4

ASH

Marcus stops midsentence and turns to me. "Ash, what's wrong?"

I wish I knew.

My best friend has had one of the most important successes in his life. So why am I unhappy?

I twist on the marble bench to face Marcus and smile sheepishly. The sun has set, and the training field is quiet. We've met at this spot many, many times. Only this night is different. From now on…

"Things will never be the same?" my inner voice says, and my stomach sinks.

Stop it. I'm here to celebrate with him.

"Is that why you look like you're about to cry?"

Right. I try for a better smile and nudge Marcus with my knee. "Your phantom holds to form, a giant *warrior*, ready for battle. He has…" I hesitate.

"Gold hair!" Marcus says in a rush.

"Like yours." I was not on the field today, but thankfully, word spread quickly through the Sanctuary. "Brown eyes, also like yours, and huge limbs." Not quite like his, but even in the short time I'd been in Tangeen, I can see that Marcus is bigger, his arms and shoulders more muscled.

"It was incredible, Ash."

We stare at the training grounds where gardeners, under the lantern light, rake the turf *called* fresh to the field. Though phantoms can't *call* new grass to life, they can bring sod to the gardeners in a fraction of the time it would take a non-savant to roll it in. I wave to Rustin, the chief groundskeeper, and he waves back.

"I'm so sorry I missed it." I'd been deep in the Sanctuary archives translating texts at Master Brogal's behest when Marcus brought his phantom to form.

"There will be plenty more times."

I change the subject because I can't see how that's true. When will I get a chance to see it, let alone spend time with Marcus like this again? He's off to the Isle of Aku for his initiation journey now. There won't be any non-savant recorders going, even if I am skilled enough to do the job. By the time he returns, new duties will take him, and I'll be who knows where.

I smooth down the sleeves of my dress, focusing on the faded lace cuffs until I'm certain my voice is under control. "Was your father present?"

Marcus's cheery tone flattens. "He was informed of the event."

The training field's an arm's reach from the palace. Would it have killed the Magistrate to make an appearance? To offer his only savant son a bit of encouragement or advice?

Even when Marcus and I were brown-robed potentials and touching knees to earth for the first time, the Magistrate had scarcely shown any interest. It made no sense to me then; it makes no sense now. With the Magistrate's eldest child lost, wouldn't he care for his remaining children *more*, not less? Especially with as hard as Marcus tries to please him?

I clasp Marcus's hand and pour all the enthusiasm he deserves into my praise. "I'm so proud of you. And I know your father is, too. You've done it, Marcus!" I can imagine the crowd roaring, arms in the air, as he stood side by side with his *warrior*. It's what we've all been waiting for.

His smile trembles for a moment, then spreads full on his face.

Yes, things will be different now, but they will be better, too, certainly for Marcus.

There have been so many rumors—even amid my travels in Tangeen, I'd heard them—and speculation on whether Marcus would, or even could, contain his phantom. Now, at least, his right to the throne cannot be contested.

The sound of crashing waves flows up from the sea, carried on the cool evening breeze. I scoot closer to Marcus for warmth.

"Is that the only reason?" my inner voice asks, all sweet and curious.

Don't you ever sleep?

"Only when you do."

Ha!

But I guess the question has some logic. Marcus has always been more than a friend. Years ago, when the other brown-robes teased and taunted, calling me *non-savant*, he stood up for me. And we've been supporting each other ever since.

The thing is, when Marcus and I are alone, we are just two people, no class or rank, simply best friends for life. Well, a little more than that for a short time a few years back. But the Magistrate wouldn't stand for it.

Of course he wouldn't. What fire burned between us, the Magistrate and Master Brogal stomped out quickly.

"Tell me," I murmur. "What's it like in phantom perspective?"

"The best feeling." His voice softens. "The link was light at first, but it was there, his form unshifting."

I nod for him to continue.

"He said, *I am De'ral.* It boomed in my head and—" Marcus flushes red. "Forget I said that."

"Forgotten." I hold his gaze so he doesn't panic.

"Seriously. You can't ever—"

"I won't speak it aloud." A phantom's name is known only to their savant, not shared even among close family members. I delight that Marcus feels so relaxed around me that he let it slip, but I understand his embarrassment and concern. "I promise, Marcus. No one will ever hear it from my lips."

De'ral…

Marcus is silent for a while, no doubt debating in that big, logical mind of his if he should swear me to silence or if doing so would compel me to blurt about De'ral even more. I take pity on him. "You have my word, Marcus. Now stop worrying and tell me more about this gorgeous phantom of yours."

He smirks. "One moment I'm studying a massive *warrior* and the next, I *am* the *warrior*, looking down on a green-robe savant. Together, we raised our arms and hollered a war cry into the crowd."

"I know. I had to cover my ears in the library. I'm so happy for you." I say the words and mean them. I *am* happy, of course I am. It's just that—

"Things will never be the same?"

Can you stop saying that? My eyes burn at the thought.

"The initiation journey to Aku?" I keep my voice neutral, determined not to give in to the rising emotions. I refuse to blink, lest the tears escape. "Will you make it before winter?"

"The Bone Throwers think so."

"With the cold season around the corner and the trade disputes in Northern Aturnia…" It's no small matter, the unrest among the realms. "I know they're in talks, but the tension still builds. And those spies you caught behind the palace, they were Aturnian, so the journey will have more risks. Unless you sail the whole way from Baiseen, which could slow you down if the wind's not right…" I stop my running thoughts to study his face. The bright victory is gone, and he looks away. "Marcus?"

"We haven't confirmed if the trespassers were actual Aturnian spies."

I reach for his hand again and give it a squeeze. "It must have been awful." The thought of the execution makes me nauseous, and I can tell it does him, too, though we barely had a chance to talk about it.

He nods and comes back to the present. "If we sail from Port Cabazon instead of Baiseen, we avoid the crosscurrents, saving two days there. Five days at sea and we touch Northern Aturnian soil only once at Capper Point to change from the ocean-going ship to a shallow draft sloop. Then it's over the shallow reefs and we're there, safe on the Isle before the gates close."

I quote Master Brogal's favorite saying. "Sometimes the Bone Throwers get it wrong."

Marcus frowns.

"Sorry. Ignore me..." What's wrong with me? I will not let my mood dampen this win just because I can't see myself in his future. "When are you going?"

"I'd be ready to ride tomorrow, but we have to wait for the new crescent moon. At least, that's what the Bone Thrower said. *Mind the protocols.*"

I look to the west, but the dark moon has set with the sun. "In three days?" The truth of it hardens in my heart like a brick. "That's cutting it close."

"We'll make it."

There he is with that *we* again, when he knows it's never going to happen. He'll go to Aku, and rightly so, to earn his yellow robes—doing whatever trials and tests are deemed necessary for warriors. It's rigorous and not all initiates will pass, but that's all I know. The trials, like so much of Aku, are shrouded in secrecy. Even the savants who have gone and returned are close-lipped about it. Something about honoring the traditions.

Anyway, after that, he'll return to Baiseen to take up his duties as Heir. I, on the other hand...well, I can't get *any* answer from Brogal about my future.

I take a deep breath and let it out slowly. Tonight is not about me. "Who will accompany you?" My voice catches and those blasted tears slip free because my dream of Aku is over. "Ash..." He brushes my cheek, his smile crooked. He knows me well enough not to coddle, which would only make tears run in earnest. "I've asked Larseen, of course, as my guard."

Right. Larseen and Marcus have been friends since brown-robes, training together almost every day since. Lars took his initiate journey last year and came back a yellow-robe. I thought Marcus would be jealous, but he has nothing but respect for Larseen.

"And Piper as my healer."

"That's perfect. Her third journey to Aku, so she knows the way. Who else?"

"Samsen will come as a second guard."

"Good choice, and I'm happy for Piper." Those two are inseparable.

Marcus grins at me. "I'll need a recorder."

Any spirits I have left drain away . The recorder is the wordsmith responsible for narrating the initiation journey and the events upon Aku, their scripts are later bound into a book and kept in the library for all to read. It is the job I've dreamed of doing for Marcus, when his time came. I have proficient skills as a scribe and have studied the laws of the realms, the languages, and histories. But with no acknowledged standing from Master Brogal, they would never approve of me.

So as much as this is a dream come true for Marcus, it is the end of mine. Passage to Aku is only for savant initiates and their company. Not for the likes of me.

"Still, he should have the best wordsmith recording."

Indeed.

"I recommend Allenren," I say, my feelings contained. Mostly. "He's from Tangeen. Raises a *caller*, and you know your father's on a campaign to reinforce ties there."

"Uh-huh." Marcus nods. His thumbs brush my cheeks again. "Allenren's fine, but he's not who I want."

"Don't choose Greker." I sniffle. "The least little thing goes wrong and—"

"I agree. Not him."

"That leaves Katren or one of her yellow-robe apprentices."

"Excellent suggestions, but I don't think so."

His expression blurs before me, and I give in and swipe my eyes against my sleeve. "Who, then?"

Marcus leans close, his breath apple-sweet and warm on my cheek. "I want *you*, Ash."

Warmth floods through me for all of two seconds. Then I turn and punch him hard.

"Ouch!"

"Don't tease! You know it's not possible."

He rubs his arm and grimaces. "I thought you'd be happy."

I'm off the bench and facing him. "Look at me, Marcus. What do you see?"

"You, barefoot as usual, to start," he says, still rubbing his arm.

"That's not what I meant!"

He makes a show of further appraisal. "I see my favorite teal-eyed girl… Well, your eyes are red tonight. As are your cheeks—only a few shades lighter than your hair."

"Keep it up." I raise my fist.

He talks right over me. "And while we're on the hair, I liked it better long."

"Nobody asked you," I huff. "Besides, you're completely missing the point."

"Which is?" He leans back against the bench.

"Dog stuggs for brains, Marcus, have you forgotten I'm non-savant?"

"I haven't forgotten you can curse like an Aturnian sailor. That won't be going in the records, I trust."

"It's a Sierrak curse," I correct him without thinking. "And I'm telling you, they won't let me go."

He pulls me back beside him and digs a handkerchief out of his robe pocket. It's an embroidered handkerchief—of course it is—and here I sit with dirt on my feet. "Ash, we promised we'd journey to Aku together. Remember?"

I blow my nose loudly in response.

"You swore an oath to set foot on every realm in Amassia. This is your chance for Aku."

"You don't have to convince me to come along. I *want* to go. I've *always* wanted to go, but my guardian—"

"Brogal?"

"Yes, *Master* Brogal, the *High Savant* of Baiseen." I emphasize his titles. "He has to clear it. I can't even get him to talk about my future as a wordsmith!"

Marcus grins stupidly, and I'm tempted to punch him again. "Ash, you're coming to Aku as my recorder. That's all there is to say."

"Your father will forbid it, too."

He taps my nose like I'm a puppy. "Don't underestimate me. I'm Heir to the Throne of Baiseen, and I just contained the realm's only *warrior* phantom."

His heartbeat is strong against my ear. Steady and sure. "Meaning?"

"If I were you, I'd start packing."

5

MARCUS

Even as I pack my bags and hear the music echoing from the courtyard below, part of me can hardly believe it's real.

For so long, I awaited this very moment.

I take one last look around my chambers—at the mess of clothes on the floor and the rumpled four-poster bed strewn with maps and scrolls I won't be taking. Then there's the carved chest with my quiver and arrows tucked safely away—I'm not taking them, either, just a short sword and hand knife. We have to travel light if we are going to make it to Aku before the gates close.

Out the arched windows, the orchard begins to lose its leaves. It will be dead bare when I return. But when I do, it'll be in yellow robes. My chest swells at the thought.

I draw the door to my chambers closed, like sealing off the first chapter of my life, and stride toward the east wing.

"Excuse me, Heir?" A servant runs to intercept me. "The Magistrate requests your presence in the throne room."

"What?"

"The Mag—"

"I heard you, but that can't be right. My father is supposed to be out on the palace steps, overseeing my departure."

"I'm sorry." He shakes his head. "The request is for you to meet him in the throne room."

Odd. It's unexpected, but maybe Father wants a private word with me first. This moment has been so long in the making, I can only imagine he'll have advice. I'm following in our forefathers' footsteps, and Father puts much stock in our lineage. Maybe he'll have an heirloom to pass down as good luck for the journey? That would be worth a delay.

"Very well." I hurry down the stairs and cut across the hall. I'm about to greet him but stop short as I take in the scene.

My father sits on the great throne—it's a massive tree trunk carved with the likenesses of a multitude of phantoms, one for each of the savants who have sat there before him. The image of his wolf dominates, slinking down the back, jaws wide, nose creased in a snarl.

And the Magistrate is not alone. Beside him in arranged seats are Petén, a smug expression on his face; five orange-robes; Master Brogal; and a black-robe Bone Thrower, Oba, I think. Her cowl is up, so I can't be sure. All the war council members are assembled as well. They sit in a semicircle before the Magistrate as if in a formal meeting.

"Marcus, you're here." My father's voice is grim.

There is no place for me to sit as the council members twist around to get a better view. "You called for me?"

"Two things." He nods to Master Brogal, who stands to speak.

"First, Belair Duquan, a green-robe initiate from Tangeen with a *warrior* phantom will take Larseen's place in your company. He's packed and ready, waiting in the courtyard."

"Why?" I blurt out, unable to control my voice.

"It's deemed prudent." He looks at Father. "Seeing that he's in a similar situation, raising a *warrior* in a sanctuary of *callers* and *alters*. He needs the guidance of Aku as much as you do, and it's his time."

It makes sense, but my throat constricts at the news.

"Belair is the son of a Tangeen delegate," my father adds.

Oh, so this is a *political* decision. My irritation flares. "Larseen's—"

"Don't worry. He took it well," Petén says, savoring my distress.

Why is my brother even here? He has no interest in politics and certainly none in my initiation journey.

"And the second thing." Father uncrosses his arms and rubs the head of his carved wolf. "Petén has petitioned the council for your seat and full voting rights."

It hits me like a slap. "What? He can't! It's mine, and he's..." I'm about to blurt out *non-savant*, but I can see by the smile on my brother's face, it's already been done. "Why now, Father? I'll be back in a few months, my *warrior* ready to defend Baiseen beside your wolf." I'm nearly shouting as De'ral pushes to the surface, filling my head with a pressure I can barely stand.

"The truth?" my father asks. "It's taken you nine years to hold your phantom to form. Why should I think Aku will be any different?" He shakes his head. "I honestly doubt you will gain the next level, which means the black-robes can have you." He's careful not to let his distaste show, not with a Bone Thrower in the room. "I need one of my sons to add his voice to the cause."

I try to swallow but can only gasp. "I will succeed!" Why won't he believe me? "You think Petén…?"

"I've turned over a new leaf, brother." His pompous face sickens me. "And am learning a new respect for Father's policies."

Rage runs up my spine and slams the back of my skull as I turn on my heel and walk out.

"Stay!" Father shouts. "We will consult the bones again. Perhaps the journey isn't even necessary for you."

His words knife into my mind. Not necessary? I try to protest, but no air will escape my throat.

But others speak out, all of them at once. I can't tell if they agree or disagree.

"Silence!" the Bone Thrower commands the room.

The old woman lets down her cowl, and it is indeed Oba. White hair falls to her waist in a mass of wraps, feathers, braids, and bone beads. Her black eyes pin me while she taps her thumb ring on the edge of the council table.

I swallow hard, watching her phantom waft away from her. It takes no solid form but ripples in curtains of red and purple light. It's enthralling, and even though I want to, it's hard to look away.

She claps her hands, breaking the spell. "The bones will speak to this, Marcus Adicio." Without a further glance at me, she rolls her sleeves up to the elbows. Bangles clink and shift. One by one, she takes them off and stacks them to the side, but some will never budge. They are woven through her dark skin. "Back away," she says to those leaning in.

They scoot their chairs back and wait.

The Bone Thrower lays out a dark hide and rattles her bag. Everyone knows what's in it—the array of etched whistle bones, one for each round on the path to An'awntia.

A breeze comes in through the open door, and I can smell the sea as the Bone Thrower's phantom drifts farther away from her body, whispering like a shadow with a life of its own. I don't want it to touch me, but it draws close to my face, like a dog wanting to smell my breath. She chants as she digs into the bag and pulls out twelve carved bones, gives them a shake, and scatters them across the hide.

I hold my breath.

In three heartbeats, she turns to my father and nods. "The Heir must attempt the journey."

Attempt?

"Ink and parchment," she commands. Her eyes find mine. "Go. I'll bring this to the courtyard." She begins writing and I numbly turn to the door. My confidence is shattered, but I keep walking, my feet moving on their own accord.

When I reach the door, Father calls back to me, and I turn. His eyes soften for an instant, or did I imagine that?

He reaches into his pocket and pulls out a gold coin. "Marcus, I wish you to prove me wrong." He flips it in an arc toward me and I catch it, knowing exactly what it's for. I give him a curt nod and leave.

As I head out the palace doors into the fresh air, I'm numb, completely numb to the core. As soon as I appear to the crowd, music strikes up in a brassy sound of horns mixed with kettle drums and flutes. Phantom voices join in and everyone cheers.

I stand tall, head high, in spite of the blow. This is the start of my initiation journey, and I'll not let them see my anger—or my shame. And by the bones, there is no shame. Seeing the council, my father, so many people assembled to discuss my shortcomings as if all I've ever been—or can be—is a failure... It hurts in a way that I can't acknowledge lest I embarrass myself further and in front of all of Baiseen.

Father, Petén, and the council members catch up at the top of the steps. We wave to the people, smiles frozen on our faces. The onlookers don't know. To them, this is one big festivity. Ash looks up from the courtyard, her expression concerned. Piper and Samsen flank her, their phantoms raised—Piper's twin-headed snake draping across her shoulders, Samsen's eagle circling overhead.

I take a last look at the terraced city and out to the sea, then force myself to turn back to Father and extend my hand. He shakes it, but I'm too crushed to feel anything.

"Take this." Oba steps up and presses a folded parchment into my hand. "Heed the words."

I start to open it.

"Not here." The faint red aura of her phantom glows around her. "When you're out of the city." Dazed, I tuck the note into my robe pocket and squeeze through the crowd, accepting pats on the back and cheers. It takes a while to reach the others. When I do, Samsen hands me Echo's reins. Her ears prick, head high and nostrils flaring. She's as ready as I am to be off. I mount up, and she paws the cobbled stones, my stirrups clinking into Ash's as our horses sidestep into each other. "Let's go."

She frowns and tries to see past me. "Where's Larseen?"

"Replaced," I snap. The newcomer rides toward us on a big bay gelding. "That must be him." Tall in the saddle, lanky, and… Is that his hair? It's a flame atop a matchstick. A pack donkey trails behind him. "Does he think we're staying all winter?"

"Be nice," Ash says out the side of her mouth before waving.

The Tangeen reaches us and salutes me, bowing his head. When he looks up, his eyes brighten. "Ash!"

"Belair! Good to see you." She smiles and makes introductions to the rest of our party. "I'll be recording for you as well, then. Splendid!"

I frown. She seems delighted with the thought of doubling her workload. "How do you know each other?" I ask, trying to keep the accusation out of my voice. I do realize friendship is not a crime.

"We met in Tangeen, at the library."

"That we did." He sidesteps his mount closer and tousles her hair. "Missed you, Little Scribe."

Little Scribe? My frown deepens. How good of friends are they, and why haven't I heard of it before now? It's like everything I've known is dissolving in front of me.

Trumpets sound the hunting call, and the people follow after us as we trot through the streets toward the east gate. Once we are beyond the city walls, the crowd stays behind and, in the span of a few minutes, the show is over. The moment I've been waiting for these last nine years, the start of my initiation journey to Aku, has arrived and I can't enjoy a minute of it, thanks to Father and his utter lack of faith in me.

"Marcus," Ash whispers. "What's wrong? Is it Belair? I know you chose Larseen, but he's—"

I shake my head. "It's not just him." I wish it were as simple as that. "I'll tell you later, Ash."

...

"Empty?" I repeat the word because it makes no sense, even though I see it with my own eyes. Cabazon Harbor lies deserted, not a boat among all the roped-off green water. It's a day for disappointments, it seems. The pounding in my head starts to increase.

"Fish are running," the Harbor Master says. "You'll not find passage to Aku from here."

"No ships?" Seems Ash can't believe her eyes either. She turns to me. "What should we do?"

"It's obvious," I say, facing my company. "We ride to Toretta and sail from there." Toretta, a city two or three days away, on the northern border, is full of Aturnian spies—or so they say. Not the ideal destination, especially with how long it will take to get there, lack of supplies...

"We didn't plan to camp." Ash eyes Belair's donkey. "Did we?"

"I have camping and cooking gear." Belair shrugs. "And some food. But most importantly, I brought a full bag of Ochee."

I stare at him blankly. "What's that?"

"Tangeen spiced tea, of course." He rubs his chin. "Don't say you've never tasted it."

"This isn't a picnic," I grumble. *Who cares about tea?*

The Tangeen does, De'ral says.

I'm so shocked by my phantom's voice in my head, I nearly lose track of the conversation.

"Toretta is out," Piper says. "Aturnian sympathizers would love nothing more than to capture the Heir of Baiseen and use him as a bargaining chip for trade talks."

"A Tangeen delegate's son wouldn't go astray, either," Samsen adds.

"The governor there has always supported Baiseen," I point out. "We could go straight to him."

"And announce to the city the Heir is in town?" Ash shakes her head. "And the time it would take to gain an audience to secure his help? The gates to Aku would be closed before we set sail."

"I'd like to see the Aturnians try to take us." I punch my fist into my hand and feel De'ral do the same. It's new, this unity with my phantom. The only light in what has been one of my darkest days.

"How many days do we have to reach Aku, exactly?"

"Eleven, as of this morning," Ash says.

No one speaks.

"Did the Bone Throwers have any advice?" Samsen asks. "All I heard was that our number should be five."

"That was it, on the first cast, besides the usual, stick to the protocols."

"First cast?" Belair says and everyone looks up. "There was a second?"

"Just this morning." I force my face into a calm mask. "It surprised me, too."

"What does it say?" Belair asks, his eyes narrowing. "Anything about this?"

I open the note from Oba and read it aloud.

Remember to keep the company's number to five.

In spite of autumn chill, optimism wins out.

When in doubt, go north.

A sword brings truth and deception.

Do not raise your phantom until safe on Aku.

Surprise comes from the sea. Don't resist it.

The Heir will not be stopped.

Out of Aku, the warriors triumph, and the southern realms are changed forever.

A surprise certainly has come from the sea, and not a good one.

None of the rest makes much sense, really, except for, *When in doubt, go north.* Also, *The Heir will not be stopped.* It's enough assurance for me. After that debacle with my family in the throne room, it is this one tenet from the Bone Thrower that I cling to. "It's settled," I say. "We pick up supplies and ride north."

Ash frowns. "But can we make it in time?"

"Maybe not," I say, reaching out to squeeze her hand, "but we have to try."

6

ASH

After two sleepless nights and long days in the saddle, my body feels like it was pounded with a bone bag—then trampled by a team of mules.

But we made it.

Here on the cliffs overlooking Toretta with an hour to spare before dark, the whitecaps sparkle and the breeze is fresh with moist, salty air. I can't see the harbor, though, so I wouldn't know if anyone is shouting *empty,* or *full of boats*. But I'm optimistic.

"You're always optimistic."

Well, hope is the currency of the scribe, is it not?

Marcus leads us down the winding path, the dry red soil clouding beneath our horses' hooves. Where the dirt roadway yields to cliff and plain, the knee-high grasses ripple in waves. It's beautiful, but oh, the dust. My once-white shirt is brown, my mouth and eyes full of grit. No price is too high for a bath tonight. And, dear gods of the deep, may we all sleep in beds.

"Clean ones."

Agreed.

It's not long before we are through the gates and slap in the middle of Toretta's noisy city streets lined with vendors peddling aromatic foods, bowls of steaming white rice, red chili soups, salads of bright-yellow mangoes and green papaya. My mouth waters.

Chickens in coops cackle and peck at the ground. Spotted goats with long, drooping ears are milked on the spot. In one stall, a big woman in an apron fills baking pots with apricots, dried fruits, and raw meats, ready to pop them into the hot wood oven behind her. Farther down, a short man sells plates of noodles and fish; the delicious smell of curry wafts from his stall. After two days of thin soup and rock-hard bread, I'm drooling like an old dog. We all are, though I don't rest my eyes on the butcher skinning eels. I'm no fan of those. Too slimy.

Savants of various colored robes, mostly green and yellow, stand out, including Northern Aturnians with their breastplates of armor and streaming capes. Our group is strung tight as a bowstring, no doubt thinking about what, exactly, a host of Northern Aturnians would do if they discovered the Heir of Baiseen in their midst.

For once, thank the bones, Marcus isn't drawing attention to himself. We seem to go unnoticed and I guess, with his green robe covered with grime and hood up hiding his golden curls, he's as far from an image of the Heir of Baiseen as anyone can be.

Belair helps, too, riding close to Marcus on his tall bay, obscuring him even further. They seem to be getting along better now. I was worried Marcus would resent him all the way to Aku, but Belair's too amiable for that, and the replacement really wasn't his fault. I'm still shocked by the Magistrate's decision to give Marcus's seat on the council to Petén. Marcus kept his voice even when he told me, but I felt the bitterness underneath his words. A father should support his son, not betray him.

They'll have a different opinion once De'ral, fully controlled by a yellow-robed Marcus, returns to them from Aku.

I smile at the thought.

We ride out of the main district and past quaint pastel buildings with bright flower boxes under the windows. Many of the older inhabitants are on the stoops, playing games of cards and dice.

Marcus twists around in the saddle when we come to a crossroad.

I draw out the map, balance it on my mare's neck and the pommel of my saddle, but it's not necessary. "Can't you smell it, sir?" I point ahead, using the new title to remind him to be covert with his name. If I know Marcus, he'll need it.

Young children kick balls and hoops back and forth in the street, darting out of our way as we approach. An elderly orange-robe savant with a lined face and skin dotted with spots from the sun snores from his low chair. Beside him, a phantom sits on its haunches. The brown bear is huge, easily eighteen hands high. It watches our approach, its gaze shifting between us and the children it appears to guard.

My mount tenses beneath me. "Easy, girl."

We progress down the road, the bear's black eyes locking with mine. In Baiseen, I'm used to the phantoms engaging me. Here, I don't find the habit nearly as endearing.

My hands shorten the reins of their own accord. This isn't Rhiannon's little meerkat, twitching a whiskered nose about my bare feet, that's for sure. I feel the bear's eyes on my back as I follow the others, but we pass uncontested, finally reaching the entrance to the harbor. Still, the water is blocked from view.

"Half the size of Baiseen with twice the stink," Belair says, a kerchief covering all but his eyes. I doubt anyone but me heard him over the cries of the gulls. The sky is full of them, and why not? There are at least ten cartloads of reeking garbage lined up, waiting to be loaded onto a barge and sent out to sea. The barrels of fish bones and shrimp tails are quite an attraction for the birds as well.

A few peddlers crowd the entrance, but this section is more for offloading goods and supplies than selling them. Winches and pulleys dominate the space, and giant cranes topped with bright flags stand out against the sky. One long building, a warehouse, I'm guessing, runs the length of the avenue, its peaked roof decorated with noisy gulls, cormorants, and the odd pelican.

"Come with me, Ash." Marcus swings out of the saddle and motions me to follow while the others water the horses at a communal trough. He acts more like the Heir of Baiseen every step down to the wooden dock, as opposed to a humble initiate on his way to Aku.

"We need to cut right to reach the individual piers," I say as I rush to match his long strides. Signs written in Aturnian, Tangeen, Gollnar, and Palrion point the way.

"I can read." He continues on at a demanding pace.

I rub my aching shoulders, struggling to keep up. "Please slow down."

For someone who wants to travel, I'm quite aware of how lousy I am at it. I train in hand-to-hand combat; I do. But I was not prepared for the long days spent in the saddle or sleeping on the ground.

When I catch up to Marcus as he rounds the corner, my physical complaints vanish and I let out a gasp. Thick tan ropes section off fifty berths, but everywhere I look, they are empty.

"That must be some *fish run,"* my inner voice notes, not the least perturbed.

Dak'n spit, it must. "Not here, too?"

"There's one." Marcus points to a large carrack near the end of the dock.

The sails are down, but the late-afternoon breeze ruffles the edges of the boom. I can't be certain, but I think I catch a glimpse of black sailcloth.

"That may not be the one for us."

"Why not?"

I point, but all I can see now are white sails rolled up tight. Maybe it was a trick of the light.

Marcus heads straight for it, his boots clipping with each stride. "It's the only one left."

I follow and tug on his sleeve. "Don't let your royal blood show or hint that we're desperate for passage," I remind him. We'd practiced bartering over the last few days. Marcus wants to do this himself, as he should, but... I guess seventeen years of commanding a palace full of servants doesn't wear off overnight. "And check the sails," I add. Just to be sure.

"It looks good to me," he says.

I want to agree with him. The ship has a wide ramp for boarding horses and livestock. It sits high in the water, too, and the boards are wet. "Fresh in and unloaded," I say to Marcus. "But the sailcloth."

He studies it. "White."

It does appear so. "I thought I saw—"

"Let me do this, Ash." He marches up the gangplank. Tension vibrates from him.

I get it, I do. We can't turn back. So much is riding on this, now more than ever.

"Ahoy!" Marcus shouts. "Is the captain about?"

"He ain't." An unshaven man in drawstring pants and a wrinkled shirt leans against a stack of wooden barrels off to the side, drinking from a large jug.

Marcus turns to face him. "We seek passage to Capper Point."

The sailor grins. "That'll have to wait."

"We must book it tonight."

"Not urgent, remember?" I whisper behind a cupped hand.

"Tomorrow is fine as well," Marcus quickly amends.

"Sorry, mate. You'll have to speak to the cap'n and, like I said, he ain't here."

Marcus draws himself up straight. "Listen to me, 'mate.' I'm the—"

I jab him in the ribs with my elbow. He grunts and clears his throat. "I'm a green-robed savant from Baiseen, on my initiation journey to Aku."

"And I am the recorder for the journey," I butt in. "May I ask where the captain is?"

The sailor looks me up and down. "Try the nearest pub, miss."

I'm disgusted, but more worrisome is the snarl on Marcus's face.

"Mind your eyes," he snaps. "We'll find another boat. C'mon, Ash." He walks back down the gangplank with his long, I'm-the-Heir-of-Baiseen stride. I'm about to follow but my inner voice stops me.

What are we waiting for? I ask.

"Listen."

The sailor toasts Marcus's back and then turns to me. "There's no other vessel sailing to Capper Point this week. Fish are running. Biggest catches on record." He caps the jug and closes the distance between us, blocking my way off the ship. "Came up out of nowhere, just like you."

The hairs on the back of my neck rise. *Is* this *what you wanted me to wait for?*

I take one step back, but he presses in. His eyes are glassy and his legs unsteady. But I won't underestimate him.

"He's no threat."

Thank you. I feel so much safer now.

I pull out my belt knife, eye on his next move. He gets one warning. "That's far enough."

"Can I help you, lass?" a voice calls from above.

The sailor backs off immediately. "She wants passage to Aku. I was discussing the options."

I don't comment on his version of the story. All my attention is drawn toward the young man descending from the crow's nest.

He jumps to the deck, landing light on his bare feet, and I promptly forget how to breathe. He's tall, with black, curly hair falling past his shoulders. His chest is broad and hairless, his abdomen ridged like a pan flute. He wears cutoff pants. That's all. Not another stitch. I've never seen so much skin, such a deep, smooth brown, in my life.

I'm still holding my breath and it's starting to make me dizzy.

"Then breathe."

I exhale, and it comes out as a whistle. He blinks, but then a crooked smile tugs at his mouth. Oh, by the Deep, let the deck swallow me whole. As he steps closer, the hairs on the back of my neck rise again, albeit for an entirely different reason.

"Worth the wait?"

I ignore my inner voice and meet his dark, gray-green eyes.

"Did you plan to do more than stare?"

I reach for the ends of my long curls, remembering too late they've been recently cut. "I…um. We…" Oh yes, I'm truly a wordsmith just now. I point at Marcus, who is walking back toward us. "My…*brother* and I are traveling to Aku with three other savants." My arm swings vaguely toward the north, but the belt knife is still in hand and he has to lean back, out of range.

"Maybe put the knife away?"

"Initiation journey?" He taps his fist to his chest, a traditional show of respect to savants. "Congratulations, but you're cutting it a little close."

"Thank you, and yes, we are. Circumstances beyond our control. Seems the fish are running." I tuck the knife into its sheath. It takes two tries. What is wrong with me? "I'm the recorder but non-savant." I turn my palms up like it can't be helped, because it can't. "Two of our party are going to train and compete."

"You travel much?"

Why is he asking me that?

"To see if you know how to barter."

Ah.

He ties his hair back, biceps flexing, and I lose my train of thought. He's handsome in a way I've not encountered amid all my vast travels. I don't know if it's something earthy—er, oceanic—about him, or just something in the way he looks at me, but I'm captivated. Silly that.

"Travel?" my inner voice prompts.

"Actually, a bit," I say. "Around Palrio. Nonnova Islands to the south and Tangeen as well. Once to Gollnar."

"'Yes' would have sufficed."

The unmistakable heat of a blush spreads up my chest and through my cheeks. "You travel much?" I ask him back.

"Did you not notice he lives on a boat?"

I laugh, completely out of context. The old gods can drown me at any time, please. It's like I've never talked to a boy before. But I have! Plenty of times. And in multiple languages, no less.

He glances up at the mast. "I've been nigh everywhere."

I can't stop the sigh from escaping my lips. "Aku?"

"I was there last summer. We're heading that way in the morning."

"The sailor said—"

"He doesn't know his left hand from the anchor chain. Pay him no mind."

I turn to call Marcus back and bump right into him.

"Ash. Stop yammering to the crew." He glares at the first sailor, who has gone back to his bottle. "We need to secure a ship, and this isn't it."

"They're sailing for Aku in the morning," I whisper.

"They're all *drunk*." Marcus isn't whispering.

"Excuse my brother," I say to the young sailor. "We're looking for passage to Capper Point, but I understand your captain is indisposed?"

"I've never heard it put quite that way, lass, but the *Sea Eagle*'s captain is very much, as you say, indisposed." His smile returns, and the sun shines brighter in the sky. "It's his natural state when onshore. He leaves me to make the arrangements. Captain Nadonis will verify them in the morning."

"He'll be sober?" Marcus asks.

"Aye. We sail with the morning tide." He nods at the barrels stacked on the dock. "We're taking apples from your lovely Palrio coast to Capper Point." His eyes wash over me at the word "lovely." At least I'm inclined to think they do.

Either way, I'm a little breathless. Again.

"Then come back to the ground and check the boom."

I barely hear my inner voice giving guidance, but I glance at the sails rolled tight around the boom. They are white, until the breeze catches the edge again, revealing black cloth beneath. Marcus spots it, too.

"No," Marcus says flatly and tugs on my arm, trying to lead me away.

The sailor raises his brow.

"He's disturbed by the black sails, and so am I."

"Our voyage to Aku is under white sails, but in any case, the winter currents are coming early." The lad looks skyward, as if he expects the season to change at any moment. "The *Sea Eagle* is your last chance to reach the Isle by ship." He turns back to me.

There's no argument to that, so I keep my mouth shut.

"What's your name, lass?"

"Ash, but about the sails—"

"*Ash*." The sailor picks up a loose rope and begins to coil it. "If you do decide to join us, how many in your party?"

"Five."

Marcus throws up his hands and stalks away.

"Luggage?"

"Saddle, bridle, and halter for each, saddlebags, and a double-sided mule pack, half full."

"Stock?"

"Five horses and one donkey."

"Seaworthy?"

"The horses are. I'm not sure about the donkey."

He nods. "Thirty-five gold each, two meals a day, and hammocks in the commonhold. Twenty per head for the livestock, more for the donkey if it gives us strife. You'll be liable for damages." He assumes it's a done deal and holds out his hand to shake on it.

Oh, how little the sailor knows me.

I draw in a breath and counter. "Twenty gold each, three meals a day, and fifteen per head for the horses. Ten for the donkey." I jut out my chin, a challenge, even though, on the inside, my thoughts are swimming in his features, the smiling eyes, strong jaw…

"Perhaps pay more attention to how you are spending the Magistrate's coin than the merits of the sailor's form."

My face heats at that, and I catch him noticing.

"You're letting him gain the advantage."

I am not.

He leans forward. "Thirty gold," he counters in his lilting accent. "Three meals, fine, but eighteen for all stock. I know how much those little beasts can eat."

I scoff and fold my arms across my chest. "What, a mere donkey's appetite? Twenty-two gold, and sixteen for the horses, twelve for the donkey, my top offer." The words sound confident, but I'm shaking inside. From excitement? Fear? I can't even tell how I feel.

And yet, he's the one who falters. It's only slight, but I catch it, his gaze lingering on my face. Unless he's shocked by my short hair?

"Maybe he marvels at the dirt on your neck."

Shut up. I brush at my collar.

He clears his throat. "Twenty-five and sixteen for all stock, three meals, my lowest offer." He's on his back foot and I could push for more.

But I don't.

"Done."

"So soon?"

No choice. Whether I'm excited or scared no longer matters. My upper lip is starting to twitch, and if he sees that, we'll be back to thirty a head and I'll never live it down.

I automatically thrust out my hand to conclude the barter. It slips into his, and this time it's the hairs on my arm that rise. I try to say the usual square, or even, but no sound makes it out of my mouth.

"Done and square." He speaks for us both, his voice just above a whisper. His eyes are full of questions, but he doesn't ask them. Finally, he lets go and steps back, all business now. "Have the horses here an hour after dawn. We like to load them first."

"What about the black sailcloth?" I insist, my gaze tearing away from him and going to the boom. "Are you visiting the Drop?" The deep-sea trench off the coast is the haunt for sacrifices of marred children—or was until the Magistrate banned them.

"I'm just the bosun's mate and can't speak of it either way. But I *can* promise you, lass, no harm will come to any on this voyage. I stake my life on that."

His words sound earnest, still… "I'll have to confer with my brother."

"Do so, then. We sail, with or without you, on the morrow."

I have to make myself turn away, because he hasn't. He's just standing there, slowly coiling the line, eyes on me. At last, I nod and walk away, but turn straight back. "Wait. What's your name?"

"Kaylin," he answers in his warm, swaying voice.

"Kaylin? Like the waterfalls in Tutapa?"

"Aye, lass. Like that."

Which explains the island accent.

He smiles and disappears below while I hurry away to find the others. My thoughts should be on the very difficult task ahead, but I can't help wondering what Marcus will decide, meaning if I'll ever see Kaylin again.

"And this matters because?"

I can't answer that. I just know it does.

7

MARCUS

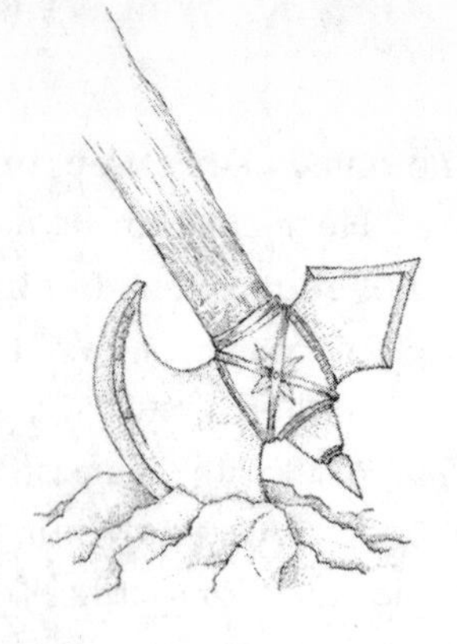

I've never seen Ash happier than when she came back from the bathing room, towel around her shoulders, hair and skin scrubbed clean. She seems lighter, like a weight's been lifted. And that smile… I guess we're all better for a wash, warm food, and a night's sleep at Toretta's Harbor Inn. If it weren't for the hair-bristling argument we've been having since after midnight, the good feeling might have lasted.

But it hasn't.

I know *why* we're fighting. She thinks we have enough facts to go on and I…well, I'm going in circles. I must reach Aku before they close the gates for the final session of the year, but I can't break Palrion law to do it—laws that I will someday have a hand in making and upholding… which won't happen if I can't reach Aku in time.

Ash keeps repeating the bosun's mate's promise that "no harm will come to any *on this voyage*." Does she not hear the contradiction? Can it excuse the captain if children are tossed overboard on *other* voyages, even if they do it beyond our territory?

"What's the alternative?" she asks.

"We ride over enemy lands."

"Marcus, it's incredibly dangerous and may take far too long." She's packing while we talk, being careful with her parchments and inks but shoving her clothes in roughly. She pulls the straps and buckles them tight, like at any moment, her possessions will escape. I can see the frustration in her rise, turning her cheeks pink.

The problem is, she's right. No other choice presents itself. Samsen, Piper, and Belair weighed in last night—all three are willing to follow me either way. Back to Baiseen, the journey failed, or on to Aku aboard a suspicious ship. They've gone down to the stables to oil our blades and tack. Sea journeys are rough on equipment, and we want the gear protected—that is, if we board the ship at all. It all comes back to me. It's my decision, and I still haven't made it.

The Bone Thrower's list of advice doesn't help much, either, except the urge to go north.

"The *Sea Eagle* is our best bet—"

"Black sails, Ash." I slam my empty mug on the table. "Don't you see? It's the principle of the thing. Human sacrifice. We've outlawed it in Palrio." I take a deep breath and blast it out in a rush. "My own brother was sacrificed before that, remember?"

"I do." Her eyes soften while holding my gaze.

"You can't be so nonjudgmental that you condone it." My face heats. Part of me suspects Ash is further along the path to An'awntia than any of us. Except she can't be. She's non-savant.

"The thought of children dying from the throw of the bones, just because they are different, makes me sick. You know that."

"But?"

"The ancient texts—"

I hold up a hand. "The short version, please. It's already near dawn."

"It's a complex issue, with different ways of viewing it."

"What different ways?" Is she kidding? "A child is thrown into the sea. A garland follows. Done. Over. Atrocious!"

"And pulling the heart out of a man's chest isn't equally barbaric?" She gasps and her eyes flood with guilt after she says it, but it's too late. The words are out.

My shoulders want to cave, but I don't let them. "I won't apologize for my father protecting our realm."

"I'm sorry, Marcus. That wasn't your doing. Neither practice is civilized, but—"

"No more buts. The sacrifices must be stamped out." I'm not going to debate the Magistrate's actions with her.

"Forcing people to stop something they believe in won't take them further along the path. They must see it for themselves."

"We could be waiting millennia." I press my hands to my temples. I would sooner die than go home and admit defeat, and by land, we'd never make it to Aku in time—if we made it there at all. Piper's right, and the Tangeen is, too; beyond our borders, even here in Toretta itself, enemies are plentiful. None of them would want to see me make it to Aku.

And to venture straight into Aturnia? My father would likely have my head on a pike solely for taking the risk. I can't say I'd fault him. Who knows what the Aturnians might try to exact from Baiseen if they were to take me hostage.

De'ral rumbles, letting me know that won't happen.

It's odd, feeling him there, beneath my skin, a weight and heat in the center of my chest. He's always been with me, I suppose, but now that my phantom has taken form—shared his name—he's more present. More *real*. I'm not assuming our struggles are over or pretending to know what caused them in the first place, but it's progress. And once we're safe on Aku, with a warrior savant to teach me?

We have to get there first! De'ral blasts the thought into my mind, and for a moment, I'm dizzied. When I recover, Ash is still speaking.

"We could talk to the captain. Confirm Kaylin is right, that no one will be harmed."

I bark a laugh. "Talk? With a captain of a black-sailed ship?"

"Mother of Gaveren, at least *consider* it. Change begins with communication."

"Upholding the law brings faster results." Damn it, it's the reason for having them.

Ash lowers her eyes. "This is why war threatens the realms. People trying to force one another to do as they see fit. There's no respect for their path."

"Shouldn't be, when their path is wrong." Somewhere deep down, I know this isn't right, but I spit it out anyway. And philosophically debating a practice is not the same as standing idly by and condoning it—

"We have to go!" Belair runs into the room, nearly bowling us over. "Armed guards are headed our way."

"How do you know?" I dart to the window, but there's nothing to see. De'ral surges under my skin.

"Samsen's *alter's* been keeping watch from above. They'll be here in moments."

Ash quickly grabs our gear.

"They're knocking on doors along the way, questioning the early-rising marketeers. Everyone points to the inn." Belair's hands shake as he speaks.

"Could be someone else here?" I'm grasping for a different reason.

Ash hands me my pack. "Didn't you notice? We're the only guests."

Seems Toretta really is full of spies, and the thought paralyzes me.

"We have to go, Marcus." Ash grips my arm tightly. "The governor may be an honest man, but by the time we explain ourselves, the whole city will know you are here, the ship will have sailed, and any chance of riding out unseen will be gone." She shoulders her pack and checks the room one last time.

"Curse it. You're right." I pull on my coat. "Where are the others?"

"Outside, horses and gear in hand."

"Go." I wave Belair ahead and take Ash's hand as we run after him down the stairs.

8

SALILA

"*Sa-lee-la.*"

My eyes fling open. The night water surrounds me, cool and undulating with lacy bioluminescent creatures—sea pens, nudibranchs, firefly squid—sleeping coral fish, and a cookie cutter shark in the distance.

I let go of the reef anchoring me to the ocean floor and rise a few fathoms. The current ripples over my body, tickling me from my head to the tips of my toes. Water plays in my hair, fanning it about like a waving kelp garden. Nothing on land compares to this feeling, though I do like wearing dresses and sampling the delectable candies and sweetcakes found in the world of landers. After eons up and down, I can still pass as a girl of twenty years—when Father lets me rise, that is. Which hasn't been for some time.

I find a new anchor in the craggy reef and stretch my free hand into the current.

"Salila?" Teern's second call wafts gently through my mind.

"Yes, Father?"

"Were you dreaming?" Teern, the king of the Mar—known as Father to us all, though there's no blood relation for any of us—couldn't care less about my dreams. He's deceptive like that, making me deceptive right back.

"Of course not, Father. I'm wide awake." Also a bit bored, considering how long it's taking. *"Are they rowing out in a canoe?"*

"Patience."

Eventually, a keel glides through the water overhead. I roll onto my back and track its progress. Its shadow drifts over me, momentarily blocking beams from the waxing moon.

"Black sails?" I ask. Impossible to tell from this angle, and I'm not surfacing unless Teern gives the word. He thinks there have been too many Mar sightings. Of me, in particular. It's the one rule he's sworn us all to uphold, and for my transgressions, I'm paying heavily. Just look

at me—under Teern's constant eye, tasked with saving *all* the marred children tossed into the sea and rushing them to the nearest Ma'ata grove. Granted, bringing new little brothers and sisters to life in the sea is rewarding. But it's been years now, and I could be doing endlessly more entertaining things with my time.

I snag a sleeping parrotfish, shake it out of its cocoon, and pop it down my throat. A moment later, I pull out a filleted skeleton.

"Sails are black as night," Teern says.

I push off the reef and stream after the ship, kicking effortlessly through the water. Stupid, idiot landers. Throwing away a perfectly good child. But then, if they abandon the practice completely, what happens to us? It would be much easier if they handed them straight over and—

"Focus, Salila!" Teern's voice booms, nearly shattering my skull. Father isn't one for subtleties.

Anyway, landers have their uses, and this is one of them. Of course, they don't believe in us anymore. They think they're sacrificing marred children to appease the old gods. Let me say it again: stupid, idiot landers. There are no old gods at the bottom of the Drop, haven't been since the last Great Dying. But, lucky for the children, there are Mar.

The hull slices through the waves, splitting the water apart to leave a frothy wake behind. They lower the sails when over the Drop, a long crack in Amassia's continental shelf. It runs for leagues from the coast of Palrio to the Isle of Aku. A nice, deep hole in our watery wonderland. Partway down the Drop, there are large pelagic fish. A moderate concern tonight. Below them lurk enormous, graceful squid, a problem only if they notice the pelagics thrashing about. Even lower, where no vertebrate can survive, are ancient things without bones—aquatic novelties that have survived many a Great Dying.

So, no. There are no gods, old or new. Something is sure to enjoy a feed of lander babe if I fail, but it's made of flesh and bone, not spirit.

"Be ready."

As if I'm not.

I rise under the ship and cling to the barnacle-covered keel, rocking side to side with the boat. *"Need some maintenance down here, boys,"* I say. The sailors do not hear me. They're stunted when it comes to mind speech, though I can hear them under certain enjoyable circumstances, which involve proximity and blood. The thought makes me hungry.

"Salila!"

Hollow drumbeats echo through the hull, sending vibrations into the water. Landers think it alerts the gods, but really it attracts only sharks. Stupid, stupid, stupid…

Teern appears out of nowhere, the rush of countercurrents ripping away my handhold. He always makes a showy entrance. I mask the thought, but maybe too late.

Teern nods. His long black hair dances around his bearded face and broad shoulders. "*Don't lose this one,*" he says.

"Not planning to, Father."

The drums stop, and a splash breaks the surface of the water.

A flurry of silver bubbles race upward through the dark as the offering plummets into the mouth of the Drop. All I can see is a bundle of iron chains. Honestly, do they think it can get away?

"*Go!*"

I push off. The ship is already drifting back from the ravine, so it takes a few kicks to go over the edge and toward the child. The water is thick, ice-cold to lander flesh. It doesn't hamper me, but it will kill the baby in no time—that, and the prolonged asphyxiation. This would be so much simpler if Father would let me snatch them while still on deck, but oh no. We mustn't reveal ourselves to the landers. Ever. If I were in charge, that rule would be the first to go.

I kick harder, fingers stretching, touching. Grasping. The moment the little boy is in my arms, I roll back, pumping my legs to reach the surface, angling away from the ship at the same time. *"Gotcha!"*

His rapid pulse throbs against my fingers. "*He's alive.*" Sometimes they're not. I untangle the thick links of chain and let them fall into the pitch-dark below.

"Follow me." Teern shoots off toward the Ma'ata coral groves, clearing the way.

Bubbles no longer escape the baby's lips, and the smooth pink skin turns gray. His eyes are wide, staring at nothing. *"Don't worry, little Mar. Salila has you."*

I break the surface and suck in air. Not for me, for him. On the dive back down, I cover his mouth with my own and gently fill his lungs. I hear his heart pulse, once, twice, then more frequently. I swim under the waves, repeating the process, trailing Teern. The Ma'ata corals are near. *"Almost home."*

A part of me envies the deep-sea dreams he's about to have.

When we arrive, his pulse against my finger is slow and thready. I weave through the sunken graveyard, stirring up sand and parting kelp.

"It's a beautiful boy!" The Ma'ata Keeper directs me to an empty tomb. "*Lay him here.*"

More of us gather around to chant and fend off predators.

The Ma'ata Keeper pricks the baby's heel with her eye tooth, and a few drops of blood drift over the tomb. My body trembles as the Ma'ata corals stir, opening their polyps, sending out tendrils. The Keeper places her hand on the baby's heart. Teern joins her, as do I. *"See, little brother? The Ma'ata has you safe."*

In seconds, the corals, sparkling with their own violet bioluminescence, elongate and wrap themselves around the child like mummy cloth. Soon there is no hint of tiny hands save for a thumb, no sight of his face but half a vacant eye. Then even those last physical features disappear.

"*Success.*" I smile and turn to go.

"Too soon to tell," Teern says, blocking my exit.

Such a pessimist.

"He has a good chance." I toy with the tip of a feather duster worm until it snaps back into its tube. I can tell Teern has more to say, and I don't want to hear it. *"Tallyho, then."* I shoot toward shore.

"Salila!" His voice stops me dead in the water, and I sink to the bottom. *"Where are you going?"*

"*Me?*" I lift my chin.

The look he gives is not pleasant. *"You will follow the carrack."*

I fidget with my hair. *"Really? You don't think he can do the job on his own?"*

"Remains to be seen, but you will keep me informed."

"Spy?" I brighten.

"If you like calling it that."

"*I do.*" I've already been following the new passengers on the *Sea Eagle* since they left Baiseen. The young Heir especially catches my eye. All Mar know the leaders of the realms by sight, but Marcus Adicio…he's a sight for hungry eyes.

"What's that, Salila?"

"I said it's a delight to serve at your pleasure, Father."

"Then catch up, and don't be seen."

9

ASH

Vez venom and spit, I moan to myself. *Death would be preferable to this.*

"Not necessarily," my inner voice says like it's a fine spring day.

How would you know?

I rock in the corner of the ship, arms around a wooden bucket. Seasickness absorbs my every thought, leaving little room to ponder what may or may not be happening topside. My stomach sloshes out of sync with the rise and fall of the *Sea Eagle*, and bouts of sweats alternate with sudden chills. I've suffered seasickness before, but never as bad as this.

Marcus brings me herbal drinks, Piper mixing this concoction and that… I appreciate their efforts, but it's not like I can hold any of them down. Still, it hasn't completely addled my brain. I remember to question Marcus about his conversation with the captain. He says there's nothing to worry about. Upon hearing his title—because apparently the Heir can't go a minute without letting it slip—Captain Nadonis spouted assurances, swearing on all sorts of oceanic treasures that there never was, nor will be, a breach of Palrio's law.

Marcus was satisfied, and I'm going to hang on to that.

"Kaylin did say none would be harmed…"

I'm hanging on to that, too.

The thought of the sailor makes me want to go topside. Not to find him! Oh no. Not feeling, and looking, like this. But I can't stand to be trapped in the hold a moment longer.

After a few deep breaths, I let go of my bucket and stagger to the galley. There everyone sits, enjoying the evening meal.

"Ash." Marcus gets up to help me. "Can you eat?"

I warn him back with a weak hand. Words are too hard to form, and nodding my head? Out of the question. The smells of fried fish and hot oil are not helping. Piper offers to brew more of her concoction. I lurch past, mouth turned down, my throat full of bile. They don't appear bothered at all by the rise and fall of the creaking vessel. Or the strong smells coming from the galley.

I catch the eye of the chef, a massive man wearing nothing but drawstring pants and a stained apron over his hairy chest. It's not a pretty sight. He stares at me for a moment, then turns his gaze on Piper, all while paring his fingernails with a long kitchen knife. It's as if my mind is homing in on the details that might make me sicker. The ship rocks again, and I stumble to the ladder. Belair rushes to offer help. My hand's up, warning him back, too.

The climb out of the hold saps what little strength I have left. But I reach the hatch, and thankfully, it's wide open. As I emerge onto the deck, the sea air slaps my face, fresh and salty. I take a breath, lunge to the rail, and dry heave over the side. There's nothing to do but hang on while the sun lights the horizon on fire. The coast is near, shadowy purple hills pitching up and down, gray mountains beyond, reaching for the clouds. I heave again. The sails, when I point my nose skyward to see them, are red like the brilliant sunset.

"Not found your sea legs, lass?"

"Demon's f'qud!" I look over my shoulder at Kaylin. "You startled me."

"And you swear in Aturnian." He looks quite pleased about that.

"I swear in every language. I hope it didn't offend you." Mostly I hope he doesn't notice how wretched I must look.

"Offend? I'm a sailor. Your vocabulary's a delight, but I can see you're unwell."

"*So astute.*"

Not now—hush!

He steps closer, fortunately unable to hear my inner dialogue. "Give me your hand."

I grip the rail tighter. "I don't think I can." For several reasons, staying upright for one, but the fear of him smelling me runs a close second. "I think I left my legs back in the hold." He's still not wearing a shirt? All that smooth tan skin exposed. Doesn't he feel the cold?

"May I?" He stands next to me at the rail and pushes up the cuff of my embroidered sheepskin coat. His long fingers wrap around my wrist, searching for a particular spot on the inside of my arm. "There." He presses two fingers into my skin quite hard.

I flush from head to toe and feel the fine hairs on my arms lift. But the pain is good. It takes my mind off the next wave of nausea. "I, uh, need to wash."

"Let's get you steady first." He presses even closer, putting his arm around me to reach the other wrist as well.

Gods of the sea, what this does to my nerves. Could a leaf tremble more? He puts pressure on the points, on both wrists, leaning in to my back, the rocking of the waves like a slow dance. Or it would be, if I weren't unbearably ill.

"This will help you make peace with the sea," he whispers in my ear.

I close my eyes and swallow another surge of bile. It stays down. Thank the Deep. He holds me like this for minutes. I don't know how many. I start to lose track of everything, including my limbs. But my stomach…

"Better?" Kaylin asks.

I hesitate to admit it, in case it's too soon to tell, so I say nothing.

"See if you can stand now." He turns me around to face him. His eyes dance when they find mine.

I need only one hand on the rail as strength returns to my spine.

"Drink of water?"

I nod, and my brain doesn't slosh up and down like a bucket of swill. No sickening cold sweat breaks out on my forehead. Warmth swells in my chest as I praise every divinity that has ever lived. I think he's cured me!

Kaylin demonstrates how to apply pressure to my own wrist. "Keep it firm. I'll get you a drink." He heads to the foremast, where the water barrels are lashed down.

While he's gone, two sailors walk by. I recognize one from the other day in Toretta, the sailor who had me drawing a knife to defend myself or, at least, stand my ground. He's tossing a coin. When he slaps it onto the back of his hand, he shows his mate and they both laugh. I don't want to think about their wager, but when Kaylin returns, they move off, suddenly busy with work.

"Sip slowly." Kaylin hands me a wooden cup.

"I'm scared to let go of my wrist."

"Let me." He takes over the pressure. It brings his hands, and bare chest, very close. He smells clean, like the ocean.

The very air around me feels vitalized. The drink washes away the sour taste in my mouth. It reaches my stomach and spreads from there like a soothing balm. "This is more than just water?" I've never tasted anything so good.

"Water from the springs of Tutapa."

"Ah." I drink more. "Your home. Those fabled pools are known for their healing properties. I thought that was a myth."

"And now?"

"A truth I am willing to boast from every rooftop."

He laughs, and I join him, though I want to roll my eyes at myself. Boast from every rooftop? Who says that?

"Apparently, you do," my inner voice chimes.

When the cup is empty, I lick moisture from my lips. "I'm feeling much better."

"What are you doing on a sea journey, lass, if it affects you so?"

"I'm always seasick, even crossing from Palrio to Nonnova, but it's never been this bad." I press my lips together and raise my chin. "It's worth it, though."

"You love your work?"

"That." And then, more softly, "I plan to set foot on every realm in Amassia."

"Is that right?"

"You think it ambitious?"

"Not in a bad way," he says. "It's a worthy goal."

I realize he's still holding both my wrists, standing close enough to, well...be close. A fresh wave of heat rises up my neck to my face.

"You're getting your color back."

And then some.

"I...am?" Is he teasing? We rock up and down with the swell, comfortable in a gentle silence, until I remember how I must smell. "You said I could wash?" I wonder if there is any privacy. The "toilet" certainly has none.

"This way." He takes me by the hand and leads me aft, where we duck behind a stack of water barrels.

"Where did you learn this?" I ask when he hands me a sponge and bucket. "The seasickness cure?"

"A healer from the far north."

"You have to show Piper."

He gives a half smile but says no more.

"Thank you, and to the northern healer. I thought I was going to die."

"If the sickness comes back, press again. Use these two fingers." He shows me one more time. "Eat something as soon as you can. There's broth on the stove."

I don't want him to leave in case he takes the well-being away with him. "I'm very grateful."

"My pleasure. Have your wash, lass. You're safe here." He bows to me, and when I can't think of anything else to say, he heads up the mast to the crow's nest.

I watch him climb while the sun fully sets. The sky is beautiful with its shades of purple, red, and inky blue. I can't believe how much better I feel. It makes me want to sing, though I content myself with humming in the near darkness, not wanting to attract attention.

"You're safe." My inner voice repeats his words, as much a comfort as the cure.

I take off my clothes and wash. The water is cold, the wind colder, but the salty breeze quickly dries my skin. I shake out my pants and dress myself, feeling a renewed, inner strength. My sea legs become stable beneath me, and I rock easily with the motion of the ship.

"You're looking much improved." Marcus is there when I step from behind the water barrels.

I take the mug he hands me. "Have you been watching out for my privacy this whole time?"

"Didn't want the *Sea Eagle*'s crew to have the pleasure. They've been very liberal with their eyes on Piper."

"Have they?" I frown into the dark broth, gripping it tightly. If they so much as touch Piper, they'll have to deal with all five of us. "Thank you, then."

The mast creaks, and I gaze up at the night. There's a silhouette in the crow's nest, an outline against the stars. "Kaylin healed me."

"Who?"

I tip my head to the top of the mast, and Marcus follows my gaze. "Kaylin, the bosun's mate."

"Glad someone did. I was about to ask Piper to raise her phantom and heal you if it lasted one more day."

"As if she could." Phantoms cannot be raised or put to ground over water. As with all things, they are born of the earth and so must pass through it to take form.

"Let's get you below." Marcus leads the way to the hatch and down the ladder. He sits me at the table while the carrack smashes through wave after wave. I keep pressure on my wrist and manage another cup of broth and a chunk of bread. Finally, he retrieves my satchel for me so

I can work on the records. He must be bored. *Really* bored. I've never seen him quite this helpful before.

"He was worried about you," my inner voice says.

I smile at him. "Tell me what's happened while I was sick—and don't embellish. That's my job."

Marcus laughs.

He relays our exact position and details the conversation with the captain. "The ship, as far as I know, did not change sails or pause at the Drop. We're headed straight to Capper Point, as a crow flies, the captain told me."

"That's the best news." I make notes for both him and Belair, whose records will be separate, of course, but with some overlap, especially on the journey to and from. The horror of child sacrifice is still with us, but at least the controversial black sails won't be in the journey records. It sidesteps a much greater set of problems, but for now, I don't see what else we can do.

I start to put my quill and ink away, leaving the parchments on the table to dry, when the all-hands whistle sounds. A few crewmen run up to the deck, and the next thing I know, I'm slammed against Marcus, my gear sliding into his lap, ink bottles hitting the floor and rolling into the galley.

"That was abrupt." He helps me put everything back in my satchel.

"Feels like we're coming about." I look out the porthole, but it's pitch-black, mostly. As the ship rises and falls, I see a golden flash on the horizon. "Are those running lights?"

"I'll find out." Before Marcus can reach the hatch, a sailor sticks his head in. "Stay below. Cap'n's orders." The hatch slams shut and locks.

Marcus and I stare at each other, eyes wide while the *Sea Eagle* bobs up and down.

"What could be happening?" Marcus asks.

I press my wrist hard. "Don't know why, but I swear we're dead in the water."

10

MARCUS

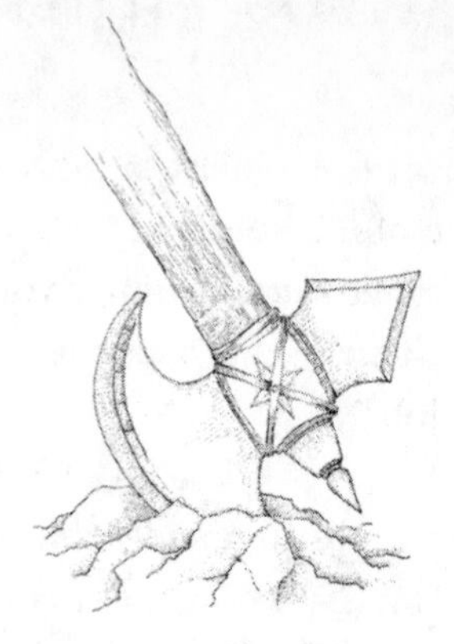

The sun is just starting to come up when they finally unlock the hatch. I'm on deck immediately, keen to talk to Captain Nadonis about our unscheduled stop.

"Change of plans," the captain says without the slightest apology to me.

"Pardon?" I must not have heard him correctly.

"There's been a change of plans." He stands with his broad back to the wheelhouse, his legs wide as they absorb the rise and fall of the ship. He holds the wheel lightly with his thick, meaty hands. His eyes are dead ahead, as if in all this expanse of ocean, we're going to collide with something any minute.

I step closer and look down on him. It's not hard. He's short, though nearly as wide as he is tall. "What kind of change?" I reach out to the man-size wooden wheel for stability as the ship lurches to the left.

"We're putting you and your party ashore at Clearwater."

"That's not what we agreed."

"Near enough." Nadonis pivots to the chart table and stabs his thumb at the coastal town on the map. "Clearwater's south of— "

"I know where Clearwater is."

De'ral rolls under my skin, awakened by my irritation. We are nearly there and now this? I tap the map. "It's a day's ride to Capper Point from Clearwater, if the horses can do more than a dog trot after this voyage. More likely two."

"Bad luck for us both. I have to hand off my cargo there, too."

"Why?"

Nadonis picks at his bearded chin. "Captain Radin on the *Green Turtle* reported last night. Seems there's a Northern Aturnian warship moored at Capper Point. They're searching all incoming. We can't let them find you aboard the *Sea Eagle*, can we, Heir?"

Too many thoughts run through my head at once. The risks to my group, to me just setting foot on Northern Aturnian soil. And what does it mean, an Aturnian warship searching vessels from the south? Do they want to incite war? I blame myself for not controlling my phantom sooner and making this initiation journey last year or the year before.

"Clearwater?" I say it again. "This is unacceptable."

"Can't be helped."

"Why not go around and drop us directly at Aku?" I remember the answer as soon as I ask.

The captain's gaze returns to the sea. "We draw too deep. Never make it over the reefs."

I cross my arms. "That's it? No other possibilities?"

"Like I said, it can't be helped."

I take a long sniff of air. "Then you will reimburse me."

Nadonis frowns. "How do you reckon?"

"You didn't hold up your end of the bargain. I want my coin back."

"Mitigating circumstances," the captain says, as if that's the end of the topic.

My head starts to ache; it's like a blacksmith shaping horseshoes on my skull. De'ral's building rage and impatience aren't helping.

"De'ral, ease up."

He relaxes a bit, making it possible to think. "You're cutting the contracted journey short." I speak slowly to keep from spitting each word. "That merits a return of fifteen gold pieces a head, man and beast alike." Ash always says to start high.

"Two gold each for the party; one each for the equines."

"Absurd." De'ral is right behind my eyes, a sensation completely new to me. It must show in my expression because the captain takes half a step back. "Twelve gold each for us and ten for the beasts," I counter.

"Seven and five," the captain says.

"Ten and eight."

"Done." Captain Nadonis thrusts out his hand.

I grip it hard, trying not to look surprised. It's twice what I'd hoped to get.

Nadonis grips back a little harder.

Heat rises from my core, and my eyes burn. When I come back to myself, I'm squeezing his hand like a vise.

Nadonis is red-faced and sweating.

"De'ral, let go!"

The captain exhales as he retrieves his throbbing hand.

"Done and even," I say, pretending I didn't nearly crush his bones. "I'll tell the others." My footsteps clip across the deck. I should be worried about being dropped at Clearwater, but I'm more concerned with what just happened. De'ral wasn't even raised, and he had that much influence on my mind, my actions?

From my core comes phantom laughter.

I rub my temples and head for the hatch. Warmth hits me as I climb down the ladder to the galley. All four tables are occupied, the cook serving up the midday meal. I spot Belair sitting opposite Samsen, who has his arm possessively curled around Piper. "I've got news."

"One day to Capper Point, then we reach Aku with a day to spare?" Samsen guesses.

I shake my head. "We disembark at Clearwater. The *Sea Eagle* will go no farther."

Piper nearly drops her spoon. "What? And ride across the border into Northern Aturnia? That's what we were trying to avoid."

"Troops could be anywhere," Samsen says. "If they stop us..."

"I don't understand." Belair pushes his bowl away, half finished.

"There's an Aturnian warship checking all incoming passengers. If they get wind of who I am..."

Belair groans. "Tell me what the Bone Throwers said again? Anything like this?"

I pull the note out and read aloud. "*Remember to keep the company's number to five*." Obviously. "*In spite of autumn chill, optimism wins out*." I don't know why, but that one just irritates me. "*Surprise comes from the sea. Don't resist it*." My neck cracks as I rock it side to side. "That was the fish run."

"Or maybe it's—surprise! We're being put off at Clearwater," Belair says.

I ignore the comment and keep reading. "Then, *when in doubt, go north*." Well, yes, Aku is still to the north. "Also, *a sword brings truth and deception*."

"Riddles to me," Samsen says.

"Agreed, but this, *do not raise your phantom until safe on Aku*, that I understand. And the next two are comforting. *The Heir will not be stopped*, and *out of Aku, the warriors triumph, and the southern realms are changed forever*."

“Black-robes and the mysterious threads they weave,” Piper says.

“Yet this detour can’t be helped.” Nadonis’s words come in handy. “But I’m certain we’ll make it to Capper Point in time and not be stopped.”

Belair wipes his mouth and stares glumly at his bowl. “Let’s hope so.”

“Where’s Ash?” Sometimes a subject change is best in situations like these. It’s a tactic I’ve employed with my father, not that the Magistrate is easily distracted.

“She’s down in the lower hold with the beasts.” Belair finds his feet. “I’ll let her know.”

“I can go.” But the Tangeen is already to the lower hatch. It would look silly to dart after him. “What’s his big interest?” I ask Piper as I sit back down. “He seems in quite the hurry to get to her.”

“It’s not so much our recorder who has his attention,” Samsen says, “but the company she keeps.”

“Horses?”

Piper and Samsen both laugh. “There’s more than beasts below,” Piper says.

I only half listen as I catch the sailors at the main table glancing our way, talking under their breaths. I reach for a chunk of bread and pop it into my mouth, staring back. Belair is right about one thing. If the Bone Throwers saw this turn of events, they didn’t share it with me.

11

ASH

"Manta Bay?" Kaylin asks, leaning on a stack of hay, watching me tend to the horses. He wears a teasing look, mainly because that's exactly what he's doing. Teasing me. "The waves are extraordinary below the cliffs of Kutoon," he goes on. "You can ride them all the way to the beach."

"Haven't been there, either." *Please remind me never to boast about my travels to a sailor.*

"After this humbling lesson, I doubt a reminder will be necessary."

Ugh…

"The terraced temple grounds of Whitewing, then?"

"I've seen paintings of them in Pandom City but haven't visited yet."

"Asyleen?"

"Stop!" He's having too much fun with me now. "You outdistance me many times over." I pour water into the horses' buckets, standing easy on my sea legs in the bowels of the ship. There's much less rocking down here, or maybe my mind is just absorbed with other things.

He smiles. "I'm sure you've done things I haven't."

"He's very polite," my inner voice observes.

I tap my lips, thinking. "Have you ever ridden horseback through the palm forests of Tangeen? They are magnificent in the autumn, the paths littered with giant fronds as red as volcanic earth. The flamingo water holes look like shimmering pools at sunset until the birds all take flight. It's amazing."

At last, it's his turn to shake his head. "Never been on a horse."

I blink. "How is that possible?"

"My life is the sea, lass."

My knees wobble a bit, and not because of the rocking ship. It happens every time he calls me "lass" in that melodic accent of his. "But surely you've patted a horse, at least."

He shakes his head.

"Show him."

I smile right up to my eyes. "Come with me."

We move in and out of the shadows as the light, a single lantern hanging high overhead, swings from side to side. It makes our elongated silhouettes rise up the planks of the hold. They splash across the ceiling and then shrink back to the floorboards. Up and down. Up and down. Like ghost phantoms rising to watch over us before slinking back to the earth. We stop at the tie stalls, and when I turn around, he's right there. I lose myself in Kaylin's eyes for a few seconds longer than would be considered proper, but he's staring right back. Then I'm not sure where to look…

"Mind on the task so you don't trip over yourself?" my inner voice suggests.

I cough into my elbow to clear my throat. "This is Rita. She's my dapple-gray mare." I rephrase. "Mine, as in the horse I'm assigned to ride." I make a formal introduction while unbuckling her blanket and pulling it off over her rump. "Oh dear."

"What's wrong."

"She loses more condition every day we're at sea. They all do, but look at her legs. So swollen, poor thing."

His hand hovers over the mare's neck like she's made of glass.

"She won't break." I hand him a stiff brush. "Start behind the ear and go right down to her shoulder. It will help her circulation, a good grooming."

"What about her face?"

"There's a softer one for that and her legs." I grab another brush from the bucket and go to her off side—equestrian talk for the right side of the horse. Rita turns to me and flutters air from her nose.

"She likes you," he comments.

"Most animals do."

"Smart creatures, I'd say."

Unlike his earlier teasing, this feels more like flirting. My pulse quickens. I go up on tiptoe to eye him over the horse's withers.

But Kaylin seems fully focused on the task. "Did your parents have a stable?"

I let out a dry laugh, trying to remember if I told him I'd been orphaned. "Not hardly. They were too poor."

"But you ride?"

"Only because Marcus taught me. We spent half our youth in the palace stables and the hills beyond."

I come back around and exchange the brush for a curry comb. "She loves her belly rubbed."

"How can you tell?"

"Watch."

He makes room for me, but not much. I sense him inches away as I bend to curry Rita's belly in fast, vigorous circles, one hand gripping her mane for an anchor. The mare extends her neck, closes her eyes, and tilts her head, her upper lip twitching.

"She *does* love it." Kaylin leans down and puts his hand over mine. "Let me try?"

Tingles run up my arm at his touch. His ocean scent surrounds me, and I fumble the curry comb as I pass it over. An unintelligible bubble of sound erupts from me. Please, grant me some self-control! With a wide-tooth comb, I return to the off side to untangle her mane and calm down.

"This is odd."

I come back to find him brushing a small indentation in the mare's chest.

"That happened when she was a yearling. Marcus's black palfrey, Echo..." I tilt my head to the tie stall next to us. "She kicked her when we were leading them out of the stables. It left a permanent mark."

"That's un—"

"Putting the sailor to good use, I see." Belair appears from out of nowhere, clomping noisily down the ladder.

Rita spooks, pulling back on her lead, her haunches nearly on the ground. It triggers the same reaction in the rest of the horses and the donkey, right down the line.

Kaylin puts an arm around me and leaps aside. I trip over the groom bucket, and we end up in a tangle on the hay bales. I'm back on my feet like a spring and hurry to calm the stock. "F'qnon, Belair. A little warning around these animals."

Kaylin is up beside me, pulling straw out of my hair. I laugh and make to brush hay off his shoulders, stopping before I touch his bare skin.

"Sorry," Belair says. "I wasn't expecting to find you two like this."

Like what? I mouth at him, straightening my clothes. "I'm teaching Kaylin horsemanship."

Belair comes all the way down the ladder and leans his back against it. "Obviously."

I prepare to deliver a witty quip, but the first mate's whistle blows topside.

"That's me." Kaylin tips his head, returning his brush to the bucket and righting it. "Perhaps we can continue this later, Ash." He nods to Belair and is out of the hold like a shot.

Belair's eyes follow him. "Have you ever known a more divine chap?"

"Ha!" I pick up Rita's hoof and clean it with a hoof-pick. "I knew you liked him, but I don't think he's your persuasion."

"I can hope, can't I?"

"Of course, and while you're hoping, please give me a hand with the rest of the horses."

I fill their hay nets while Belair unbuckles his bay gelding's blanket. He rubs his horse's haunches before moving to inspect the bay's legs. "You'll be hard-pressed to carry me."

"What's that?"

"I came to tell you." His expression turns serious. "Our sea journey's been cut short."

I pause what I'm doing. "Kaylin didn't mention."

"The captain only just told Marcus. We're being put off at Clearwater."

My muscles tense, mouth goes dry. "What possible reason would there be?"

"Something about a warship at Capper Point searching incoming vessels." He finishes grooming the bay and moves on to the donkey. "Marcus wants us packed. We reach the port by tomorrow morning. Obviously, we can't have any delays."

I pick up Echo's hoof, keeping my head down, not wanting to show my concern. "I'll be ready."

"Me too." Belair frowns at his mount's swollen legs. "But I don't know if we can say the same for any of the horses."

I wish it wasn't true, but he's right.

It wouldn't matter if we were in our home realm, with endless days to reach Aku. We could take it slow. Rest along the way. But we have three dawns left before the gates close, and this is Aturnia we are about to set foot in. Enemy soil. Unknown territory. Marcus's future and our very lives depend on these horses being sound, and danck the bones, a small child could see they are not.

12

MARCUS

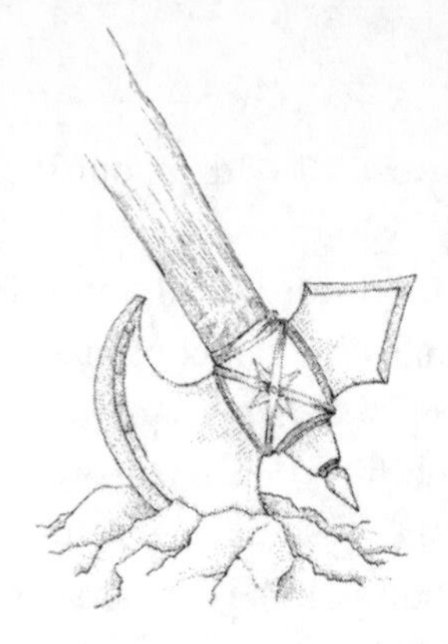

I stand on the main deck, wet with fog. Apparently, Clearwater Harbor is coming into view, but I can't see anything in this soup. Ash kneels next to me, rummaging through her pack, muttering curses.

"If you're looking for the bosun's mate, you won't find him in there."

"What? My gloves are missing." She pulls out a dark-green knit hat and plops it on her head. "That's all."

"If you say so." It seems about more than missing gloves to me. "The captain recommends we ride the coast road until dark, camp the night, and then on to Capper Point in the morning before the sloops sail for Aku. We'll make it, he says, with time to spare."

"Is the road safe for us?" She's given up searching her pack and stares up at the crow's nest.

"Both Southern and Northern Aturnia are bound by custom to let initiates pass." I say it with a little less confidence each time. "The Bone Throwers didn't suggest any trouble."

"They didn't suggest the fish would be running, either."

"But Oba did say, when in doubt—"

"Go north." She exhales forcefully. "What other direction would we take? Aku is due north."

Exactly. Which makes me think perhaps we put too much stake in the bones.

"Marcus, promise you'll keep your identity hidden. And let me speak in public from now on. We don't want people overhearing our accents, just in case customs aren't being honored. If you have to say something, use the Aturnian words you know. Tell me you remember some."

"Don't worry so much." I rub her shoulders. Somehow her concern helps me stay calm. "On the bright side, you'll be setting foot in both Southern and Northern Aturnia today. Two more realms to tick off your list."

She huffs out a laugh. "Not quite how I envisioned experiencing it, but true."

The captain wants the horses off-loaded first, so we head for the hold. Once there, it's as feared.

"They aren't sound," Samsen says.

Ash's mare stumbles down the ramp. She comes back up fast but walks so stiffly, I can't tell if she's injured or just sore. Echo and the donkey aren't too bad, but the other three are completely stove-up—their legs swollen and joints puffy.

"Don't consider it." Samsen rests his hand on Piper's shoulder. "I know you want to, but at what cost?"

He's right. Our healer might be able to help one of these fifteen-hundred-pound horses, but all five? And then struggle to hold them still while a two-headed snake latches onto their throats? Not going to happen.

Ash holds Rita and the donkey to the side of the dock while I help Belair bring his bay gelding down the ramp. He's the worst off, and cranky for it. Suddenly I have a tall and wobbly horse to manage along with Echo, who pins her ears back at the bay when he tries to bite. Samsen and Piper are still trying to coax their mounts onto the ramp. I turn to Ash for help, but the bosun's mate is in her ear. Whatever he's saying, it has Ash turning pale and then red.

"What was that about?" I ask when he's gone.

"I'll tell you when we're clear of the crowd."

Piper arrives with her horse and Samsen follows with Frost, his winter-white mount, Belair clucking to him from behind. I lead the way, but the dock is a logjam. People are shouting, the donkey keeps braying, and longshoremen run up to unload the apple barrels and other cargo, crates of various sizes I hadn't noticed before. "Chicoopa!" I shout the Aturnian word for *make way.*

"You mean chiroop?" Ash says under her breath.

"Chiroop! Chiroop!"

Eventually we push through, walking single file down the dock. The animals stumble to a halt at the harbor entrance, where we lead them up the final ramp to the main street of Clearwater.

"Blacksmith?" Ash is up on tiptoes, searching the thoroughfare.

Having the advantage of height, I spot their shingle, an anvil and hammer. "This way." I lead my company straight for the noisy, open-air barn where hot forges give out a welcome warmth and the sound of hammers on anvils rings in my ears. The scents of coal fires and burned hair hit me at the entrance. "A blacksmith shop in any realm is exactly the same."

Ash catches up. "Not exactly."

I look again and realize they are all women. Not big and burly but lean and hardened. One shapes a red-hot horseshoe using rhythmic hammer falls, tapping the iron, then letting the hammer bounce on the anvil and then tapping again. She says something in Aturnian without looking up from her work.

Ash does the talking and I wish, not for the first time on this trip, that I'd taken my language classes more seriously. For years, my main focus was on field training, but now that I can hold my phantom to form, I realize how much more there is to advancing as a savant. I'm glad that Ash is here.

The farrier straightens, tossing the horseshoe into a bucket of water. Steam hisses up around her as she and Ash exchange more words I don't understand; then the blacksmith turns to the horses. She feels down the big bay's swollen cannon bones and clicks her tongue, not too hard to translate.

I nod as she flips Echo's blanket up. The mare's flank is caved in like a canyon.

Ash gathers us around. "She's going to check their shoes first and watch each one walk. There's a trough at the side of the shop for a good, long drink and hay nets for a gold coin each."

The blacksmith picks up the bay's near foreleg and rubs a callused thumb across the nail heads. The shoe's obviously loose. Must have clipped it unloading.

On the spot, the woman pulls a couple of thin, beveled nails from her tool belt and sticks them in her mouth. She taps a nail in the bottom of the shoe with a small hammer and block. And then she strikes it with one hard drive to catch the bevel, and it pops out the side of the hoof wall, perfectly in line with the other two nails. She's a master at her craft. She wrings the nail off flush against the hoof and clenches it with wide-mouth pliers.

"And liniment?" I ask Ash.

More words are exchanged before she turns back to me. "They're out, but the apothecary's across the street, six doors down."

"I'll go with you." I hand Echo off to Piper and retrieve the shrinking sack of coins from my saddlebags. There are a few unmarked half pieces of gold, and I hand them to Ash, hesitating when I pull the single gold coin from my pants pocket, the one Father tossed me when I left Baiseen.

"Oh?" Ash studies it until realization dawns on her face. "For the fountain on Aku!"

I nod.

"You're *not* spending it here."

She's so adamant, I agree, though Aku's wishing fountain is not high on my mind. Making it out of enemy territory without starting a war, yes, that takes priority.

"We'll be right back," Ash calls to the others and leads me out.

On our way down the street, I raise my brows at Ash. "So what did he say?"

"Pardon?"

"Kaylin. You looked upset."

Her brow pinches. "He gave a warning, but it clashes with the captain's advice."

"Tell me." My stomach sinks. We can't have more bad news today.

"He said a storm's coming. To ride straight to Capper Point and be there by tonight, secure on a ship to Aku. No matter what."

I point my nose to the sky but can't see through the fog. "Storm's coming?"

"It's what he said."

"Is that all?"

"More or less."

She's blushing, so I assume *more* that has no relevance to the journey. It also makes me think I should try to get my own warning back to Baiseen. The Aturnian warship might be working its way south, port by port.

"Here we are." She points to the shingle.

It has lettering that I can't read, and below it is a painting of a man and woman in a garden.

"It says, *Herbs, Medicaments, and Soaps*," she translates.

"That's promising."

I'm about to pull the door open, but Ash plants her hand on it to stop me. "Wait." She studies a notice on the door. It's in Aturnian, I assume, and has symbols at each corner. In the center are two circles, spirals really, one large and one smaller, overlapping and curling into each other like script. "What's it say?"

She shakes her head. "The symbols I don't recognize, but the words, if I'm translating right, say, *Heed the warning. The dark sun draws nigh.*"

"Dark sun?"

"I must have it wrong." Her brow is creased. "The symbols remind me of— "

The doorbells jingle, and a young woman exits the shop. I move aside to let her pass. "Let's go," I say quietly, tilting my head toward the door.

The air is cloying inside, thick as syrup. A middle-aged man and woman fill orders from the wall behind them, stacked to the ceiling with jars of herbs and colored liquids.

"It's a library of flowers and essence." Ash points at the containers, smiling. "And look there." She tips her head up to the herbs hanging from the rafters and lists them off. "Chamomile blossoms, lavender, bay leaves, lemon grass. Is that comfrey or tobacco?"

"No idea." I take shallow breaths and try not to choke.

Ash, on the other hand, is perfectly at home. She chats in Aturnian with the elderly woman in front of us who speaks with a toothless smacking. She's wearing so many layers of clothes, it's a wonder she can move her arms.

"Apparently, this is the only apothecary in town, but they could do with another," Ash interprets.

I give the woman a polite nod but don't risk saying a word, even hello.

Ash seems pleased about that. She says everyone in front of us is after something for a headache. By the smell of their clothes, I suspect they all drink too much, though that pastime is not uncommon outside of the Sanctuary, in the homes and taverns of non-savants. Master Brogal says it's because the communion with one's phantom is its own ecstasy, in a way, its own escape onto another path, something the non-savants all long for. I don't know. Ash has never complained of such longings, and "ecstasy" is hardly the word I would use to describe my relationship with De'ral.

When it's our turn at the counter, Ash asks about the best horse liniment. The short man serving us recommends aberlac, a word she tells me means "muscle relief."

"Best get two bottles," I whisper. "And that tincture for headaches, as well." Maybe it will help me with mine.

After she pays, we head out the door, but I have to drag her away from the notice again. "If the sailor is right, and we need to be in Capper Point by dark, there's no time for this." I take a swig of the tincture and tuck it into my pocket. "Come on!"

She sighs and hurries along beside me to the blacksmith's.

The horses are saddled outside. Everyone gathers around, and Ash and I pour liniment into cupped hands to rub the horses down, elbows to pasterns, gaskins to fetlocks. My hands instantly heat, and fumes go up my nose.

When finished, Ash gives me an expectant look. "Ready?" She has her map out and is measuring the distance with her thumb and forefinger.

Liniment fumes burn my eyes. "We can't go yet."

"Why not?"

I lean in so she can hear my whisper over the sound of the hammers and pumping bellows. "I need you to script a message."

"Now?"

Belair joins us. "Why are we whispering?"

"I want to send word to the Mag—my father. He needs to know about the warship in Capper Point that's inspecting vessels."

"Tangeen must know as well, but how can we send a message without exposing you as the Heir?" Belair rubs his scruffy chin.

Ash's mouth turns down. "And who'd carry it?"

"If you write it in Aturnian, it can go with the next merchants' caravan," Belair suggests as Piper joins us.

"Addressed to the Magistrate of Palrio?" Ash shakes her head. "They'll read it, burn it, and hunt us down."

Definitely not a good choice. "Other ideas? Anyone?"

Ash drums her fingers on the railing, eyes hooded.

"Watch out." I pull her hand away from a line of green ants crawling toward her.

"Look at that color," Belair reaches toward one.

"I wouldn't—"

"Ouch!" he cries and shakes his hand.

Ash examines his finger and drops some aberlac on it, which only makes him glare and fume.

"Maybe we have to forget the message and ride?" Belair says when he's stopped shaking his sore finger.

"We can do it." Ash tugs on my sleeve. "But we have to be smart." She leans closer, keeping her voice low. "If any one of these good citizens of Clearwater suspect the Heir is walking in their midst, their minds will turn to ransom and reward. The message can't reveal us. So…how about we send it to Toretta?"

"The border city full of spies?" I don't follow.

"Specifically, to Farin Blane." Ash is already nodding to herself. "He has a difficult job," Ash allows, "governing a border city, but he's loyal to Baiseen—isn't he?"

"Father always says so." I think I know where she's going with this. "We address it to him?"

"And when he breaks the seal, he'll see it's for the Magistrate and courier it to the palace. As long as I word it right, it won't give us away if intercepted beforehand.

"It'll warn him as well, if Aturnians are breaking treaties. He may ride it straight to Baiseen himself, to consult with Father."

She's already pulling out parchment, quill, and ink. While she writes, the others repack the saddlebags. Piper and Samsen buy bread, grains, and parched fish from the store. The ink is dry when the others are ready, and Ash reads it aloud to us.

Dear Father,

It is my hope this letter will find you and the family well. We are nearly to our destination, though the seas were not so smooth. Of note, a single eider duck roosts at Capper Point. We wonder if a flock will follow and migrate to Palrio before we return. Perhaps you will have some fine hunting. I wish I could join you! As it is, time chases us to the halls of Aku. I shall write again before our return if there is a messenger at hand. Indeed, you will hear from the High Savant Yuki in due course.

All loving regards,

Your son.

"All loving regards?" I shake my head. "That's not something I'd say."

"And your Father knows it." Ash looks quite satisfied.

"Ah." I pull her into a quick hug. Over the top of her head, I ask Samsen to run it down to the station. "They have one, don't they?"

"I'll ask."

I unbuckle my belt knife. "Use this to pay. I'm out of unmarked coins."

My heart sinks. Fifty hours before the gates close, lame horses, enemy lands, and a storm hitting before dark? Am I deluding myself that we can make it in time?

"Are we ready now?" Ash asks.

"Let's go."

It's midmorning by the time we lead the horses out of Clearwater and into the countryside. The animals are slow and hobbling, worse off than I thought.

"I can't believe how cold it is." Ash is rugged up in a knee-length sheepskin coat and scarf. Her green knit cap flops up and down as she walks.

More than a few times, she looks over her shoulder, back toward Clearwater, the harbor, and, I'm guessing, the *Sea Eagle*, not that anything can be seen in the fog.

I try to keep my voice neutral, but I can feel the gruffness slip out around the edges. "Did you leave your gloves behind?" Like earlier, it's not the gloves, but the bosun's mate, I'm betting. It shouldn't bother me, but it does. "We can get you another pair."

She shakes her head. The mood around her is thicker than the fog.

My heart pinches as she lets the sadness in her eyes show. Stuffing my conflicted feelings down deep, I smile at her. "You know what?" I ask with a light voice.

She doesn't respond so I keep talking. "If we traveled with a black-robe, they could cast the bones and tell you exactly where to find your gloves."

She rewards me with a small smile but it fades. "A black-robe wouldn't waste time on something so trivial, Marcus. Not for a non-savant."

"No ordinary non-savant." I reach in front of Rita and gently push her shoulder. "The recorder to the Heir of Baiseen."

"And the delegate's son, Belair Duquan." He comes up behind us.

"Thanks. Both of you." A genuine glint shines in her eyes as she raises her chin.

That's better.

A few miles out of Clearwater, I give the signal to mount up. There's nothing to see ahead or behind but fog, making the road a cloud tunnel, the hoofbeats echoing, each thud giving me shivers. It's hard not to keep looking over *my* shoulder. "What can we expect ahead?" I ask.

Ash studies the map. "The coast is not heavily traveled, it seems."

"Nothing to it, then."

We walk and jog for several hours and rest at a creek that cuts through a trampled cornfield. There's no crop left, but the horses enjoy chewing on the pale, dried leaves and husks.

"Shouldn't this be the start of the harvest season?" Belair asks, snapping a dry stalk in two.

"Should be," Piper answers. "Looks like winter's come early to

Northern Aturnia."

"Have we crossed the border, then?" He throws the stalks like short spears into the field.

"Hard to tell," Ash says, studying the map. "But if not, we're close. They should post a sign."

"Be glad it's not marked or patrolled." Samsen pokes around at the remnants of a fire. "A small party camped here recently. Raised a phantom, too."

"How long ago?" I ask.

"Seven days?" Piper says, investigating the tracks. "Maybe ten. They were on horseback."

A wave of unease tickles up my spine. "Let's go." I glance at the remnants of the fire as I tighten Echo's girth and mount up. Scouts? Phantoms? Troops patrolling the border? The last thing I want to do is test the initiate laws of safe passage to Aku. With the sanctions against Northern Aturnia, they might not be feeling all that generous, putting not just me but my whole company at risk.

I haven't voiced it aloud yet, but it's possible the Aturnian warship is searching for us. Me, specifically. I recall how Father handled the purported Aturnian spies, and I swallow hard, imagining that if I were captured, Aturnian officials might like to return the favor. Truth, there may already be worse repercussions in play, to retaliate for my father's actions. Damn the bones, my father is too smart not to have known that would be the result.

And now here we are, journeying through Aturnian land. It's as if we've been played right into the enemy's hands.

De'ral rumbles at the thought.

Kaylin's right. We need to reach Capper Point before dark. I cluck to Echo as Piper and Samsen take the lead, Samsen's eagle phantom scouting ahead. Belair jogs beside me, Ash bringing up the rear.

"They're adorable," Belair says, nodding to Samsen and Piper, who are riding close enough to touch.

"I guess." It's not how I would put it.

"There's a story there, I'll wager." He sounds more than a little curious. "She's older, right?"

"Not that much."

"How'd it happen?"

I'd rather discuss training on Aku, or learn about his *warrior*, or focus on navigating these enemy lands. Ash clears her throat. The sound is a familiar one. It's her way of telling me to play nice.

I sigh. "Ten years ago, when Piper was sixteen, she'd just earned her orange robes."

"That's young."

"She's an excellent healer. Anyway, she was in the hills behind Baiseen, gathering herbs, when a band of Gollnarians cornered her."

"They were far from home."

"A scouting party." It occurs to me in this moment that the incident with my father's dire wolf was one in a string of many. "Piper was badly outnumbered."

His brows rise. "What happened?"

"Samsen, thirteen at the time, was out hunting. He heard the fight and sent his phantom in."

"Form?"

"Golden eagle, talons like grappling hooks. But by the time Samsen reached her, his phantom was pinned under a Gollnar winged demon, and Piper was cornered in the bottom of a ravine, her snake chopped in half, going to ground. Sam refused to let his phantom go to ground. He stayed in phantom perspective. Fought them off. Killed or cut up every last one. By then his phantom wounds were so severe, he nearly bled out."

Belair winces, squeezing his shoulder.

"You've had phantom wounds?" I ask, keeping the envy out of my voice, though Brogal says it's nothing to yearn for, the injuries a savant's body can incur when the phantom is harmed.

Belair lets his hand fall. "Hunting accident. Entirely my fault. I wasn't supposed to have my phantom up, let alone be in his perspective. A wild sow attacked. I didn't get out of my phantom's eye-view in time." He tilts his head to Samsen and Piper, who are a fair way ahead. "So…the healer saved the hero?"

I nod. "And they've been bonded ever since."

Belair says nothing, and the silence between us feels awkward. I cough. "Do you have much riding on this journey? A vote at the Summit?" Certainly not the throne in Pandom City, but his father may be higher up than I first thought.

"There is much I must prove on Aku," Belair replies cryptically. And with that, he nudges his horse to catch up to Samsen and Piper, leaving me wondering why exactly Belair is *really* on this journey.

• • •

By late afternoon, everyone's dripping wet and shivering. Dew beads the horses' eyelashes and manes, and our leather saddles are soaked and squeaking. Our mounts stumble repeatedly until Belair's bay falls, spilling him out of the saddle. I raise my hand, calling a halt. "Make camp."

Ash is about to protest. "Kaylin—"

I gesture to the group. "Look at us. We can't make it a step farther."

Belair is with me on this as he feels down his horse's swollen leg. "Plenty of dead wood for a fire. I bet those husks in that field will burn hot, too."

I point my nose to the sky. "Send your eagle up, Samsen. Let's have a bird's-eye view. If there are no troops about, we'll camp here the night and ride into Capper Point at first light."

"And if there are troops?" Samsen asks.

"We head for the woods, fast as we can…"

13

ASH

"*Wake up!*" The warning booms in my head.

Startled, I listen to the sea crashing on the rocks below. Nothing else moves, no crickets, no flutter or shuffling from the horses picketed nearby, not even Marcus's snoring. Is he still on watch? When he took over for me, there hadn't been a whisper on the road, and I felt safe next to the cheery fire. The flames are all but gone now, though the embers still glow hot, and I sit up, reaching out from under my blanket to grab a log. As I plunk it on the coal bed, my inner voice warns again.

"*Enemies!*"

Where?

Without answer, I'm grabbed from behind and pulled to my feet. I cut loose a scream to warn the others, but a large, callused hand clamps over my mouth and lips press against my ear. "Speak a word, and I'll cut your throat."

He's not hard to visualize. Male. Large. Armed.

His beard scrapes my cheek as I'm assailed with the stench of rum and garlic. It's impossible to breathe in the crushing hold, but I'm not so stunned that I forget my training. I kick back like a mule, catching his kneecap; he smacks me to the ground and curses while I wail.

Before I can scramble to my feet, he hauls me toward him again, a blade pressing my jugular. The log catches fire, and the camp is suddenly full of men circling us, their swords raised high. Belair is wrestled down in front of me, also held by a knife. I see Piper from the corner of my eye—a guard on each of her arms. The ground rumbles as she starts to raise her phantom.

"None of that!" The captor stabs his knife deep into her thigh.

She cries out into the night. There's no sign of Samsen or Marcus.

"What do you want?" I shout as they bind my wrists with rope.

"Shut up!"

"You can't—"

I don't see the swing coming until it connects, my head whipping back from the force, my cheek stinging like salt in a cut. My eyes tear up. The blade is back against my throat, preventing me from moving my head and scanning the whole camp. I try to count the attackers as they move in and out of my vision. There are ten in front and an unknown number behind. Some of these men are Captain Nadonis's crew. Among them, one man roars for silence in Aturnian, and my heart sinks.

Ride straight to Capper Point. Kaylin's warning comes back. Did he know this would happen? And that's all he said?

"Line 'em up." I recognize a longshoreman from the pier.

They drag me forward. Everyone is forced to my side of the fire, including Samsen, who is bound and unconscious. Surely they wouldn't hog-tie him if he were dead, right? Belair and I lock eyes as they shove him next to me. I'm shoulder to shoulder between the Tangeen and Piper, who is panting on my other side. I want to scream at the savants to raise their phantoms, but we all have knives at our backs, and every few moments, a fist comes down hard on the kidneys or ribs. There's no way Marcus or Belair can raise their phantoms under these conditions, let alone control them. I finally see Marcus as they drag him forward and push him to his knees. His nose is bleeding, hair falling over his face.

One of the crew holds up Marcus's small purse. "That's all we found in the saddlebags."

"Where are the plans?" The leader points a knife at Marcus and rests it under his chin. When Marcus doesn't speak, the man lifts the blade, forcing Marcus to raise his head. "I know you're taking battle strategies to those traitors on Aku."

"Not true!" I say. "These are savants on their initiation journey."

Bright light explodes behind my eyes as I receive another knock on the head, this one from behind. When I can focus again, they have my satchel and are tipping it out on the ground, raking through the scrolls, writing tools, inks, and notes.

I struggle against the restraints, and the knife presses harder against my throat. Blood drips onto my collar, or maybe it's sweat. Pressure in my chest builds, a volcano smoking, ready to erupt.

"These must be it, but they're not in Aturnian." The man spits. "Foreign spies!"

"Bring them here." The leader indicates next to Marcus. "All except the girls." The leader laughs at Piper and me.

A cold chill replaces the heat in my veins. Marcus moans out a feeble "no" and tries to make a move, but his captor rams his jaw with the hilt of his sword. The others are dragged over to Marcus, pushed to their knees, heads bowed. My heart stops beating for a moment because I've studied enough history to know an execution line when I see one.

The leader sneers. "More coin will be in the reward." He nods at Marcus. "Off with his head. Nadonis says he's important, and what easier way to deliver him?"

Two captors flank Marcus as a young, barefoot man comes out of the shadows. My muscles go rigid, breath trapped in my lungs. I recognize him, through tears, through a heaviness so immense, my body threatens to crumble. He has a long, curved sword in his hand.

Marcus looks up at me and starts to mouth something.

They shove his head down, exposing his neck. "Kaylin, no!" I shout, and the knife presses harder against my throat.

Inside me a storm rises, black and threatening. The ground trembles and I feel the sand slipping away.

Kaylin raises the wicked sword high over Marcus.

"No! No! No!" I close my eyes and scream the word, over and over, pressure building until I'm sure my heart will explode. The pain of it shatters me, and I howl, the sound tearing from my body like a caged beast. If the old gods could hear me, I would pray that death had taken me from the path before I reached this awful night.

Nausea swells my throat as the sword whistles through the air. The high-pitched sound slices me open, and I cry again, eyes squeezed tight. It doesn't stop the blade, but when I run out of air, there's an odd moment of silence.

It's immediately followed by shouts and weapons clashing.

"Duck!" my inner voice shouts.

My eyes fly open as the captor behind me drops his knife and falls face-first to the ground.

It takes a moment to register that the man lying beside me is headless, neck stump gushing blood so close to the fire, the edges sputter and boil. But the horror can't be Marcus. He was too far away.

I take a deep breath and force myself to look across at where Marcus kneeled. His guards are dead, cut clean in half. It seems Kaylin's blade swung wide of the mark, twice—and it hasn't stopped swinging yet. He's taking on all the attackers, one young sailor against a horde of angry men.

My knees buckle from the relief, and for a moment I am in an eerie bliss, thinking we are saved. That sensation falters when a knife flies by, hitting Marcus square in the chest. Air rushes out of his lungs and he caves in on himself, hands reaching for the hilt where blood spreads like black oil across his robe.

"No!" I try to reach him, struggling against the bonds cutting into my skin. Piper appears next to me, slicing the ropes. Circulation rushes back into my limbs, and a thousand needles prickle my nerves.

"Go to him." Piper nods to Marcus and sweeps up a sword from the ground. "Stop the bleeding." She's fighting attackers before the sentence is out.

I leap to my feet and come face-to-face with Kaylin.

"Careful, lass." He winks as he glides by and runs through another of the attackers. "This will take a moment longer."

I run toward Marcus. When a marauder leaps in to clamp meaty hands around my neck, I press into the chokehold and drive my knee up into his crotch. He's down, but another reaches for me. Before I can dodge, Piper's phantom, lashing like a sea serpent, wraps around his legs and trips him. Fast as lightning, the twin-headed phantom bites both men in the large artery of the thigh. Blood spurts like geysers, spattering my face and arms.

"Free me!" Belair yells. He's on his knees, hands tied behind his back.

Piper cuts him loose, and he takes a deep breath. Instantly the ground rumbles and cracks. I stagger backward, the sand dropping away beneath my feet. Out of the earth come two huge red claws, then a head, body, and tail. The sun leopard leaps free and throws back its head. The roar echoes through the camp, hammering my eardrums. Belair remains on his knees as the feline spins, bringing down an Aturnian who rushes in from behind. The phantom cat shakes the man like a rag and snaps his neck. I swerve out of its way and hurry to Marcus. He's on his back, eyes closed.

"Ash." His voice is strong but breathy. "What's happening?"

"We're winning." I press his coat down around the edges of the blade, trying to stop the flow.

"Are you sure?"

Belair's cat tears around the headland, slashing at trees, saddles, bodies. It's out of control, baring saber teeth even at me as it leaps by. The attackers left standing spread out. Kaylin has a sword in each hand and fights them all at once. He's covered in blood, but I don't think much is his own. Piper guards Samsen, and Belair, with his sword raised, guards me. "Definitely winning," I tell Marcus.

Then one of Nadonis's men rises behind Piper and strikes the back of her head with a thick log.

"Piper!"

The healer falls hard, and her phantom goes to ground.

I take Marcus's hands and press them around the knife. "Hold here. Don't let go."

He groans.

I run to Piper as the sun leopard chases the man into the trees, and then I find a pulse. Our healer's alive but knocked out cold. I pull off my coat and elevate her head, realizing her leg wound is bleeding through a hasty wrap. Marcus is behind me now. I can't see how he's faring.

Kaylin's blade whistles through the air. Is he…*singing*? His face lifts as he dances over bodies, cutting the marauders down. In a blink, only the longshoreman is left standing. The burly man runs at Kaylin, who leaps out of the way, arcing his sword over his head double-handed. When his feet touch down, he turns back to the man. The longshoreman's expression doesn't change, even when he drops to his knees and his head slides from his shoulders.

The camp goes suddenly quiet again, only labored breathing to be heard, mine and Belair's, and groans from Marcus. My heart gallops inside my chest so loudly, the others can probably hear it, too.

I look up at Kaylin, speechless.

Scattered about are the slashed and severed bodies of at least fifteen men. It's hard to count, as they are in pieces. Piper and Samsen are still unconscious. Belair's unsteady, his phantom chewing on a boot with the foot in it. Behind me, Marcus coughs, holding the knife that protrudes from his chest.

Something twists and turns inside my chest as well. Fury at the attack, at us all nearly being killed, and also a sinking pit of helplessness I'll do anything to avoid. Because if I were savant, this wouldn't have happened.

I let my breath out in a rush. It's not true. Our entire party is savant, except for me, and it didn't matter. The non-savant bosun's mate saved us.

I ball my hands into fists and back away from the rushing emotions, pushing the feelings down. Now's not the time. "*This* is your storm?" I ask Kaylin.

"Aye, lass." One brow goes up.

"Then thank you, but your warning was badly understated."

His eyes move over me, like he's checking for injury. Finally, he expels a deep breath. "I wouldn't let them harm you."

The sun leopard crouches, stalking forward by Belair's side.

"I'm afraid that's not good enough," Belair says between gasps for air as he draws near. "Drop the swords."

Kaylin raises his hands but doesn't let go of the weapons. "I can help you." He glances around the camp. "Already have, but you need me still."

"As delightful as that sounds, I think we can manage from here," Belair croaks. The cat lashes its tail, sweeping the sandy ground. "I said, drop your swords."

"Wait." I leave Piper's side to stand between them. "Kaylin's right. We need his help."

Belair doesn't back down. "They were his crewmates, Ash. He was with them." But as Belair glares at Kaylin, his leopard's eyes turn to me, whiskers twitching. Its tail stills, and I get an image in my mind of a cat with a mouse pinned under its paw. I turn to Kaylin, unsure where the vision came from—or which one of us, in this scenario, is the mouse.

"You can trust me or not, but know this," Kaylin says. "I've risked my life for yours." His eyes are on me alone. "I cannot go back to the *Sea Eagle* or any port without disguise. Nadonis must believe I died with this lot. If I'm spotted, he will know I betrayed him, and there would be no place to hide save the bottom of the sea."

"It was Captain Nadonis's doing?" I ask.

"He and Levvey there." Kaylin points his sword at the longshoreman's headless body. "They thought you were spies."

"That's ridiculous," I say.

"Spies sent by the Magistrate to track black-sailed ships. Keen to report them. To execute them."

I want to say that the Magistrate wouldn't do such a thing, but I stop, realizing it's exactly something he would do. Then, beside me, there comes a padded thump as Belair buckles to the ground, his phantom melting away.

It's my decision now.

"Trust him," my inner voice says. *"How else to save the others?"*

"Hurry." I shove wet hair out of my face and go to Marcus. His pulse is strong, pumping blood out of his body and onto the ground at an alarming rate. "Keep pressure around the wound."

Kaylin sheaths his blades and kneels by my side. "He needs the healer."

My thoughts exactly. I check Samsen and cut his bonds. "Unconscious." I run to Piper. The knife wound in her leg looks bad. I untie a cloth sword belt from the nearest body and bind her wound.

"I can wake her," Kaylin says as I wind up and slap Piper's face.

Her eyes fly open on contact and she gasps, hand going to her cheek.

Kaylin smiles. "Or you can do it."

"Piper, how do you feel?" I adjust my coat under her head and check her eyes.

"Like a bear gnawed off my leg." She scans the camp. "Samsen?"

"Still breathing."

Unfathomable relief floods her eyes, and she blinks back tears. "And Marcus?"

"Still bleeding."

Piper tries to rise, and I help her to her knees. "Mend yourself first. We all need you strong."

With eyes closed, Piper raises her phantom. It shoots out of the ground, larger than I've ever seen it. Its long black body winds over Piper. Sand and grass fall from its scales and gently, purposefully, the phantom sinks two sets of fangs into her neck, a head on either side of her throat. Piper's agonized expression intensifies for an instant, then dissolves into nothing short of bliss. I'm embarrassed to keep watching; it seems so…intimate. The fangs soon retract, and Piper is on her feet, stunned and stumbling, but she goes straight to Marcus, and I follow.

"They stabbed him in the heart." My eyes well.

"If that were true, lass, he'd be dead." Kaylin seems to have stopped the bleeding. "Luckily, the knife stuck in the sternum, the body's armor doing its job."

"You have any pressure points for hemorrhage?" Piper narrows her eyes at the sailor. "Or is seasickness the only thing you can cure?"

"Have and using them." He keeps one hand on the wound and the other pressing various points around Marcus's head. It all looks like a bloody mess to me.

Piper doesn't soften. "You could have killed these marauders *before* they started carving us up like steaks."

"All the bloodshed could've been avoided had you reached Capper Point like I warned."

Piper ignores his words. "You were with them." Her eyes blaze, the accusation thrown like a spear.

I kneel in the middle, a barrier between the two. "Let's heal everyone first, before we start fighting again, please?"

Piper exhales. "I'll need water and my kit." She glares at Kaylin.

I take over the pressure around Marcus's wound as Kaylin rises to his feet, not a limp or complaint to be seen.

"The healer's bag is by the fire." I point with my elbow. "There's a bucket with the saddles and a stream…"

"I can find water, lass." Kaylin brings the kit and disappears with the bucket.

"He's quite a swordsman," I say, watching him go.

"But whose side is he on?" Piper readies a cloth bandage as her phantom snakes over Marcus.

"I think it's obvious." I glance meaningfully at our massacred enemies.

"You *think*, but can you be sure?"

"He saved our lives."

After a moment, she nods. "And the other two? How bad?"

"Belair's been beaten and is exhausted."

"And Samsen? Are you sure he's—"

"Out cold. A lump on the back of his head. Nothing else I can detect."

Piper nods, and her phantom entwines Marcus, one head sinking fangs into the left side of the Heir's neck, the other head tasting the air around me. "Help me with his coat."

Between the two of us, we keep pressure on the wound while taking off the coat. "Pull out the knife, Ash. Dead straight, like this." She demonstrates in the air. "You'll have to straddle him. I'll bind his chest the moment you do."

I bend over Marcus, a foot on either side of his body. He's unconscious now, which might be a blessing.

"On three," Piper says.

I wrap my sticky hands around the hilt.

"One."

"Marcus, hold on," I whisper.

"Two."

I'm ready.

"Three!"

All my might goes into it, but my hands slip off the knife as I fall backward onto my bottom.

"Let me." Kaylin returns with the water and takes my place. He pulls the blade out, quick and clean as if it had stuck in butter, not bone.

Piper wraps the bleeding wound, Kaylin helping roll Marcus from one side to the other to keep the bandage flat and tight.

"Sit here, Ash." Piper nods to the area beside Marcus's head.

I obey, and the free head of the serpent again tastes the air in front of me. A lump rises in my throat. "You're not…"

"Marcus needs blood." Piper sponges off my neck.

"*My* blood?" I look at Kaylin. Maybe he wants to take over this task as well? He crosses his arms and shakes his head. No, he does not.

"Remember two years ago?" Piper prompts. "The riding accident? Your blood and his match."

"But…" It's not a memory—or experience—I want to relive. "Maybe—"

"Relax." Piper tucks hair behind my ear.

I am the complete opposite of relaxed. The phantom is so close to my face, I can count the tiny black scales on its head. The mouth opens, white fangs glistening in the firelight. I instinctively lean away as it strikes. I feel the prick, followed by the plunge of two sharp daggers into my jugular vein.

"Breathe, Ash." Piper and Kaylin speak as one.

I exhale through tight lips. It isn't too painful, but I noticed Kaylin looking at me strangely, keeping a distance. "You can't tell me you're squeamish," I say.

Kaylin shakes his head. "No, lass, not that." He doesn't say more.

"I'm injecting an astringent to stop infection and a soporific to help with the shock. And you're giving him a milk bottle's worth of blood." Piper puts a hand on my shoulder. "Best lie down."

"I hope you appreciate this," I whisper to Marcus as I lay by his side, a phantom snake between us, sucking at our necks. The salt-crusted grass prickles my cheek and the smell of blood mixes with smoke from the fire. "And, dak'n crips, you better heal fast."

14

ASH

Dawn breaks without the sun, though the sky lightens, and a commotion of birds comes alive all at once. Gulls sweep the cliffs with their endless riot, and the lone whistle of a turkey buzzard sounds from high above. They can smell a dead body from miles away, it seems, and, on this headland, we have more than one.

Piper and I lean over Samsen, applying cool cloths to his face. His eyes flutter open, and he focuses on us with a look of disbelief. I understand why. My clothes are blood-soaked, my arms and, no doubt, face streaked with blood as well, and Piper's face is bruised, one eye swollen nearly shut, with gashes on her arms. Sure, she's given herself a healing, but only enough to get her on her feet. She has to pace herself, and her phantom, to help Marcus, whose injuries are more severe.

"Piper?" He gasps her name.

"I'm fine," she says quickly, though it must seem like a lie. She feels the lump on the back of his head so tenderly, I look over my shoulder toward the sea.

"Marcus?"

"Hale enough, or he will be after a little more rest."

Samsen tries to sit.

"Not so fast." Piper's serpent retracts its fangs from his wrist. "You have a concussion."

"Not fast enough, you mean." Before we can stop him, he's up on one knee. The ground rumbles and churns. I shield my eyes as a black vulture flies out of the earth, dirt and grass falling from its wings. The bird gains altitude and circles over us, a silhouette against the early dawn sky.

"Who attacked?" Samsen's voice sounds distant, though he's right next to us.

"Aturnian mercenaries, some of them Captain Nadonis's crew."

"Apparently, he thought we were spies," I say.

Samsen frowns. "I suspect the attack was more about killing the Heir before he reaches Aku than some purported spying. They may not have even known the true purpose."

I have the same fears.

"Can you look for the horses while you're up there?" Piper asks. "They pulled their pickets."

"Got 'em. A stone's throw north in a dry cornfield, eating husks."

"That's good news." I leave Piper to fill him in on the details of the attack and check on Belair. He's awake, and I offer him a strong lemon-balm tea. Sadly, his supply of Ochee perished in the battle.

"Never thought our adventure would come to this," he says quietly. "Hope you'll put me in a good light in the records."

"Let's not worry about it just now." I pat his arm. It hasn't occurred to him what this delay might mean. I move to check Marcus. He's more like a peacefully sleeping person than a corpse now, which is a relief. A blessing, no doubt, until the serpent's healing takes full effect.

Kaylin drags bodies and various amputated limbs to the edge of the cliff and tosses them to the sea. I am lost for a moment, watching him work.

"Aturnians to the north!" Samsen calls out. "We need to round up the horses immediately." He lifts his head, back from phantom perspective. "But first I want to talk with the bosun's mate." His eyes narrow on Kaylin.

I hold out my hand. "He's not the enemy."

"Still need to talk." Samsen draws his sword.

"Talk or fight?" I say as he walks by, brushing me aside.

"Depends." He approaches Kaylin and stops a few feet away. "You did this?" he asks as he taps the lump on the back of his skull.

Kaylin drops the body he's dragging. "No, but I see you want an explanation."

"It might give me a reason not to kill you." Samsen isn't smiling.

Kaylin shrugs. "I did what I was ordered to do. Assisted Levvey. At least, until the orders clashed with my own better judgment."

"You do this often?" Samsen glances over the camp. "Attack your passengers once they disembark?"

"You had Nadonis and Levvey suspicious."

"Did you know you were to execute the Heir of Baiseen?"

"Nay." Kaylin glances at Marcus, who hasn't moved.

"It sounds like you came very close to doing it."

"Looks can be deceiving." He nudges another body off the edge of the cliff with his foot. "I wouldn't have done it, even if we had never met."

"Why not? You're clearly adept with the sword and have no second thoughts about taking a life from the path." Samsen shakes his head at the body count, as if unable to believe his eyes. "Astonishing, for a non-savant."

I plant my hands on my hips. "For a non-savant?" I never thought I'd hear bias from Samsen.

"You cannot know my thoughts," Kaylin answers, taking no offense.

"Then explain them to me."

One side of Kaylin's mouth turns up. "Your party is savant, granted safe passage to Aku, and I believe in and protect that right. What they were going to do to Ash, and your healer, could not go unpunished."

"You didn't mention that part." Samsen glances at Piper before rubbing the lump on his head. "And you take it upon yourself to be judge and executioner?"

"When the circumstances warrant, aye."

Samsen studies him in silence. "You're a dangerous lad."

"That I am."

Before he can say more, Samsen's phantom swoops in and perches in the low branches of an ironbark tree. It spreads its wings, showing off the intricate charcoal and gray herringbone patterns beneath the primary feathers. The span is as wide as I am tall as it fans the air.

"The Aturnian soldiers are breaking camp, heading south. Toward us. Less than an hour off." He looks out to sea. "We must ride."

"We can't move Marcus," Piper says. "Not until he regains consciousness and I'm sure the bleeding has stopped."

"No choice," Samsen answers. "We'll head into the forest. They may not be scouting off the road."

"What would they be doing, then, if not scouting?" Marcus asks from the other side of the fire, startling us all. He's not only conscious but on his feet.

It's all I can do not to rush to his side and throw my arms around him. "How are you feeling?"

"As well as I look, I imagine." He winces and rubs his chest.

"I wager the troops are heading for Clearwater, not searching for you," Kaylin says, not in the least surprised to see Marcus recovered. "They do regular sweeps of the coastal towns this time of year."

"On their way south?" Marcus asks.

"Aye."

But the mood is darker, more ominous, and I can't help but wonder if this journey will be remembered as the one before chaos consumed the realms. Surely the events of the last days—on both sides—will not go unchecked. But I'll not voice these things. Not now.

Marcus bats Piper's hand away when she tries to sit him down. "Leave off. I'm deciding whether to thank this sailor for saving my life or kill him for betraying us."

"I suggest you do it quickly." Kaylin tilts his head to the north. "It's time to go."

"How do I know you weren't setting us up?" Marcus asks.

"You don't." He turns to me. "If you'd gotten to Capper Point before nightfall," Kaylin reminds us again, "this could have been avoided." He shrugs as if it is a small matter and eyes the eastern horizon. "Samsen's right. The headland may betray us, but soon rain will wash it clean. Shall we go, before the Aturnians arrive?"

Brown leaves fall from the ironbark trees and blow across the camp as we chew on his words. I look to Marcus, beseeching.

"He will make the right choice," my inner voice says.

The only thing is, I'm not entirely sure what the right choice is.

"Break camp!" Marcus orders, and I'm flooded with relief from head to toe.

"Now you know."

Marcus limps over to Kaylin. "Thank you." With a curt nod and an offer of his hand, he adds, "Don't make me regret this."

15

KAYLIN

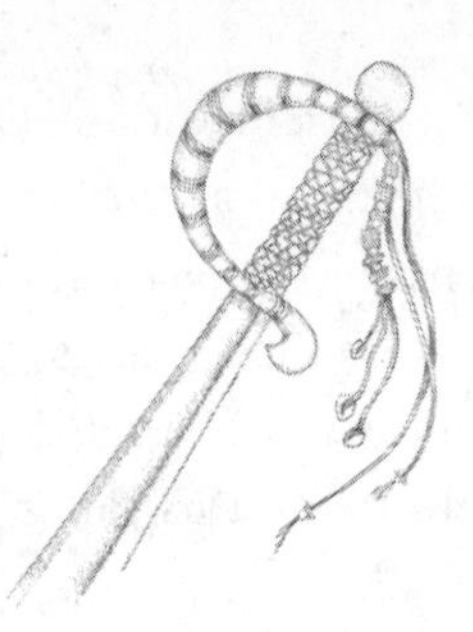

A lot of things fall under the definition of bliss—the sunset currents streaming around the isles of Tutapa, bioluminescence under the full moon, the taste of oysters fresh from the rocks, battle with a just cause…

Now I have one more to add: finding myself on a high Aturnian headland, enemy slain at my feet, fresh blood on my face, and a beautiful lass from Baiseen sending curious glances my way. The new feelings are inexplicable. I don't even know how I got here.

One thing led to another…

True, and the fact remains there's no going back on any of it, nor would I wish to if I could.

I keep my head down, tossing the corpses into the sea. It's the best use of my time while the others argue about how to proceed. It also gives me a moment to work out an alternative strategy, in case theirs is bad enough to get them all killed, which it likely will be. It's an interesting lot, these initiates. For as strong and capable as they appear, their survival instincts are sorely lacking.

But what a spectacular bout! I keep that thought to myself, too, since the others are not inclined to share in the glory of battle. I understand. They have injuries and no clear way ahead, at least until I suggest mine.

Ash mostly listens while she tries to salvage her writing tools and the coins spilled from the Heir's bag. I want to help her pick up every last one and assure her, again, that I never meant her harm. That, in fact, I will protect her life as if it were my own. But she might want more of an explanation for my cryptic warning to leave Clearwater.

In hindsight, I could have worded that better. And then there's how I turned up at precisely the right moment, if I'm truly not in league with Nadonis. I have no rationale to offer without giving away too much.

One thing led to another? I repeat to myself. It wouldn't satisfy me. How can I expect it to satisfy the lass? Then there's my absolute willingness to help her. I daresay I don't understand it.

Maybe it was seeing her with knife in hand, squaring off with one of the crewmen, that first time on the deck of the *Sea Eagle*. Or hearing her pine for far-off lands with such heartfelt passion that piqued my interest. Or watching her curry animals in the bowels of a boat just to bring them comfort. I'm not sure. But I'd given her my word that no harm would befall her, and the truth of that unexpected promise won't change.

When the others reach a stalemate, I step up. "Have you considered riding up the north road?"

"Toward the enemy?" Marcus says, as if I suggested jumping off the headland into the sea.

"What good is that to us?" Samsen asks. "We'll run straight into the troops. Do you want to take them all on, too?"

I actually wouldn't mind, but it's not what I say. "We can ride inland along the Navren River, hiding our tracks in the water. If you send a rider south with the donkey..."

"Our tracks will lead both ways." Ash catches on. "Confusing them, at the very least. At best, sending at least some of them along to Clearwater, quick sharp."

"Aye. Our decoy can loop around and meet us inland. From there, it's up and over the hills of Mount Bladon and on to Capper Point by ferry down the Ferus River, none the wiser."

Ash raises one brow. "You certainly know the lay of the land."

"I know the lay of the *rivers*."

I thought it would take more time to convince Marcus, but he nods, saying something about, *when in doubt, head north*. An interesting lot, these initiates, I think again. That's for sure.

We ready to ride, and to my delight, I find myself in the most pleasing occupation of helping Ash repack her satchel. It's all I can do not to breathe her in. She's over the shock of being attacked and on to bone-cracking anger. Who would blame the lass? Her life was threatened, her trade tools strewn everywhere, texts ruined, and ink bottles broken.

Red-faced, she finds her map of the realms and unrolls it. "A slow, naf'n demon's death to all marauders. How will we make it in time now? Sark f'qud."

"A Nonnovan curse?" I ask. "Excellent choice."

She turns hooded eyes on me, and I cough to cover my smile. The scent rising from her skin is like nothing I've ever known. Even in her anger and the hasty wash, she smells of lilacs and summer seas. "At least this is in one piece." She shakes the map and checks our location, the distance to Bladon and then to Capper Point, and rolls it back up. "We *can* make it, if there are no other delays." She repacks everything, cursing now in Tangeen. I hand her a bottle of ink she missed in the tall grass. "Maybe we can track down these Aturnian miscreants and cut their throats," she mutters.

"You're a girl after my own heart, lass, but you realize I've already done that." My hand goes toward the cliff and the wet drag marks leading to it.

"Peace be their paths." She says it with reverence, revealing her well of contradictions. Then the full gaze of her sea-storm eyes locks onto mine. "Thank you, Kaylin. I want you to know—"

"She's not serious." Marcus steals the moment from us as he walks by. "About wanting to cut their throats. She isn't like that."

"Part of her seems a bit like that." I don't mind the pride in my voice, but I can see the Heir does.

We stare at each other until Ash punches him in the arm, a habit of hers I've noticed before. I thought it was affection, but maybe it's more complex than that.

"Let's mount up." Marcus scowls at her, then heads for the picket line without waiting for a reply.

When I turn to see if Ash and I might resume our conversation, she's already halfway to the horses.

Once packed, Marcus gathers us around him, his authority back in place. "Samsen, you take Frost and the donkey and ride at good speed back toward Clearwater. Cut into the forest over ground that leaves no tracks, then turn back toward the Navren River. We'll meet upstream in one hour." He confirms with the Tangeen, who nods once.

"We should keep silent and to the port side of the road," I add.

"Left," Ash says to the others and mounts the gray mare, the one we groomed together just two nights ago. Rita, she called her.

Marcus and Piper jog horseback around the camp and muddle the tracks, churning the drag marks and bloodstains into the ground. Belair's bay lets loose a shrill whinny and paws the ground, staring after Samsen and the donkey. "They'll catch up, lad," Belair says to his mount. "Easy now. Silent."

"Ride with me?" Ash extends her hand and kicks her foot out of the stirrup.

"Delighted to." I grab a handful of mane, as I saw her do, and swing up behind her, landing lightly.

"Just hang on and move with her." Ash turns to me. "Like a raft on the waves."

"Aye, lass." I encircle her waist. I mean, what else can I do with my hands? Rita's gait settles Ash against me. For a moment, I'm lost in the rise and fall of her breath, her heart beating through her back and against my chest.

I decide I like horseback riding very much.

The mare trots over the short grass beside the road as the sun burns off the fog. Below the headlands, a good six fathoms down, waves crash against the shore. Buzzards circle and gulls already feast at what their short beaks can pry from the bodies that have yet to be washed out to sea.

Ash frowns. "First glance over the cliffs and the Aturnian troops will know there was foul play."

"Maybe not. The tide is rising." The mare stumbles, and I fall against Ash, tightening my grip around her waist.

"Are you all right back there?"

"Not used to the world from this perspective." I close my eyes and lean closer; the heat of her blush warms my cheek.

"Spent your whole life on the sea?"

"Aye." Thank the deep sea she's not inclined to quiz me on those details yet.

"I spent my whole life in the Sanctuary until—"

Marcus hushes us.

I don't mind. It's something to ask her later. Perhaps tonight. Oddly, I feel we have all the time in the world, which I know is a lie.

Ash urges Rita into a lope. It is much like a dinghy in choppy waves, and I keep my seat once I find the rhythm. The road drops down toward the river mouth where the grass grows tall and the trees give way to a wide mudflat.

"This is your plan?" Marcus halts at the edge of the mud. "We might as well paint a red arrow to point which way we went."

"It's an estuary ford," I explain. "If we follow the bank from a distance, sticking to hard ground, there will be a rock crossing soon enough. No tracks."

"You really do know your rivers," Ash says.

"As a good sailor does."

"And you're a good sailor?"

It's my turn to flush. "Aye." But it comes out more like a question.

"There it is." Marcus surprises me with an appreciative nod. "A rocky ford, as you said."

Not a hundred feet from us, the mudflats give way to a deep riverbed, the water running fast and clear over large, round stones. The banks are hemmed by slabs of granite with gravel beaches between them. Ash twists around in the saddle, her face inches from mine. "Well done."

"Pleasure's mine." This beautiful lass will be the death of me as sure as a sunken ship turns to reef.

"How in all of Amassia did we end up riding through Aturnia together?" Her voice is barely more than a whisper.

"As I recall, we were docked in Toretta, loading apples on a carrack, when a lovely lass bartered for passage to Aku..."

"And then one thing led to another," she says with a half smile.

My body stills. She says this as if she heard my earlier thoughts. But that's just coincidence...right?

16

ASH

"Lean back a bit," I say to Kaylin as I urge Rita down the rocky bank, never more aware of anything so much as his arms around me, the warmth of his body against my back. The water runs gentle but deep, the surface green as spring grass, smooth enough to mirror the giant weeping willows that grace the banks. It's a beautiful river.

"Tell me horses can swim." he whispers in my ear as the mare wades into the stream.

His lips so close to my skin send shivers up and down my neck. If there wasn't a thread of worry in his words, I might have laughed. As it is, I can't control my pounding heart, and I'm sure he feels it through my coat. And then there's the blushing. If I would just stop turning around to look at him, he wouldn't see my glowing face. But here I am, looking over my shoulder, our faces only inches apart, his eyes smiling in his tanned face.

"It's a fact," I say. "All land animals can swim from birth—all but us. We have to be taught."

"An animal expert, are we now?"

Hardly.

But my inner voice is zeroing in on semantics, and I'd much rather it tease me about those than him. I face forward and use my knees to urge Rita into the water.

"And were you taught?"

Huh?

"To swim."

I turn, *again*, and blush. "I must have been because I can, even though I don't recall. I promise it wasn't Master Brogal, though I could ask. Not that he'd answer—"

"Babbling like this creek," my ever-helpful inner voice comments.

"Do you not remember at all?" Kaylin asks.

"I have a strange half memory of diving for copper pennies in the deep tide pools near the harbor."

"Do you really want to explain your orphan, non-savant upbringing at the Sanctuary?"

No. All stocked up on pity here.

I direct the conversation back to Kaylin. "I'm guessing you swim like a dolphin."

"People from Tutapa start out as landers, just like everyone else."

"Start out as what?"

He leans in close and repeats the word in a low, rumble of a voice. "Landers. It's what we call those who cannot swim." In the next breath, he vaults off Rita, his feet plunging into the knee-deep water without making a splash.

"What are you doing?"

"I prefer to swim alongside at this point." Kaylin peels off his bloodstained shirt and ties it to the back of the saddle. "I had no time to wash."

He has his hand on the mare's neck as he strides into the middle of the stream with us.

"Isn't it a little cold?" The water seeping through my pantlegs is decidedly frigid.

"You'll feel it for yourself soon enough. The Navren runs cold and deep this time of year."

The morning sun filters through the willow branches as the trees close in, making it hard to see much farther ahead. The banks are narrow and steep, and as Kaylin warned, the water is soon chest-high on the horses. I'm glad the donkey went south with Samsen; otherwise she'd be dog-paddling the whole way.

Rita bobs before kicking harder, her hooves meeting only water as the river deepens dramatically. I float off the mare's back and hold on to the pommel of the saddle as the water reaches the horse's neck. "It's freezing!"

Kaylin chuckles.

This will test my scroll cases, the ones not ruined by those marauders. They are meant to be waterproof, but I've never had the nerve to fully submerge them and find out. My skin prickles with goose bumps. "You do love the—"

Marcus signals us. "Hold back!"

It's impossible to follow the command. The horses are not going to tread water like we can. And saying "we" is generous, as only Kaylin,

Belair, and I swim in this group. The others, by my sailor's definition, are "landers," holding on to their saddles and letting the horses lead the way. Even Marcus can't follow his own advice.

"Did you just say, 'my sailor'?"

Shh. This is serious.

"I'll see what it is." Kaylin swims to Marcus and then quickly drifts back to me. "Aturnian soldiers crossing upstream. Back the way we came."

We manage to turn around, which puts Kaylin and me in the lead with Rita. We're the first to spot a break in the sheer banks, and Rita lunges out of the water and up it without hesitation. The others follow, crashing through the undergrowth behind us.

Marcus signals for quiet, waving his hand downward in short, quick motions, but the horses don't know the command. They lower their heads, stretch out their necks, and shake like wet dogs, brass buckles and stirrups clanking, leather slapping their sides. We are all dripping wet, holding our breaths, but there's nothing to be heard save for a few blue jay calls and distant crows.

"We better scout the area, track where they've gone," Piper says.

"No phantoms," Marcus whispers. "We each take a different direction from the crossing point."

Kaylin is already slipping away, heading north after a quick wink at me. Happily, I'm too cold for my face to heat this time, and I simply smile back. The others fan out, stiff and limping from last night. I'm left holding all the reins, not an easy task with four wet, restless horses on my hands. I take a deep breath and hope with my whole heart that they won't whinny or startle while I'm on my own. Peeking through the undergrowth, there is nothing but endless woods, brilliantly colored oaks, hickory, birch, and sweet eucalyptus. Like living fire, the autumn leaves are a wash of red, burnt orange, dark yellow, and pale green. No troops in sight.

If I can't see the enemy, they can't see me. Right?

"Not really the case."

I'm compelled to correct myself, it seems.

By the time they all return, I'm shivering uncontrollably. The Aturnian scouts have ridden past, I'm told, their tracks lost as falling leaves cover them like ochre snow. "So it's find Samsen, then on to Mount Bladon?" I ask through chattering teeth.

Marcus's eyebrows go up. "If Kaylin knows the way."

"I do." He moves next to me and vigorously rubs circulation back into my arms.

Before we mount, a very large falcon lands in a nearby oak. It's blue-black with huge talons and a yellow beak. "Samsen's phantom." Piper has no doubt.

Soon Samsen appears on Frost, leading the donkey. Unfortunately, the donkey and Belair's bay gelding see fit to greet like long-lost friends. The donkey sticks out her head, opens her mouth, and brays for all she's worth, sending hee-haws echoing throughout the woods. The bay gelding whinnies a reply and paws the ground.

"That's going to give us away!" Marcus shoots a glance to Belair.

"Don't just stand there." I give the Tangeen a push. "Quiet her down."

Belair leads his tall bay to Samsen, churning up leaves and snapping branches until their urgent greetings are replaced by soft whickers. Samsen dismounts, drops to one knee, and calls in his phantom.

"Water," he says, and Piper trades his empty skin for a full one. "They need a drink, too." Samsen nods at Frost and the donkey before taking a long swig. He wipes his mouth with the back of his hand. "Ten Aturnian guards cut very close to you. I've been hiding until they were well past to the south."

"Then let's ride over this hill and on to Capper Point. There's still time." Marcus squints at the late-morning sun.

We mount up and are off quickly, but the deeper we go into the woods, the less sure I am of direction. "Where's Mount Bladon exactly?"

"Over that rise." Kaylin points as he pulls on his damp shirt.

"You've a scope?" Marcus asks from behind us.

Kaylin nods to the donkey. "In my pack. If there are any tall masts in the harbor below the cliffs, we should see them from Mount Bladon."

"Tall masts are bad?" I keep my eyes forward this time.

"Not inherently." Kaylin tightens his arms around my waist even though we are at a walk.

I know he's been doubling with me for only a few hours, but already his touch feels familiar.

"Does it now?"

I huff.

"Too tight?" he whispers in my ear, sending tingles down the left side of my body.

Marcus clears his throat. "You were saying, about the tall masts?"

"Here they mean the Aturnian Navy. I trust you don't want your identity revealed to them."

My blood runs cold at the thought.

"We are savants on our journey to Aku," Marcus says in a rehearsed voice. "But you're right. I'd rather not. In any case, we'll check the view from Mount Bladon before riding on to Capper Point. From there, with all speed, we sail straight to Aku, hours to spare before the gates close."

We all give a round of hushed, "Hear! Hear!" and ride on.

I find myself in the lead as Kaylin guides us. The ground begins to climb and the trees thin. There's a stream of midday sun warming my head and shoulders. My clothes dry out, limbs thawing, but I jump at every twig snap and birdcall.

It isn't spoken, but we all know we're sitting ducks if they're watching us.

"I don't think they're watching, lass." Kaylin's warm breath tickles my neck.

Oh, I guess I let that last fear slip. "How can you be so sure?"

"Because we're all still alive."

17

MARCUS

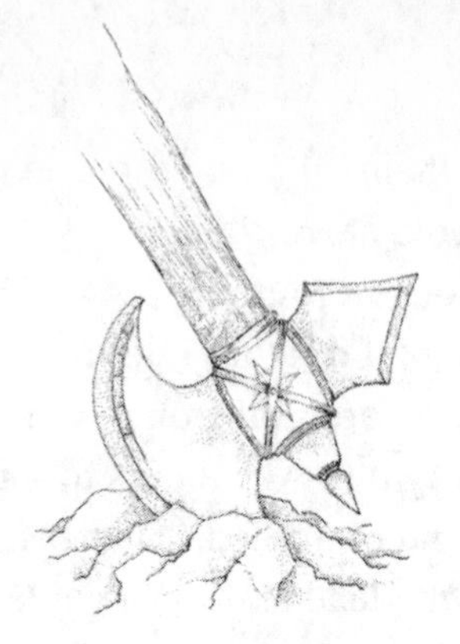

Every plod of Echo's hooves sends stabbing pain through my chest and a pounding in my head. Piper brought me back from the brink, and I owe Ash my thanks for her blood, but I'm far from fully healed, and by the bones, each step this horse takes feels like an ice pick in my brain. I keep telling Piper I'm fine. She knows it's a lie.

De'ral sulks somewhere in the depths without a word. Maybe he feels the failure on the headlands as much as I do. *"But how would I know what you feel? Because you say nothing to me."*

I drill him mind-to-mind, but there is no reply. He doesn't speak, and yet I feel his presence. It's a growing, angry pressure behind my eyes.

My ears burn, not just because of the midday sun. It's also my current view—the rear end of Ash's gray mare and the sailor's arms wrapped around her waist. It shouldn't bother me, and in theory, it doesn't. Ash's happiness is mine, and I won't let this irrational ire show, but curse it, I feel…agitated. What do we even know about this Kaylin? That he saved our lives, all right, but must he cling to her so tightly?

My anger seeps into De'ral—as if he doesn't have enough of his own—and Echo senses it. Every new noise has the mare jumping. I want to order phantoms up to travel beside us, knowing Aturnian scouts could be nearby. But Samsen and Piper are exhausted, and Belair and I are too inexperienced to have our *warriors* careening about uncontrolled.

Brogal's words come to mind, the High Savant's face menacing and his voice harsh. *The journey may prove hazardous, requiring every able body to protect you. Ash is non-savant. Don't even think of taking her.*

I look again at Ash riding in the lead—what I can see of her around the sailor's broad shoulders, anyway. *It wasn't a mistake,* I think, continuing the imagined conversation with Brogal. *I have needed her, just as she is. Already her language skills and counsel have helped enormously, and her blood!* But to myself, where no one but De'ral can hear, I admit it would help if she raised a phantom. I'd told Brogal that with five of us on the journey, I would be in good hands…

Then it dawns. *Five* of us.

Of which we are now *six*. That explains the avalanche of bad luck! The Bone Throwers did have it right.

I chew on the thought. Not four companions or six or seven, but five were needed to ensure success. This has to be the problem, but until we reach Capper Point, I don't know how to fix it. We *need* Kaylin. I'm not going to send him packing now, no matter how mixed my feelings are. His sword, and sense of direction, stays.

A hawk calls in the distance, and the grass rustles. Echo spooks, jumping to the side before I can control her. All the horses stop, heads flying up, nostrils flaring, ears rotating forward and back to locate the source of danger. Kaylin leaps to the ground and draws his sword. Not far to the right, in low-growing scrubs, a flock of birds takes flight.

"Pheasants is all," he says. Relief floods me. "Carry on."

Ash continues in the lead, and Kaylin sheaths his sword, swinging up behind her again. I don't know if we are being flanked by the enemy or not, but Kaylin's hand stays close to the hilt of his sword. I follow his example and do the same.

Horses and riders swivel their heads left and right, flinching at every new sound, real or imagined. The ground continues to rise, and Kaylin points to a steep climb.

"We'll have to walk the horses." I dismount, stifling a groan as I hit the ground.

"Can we pass the waterskin around?" Kaylin asks before I can order it. "Hard climb, but we're nearly there. Bladon is a giant, flat hilltop surrounded by a scattering of trees and dense scrub."

"Bladon," Ash says. "It means—"

"—flattop in Aturnian." She and Kaylin finish the sentence together.

"Helpful information." I pass to the head of the party, and Ash's mare whickers to Echo, our horses briefly touching noses. Ash looks exhausted, though her clothes are drying and she's stopped shivering. I survey the others and realize what bad shape we're in, all except Kaylin. He seems untouched by the battle, which I can't fathom unless Piper gave him healing I don't know about.

There are grunts and hushed exclamations as the others dismount. We pass around the waterskins, Kaylin taking a deep drink right along with everyone else. Then I lead our party up the hillside.

The sailor is right about one thing—the climb is short but steep. I'm breathing hard when we reach the top. "We'll let the horses rest a moment, check all directions, and carry on, quick as we can."

"Thank the dry flar'ned bones for that." Ash guides her mare toward the deepest grass and flops to the ground.

The plateau is lush and ringed with trees. In the open spaces are patches of yellow flowering fireweed. The horses go straight for the grass with little encouragement. They've had no chance to graze since the dried cornfields we found them in this morning, and that was hours ago. "Mind the fireweed," I warn the others. Horses won't usually touch it if there's a better choice, but I don't want to take any risks. The crossing was hard enough on them without further challenging their digestion. "Kaylin, give us a look at the distance viewer?"

Kaylin goes to retrieve it. The others run up their stirrups and loosen their girths a notch, letting the animals breathe deeply. Samsen and Piper spread out to check the paths on the other side of the hilltop. The healer walks with a limp but doesn't complain. I've known Piper all my life. She's never been one to complain about anything.

Kaylin and I head to the north edge of the hill and check the docks at Capper Point.

"Socked in," Kaylin says, handing the viewer to me to take in the fog blanketing the harbor. "We'll not know until we get there. In any case, I'll find you a sloop with no one the wiser. Your horses will be a problem, though."

"We'll deal with it at the time." My guts knot at the possibility of leaving Echo behind, selling her off to an Aturnian farmer or hunter. It shouldn't have come to this. Five instead of six. I grit my teeth and look through the distance glass. "You're right; there's nothing to see but a mass of gray."

"At least it's sunny up here." Belair sprawls in the grass, lacing his hands behind his head for a pillow. "Storm clouds to the south, though. I think Kaylin's right about the rain."

"Don't get too comfortable. We mount up again as soon as I check west and south." I pan with the viewer. Endless trees and sky and distant fog. "Let's not forget we're in enemy territory."

"What an odd bird." Ash points skyward.

Belair frowns. "Turkey buzzard?"

"Too big."

I follow her line of sight with the distance viewer. The sun dazzles my eyes, and bright spots cover the image. "Can't tell." I leave them and check beyond the eastern ridge. I have to smash through the lantana, but once I have a view of the valley, I feel a slow smile rising. Finally, open vista, clear as far as the eye can see, all the way to the south of Clearwater. Footfalls sound behind me and I spin, drawing my sword.

"It's only me!" Ash holds up her hands.

"Don't just appear out of nowhere like that." I sheath the sword, glad I didn't lunge before I recognized her.

She stands next to me and breathes deeply. "What a spectacular view."

"As long as there are no Aturnian troops milling around below, it's not bad."

"Is that likely?"

"I don't know. This is *their* realm we're traipsing through. It's easier if I think Nadonis and those mercenaries were after ransom, or if they feared some kind of retribution if they hoisted black sails. But if they're Aturnian sympathizers..."

Ash threads her arm through mine. "Shall we wade through the lantana and view the western valley, my Heir?" Ash asks with a twinkle in her eyes.

"With all speed." She's not called me *my heir* in a long time. It's always said in a teasing tone, and it reminds me of childhood and makes me feel lighter. I take her hand, and we hike to the other side of the plateau. As I push back the last barrier of tobacco bush leaves, I drag Ash back. "Down!" I whisper at the same time that De'ral shouts it in my head. I pull Ash flat to the ground with me.

"What is it?" Her cheek presses into the dirt.

"A camp." A *large* camp.

Slowly we worm toward the edge and peek through the tall grass.

Ash sucks in her breath. "Gutted stuggs. Look at the size of that herd."

De'ral rumbles in the depths.

"I'm more concerned with the campsite."

"Concerned" is too mild a word. In the valley to the west of the plateau, directly below us and not far from the north road, is a camp the size of Toretta City. The camp *is* a city. And it's full of Northern Aturnian troops, judging by their traditional flag, black with twelve bright stars shooting across it. They also fly the Gollnar banner, red with a dark horse galloping in the wind. Gollnar and Aturnia? United? Chills wash over me. Father must know about this! I squint through the glass. There's a third flag, white background with twin circles, one red, the other smaller and so dark it's almost black. I pass the viewer to Ash. "Check the flags."

She puts the viewer to her eye, her hands shaking. "Northern Aturnia and Gollnar together?" she echoes my surprise. "The third is…it's…"

"Tell me," I say in a rush.

"New to me. Never seen it before except—"

"Give me the glass." I quickly scan the camp. They have been here awhile, judging by the well-worn paths crosshatching the long rows of tents, the grazed pastures, and the general industry. Everyone is busy—shoeing horses, marching on the parade grounds, lining up to a very large tent that appears to be the mess hall. I've never seen such a large encampment.

Ash taps my shoulder, hard. "We have to go. Right now." Is that her pulse beating double time in her neck? I put my arm around her before we crawl backward from the edge.

"Quickly and quietly." I take her hand and lead the way back. "Straight to Rita and mount up. I'll signal the others." She squeezes my hand once before letting go. We sprint out into the field.

But it's too late.

Samsen shouts a warning as a dozen riders crest the unguarded track on the northeast ridge. They're on Gollnarian horses—pintos and blacks with white spotted rumps—and carry long, metal-tipped spears. Their dress is Gollnarian, too, with their round shields and long bows. I know that much. Quivers of arrows, feathered in red and blue fletches, are slung at their backs. A party from the encampment, probably their scouts, but are they savant? I come to an abrupt stop and let the distance viewer slide from my hand into the tall grass. No matter how this goes, being caught holding a spying glass won't help our cause. Ash, who was running behind me, slams into my back. "I told you to get on your horse."

She raises her brows. "Thought you might need a translator."

I call to the others, and she slaps my arm.

"Speak Aturnian," she hisses under her breath. "Better yet, don't say anything." She steps in front of me. "Hello!" she sings out in the common Aturnian dialect. Even I recognize the greeting. She says more, keeping her voice light and carefree; I don't know how. Belair is on his feet, sweeping up his coat. The others retreat toward us as the riders flood the hilltop. Samsen's phantom circles overhead, and Piper's serpent coils around her neck and left arm. All hands are ready to draw weapons. De'ral pushes up toward the surface of my mind, making my temples sweat.

I give a quick shake of my head to them all. "Wait and see. Ash might talk us through this." I tip my chin subtly toward her so they understand. The faces of those Aturnians we caught flash before me. What if they really were lost, just like us? The irony turns my stomach cold.

The riders shout as they approach, but the dialect is no Aturnian I recognize, not that I necessarily would. "What are they saying?" I ask Ash without moving my lips. I glance at Kaylin, who stands on her other side.

Ash turns briefly to me. "They're speaking Gollnarian."

"They are Gollnarians, by the look, but what are they doing half a world away from their realm?" Samsen whispers.

Whatever the answer, it's not good news.

"Remember, we're savants traveling to Aku," Ash says quietly. "They must let us pass. Just let me talk."

"But be ready to make a break," I say, though I'm not hopeful about our chances. The horses are at the other end of the plateau, startled by the new arrivals, and the Gollnar riders have us surrounded as they gallop the hilltop in ever-tightening circles.

Ash stands tall, waiting for them to bring their horses to a halt. When they do, she steps forward a pace, directly in front of the lead scout. Her hands are open in a gesture of goodwill, not an easy stance when hedged in by armed riders. She speaks fluent Gollnarian. I recognize a word or two now that she's identified the language, and of course the repeated "Aku initiates," the meaning all realms know and respect. The conversation goes back and forth for some time—the captain fires questions and Ash answers back in short, concise, and very formal-sounding words. At one point, she turns to Kaylin and asks him something in Aturnian. He, apparently understanding her perfectly, goes to the donkey pack to retrieve something.

De'ral growls, and it vibrates in my throat.

"Steady," I say, but am glad for his presence.

Ash and the captain keep talking. Again, I wish I'd taken my language classes more seriously. But some things need no translations, like the way the captain sizes up Ash and Piper, perceived as the weaker of our group or, worse, as someone to victimize. Can I just rip his arms off and throw them over the cliff? Judging by Samsen's face, he feels the same. We have laws against harming women in Baiseen, against harming *anyone*.

It appears the same tenets don't hold true here.

Crush them, De'ral says. So far, we haven't agreed on much, but he'll find no argument here. My phantom pushes hard, but these scouts have each of us in their sights. If I drop to my knee, I'm sure to find an arrow in my neck before De'ral breaks the surface.

Kaylin steps between Ash and the captain, handing over our travel documents. I can tell instantly that the captain is not happy with them, and I know why. There are six of us traveling and only five documents.

Keep the party's number to five. The Bone Thrower's instructions echo in my mind, much too late. Damn it all.

The captain dismounts and passes his reins to the man beside him. His long spear he keeps to hand.

Ash talks fast, pointing to Kaylin, the coast, and the donkey.

The captain chuckles, his dark beard wagging. I doubt she has told a joke. The other scouts join the laughter. He then makes a show of reading the scrolls and glancing at the corresponding savants.

If we bear the harassment, they'll probably let us go. It's law in all the realms. A little loss of face and then on our way.

Another dozen scouts crest the rise and flow over the plateau. Our horses are caught and led back to the circle. An order is barked, and another three scouts leap to the ground. With their spears at the sailor's throat, his sword is confiscated.

And just like that, our best weapon is gone.

Our saddlebags are brought to the captain's feet. He takes his time going through them, pulling things out and stuffing them back in again, especially Piper's and Ash's. He whistles when he finds their underthings.

The other scouts, both men and women, laugh.

Ash keeps her face neutral while the captain holds her favorite purple dress up like a dance partner and goes through the motions of a Gollnar tanglok. My blood heats at the disrespect, and De'ral slams into the back of my mind, enraged. I make to step forward, but the captain has moved on to my pack.

A cold sweat breaks out across my forehead when I realize what he's found—the sack of gold coins marked with the Palrion shearwater and my Baiseen family seal. I curse to myself. What was I thinking?

Now we must admit we are from Palrio and then explain why we are so far off course, given we are not spying but savants on our way to Aku. If they suspect we've seen the camp, none of us will be going anywhere,

I am certain.

The captain drops the items back in the saddlebag and stands in front of Ash.

Too close! De'ral's rage echoes in my mind.

My only thought is to snatch the captain's spear and impale him with it. De'ral is so near the surface, I think my skull will crack. Behind, we are outnumbered four to one.

If they are non-savant, though, we have a chance. It should be obvious by robes, but what if these scouts are hiding their rank? Then I hear Ash blurt a question, catching the word "non-savant." Has she outright asked?

"Non-savant?" the captain repeats. He follows with a deep belly laugh and holds out his arm, his cuff riding up. Ash stares at his wrist, but I can't tell what catches her attention. The captain's eyes go skyward, and we all follow his gaze. Coming out of the clouds is a dark-winged creature, the bird we saw earlier. Only it's not a bird at all. It's a phantom, up scouting us the whole time.

I should have known.

It dives, the wind whistling through its wings, making a high-pitched searing sound that grows louder by the second. The creature folds into an arrow and gains such speed, a boom cracks over the mountaintop and shakes the earth. The horses try to bolt, but the scouts hold them back.

"Ash, to me!"

She turns to run as the phantom hits, diving into the earth, burying all but the tail. Grass and rock fly up like a geyser as the remains of the phantom turn into a tangle of barbed, lashing vines, growing at a terrible rate. An *alter*!

"Look out!" I warn as vines wrap around Ash's legs and trip her to the ground. I bolt toward her, but a scout tackles me from behind and pins me with his spear. De'ral roils, but the scout has me on my feet before I can raise him.

Ash is trapped, my whole company guarded, unable to respond. The phantom sprouts new vines, reaching toward her and out to the others. Kaylin ducks his captors in a blur of movement I can't follow and rushes to Ash's side. She buries her face in his chest, but a dozen spears point at their heads.

The captain smiles. "*Alter* phantom, didn't you know?" He speaks Palrion? "I wouldn't anger him if I were you."

"Last thing on my mind." Ash chokes out the words.

"Release the little non-savant," the captain commands his phantom.

The vines loosen, and Kaylin helps Ash to stand. The phantom spirals around itself and shoots toward the darkening clouds, altering once again into the monstrous winged demon. The spears remain leveled on Ash and Kaylin, but it looks like only the captain of this band is savant.

"You'll need to come along and explain to our High Savant what you're doing so far from the road to Aku." The captain turns to the scouts and shouts orders.

A spear jabs my back, and a scout binds my hands in front of me. A tall Gollnar woman with multiple yellow braids, she nods to the horses. "Which one?"

They *all* speak Palrion? What is happening here?

Thoughtlessly, I incline my head in the direction of Echo. The captain watches, eyeing Echo with the same interest he showed the Baiseen coin and seal. Of course he does. She's the finest horse here. And I'm a fool for not pointing to the donkey. I'm sure Ash is thinking the very same thing.

The scout motions to the others, and I'm given a leg up into the saddle at spear point. Just as Kaylin predicted, rain begins to fall. It's too late for a distraction, at least on the spot. Samsen, Piper, and Belair are all in the same predicament. Hands tied, aboveground, and riding toward the enemy camp—the huge enemy camp they don't know about—with spears pointing at their backs.

The captain lifts Ash onto Rita, giving her thigh a more-than-friendly squeeze. "Our lieutenant will want to question you all privately," he says as Kaylin, also bound, is boosted up behind her. The captain's eyes linger on the sailor, too.

Ash looks down her nose at the man defiantly, but he's already turning to Piper with his hunter's gaze.

I shake my head at Samsen as he strains against the bindings. Not yet, but we have to do something before we reach the enemy camp.

As if hearing my thoughts, Kaylin turns and winks at me. Actually winks! For an instant, I see he's calm, unperturbed, but only because he has no idea what's ahead. The size of the enemy camp. The sheer number of troops.

His lack of fear may rise from ignorance, but at the moment, I'm grateful for the shred of hope it brings. I'm also glad he rides with Ash. Wherever my earlier jealousy stemmed from, it has vanished, replaced with a desperate need to come up with a plan, and fast.

18

ASH

The only thing keeping me from panic as I ride, hands bound, rain falling, is Kaylin doubling behind me. We don't speak, but his presence, the way he leans forward and turns slightly so his shoulder presses against my back, makes me feel like there is hope. Plus, there's his handiwork on the headland to remember. I know what he's capable of. But with his hands bound, the scouts ready to skewer us at any false move, and his weapon taken from him, how can he possibly save us?

"Wars are won in the will, not the weapons."

This is hardly the time to philosophize. And speaking of war—Gollnar in league with Aturnia? When did this happen? It's another thing to warn Master Brogal and the Magistrate about, but *how* I can't imagine. It is very likely we are being marched to our demise.

"You don't have all the facts."

What does that mean? Facts like the exact number of warriors in the camp? How we will be tortured? My stomach's in my throat.

"Other facts," my inner voice replies.

The rain falls harder. It runs off my head and down my nose, giving me a terrible itch. We're on Rita, third back from Marcus, who is being led behind the captain. They must know exactly who he is now. Palrion gold and the Baiseen Magistrate's family seal on a savant far off route to Aku equals highly prized captives, most likely spies.

"And not very good ones."

I agree with my inner voice on this. The next time Marcus plans to travel across enemy territory, I will do the packing. But in all fairness, this jaunt to Mount Bladon was never planned. "So goes the path," I say under my breath.

"Don't give up, lass." Kaylin speaks so softly, I barely hear the words, but they ring warm in my mind nonetheless.

"Thank you." When I turn to acknowledge him, he seems surprised.

There is so much more to say than a simple thanks, but I turn back, not wanting to draw attention.

Only Marcus and I know of the military encampment in the valley. If the others knew, they might be inclined to think up a way to escape before we're surrounded by a thousand swords, which by my count will be in three minutes. I have to try something.

"Then do."

I look over my shoulder, around Kaylin, at the scout riding behind us, and smile. He has light skin and curly, reddish-blond hair escaping his bone-colored knitted cap. He wears an Aturnian coat, baggy riding pants, and sheepskin-lined boots, all darkening in the rain. His face is sharp and angular—but less severe than the captain's. I hold my brightest smile in place. "It would be so nice to have someone to chat with, you know? I've been traveling with these scholarly savants for a full month! They are terribly reticent to converse."

He doesn't respond, but he doesn't tell me to shut up, either, so I keep going.

"How far to your camp?" I ask in Palrion to make sure my party listens. I feel Kaylin straighten. "Just ahead? It's hard to see around the trees." I glance forward and note Samsen's ears all but prick as well. "I caught a glimpse of your site from the plateau," I go on. "Quite impressive. I particularly like your spotty horses. Such a large herd of them."

The scout nods, and his horse, a black mare with tiny white speckles over her round rump, flutters her nostrils.

"You must have a huge galley tent to feed such a horde."

Kaylin knees me in the back of the leg. Too much? "Perhaps—"

"Silence!" the captain says from the head of the trail. His look is not friendly or tolerant. I close my mouth, hoping the others have a better idea of what we're in for, that it will spur them to some action. In any case, a few strides down the track reveals all as the enormous camp comes into view and speaks for itself. To the left of the trail, through the trees, I catch sight of flagpoles and the three banners flying from them that we saw from the summit—the Aturnian stars, Gollnar horse, and the twin, overlapping circles or suns. As I wanted to tell Marcus, it's new and belongs to no realm I know. But I've seen the image three times since docking in Clearwater. First on the notice at the apothecary, then these flags, and finally tattooed on the inside of the captain's wrist. I have no idea what kind of political mishmash this represents. Most likely I will never find out.

"*Quite pessimistic.*"

True, but in my defense, it's where the facts point.

That, and being bound and taken captive.

I realize, even as the thoughts come and pass, that I'm incredibly calm, all things considered. Shock? Suspended belief, perhaps?

My inner voice has no answer.

As we descend, the rows and rows of brown hide tents come into view, only a few minutes' ride away. Beyond the camp are rolling hills covered with horses, a thousand of them at least. My blood goes cold, and the rain makes me shiver. Although that could be the fear catching up to me.

Kaylin, on the other hand, remains unruffled behind me. He should be highly alarmed by now. His grip, where his tied hands hold a fold of my coat, relaxes, which is reassuring, but as the descent continues, the trail curves westward and "city-size" suddenly seems a conservative estimate for the enemy camp. Beside the fields of horses grazing in the hills are at least a hundred mounts being ridden in formation around a vast parade ground. The numbers are too many to count. This is no military exercise or even show of force.

It's an all-out war campaign, and we are being taken straight to the heart of it.

19

MARCUS

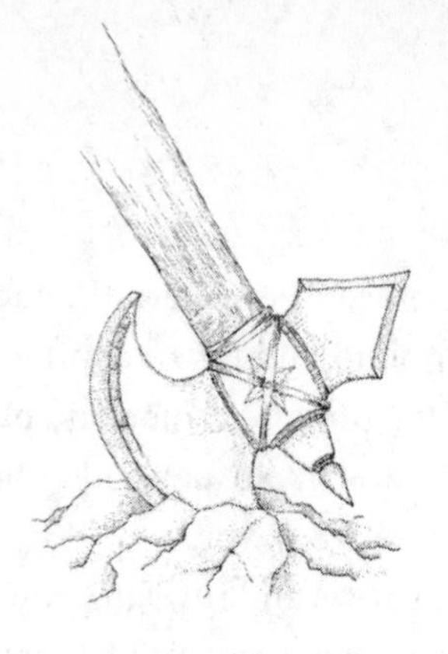

I have to do something, and it has to be *now*.

The Heir of Baiseen and his company are not going to fall into enemy hands. Not like this. Not without a fight. Ash did a good job warning the others of the sheer size of what we face, but this is one situation she can't talk her way out of. And this is all my fault.

Rain falls harder, the trail going muddy. The horses slip and slide down the track. It might be an advantage. I don't know yet. There's too much rage—both mine and my phantom's—to think clearly. And the pain in my head… It's nearly unbearable. I test the binding at my wrists, again. Nothing gives. We have to make a break for it now, before reaching a shout's distance to the Aturnian legions. But how?

Crush them, my phantom suggests once again, and I see an image of a lion breaking out of a cage and devouring its captors.

At least he's talking to me, and like last time, it's not a bad suggestion. *"How?"*

Touch ground and I'll show you.

Could it be that simple? The trail widens not far ahead with a steep cliff on my right and a stone retaining wall to the left. If there's going to be an escape, it must happen in the next thirty feet. I search for the courage to act and run straight into De'ral, his presence pressing in on my mind. He's ready. Echo knows something is up. Her ears pin back and her head juts high. Fifteen more strides. Fourteen. Thirteen.

Do it! my phantom growls.

I feign a cough, lean forward, and check the cliff's edge. It's between two to three yards to a rock ledge. It's survivable. Probably. I cough again and hunch over. De'ral must rise immediately, before they shower me with spears. Another deep breath and I inch my boots out of the stirrups until only the toes press the metal bars. I cough a third time and make a huge hacking sound at the end to clear my throat, a habit Ash hates. It's the only warning I can think of.

I fall back, slamming my spine and shoulders hard onto Echo's rump. She startles and bunches her hindquarters. I heel her shoulders and she crow-hops forward, crashing straight into the lead mount. *Sorry, girl.* But it gives me the seconds I need to scissor my legs and flip off her back. The ground comes up fast and punches the air out of my lungs. *"De'ral, be ready."* I tuck my chin and keep rolling, right over the edge.

Hit the dirt; raise my phantom. It's my only thought.

But the fall breaks me in half. I can't swallow or breathe. White lights flash in front of my eyes. Acid races up my throat and I try to heave, but that requires breathing, something I still can't do. *"Rise!"* I command my phantom.

De'ral is already exploding out of the ground. I duck, shielding my head against the rocks and dirt that avalanche down. The whole cliff face rattles apart as my massive phantom rises to full height, thundering a challenge.

"Kill the enemy," I gasp. "Harm none of our own." A phantom shouldn't have to be reminded, but De'ral's untrained. By the bones, I hope he can tell the difference between friend and foe.

De'ral climbs, the ledge crumbling under his hands and feet. I drag myself out of the way to keep from being buried alive. There's no way to gauge what's going on above me save for the little I perceive through the tunnel-vision rage of my phantom, and the wails and chaotic shouts of everyone above. De'ral's intent is so burning that I can't take full phantom perspective. But I must. This attack can succeed if it is swift and quiet, before reinforcements come from the camp. We're already far beyond silent, so swiftness is the key. The barrier between me and De'ral finally bursts and a rush of emotions flood in along with a full view of the road. Violent rage is at the top of my feelings and pooled below a sickening, oily darkness I don't recognize, though the pounding in my head is all too familiar. Only one thing is certain. The Aturnian scouts are dying under my phantom's crushing blows. For now, it's going to plan.

20

ASH

"Look out!" Kaylin shoves me against Rita's neck as a shadow sweeps over our heads.

I try to hold on, gripping her mane with my bound hands, unable to shorten the reins and hold her back as she shies toward the rock wall. Marcus's phantom is climbing up the cliff. By the Drop, De'ral is *huge*. I'd heard the rumors, but nothing could've prepared me for this.

Our eyes lock, sending chills right through me. He raises one arm high overhead then brings it down, smashing the captain flat to the ground, spotty horse and all.

My jaw drops and I can't move.

"See," my inner voice says.

"De'ral is one Barlargka of a phantom," I whisper.

"Indeed."

My attention snaps back to the present. Kaylin's untying his binds with his teeth while De'ral stomps among our captors, ignoring the thrusts of spears and slices of blades, destroying the enemy right along with their horses. I can't take my eyes away. It's the most terrifying thing I've ever witnessed.

"Give me your hands." Kaylin breaks my bonds as if they were string. The mare rears again as De'ral smashes the scouts in front of us. Kaylin and I slide off her back to the ground and Rita bolts. We run toward Piper, whose chestnut gelding whinnies, head high, whites of his eyes showing.

Piper kicks her foot out of the stirrup. "Knife in my boot."

Kaylin retrieves it as she vaults out of the saddle. I take her horse's reins, and with a quick slice, Kaylin cuts her bonds.

"Hold him and the donkey," she says to me. To Kaylin, "Weapons?" He offers her the knife and an Aturnian blade from the ground. Piper nods and pushes into the fray, carving her way to Samsen and Belair, who are stranded in the thick of it.

"Mind the battle," Kaylin says. "And don't take your eyes off that monstrous phantom." He lifts his chin toward De'ral, who is busy hammering scouts flat like a blacksmith works iron. "You didn't mention."

"I didn't know!"

Blood arcs through the air like a macabre rainbow. Horses scream and the sounds of battle ricochet in my ears. De'ral bellows a war cry and punches a scout into the rock wall that holds the hillside back from the road. The blow cracks the stone, the scout's skull smashing like a melon, blood spraying as the wall crumbles. I turn away from the bulging eye protruding from the scout's face. Spears still rain into De'ral's chest and forearms, sticking there like oversized toothpicks. They don't slow him in the slightest, but what is this doing to Marcus, who must be on his knees below the cliff? Does he have phantom wounds? Will he bleed out? While my mind races with these thoughts, De'ral picks up the body with the smashed skull and winds up to throw it over the cliff.

"He's dead already, De'ral," I say to him in my mind. It's not like I expect him to hear me, but he glances my way and drops the corpse.

Add that to the shocks of this day.

I give De'ral a faint smile. Maybe it was my look of horror that stopped him. Surely not my thoughts.

"Catch the horses!" Kaylin shouts amid the fray.

I rush back up the road, pulling Piper's horse behind, but the donkey isn't fast enough. *"De'ral, no!"* I think it fast, on the chance that knowing his name will allow him to hear my thoughts. But it's too late.

The donkey squirms a moment under the *warrior* phantom's unintended stomp then lies still. If it makes any sound, it's lost in the rest of the madness. De'ral gives me a sheepish look. So…he *can* hear me? Plenty of time to ponder this more when there is less killing and screaming. *"Be more careful, for rit's sake!"*

So many scouts are crushed, dead in the road, rivulets of blood streaming from them, aided and buoyed by the rain. Those left alive struggle to control their horses and retain Belair and Samsen. Thank the gods of the deep those left are all non-savant. Two try to bolt away, but Marcus's *warrior* backhands them off their mounts and over the cliff to the valley below, where their shrieks are cut short by resounding thuds. The phantom plucks a spear from his arm and hurls it at another of our captors. It flies past his face and impales his horse's neck, dropping it fast, but the rider rolls free.

"De'ral! Slow down. Take aim." Where in all the bones is Marcus? His hands must still be tied.

Kaylin cuts down any scouts that cross his path as he guards Piper's back. They reach Samsen first and free him, his phantom taking to the sky, talons extended, but his horse panics and runs. I turn back to catch him. We're going to have to ride out of here, and fast.

I make my way to Frost, shivering as she presses into the bank, too well trained to bolt, but clearly terrified. "Easy girl." I put my hand on her shoulder and reach for the reins. She relaxes the moment I touch her. I turn to search for Echo, whose reins are trapped, but Rita is close, so I lead Frost toward her first.

"Bring it in!" Samsen shouts over the cliff to Marcus. "We have this." Samsen's pale hair is wet with rain and blood. He dashes out of the way as De'ral sweeps a stray scout off his feet and hurls him into the distance. When another makes a run for the enemy camp, the huge phantom plunges his fist into the rock wall above the scout's head. It collapses, burying the man alive, and half the road with him.

Belair points wildly. "One's getting away." He falls to his knees and up comes his sun leopard, rising through the middle of the road, rocks and gravel and bodies flying. It attacks a scout who is near dead, shaking an arm until it detaches from the socket. Then the big cat sees the one running toward camp and streaks after him.

"Marcus," Piper calls over the cliff. "Call him in!"

He must hear her, because his phantom disappears into the earth, leaving a pile of broken spears behind him. De'ral looks at me again before his head vanishes, his grimace softening.

As I stare at the muddy mess in the road where Marcus's phantom went to ground, a wounded scout climbs onto the nearest horse and gallops away. At the top of his lungs, he shouts, "Marcus Adicio! Marcus Adicio! The Heir of Baiseen is among us!"

"Stop him!" I shout at the savants. "He can't reach the camp."

Samsen's eagle is high overhead. It folds its wings and dives, dropping the scout on impact, rising again with a red ball in his talons, streaming ribbons. I squint. Not ribbons, blood vessels. The phantom has ripped out his heart, but not before the enemy's warning sounded through the valley. The rain turns into a downpour and for a moment, all we can do is stare at one another and pant, water streaming down our faces.

And pray to the old gods no one else heard.

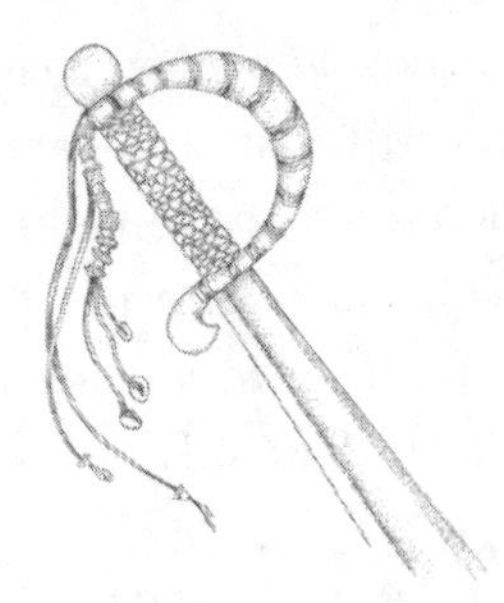

21

KAYLIN

It's a fine battle. I'm drenched in blood and water, smack in the center of the best massacre I've seen for some time. No reveling in it, though. A hundred horsed Aturnians and their new Gollnar friends are apparently about to run us down, with a thousand more to follow. Does Teern know about this alliance, I wonder? He'd have a spy or two in that camp, surely. But for now, I focus on escape, seeing only one way.

"They're coming." Ash jumps from her perch on the rock wall. "Too many to count," she says louder, startling when Marcus emerges from the ravine, supported between Samsen and Piper. "Is he all right?"

"He will be." Piper sounds proud. "Let's get him on his horse."

Ash heads for the frightened black mare. "Let me."

Echo stands next to the Aturnian captain's broken body, anchored by her reins tangled in his dead grip. I soften as I watch Ash soothe the animal. She has a way…

"Easy, girl." She strokes the horse's neck before prying the captain's fingers open to release the mare's reins. Once done, she lingers. Something attracts her attention on the ground.

"Quick is best, lass," I call. "Company's coming."

Ash wrenches her gaze from the severed arm and leads the horse toward me. Samsen has Rita and Frost, but that is all. Belair's bay is dead lame. He untacks it and shoos it away, tears in his eyes as the animal lingers over the donkey flattened into the road. The other horses, including Piper's, are gone. As Ash leads Echo toward me, she passes a scout's corpse slumped against the bank. His hand is up over his head, as if even in death he tries to ward off the assault. She stares for a moment and I see what catches her eye. A tattoo on the inside of his wrist. The Twin Suns.

My body stills as my mind races.

It can't be. Not yet.

Marcus stirs, his hair thick with mud, blood running down the side of his face. "Well done, Heir. They didn't have a chance against your *warrior*." I have new respect for him. My plan for escape wasn't nearly as fantastic.

Marcus gives a satisfied smile, though it obviously pains him. The fall wouldn't have been pleasant. I lift Marcus into the saddle. He flops forward and we secure him in that position with straps from the donkey's harness.

"We have to ride, and fast." I go to Rita as Piper hoists herself behind Marcus.

"There's no escape," Samsen says. "This road leads straight toward the enemy."

"Not that way." I indicate the cliff. "Take the trail down to the Ferus River."

"What trail?" Piper peers into the ravine.

I point to a deer track snaking over the edge. "At the bottom, there's a path through paperbark trees. If the river runs high, we can board the ferry and haul ourselves across."

"What keeps the Aturnians from following?" she asks.

"Once on the other side, we cut the ferry loose."

Piper nods. "And if the water's low?"

"We ford the river and keep running."

"Do it," Marcus says through his tangled hair. Piper throws her weight back as far as she can and urges Echo down the cliff. I watch until the mare's black rump fishtails over the edge.

"Belair, you take Frost," Samsen shouts above the downpour. "Ash, grab the extra saddlebags."

Ash slings them over Rita's shoulders as rain pounds her head, parting her hair down the middle.

"Ride, lass." I boost her into the saddle.

"What about you and Samsen?"

"We'll catch up." A spear zings in and lands an arm's length from us. Foot soldiers charge up the road with blades drawn. "To the river!" I shout and slap Rita on the rump. The gray mare leaps over the cliff, Ash clinging tight to stay in the saddle.

With her away, I turn to face the enemy, a grin bursting free. My blade! I spot it in the wreckage and sweep it up. Ah, but the sword feels good in my hand as Samsen and I meet the attack. There are only ten in total, but not far behind are a score more on horseback. I cut the last of the ten down and Samsen and I sprint away. The cliff is slick but the rain a blessing. I slide down and hit the trail at high speed. The rain plummets in sheets, and I can see only a few lengths in front and to the sides.

Ash, I think to myself. The distance stretches out between us and I can't quite steady my feelings. But then she appears, waiting for me, halfway to the bottom of the ravine.

"I said to run, lass."

"Just jump on the horse." She has her foot out of the stirrup, holding Rita on the muddy slope. Samsen swings up behind Belair, who waits as well.

I sheathe the blade and vault into the saddle, my arms going around her tight. "To those scrub oaks." I lick the fresh water off my lips and speak into her ear. "Thank you."

Her breath comes in a gasp, and warmth spreads up her neck to her face.

For me, the sensations are all-consuming. Who is this wordsmith from Baiseen? I will make it my calling to find out.

We take off, slowing only to negotiate the narrow turns and rain-slick drop-offs. Again, I wonder how I have come to be on the back of a horse, my arms around this brilliant scribe, my sword singing with enemy blood? It's not a question to answer but to relish.

I check over my shoulder as mounted Aturnians spill down the cliff behind us. Their horses don't hesitate, so we're barely in the lead.

Ash's heart pounds through her sheepskin coat. I close my eyes for an instant, shutting out every other sound in the world but her racing *lub-dub, lub-dub*. I deliberately draw in a single breath and with it comes her scent. I can taste it on my lips, ocean and lilacs and a drop of blood. I savor her nearness for a moment more, then jump off the horse.

"What are you doing?" Her eyes are wide, rainwater running down her nose and spilling from the corners of her mouth.

"Slowing them down." I hit the ground hard and turn to face the enemy. "Ride, Ash. I'll meet you at the river."

She hesitates as a spear flies straight toward my chest. I swerve to the side and grab it out of the air. The friction burns my hand, but I hold on and dig in my heels, sliding with it. In one quick snap of my wrist, I reverse the weapon and hurl it back at its owner. It goes right through the lead Aturnian. His horse careens in another direction as the rider falls to the ground. "Ride, Ash!" I draw my sword and charge. "All of you, ride!" But I'm not alone. The eagle phantom flies above, and the healer's serpent streams behind.

I'm impressed by the raptor. It fights well as it breaks necks with a quick twist of its powerful talons, rending its victims like down-stuffed pillows. The healer's serpent bites its prey half a chain away, injecting venom, dropping horses and then the riders. As more Aturnians attack, I slash and stab, taking an Aturnian blade in my left hand as well, cutting down the enemy.

"Tutapa!" I let loose my home island's battle cry. As I stand at the bottom of the ravine, rain-soaked and flinging blood from my blade, the road above shakes with more and more galloping hooves. I signal the raptor phantom, then turn to the snake. "Go!"

The serpent disappears into the ground and I know Piper has received the message. Now it's just dodge the arrows flying at my back and make it to the Ferus River, to my lass, ahead of this mob. The rain falls in buckets. With any luck, the river runs high.

22

"Where is he?" My pulse races as Samsen and I wait a short distance from the river, the horses' sides heaving, their sweat washing off with the rain. I peer up the trail. It's lined with wet paperbark trees, their mushroom-colored hides peeling away like layers of old snakeskin. The drooping leaves slash about in the wind, and on high branches sacred ibis ride out the storm. "We shouldn't have left him behind."

It happened so fast. One minute, Kaylin is behind me on Rita and the next he hits the ground and catches a spear midair. I've never seen anything like it.

"Here he comes!" Samsen says over the sounds of the rushing river and driving rain. Behind us, the banks of the Ferus barely contain the raging water. It splashes out of the swollen riverbed, mud brown with frothy whitecaps.

"We're trapped!" I call to Kaylin as he runs to me. I kick my foot out of the stirrup and he swings up behind. "Ferry's on the far side and it won't budge."

"We'll see about that."

We gallop back to the river and slam to a halt at the dock.

Once again, Kaylin hits the ground running. "Be ready to board!" He bolts down the dock, soaked to the skin, his white shirt saturated to transparency. He strips it off without breaking stride. His sword hits the dock, too, and he unsheathes a buck knife. With it gripped between his teeth, he throws his hands over his head and dives into the torrent.

It's a moment before I can slide off Rita. I stumble to my feet and gaze at the river where Kaylin went under. My heart tightens, air hardly able to escape my lungs. Slowly, I lead Rita to the pier where fringing trees toss wildly in the wind. Weak branches snap and crash into the water where they are quickly swept away. "Kaylin?" My eyes lift to the far side of the shore.

Piper stands beside me. "He's a strong swimmer. He'll make it."

I watch the roiling surface and wait.

"There he is." Samsen points across the river, shielding his eyes from the downpour with his other hand. "He's shouting something."

Pull the cable. I hear it loud as sanctuary bells. "Pull the cable!" I repeat.

Samsen and Piper rush to the connecting cable and haul on it with everything they have. The ferry is set up with a simple pulley system, and even in the raging current we have it snug against the end of the pier in no time.

"Load the horses," Kaylin hollers as he unlatches the tailgate.

Piper leads Echo aboard first, but Marcus is so weak we leave him secured to the saddle. Next comes Belair, on Samsen's Frost. The river continues to rise, splashing over the dock. I can't see my boots or Rita's hooves as we step onto the ferry. Bless the bones, the horses are well trained, loading reasonably well even as the raft rocks and plunges and strains against the cable.

Kaylin retrieves his sword and shirt, belting on the weapon and stuffing his shirt into his back pocket as far as it will go. "Haul!" He jumps back aboard.

Piper and Samsen pull hand over hand. I join in, but the ferry's load is heavy and we're not moving fast across the wild current.

"Let me, lass. And keep an eye on the riverbank. Our enemy has bows." Kaylin hauls on the cable and the ferry cuts across the current toward the other side.

I tie the horses with a quick-release knot, in case they panic midstream, all while watching the shore. "Marcus? Can you hear me?" I grip his calf, noticing his restraints slipping.

He rouses, looking up long enough to nod before slumping back down on Echo's neck. I attempt to retie the straps, but my hands are numb. The ties slip through my fingers, and Marcus falls onto the deck with a grunt. He tries to pull himself up between Frost and Echo. The horses snort but are careful not to tread on him.

I squat and do my best to haul him forward, yanking on his arm, but he hollers.

"Are you trying to kill me?"

"Sorry." I push a mass of wet hair from his face. "You must have injured your shoulder in the fall."

"There's not much I *didn't* injure in the fall."

"But you saved us, Marcus." Warmth spreads through my chest.

His grin is equal parts pride and grimace.

"Come out from under the horses' legs." I try to guide him. Their bellies drip mud and sweat and rainwater. The ferry bucks and plunges, water washing over the deck. With his cooperation, I drag Marcus in front of the horses and lean him against the center post. "Stay put."

"Where would I go?"

A cheer rises from Piper and Samsen. We are nearly to the other side. But the revelry cuts short when an arrow flies toward us and thuds into the post over Marcus's head.

"Stay behind the horses!" Kaylin yells.

I make a face at him. "Horses aren't shields." As I speak, two more thuds sound out. Belair screeches and Frost fires both iron-shod hooves into the tailgate. It splinters and sails off its hinges, the river sweeping it away. The ferry bobs, straining to follow.

"Belair!" I go to him, finding an arrow deep in his left shoulder. The white horse has one in the rump, blood running dark down her hind leg. "You have to get down." More arrows come at us. I haul on Belair and he tumbles out of the saddle then hits the deck hard. I clamp pressure around the wound as blood rises through his sheepskin coat. "Piper, help!"

Belair grits his teeth and pants, cursing me in Tangeen. "Tell Piper to wait and see if we survive the crossing. No point in wasting her time if I'm about to die."

"You're not about to die." My hands are drenched in his blood.

"Don't be too hasty to judge, lass." Kaylin points to the shore.

I turn back to see a wall of Aturnians skidding to a stop at the edge of the river. "C'hac no." The riders dismount, drop to their knees, not to raise phantoms, but to fit their bows. Belair is right. We're all going to fall from the path today.

Kaylin draws his sword. "Stand clear!" To me he says, "Hold on tight, lass." He raises the Aturnian blade high over his head.

"What are you *doing*?" Samsen shouts as the Aturnians release their bowstrings. A slew of arrows streams toward us like a swarm of hornets.

At the same moment, Kaylin's sword slices the cable clean in two. "Watch your heads!"

The line snakes through the pulley at lightning speed and flies free. The ferry careens downstream, arrows missing us by an arm's length. My stomach slams into my mouth as I grip the railing. By the time the archers reload, they're too far away for another shot. Meanwhile the raft races over the rapids.

Samsen clings to the narrow railing. "You're mad!"

"And you, my good savant, are alive." Kaylin slides by the horses to reach me.

"Where are you going now?" Samsen demands.

"Not far, I assure you. This vessel is small."

"It is also without a rudder. You can't just let us speed down the river."

"Aye, but there are no true rapids, yet. We'll see them when we near the falls."

Samsen wipes water from his face and pushes back his hair. "Falls? How soon?"

Kaylin tilts his head, listening. "About two minutes. We best tend to Belair. That arrow has to come out in case he needs to swim."

"Swim?" Samsen cuts loose a stream of curses, which, under more serene circumstances, would impress me. As it is, we're all swearing up a storm.

"I take it we've had a change of plans?" Belair opens his eyes.

I grip the rail with one hand and press his shoulder with the other.

"Not to worry, though," Samsen says as he squats down on the other side of the Tangeen. "Apparently, we have two minutes."

"One and a half, now," Kaylin says casually.

"Then what?" Belair asks.

"Rapids."

Belair groans.

"Shouldn't we remove it under more hygienic conditions?" I ask, trying to digest everything that's happening.

"Not with an Aturnian arrow. They do like their poisons."

Belair groans again.

Kaylin straddles him, grips the shaft with both hands, and puts one bare foot on the Tangeen's chest. "Exhale, mate."

"Wait!" Belair protests.

Samsen grabs his shoulders and Kaylin yanks.

The squeal out of Belair's mouth is ear-piercing. It rips through the rain, the rapids, and the roar of the Aturnians shouting on the distant bank.

Kaylin gestures at the horses' hooves. "Clay from the riverbank. Quickly now."

I know what he means before the words are out of his mouth. I lean against Rita's shoulder and grip her shaggy fetlock. She takes the cue, braces her other three legs, and lifts her hoof. "Good girl." Rain washes the mud off her iron shoe, and sure enough, her frog is packed with clean red clay. I unsheathe my belt knife with one hand and pry out a gooey chunk, handing it off to Kaylin.

He packs the wound and does up Belair's coat just in time for us to hear a roar above the churning water.

"Hold on." Kaylin can't quite hide a smile. "It's a bit of a ride."

"That's all we're going to do?" I say. "Hold on?"

"No. We're going to untie the horses, just in case."

"Just in case what?"

"The ferry splinters into a hundred pieces and we all have to swim for it."

The ferry pitches and drops, whitewater rapids closing in on both sides. The horses are petrified, tails tucked, heads high, and eyes rolled into the backs of their skulls. Piper and Samsen cling to the port railing, but as we crash into a standing wave, their rail rips away. Kaylin reaches out with both hands and pulls them back from the edge. They transfer their grip to Echo's saddle and tail, while the mare stands quivering.

How the deck is in one piece, I don't know. I lose my footing when another wave washes over us, but I have one arm wrapped around the center piling and anchor to it. When I think we have made it, the raft free-falls for several seconds then smacks down with a *bang*. The deck submerges, water up to my waist, before it buoys to the surface again.

And then, as if it had belonged to the raging rapids, the wind drops and the downpour fades into a drizzle.

The ferry drifts silently on a wide lake while the fading rain makes dimples in the otherwise calm surface. We're all panting, hearts pounding. The horses gingerly shift their weight to a narrower stance and flutter out soft breaths. "We made it?" I swipe water from my face and rub my eyes.

We continue to float down the middle of the expanse, far from the misty banks and overhanging trees. Forest birds call, like whips cracking in the distance, and bullfrogs moan on either shore, stopping abruptly when we approach only to start up again once we've passed. The rain trickles away to nothing, and a light fog rises from the water like steam.

"We made it," I say, more confident this time.

Samsen slaps Kaylin on the back. "That was some ride, sailor."

When I look down at Marcus and Belair, I realize what is gone. "The saddlebags?"

"Couldn't hold 'em," Marcus says.

"Our gold? The records? Everything?" Not to mention clothes and supplies and map. Piper's healing kit.

I look to Kaylin, but he's busy tying rope to a ring in the center of the ferry. I drop to my knees and check Belair. His eyes are round as an owl's.

"You all right?"

He gives his head one quick nod, but I'm not sure which of us he's trying to convince more.

I turn to Marcus. "You?"

"Sorry about the records," he says.

"We're alive. That's what counts." I rub the circulation back into his arms then suddenly stop to listen. "Do you hear that?"

His eyes close. "My heart pounding in my throat? You hear it, too?"

"No, the humming." It grows louder and turns into a rumbling drone. I tug on Kaylin's pant leg and he kneels beside me, eye level. His face is very close, so close I can see gold flecks embedded in the dark sea green of his eyes. "Kaylin, what am I hearing?"

He ties a thick rope around his waist. "The falls."

"Behind us?"

"In front."

"The Capper Point Falls?" I stand up, going on tiptoe, but can't see beyond the calm and the mist.

"Best untack the horses, everyone, fast as you can."

"What now?" Piper asks.

"We're all going for a swim." The look on Kaylin's face makes us spring to action. Buckles and straps are hard to undo with cold, stiff hands, but I have Rita's saddle and bridle off in good time. The others are untacked as well.

"We have to move." Kaylin finishes securing the rope around his waist.

"Move?" I ask. "Tell me how in the name of the deep dark Drop we are going to survive the Capper Point Falls!"

"We're going to hike down beside them." The raft twists to the side and picks up speed as he speaks.

"Shove the horses off," Kaylin commands and dives into the water.

"The horses?" Both hands go to my temples. "Shove them off?"

The roar increases, and the lip of the falls comes into view. White mist rises around it, stirred by the pummeling water below. Rita leans against me for comfort. "You want us to push the horses into the water?" I shout at the dark surface where Kaylin last was seen.

He pops up much farther away. "It's their only chance."

Marcus protests as he struggles to stand. "They'll drown."

"They can make it to shore," Samsen says. "If I were you, I'd be more distressed for those of us who may not."

Kaylin's right: we have to do this. I kiss Rita's nose and step aside as Samsen slaps her rump. The mare's reluctant but soon bunches her legs together and leaps into the water. The splash washes over the deck and Echo is pushed off behind her, all while Marcus protests.

Samsen removes Frost's arrow from her rump and she jumps into the water, leaving him standing there with the bloody arrow in his hand. The little ferry dips and shoots sideways, floating much higher now, and faster. The three horses swim for the western shore, only nostrils, eyes, and ears visible above the surface. For every length forward they gain, the current drags them farther downstream, toward the falls.

"Will they make it?" I follow their progress as the ferry moves parallel with them.

"One way or another," Piper says. "Hope we can say the same for us."

By then Kaylin nearly reaches the opposite shore.

"What's he doing?" Marcus clings tight to the central post.

I crouch next to Marcus. "Trying to save our lives." I make Kaylin out in the mist-cloaked willows. He swings up into a stout branch and unties the rope from around his waist.

"Hold on," he shouts and loops the rope around the branch twice before it pulls taut. The ferry strains to a halt. I grip the railing and wave at Kaylin. "You did it!" Though bobbing in the middle of the current, tethered to a tree branch by a straining rope isn't a permanent solution. Kaylin waves back and dives into the water.

Seconds later, his mop of curly black hair breaks the surface and his hands clamp onto the deck. He's up in one motion, slinging water out of his eyes. "You can go hand over hand to the shore," he says. "Belair first, the strongest swimmers last."

"Strongest? Only Ash can swim," Samsen says. "And the Tangeen, though not so well with an arrow wound."

"Then don't let go." He pulls Belair into the river, one arm around his chest, the other gripping the rope. "Roll onto your back," Kaylin commands.

Belair complies and manages to keep his head above water.

Kaylin flips onto his back as well and wraps his legs around Belair's chest in a wrestler's hold. He hauls on the rope, hand over hand, towing Belair quickly toward the bank. "Be at it, all of you."

We stare after him.

Marcus recovers first. "You next, Ash." He struggles to his feet.

"Strongest swimmer last," I say. "*You're* next."

There's no time for argument. Marcus reaches for the rope, holds it tight, and falls into the river. "Keep the party's number to five," he mumbles. Then he copies Kaylin's technique and turns onto his back, holding his upper body high out of the water. Probably too high. He'll use up all his arm strength. He pulls himself toward the safety of the bank, his injured arm slipping more with each new grip. Piper follows, then Samsen, then me.

I lower myself in and hold tight, arms already trembling. The weight of my coat drags me down, so with one hand, I undo the buttons and shrug out of it. The current carries it away. The water is ink black and bottomless under the clouded sky, making my mind shift to what creatures lurk below.

"Don't dally."

My inner voice needn't bother. I've every intent of hurrying to shore. Though whether the warning comes from the threat of the falls or what lies below, I can't guess.

"It's the—"

Don't tell me.

I crane my neck, trying to spot Kaylin. He is only a few lengths from the willow tree, Belair safe in his grip when the raft slowly arcs toward the shore. The line slackens ahead of me and Marcus lets out a cry. The horses shriek, and I jerk around in time to see Frost disappear over the falls. The other two are nowhere in sight. My eyes close tight. *No. No. No.*

"Ash," Kaylin calls to me. "Keep coming."

Before I can start up again, the raft hits a rock, the far side lifting out of the water, the front end plowing under the waves. Splinters fly into the air, and the rope goes completely slack.

"Hold your breath."

I sink with the rope until it slowly rises back to the surface in time for me to see Marcus, Samsen, and Piper whisk by, gulping for air. They didn't hang onto the rope!

I hear Kaylin shouting, "No!" even as I let go and swim for Marcus.

But the current's too fast.

We're all headed straight for the falls.

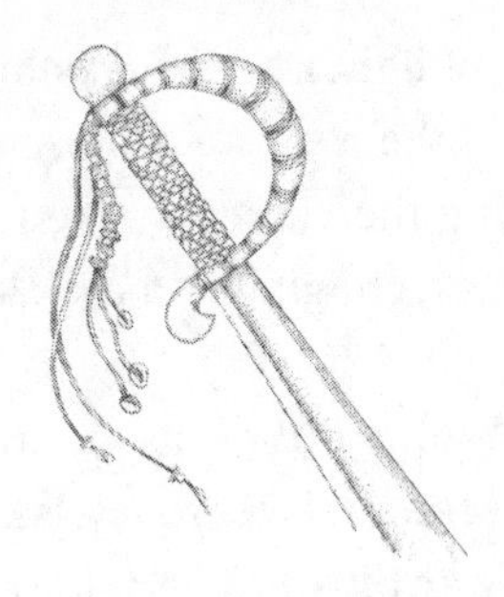

23
KAYLIN

For the love of the sea, these landers…

I pull Belair up onto the shore where he staggers, finding support against the tree. "Hike to the bottom. We'll meet you there."

I push off the bank and stream underwater, kicking hard. In seconds, I'm at the edge of the falls and take a quick look at what lay below. It's decent—plenty of water in the churning pool. Like a leaf in a stream, I glide over the lip. A heartbeat later, my feet smack the surface and I plunge into the depths. The sound is deafening until I sink toward the bottom of the gorge. There, an eerie silence surrounds me, the roar of the falls muted by an ocean of water over my head. I shoot for the surface, searching for the others. Ash is there, treading water, safe. Relief floods me, a feeling completely novel. One of many new sensations experienced since we met. Was that only six days ago? Luckily, she's not a bad swimmer, my lass. Can't say the same for the rest of them.

I dive back down and find two shadows; one swims weakly for the surface, the other drifts in the current belly-up like a dead fish.

Piper is closest but out of air, her face stricken. I circle her waist with one arm and rise. She gasps when we break the surface.

"I've got Piper," Ash calls over the roaring falls as she reaches me in two strong strokes. "Find the others, please."

I dive straight back under, flowing downstream with the current. Marcus isn't hard to spot, his heavy coat open, floating around him, hair fanned, blood inking the water from his phantom wounds. I drag the Heir of Baiseen to the surface and search for Ash. She's on the bank, sleeves rolled up, supporting Piper. She storms to the shore when she spots me. Piper staggers after her.

"Samsen?" I ask as I bring Marcus to her.

Piper's dark eyes are wide, her breathing fast. "I can't see him."

I disappear back under the water. The lowering sun cracks through the clouds and sends beams of light into the crystal depths, turning the gorge emerald-green. There, on the rocky bottom, a glint of gold shines, and I sweep it up before letting the currents take me downstream. Samsen's farther along than I expect, clinging to a rock, unable to pull himself out of the water.

"Piper?" It's the first thing out of his mouth.

"She's resuscitating Marcus. Everyone else is fine."

He tips his nose toward his left shoulder. "I've come into a bit of strife." His arm hangs unnaturally low. "Can't pull myself out."

I boost him onto the boulder. "Let me look." I take his left hand and lightly rock it up and down. "You never learned to swim?"

Samsen starts to explain and then cries out as I traction the dislocated shoulder joint back into place.

"Blood and guts of the mighty Er, that hurts!"

I nod agreement. "Better now?"

"Maybe." He rolls it and struggles to his feet.

We make our way down the other side of the gently sloping boulder, through the reeds, and onto a grassy bank. Tangles of vines and weeping willows make the way slow going, but in time we are back upstream to the others.

Ash is with Marcus where he lies on his side, coughing up half the river. Piper runs to us, opening her arms and burying her face in Samsen's chest. Her serpent has its fangs in Belair's shoulder, as he leans against a tree. Ash turns to me with a look as fierce as knives.

"Are you well, lass?" I've not seen this expression on her face before.

"No thanks to this escape route of yours."

I lock onto her eyes. They are more turquoise now than ever, like the waters of Tutapa. I start to smile but curb it. She's in no mood for fun. "A difficult twist in the path, I agree, but we're safe, for now."

"Safe? You call this *safe*?" Her voice goes up an octave. "We lost our gear, travel documents, records, seal, supplies, coin for passage to Aku, the horses—peace be their paths—and there is no time left to make it to Capper Point. Do you realize what this means for Marcus?" Her eyes well.

"We can still make it if—"

"I thought everyone was dead." Her tears overflow, the anger giving way to fear.

"Lass..." Somewhere in the depths of my chest I feel a twinge. "I didn't mean to—"

"I thought *you* were dead," she whispers.

"You see it is not so."

A neigh in the distance stops us all short. The sound blasts from across the water and I turn toward it, half expecting a line of Aturnian bows pointed our way. But it's Marcus's horse, her black coat dripping wet and turning blood red in the sunset. She stands on the far side of the river.

"Ah, the horses are back." I smile. "Things are looking up."

The mare remains long enough for Marcus to call to her. She tosses her head, rolls back on her haunches, and bolts away. Behind her streaks a flash of gray and frost-white through the trees.

"And there they go." Ash sits in the grass, hands over her eyes as if she can't bear to watch. "Samsen, can you call them?"

He shakes his head. "Not unless there's a ford. Otherwise they'll be swept away."

"We could search for one…" Her face comes up with a start. "Kaylin? What did you mean when you said we are safe *for now*?"

"As I hear it, Aturnians aren't known to give up the chase. We need to keep moving."

Marcus struggles to stand. "How long do we have?"

"Depends on that ford."

"Best guess?" Samsen tests his shoulder.

I scan for the fastest way out of the river valley. "With luck, we'll be on a sloop to Aku before they know which way we went."

"And without it?" Ash asks, taking the hand I extend and allowing me to pull her up.

I don't release her right away, the proximity like a sweet southerly breeze over cresting waves. "You should know by now, lass, luck is one thing I'm never without." I give her a wink and let go, following Marcus to the edge of the river. From deep in my pocket, I fish out his medallion and hand it over. "Your family seal, I believe? Could help when we land on Aku."

He grips it tight, rubbing his thumb over the engraving. "How did you get it back?"

"Like I said to the lass, I'm never out of luck."

24

ASH

We have a new plan, which involves getting ourselves to Capper Point at the speed of thought, but I lag behind as we trudge under a vast and velvety night sky. It's filled with brilliant stars and a waxing quarter moon gliding high overhead. The storm has passed; the air is frosty. Dirt and sparse blades of grass crunch under my boots. I don't know how I keep moving. My legs are dead weights. Inside, I beg for a rest as we climb yet another hill.

This farmland is peppered with black sheep, all camped for the night, chewing their cud and huffing out foggy breaths. We stumble through strips of chaff crosshatching the fields, remnants of where the farmer dropped hay. It's early in the year for the stock to need hand feeding. It's going to be a hard, cold season by the look of it.

"At least they have warm wool coats." My hands are shaking, my toes and fingers numb. I'm certain my nose is red as an apple.

"You're worried about your appearance?"

I'm freezing, is all.

"I would think you'd be more focused on the recording after such curious events."

Irritation warms my skin. *First of all, the weather* is *part of the recording. And second of all, curious?*

"Out of the ordinary?"

Extremely out of the ordinary is more like it. My limbs tingle with new circulation as I map out in my head what has happened in the last twenty-four hours.

"It's not far now." Marcus interrupts my thoughts. He's recovering, keeping up with Kaylin, thanks to Piper's healings. I'm sure she never thought her skills would be tested so deeply on our way to Aku.

"If they don't all mutiny at what's coming next..." Kaylin's words drift back on the wind.

Wait. Was that Kaylin, or my inner voice?

"Can you not tell the difference?"

I can barely tell my left foot from the right just now. And it's not only the exhaustion or cold wearing at me. If I allow my thoughts to sift through the last hours, from the moment the Gollnar scouts caught us and everything that transpired since… I shudder. Definitely more than curious, or out of the ordinary.

"Don't linger there."

No. I won't. I *can't*. I realize abruptly that my inner voice's banter has been intended as a distraction to help me keep going.

"Am I?"

I'm too worn-out—and grateful—to argue. I shake my head to clear it. "Why are we talking about mutiny?"

Kaylin turns to me, brows raised to sharp points, but doesn't reply.

"You're hearing things," Marcus says. "No one's mentioned mutiny."

You? I ask my inner voice and receive a cerebral *snort* for an answer.

Strange. I tap the side of my head with the heel of my hand. "Water in my ears, I guess." I want to say something to Marcus about De'ral, now that I've seen his phantom for the first time. But the horror of it all… I best leave it for a private chat.

Kaylin studies the sky as Samsen's phantom flies over us in the form of a sparrow owl this time, better to escape notice if other enemy savants patrol the air. The bird is the size of a child's hand, a brown dot in front of the twinkling stars. Being smaller than the phantom's full form, some of its mass has to be left behind, and it isn't hard to see where it's gone. Samsen sports a feather cape that falls to his thighs.

At least one of us has something warm to wear.

"Look at the lights!" Belair gasps as we reach the top of the hill.

It's like the stars have touched down to illuminate the city of Capper Point. So many lanterns. The spectacle flows in a V-shape, two fingers of settlements, one on either side of the Ferus River. We've come out on the north branch, which I hear Kaylin say is a good thing. But b'lark the bones, I don't see his mouth move. Has he said it aloud or am I delirious? Imagining things?

"Imagination is a resource," my inner voice observes.

Food and sleep are a resource, too, and I'll need some of both if I'm ever to make sense again.

"We're nearly there."

I know Kaylin spoke those words. Watched him do it, which is a relief. He's definitely excited, and I catch the feeling, too, allowing it to warm me. Still, we have problems ahead.

"How are we going to hire a sloop without a coin between us?"

"Over that rise is a ranch house." Kaylin points the way. Is he trying not to smile?

"Will they help us?"

"Not exactly."

"Then why are we headed there?" I tuck my frozen fingers into my armpits and shiver. This would be a good time for him to explain things clearly.

"It's on the way," Kaylin says.

"What kind of answer is that?"

"A true one." He heads down the hill at a jog.

I run after him. "You're being odd, Kaylin."

"Ash…" He says my name like he's pleading his case.

I give a little laugh and relax. "I'm not cross with you, Kaylin. It's just… Please, one of you, tell me what's about to happen."

Marcus steps up beside me, his hand on my shoulder. "Kaylin can get us coin and supplies for the crossing to Aku." His eyes go to the farmhouse.

I turn back to Kaylin. "Explain."

"Very well, but Marcus says you won't like it."

"Gaveren's stuggs!" I snap, my nostrils flaring. "One of you spit it out."

"Ash!" Piper chides me.

"Sorry." I send her a beseeching look. She's offended, but not Kaylin. He can hardly hide his smile.

Still, Piper's correct. I have no right to use the name of Gaveren the Great in a curse, peace be his path. As the stories go, he was the most celebrated savant of all times with a *warrior* phantom larger and more powerful than any ever raised. Well, before De'ral that is. "I just want to know what the plan is. Plain and clear."

"Lass, the plan is to sneak down to the farmhouse and steal what we need." Kaylin looks at me expectantly, like he's waiting for a thank-you.

My body stiffens and the heat of anger flushes through my veins.

Marcus must see the emotion on my face. "We don't have a choice."

Today, for the first time in my life, he frightened me. His phantom did, anyway, with the indiscriminate slaughter, and now theft? "What path do you think you're on?"

Marcus avoids my eyes. "The sheep farmer's wealthy. It'll do no harm."

"And that makes it right?"

"No. Obviously, I'll reimburse them—"

"How?"

He prattles out possible ways as I fire back reasons why they won't work. But he does want to make it right. That's something. And, when challenged to suggest a better idea, I can't, so I let it go. For now.

We continue the hike toward the farmhouse at a stealth run. The high cliffs of Capper Point are visible in the distance, the waxing moon lighting a brilliant path across the ink black sea and the deep-water harbor.

"Tall masts?" I ask.

"The port's clear of warships," Kaylin says after a glance. "They've sailed on."

"That's good news."

"Aye, and if we run the whole way, we'll make it before dawn."

We reach the farmhouse and drop down into the grass, studying it from twenty-five yards away, breaths puffing warm air into the icy night. The windows are dark, but a porch lantern glows under a wide verandah.

Belair catches up to us. "And what exactly is the plan?"

"We're going to rob these good people, race to the harbor with the spoils, and hire a sloop to Aku." I recite the plans, laughing as I do. Clearly, I'm delirious with fatigue.

His eyes sparkle. "Who's going to pull off this theft, or do I have to ask?"

I tip my head toward Kaylin.

"Go now and give the farmhouse a wide birth," he says. "I'll meet you on the main road. If you hear barking or angry voices, run!"

"Practiced at this, I see."

He chuckles. "Aye, lass, and be glad of it. Now go." But he lingers, just a second, and I know he's waiting for something from me. Something other than exasperation. So I soften, just the slightest, my lips hinting at a smile.

His face lights up, and with a grin that warms me from the inside out, he bounds off in the direction of the farm.

• • •

We wait in a culvert beside the road. It feels like ages, but according to Samsen, who is still in phantom perspective, it's only minutes, and going well. Apparently, Kaylin is sprinting toward us with an armload of loot. I don't know which I want more—dry clothes, food, or water. After going over the falls, I thought I'd never want to drink again, but jogging up and down hills for two hours straight changes that. I strain to hear his approach.

"An apple for the lovely lass..."

"He's singing?"

"I don't hear anything." Marcus cups his ear.

I yawn and rest my hands in my lap. In that moment, Kaylin appears, loaded with booty, and drops a dark red apple into my open palms.

"Oh." I polish it on my shirt before taking a huge bite. "Thanks," I say around the mouthful.

"My pleasure."

Kaylin pulls apples and pears from the pockets of his newly acquired sheepskin jacket and tosses them to the others. He has a whole loaf of bread, a waterskin, two fisherman sweaters, four more sheepskin-lined vests, and a finely woven blanket. My limbs tingle, my body energized. "For your crimes, my sailor, I forgive you." I bounce up to my tiptoes and kiss him on the cheek, intending to immediately jog off.

Except Kaylin doesn't realize what I'm doing until it's too late. He turns my way, likely to speak, and catches the kiss smack on his lips.

The light touch lasts for longer than the peck I intend, my face warming when I lower back to the ground. "That... I'm..." My finger plays on my lower lip. For a wordsmith, I'm having trouble finding a decent response. But I can't blurt out what I'm really thinking—that I want to kiss him again.

I think Kaylin is more surprised than me, if that's possible. His usual cockiness is gone, replaced by a bewildered gaze. His hands still rest on my hips. How did they get there?

I check if anyone saw our little exchange, but they are all busy donning warm clothes on the fly and stuffing food into their mouths. I keep watching, though, using the moment to collect myself before turning back to Kaylin. "Where's your food?"

"Oh. I...uh, I ate it on the way," he says and pats his belly. He's visibly off-kilter, and I can't deny that I enjoy this change in dynamic. "This is for you." He shrugs out of the coat and tosses it to me.

"But you'll freeze."

He blinks a few times, then laughs, his confidence trickling back. "Not a chance." He holds the coat for me to slip my arms into.

"On to Capper Point," he says to us all, his sparkling eyes resting on mine.

But I see through his mask.

I shocked him. I did. And against all better judgment, I hope I have a chance to do so again.

25

MARCUS

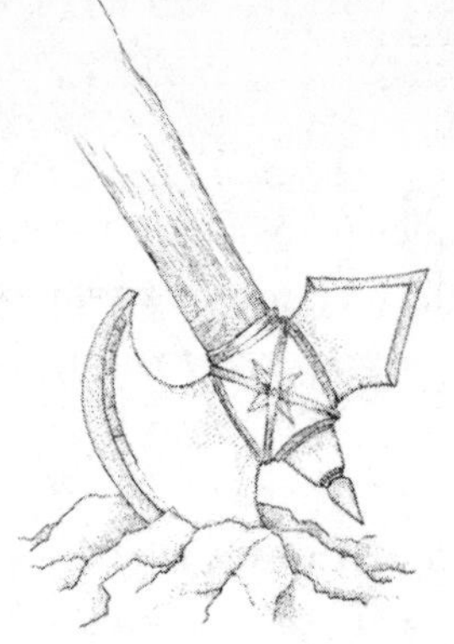

By the time we're walking the back streets of Capper Point, my limbs tremble so much I can barely keep going. The healing venom's gone, but I can't ask for more. Piper's as done in as the rest of us. I try focusing on the surroundings to distract myself. There's not much to see under the dim streetlights, but the smells are another story. Wafts of filth rise off the slick cobblestones. Wood smoke mingles with the sea air, and each lamppost has obviously been marked by dogs. Whole packs of them. We don't allow such conditions in Baiseen.

Kaylin insists we stick to the back alleys in case the Aturnian troops sent word to watch for us. He's right, but it makes the going harder as we scramble over fences and brick walls, trying not to wake guard dogs or disturb night scavengers milling through the rubbish.

"Smell the bakery?" I say as we climb yet another wall and cross behind a building with tall chimney stacks. The fresh, warm aroma makes my stomach growl. The food from the farm was good, but now I feel hungrier than ever. We pass the bakery and, another block down, are hit with the scent of herbs and spices.

"Apothecary," Ash says.

I think back to the one in Clearwater. Was that only yesterday?

Belair sniffs the air. "Any chance of getting some willow bark?"

"Good idea. But they aren't open." I scruff my hair and tug on it, wishing I still had the vial from Clearwater. I don't even know when I lost it.

We plod on toward the "steps," the long, snaking path cut into the cliff face that leads to the docks far below. On our way we pass several taverns with lively fiddle music pouring out the windows and swinging doors. Clearly the people of Capper Point have no curfew. It must be nearly midnight. There's food in there, and warmth, but Aturnians as well. Not worth the risk.

Finally, Kaylin halts us under a dim streetlamp. "We can blend in behind that donkey train." He points to the platform above the steps. "And avoid being questioned before we reach the docks."

Piper leans against Samsen and he pulls her closer, resting his chin on the top of her head. "Sounds good."

"Lead the way." I tighten the blanket draped around my shoulders.

Ash is all but swaying on her feet. "There'll be a sloop for Aku? One we can board now and sleep the rest of the night?"

"With luck." Kaylin winks at her.

It's the tenth time he's done that since the fight on the headland, or it seems so, anyway. Ash hasn't put a stop to it. On the swords of Sierrak, why not?

My jaw tightens and my head pounds, mostly from falling off a cliff, running for my life, and nearly drowning. But the sailor's flirtations aren't helping, and my previous goodwill toward his protection of Ash is fading. Doesn't he understand there are rules of conduct on an initiation journey? I rub my brow, trying to pin down my jumbled emotions. I'm being irrational, I know. Still, I'll speak to him privately. Set him straight. No, I'll speak to her. She's my recorder and should not encourage such things.

But who am I kidding?

I've seen the spark in her eyes. She's interested, isn't she? Or is that just the thrill of the adventure? Curse the bones, I can't tell, but next time we're alone, I'm going to find out. The protocols on an initiation journey aren't just for the savants!

As we approach, the harbor comes into view and, with it, a stronger scent of the sea. There are tiny boats far below with lanterns at the tips of their masts, no Aturnian imperial navy ships to be seen. Praise the bones. As I trace the steps with my eye, it's clear how far we have to go. I groan.

"Long way down," Ash speaks for us all.

"Aye, lass. But plenty of sloops. If they set sail early enough, you should be on the training grounds before the gates close."

I feel a weight lift. We *can* make it. And, when we do, the journey won't have been for naught. I *will* become a yellow-robe with an unstoppable phantom.

As it is, my *warrior's* skills, untrained as they are, did save us. But if that Gollnarian-Aturnian war party is any indication of what we might face in the years to come, then De'ral and I will need more than raw punch and the element of surprise. I look down, contemplating my boots as slowly, the weight returns. It's an effort to put one foot in front of the other.

Fortunately, donkey trains are not noted for their speed, so we don't have to work hard to keep up. I drift in and out of awareness as we follow down the steps—thousands of them, I imagine, but I don't even try to count. Ash, on the other hand, does. I hear her whispering the numbers but quickly lose track. We stick close to a string of some twenty little beasts, an odd variety of donkey with long, tufted ears, thin legs, and each packed high with boxes and crates. Beasts of burden. I think I understand the term better now even though I carry only the clothes on my back and a blanket over my shoulders.

Down we traipse, back and forth, back and forth, following the zigzag path that takes us, finally, to the wooden docks below. Once we reach the harbor, we peel off from the train and find a dark corner behind head-high piles of grain sacks. "What's the plan?"

"You all stay out of sight." Kaylin takes Ash by the hand. "We'll hire the sloop."

Hand-holding? Is that necessary? But what would I have her do? Snatch it back and push him away? I'm too tired to think. "We'll wait." But it comes out like a whip crack.

"Is it safe for you on the docks? To be seen, I mean?" Ash asks Kaylin.

"Is it safe for any of us?" I ask, rubbing my temples.

"Captain Nadonis wasn't lying when he said he'd not put in at Capper Point."

"But if someone recognizes you?" I ask.

Kaylin fishes a knit cap out of his pocket, another prize from the sheep farm, I suspect, puts it on, and tucks his hair inside. "They won't. Ash will do the talking, and I'll direct her to the right sloop, with the right captain. One we can trust."

"But can we really trust a Northern Aturnian? After what we've been through?"

"Under my guard, you'll be as safe as possible outside of Aku."

Ash looks at me to confirm the plan. At least I haven't lost all authority on this trip.

"Do it." I lean against the grain sacks and lower myself to the ground.

"Is there enough coin?" Piper asks.

Kaylin pulls a purse of gold out of his pocket. "The sheep farmer knows his business, it seems."

"I will definitely see they are reimbursed," Ash says. At this point, it's not as pressing a thought to me.

"You've enough for twelve coins a head, Ash, but don't pay that much. Eight is more like it if we can sleep below decks tonight," Kaylin coaches her.

"Leave it to me." I can hear the smile in her voice as she turns to walk away with the sailor.

Does she realize the success or failure of our journey is now entirely in her hands? And the sailor's? My jaw clamps tighter. None of this is what we anticipated. Why wasn't there more warning from the Bone Throwers? I don't have answers, but I can and will keep my eye on Kaylin's every move until we're safely on the Isle of Aku.

I sigh.

Right about now would be a good time for that *surprise from the sea*, and this time, make it a decent one.

26

ASH

I turn back to look at Marcus, and I know he's worried about me. I glance at Kaylin. Is Marcus jealous of him? The Heir jealous of a non-savant sailor? Odd as it sounds, his frowning disapproval as I wave suggests it's possible. What nonsense. I will set him straight, as soon as we have a moment's privacy.

"Is he the one you need to set straight?"

Nonsense to you, too. It's just Kaylin's way.

"Interesting. You knew who I meant, without a second thought."

Never mind. I dismiss my inner voice and focus on the task.

Black water laps the pilings beneath me as I walk the pier. The quarter moon has set, and the lamplights give off a misty yellow glow, though I can barely keep my eyes open to see.

"What's wrong with that one?" I ask, pointing to a sloop nearby.

"Too low in the water," he answers. "They won't have room."

Too low, too high, bad crew, disrepair. Kaylin, it turns out, is very particular about the quality of any ship we board. While I hang back, trying not to fall asleep on my feet, he chats to yet another sailor. I lean my head against a lamp pole then turn to study it, the crunch of fibrous paper capturing my attention. It takes a moment to focus in the lantern light, but there it is again, the twin orbs interwoven and a script that reminds me a lot of what I asked Master Brogal about back in Baiseen. What's written in Aturnian, I think I can translate. Kaylin comes back. "It says, '*The dark sun returns*,'" I tell him.

"Is the translation dark, or hidden?" he asks, reading over my shoulder.

"Could be either, or even 'second sun,' but that adjective is usually reserved for proper nouns."

He chuckles.

"Well, I am a wordsmith." Maybe whoever wrote this considers it a proper noun. "Sun is capitalized."

He points to the letters. "True, but so are all the words in that sentence. It's a title."

"We'd have to ask an Aturnian wordsmith, to be sure. And Sierrak. Look, there's some of that realm's script here, too." I clear my throat and translate the best I can. "*Heed the warning… The dark sun draws nigh.*" I underline the script with my finger. "There was a similar notice in Clearwater, on the apothecary's door, and see these overlapping orbs?" I trace them with my finger in almost a figure eight, though one is smaller than the other. "This isn't the only place I've seen them."

"The flags at the encampment?"

"You noticed them, too?"

"Aye."

"Any idea what it means?"

He opens his mouth then closes it. After a moment, his confident smile slides back into place. "You hear such warnings harangued farther north, and in Sierrak, usually by a rogue stargazer who babbles and shakes."

"Doesn't sound like a reliable source."

Kaylin props his hand on the top of the poster and leans in. "Probably not."

My heart skips as I keep trying to translate. Is the notice exciting me so, or is it Kaylin's proximity? I can still feel the kiss on my lips, and if I were to turn a few inches they would touch again. He's not mentioned what happened. Does he think it was a mistake? Or is he wishing for it to happen again?

As I drag my thoughts away from the dreamy feelings, the symbols sharpen. In my mind's eye, they pull me back to the bodies De'ral crushed, even though I don't want to go there. I see broken limbs, arms, wrists exposed… "Kaylin?" I step back a bit so I can breathe my own air. "Did you also notice the scouts had these very twin orbs tattooed on the insides of their wrists?"

"Aye." He says nothing more. Just pulls the notice down, folds the thick paper carefully, and tucks it into his pocket. "I'll keep it for later."

So, there will be a later? He's seeing us all the way to Aku?

"There's a captain at the end of the dock waiting to speak with us." Kaylin takes my hand like it's the most natural thing in the world. "I found a good one," he says, oblivious to the shooting stars going off over my head.

"Thank b'lark for that," I whisper, trying not to tremble.

I don't know myself, walking down the docks of an enemy port at midnight, hand in hand with a bosun's mate from Tutapa I met only days before, about to barter passage to Aku with coins stolen from an Aturnian sheep farm. My life is unrecognizable. With that realization, I tuck my question to Kaylin away, for later.

At the end of the dock stands a short captain with a bald head. He has a writing board in one hand and is shouting orders to his crew in Aturnian. I open my mouth to engage him and remember in the last second to speak Gollnarian. If the enemy camp had by chance gotten here ahead of us, they would have warned every captain on the docks of travelers from Palrio. Possibly a reward on our heads.

"A sizable reward," my inner voice says.

What a reassuring thought.

"Passage for six savants to the Isle of Aku, please."

The captain sizes me up, not hiding the scrutiny. I know what he sees—battered and bedraggled, muddy boots, and ill-fitting clothes. Hardly the picture of a savant from any realm, cutting it terribly close for the start of events on Aku tomorrow.

"Six?" he questions.

"My brother and I..." Kaylin stands so close, my temple brushes his shoulder when I tilt my head toward him. So close that I hear his sudden intake of breath. "We're their guide and recorder," I explain.

"Come by land?"

"We did." I straighten. "Bit of a rough crossing over the Ferus."

The captain nods. "Water's up and running for weeks."

"Early for the season," Kaylin says. "I suspect the runoff of your rich Aturnian soil accounts for the fish runs we've heard tell of."

The captain grunts. "Salmon, for one, are filling the nets."

"And grouper?"

"Aye, in record numbers." He shoves the board under one arm, making a choice. "Ten gold each for the lot of you, twelve if you want to board tonight." He points at the sloop. It's a sleek ship made of dark wood, the deck immaculate, ropes neatly coiled, and a small crew busy with the rigging. It has a single mast, a pelican banner flying from the tip. Judging by those berthed beside her, the sloop's a dolphin among gutter sharks.

I want to say "done," shake his hand, and find a place to lie down, but it would arouse suspicions to accept the first offer. Kaylin's arm goes around my waist and that has my eyes wide, tingles shooting up my spine. "Six gold a head." The words burst out of my mouth.

"Eight, and you board at sunrise."

"Eight and we board right now, plus a bowl of whatever the galley chef has on the stove." *Please, please tell me there's something warm on the stove.*

"There is something warm on the stove."

I laugh to myself at how literal I can be.

"Done." The captain smiles and our hands clasp. "It's six hours till dawn. We'll set sail with the morning tide, at sunrise, and with luck, have you in Aku before the opening ceremony. If not, there's always next year, right?"

I'm not going to say *wrong* and explain that this is the Heir of Baiseen's last chance. Instead, I say "thank you" in a rush of relief. I've never meant those two words more in my life.

Kaylin keeps his arm around me on our way back to the others, our footsteps again falling into sync. I suspend my astonishment and lean in to him. To be honest, I'm not sure I could walk straight without his support right now.

"You seem to collect brothers," he whispers into my hair.

The softness of his voice makes my legs even weaker. "Brother as in *people of a common cause*."

"I see, but do they?"

"Ha-ha." Brotherly is not what I feel toward Kaylin, bosun's mate of the *Sea Eagle*, assassin, and now guide of savants, apparently. But maybe he is just like this, enchanting, demonstrative, a handhold here, arm in arm there… Can it be more than play to him? It sure felt real when we kissed. Accidentally, yes, but still. For an instant, he wasn't the self-assured sailor I've come to know, what with his dazed expression, hands lingering on my waist…

I shake my head to stop the runaway thoughts. This is Marcus's initiation journey. There are protocols we are expected to follow. Is that why Marcus is throwing me scowling glances? He's worried I will ignore the Sanctuary rules of conduct? I'm not sure which makes me madder, that I might be tempted or that the Heir has no faith in me. Rest assured, no way will I allow doubt to be cast on the records because I was distracted by a sailor. I exhale, straightening as we approach the others. *I hope Kaylin understands.*

He lets his arm slide back to his side, though he doesn't put much distance between us. "There are conventions a journeying wordsmith follows?"

He's read my mind, which makes this much easier. "On initiation journeys, there are. Strict ones." A slow smile spreads across my face. Have we been thinking the same thing? When we reach the others, my expression is back to neutral. "I'm happy to report success."

Everyone lets out a collective sigh, patting me on the back.

"Supper, too," Kaylin adds.

They outright cheer now.

Kaylin and Samsen support Belair down the pier and up the gangplank. The clay has controlled the bleeding, and Piper's healings have helped the pain and reversed any toxins that the bolt may have held, but his exhaustion is complete.

Piper and I flank Marcus, bringing up the rear. I don't know how he is conscious, considering all he's been through. As I think it, he stumbles.

"We've got you." Piper grips his arm, and he leans heavily on us the rest of the way.

"Nearly there, Marcus. Up the plank, down the hatch, and something warm from the galley. Then you can sleep." I want to cry from exhaustion by the time we slide him onto a bench seat and settle in with the others.

"Fish chowder and buns?" Kaylin serves us, not waiting for an answer. He's made friends with the chef and fills generous-sized bowls from a pot.

I moan my appreciation, as do the others.

"Nearly to your destination."

"Many thanks to you." I speak for Marcus and the others whose mouths are full, eyelids sagging. The soup is delicious and warms me to the core. I've never had chilis in chowder, but I'm glad for them now, though my nose begins to run. When Kaylin heads topside to talk to the captain, I catch his gaze.

"I'll be back," he says, I think just to me.

When the soup is gone and the cleanup done, I climb into my hammock. Marcus is in the one next to me and I turn to face him. "My Heir?"

He murmurs but doesn't open his eyes.

"We're going to make it to Aku, just like we always planned."

Eyes still closed, he reaches for my hand and squeezes it tight, a smile lifting his face. "Ash?"

I wait for him to say more but the next thing I hear is snoring.

27

ASH

Bells ring, and the sloop pitches back and forth. Sunlight spills down the hatch where I am wrapped in the gentle swing of the hammock. In my sleep, I kept pressure on the inside of my wrist, which kept the nausea at bay, but still I awake bruised and incredibly sore from the last two days of battle and capture and escapes.

A quick count shows four sleeping forms around me. Kaylin must be on deck. I wait for the pitch to lean me close to the floor, slip out of my hammock, and gain my feet. When the sloop pitches again, I head to the hatch and climb.

I cross to the rail. The sunlight makes the deep teal water sparkle like gems. Waves roll along the channel and break on the reefs surrounding the Isle. The offshore wind blows the white water from the crests and showers me with mist. I go up on tiptoe, holding the railing with both hands, and laugh aloud. "Aku! Aku!" I call like a bird singing to the sun.

The sacred Isle of Aku is the most exhilarating sight I've seen in my life. It's a safe harbor for those who come in goodwill to train their phantoms and raise in ranks. There is no stronger sanctuary in all of Amassia, and we are here. We have arrived!

"Finally," my inner voice whispers.

The cliffs loom high and rugged, the beaches sandy white and backed by a forest of pine and spruce that climb to the top of the highest peaks. Well above the headland sits the oldest teaching sanctuary in Amassia. I make out the copper-green tiled rooftops and the brightly colored flags after the tradition of the southern savants, in order of their rank: brown, blue, green, yellow, orange, and red. I spot another tower with only two flags, one black and one white. Black for the robes of the Bone Throwers, but the white is a mystery to me.

"The lass awakes!"

I pull my attention away from the island at the sound of Kaylin's voice. "Not too late, I hope?" I shade my eyes to find him climbing down from the crow's nest.

Kaylin leaps to the deck and takes a wide stance in front of me. "It's a brilliant morning. And you are a delight to my eyes."

Something deep in my belly flutters, and I blush.

As the ship rocks and pitches, Kaylin and I turn to gaze at the Isle. My eyes linger on his profile, taking in his wind-tossed hair and open face. He's a delight himself, but I'm not going to say that aloud. "Does that mean we *are* too late?"

His smile dims. "I won't lie, lass. It could go either way."

All our struggles only to miss out *now*? "Can we go any faster?"

"We dock around the leeward side." He points north. "Nearly there."

My eyes cut to the road leading to the top of the Isle. It looks like a scaly reptile, snaking its way to the clouds. "How far?"

"A three-mile climb. It'll take a fast jog to reach the gates by the fourth bell."

"It's just after first bell. Three hours should be enough."

"It's still hard, especially after such a journey. We'll need every minute of it."

I hesitate, my lips parting. *Did he say we?*

"I believe so."

He's coming with us?

"Why not just ask?"

It's the obvious thing to do, of course. Just say, "Are you joining us, Kaylin?" But, suddenly I'm not sure how to begin or where to put my hands. "There is much to see on Aku."

"True words." He turns back to me. His eyes are smoky in the morning light, and it's all I can do to meet them before quickly glancing back to the island.

"The library alone is the most esteemed in Amassia." I lace my hands behind my back, feeling my palms sweat. When the sloop lurches, I grab for the railing.

"This is you asking him?"

Shh! "What I mean to say, to point out, really, is that it would be a shame not to partake of the Isle of Aku while you have the opportunity. Before winter sets in. As it does this time of year…"

"Really?"

Kaylin lifts an eyebrow. Does he enjoy my floundering?

I try again. "More to the point, are you staying?" My face bursts into flames, no doubt red as a High Savant's robes.

But Kaylin doesn't laugh at my unraveling. Quite the opposite. He leans in to tuck strands of windblown hair behind my ear before straightening. "Would you like me to?"

The muscles of my throat tighten as every cell in my body says yes.

"You'll need to speak up," my inner voice prompts.

"Em, indeed," I manage to reply.

His eyes gleam as he leans in again. Is he going to kiss me? My breathing falters, then I realize, no, silly, we aren't going to kiss on the deck in front of all Aku.

He simply gives me a formal bow. "Then yes, I will be most pleased to stay, for a time."

Warmth rushes through me and I sputter an unintelligible word that sounds something like "glabich," which was not my intended response. But, to be honest, I have no idea what my intended response was going to be. Maybe *great*, or *good news*?

Mother of Mar, where has my vocabulary gone?

Kaylin only chuckles.

We both do, as together we turn back to the island. It's growing larger as we glide over the reef toward the sandy bay.

Thanks to the fresh sea air, the heat in my face eases, my poise returning as we share a moment of reverence for Aku, the smallest realm in Amassia—with the greatest consequence.

"We made it," Kaylin says softly, his eyes still on the mountain sanctuary.

"We did." I reach out my hand to take his. "Thanks to you." My fingertips tingle at his touch before I pull away. "I'll go wake them!"

I hurry across the deck, too many emotions rolling through me to identify a specific one, but once down the ladder I sober. Disembarking will be anything but quick, even though we have no baggage or sea-weary horses. Oh, the horses—my hand covers my mouth to hold in a sob. We've lost so much on this journey. Not just the lovely beasts, but the introductions for us all from Brogal, the scrolls and sanctuary seal he entrusted to me. His personal translation guide… I'll have to write some b'larkin spectacular records for Marcus and Belair to make up for it.

I wonder if Kaylin will stay the whole time? He could help with—

"Maybe get the initiates to the gates before they close first, or there will

be no records to write at all."

That sobers me further. "Marcus! Belair! It's past first bell!"

My call is met with groans from everyone.

Marcus is hardest to rouse, the few hours of rest doing him more harm than good. He'd clearly been running on sheer willpower the night before. Belair fares little better, and Piper, with her phantom down, can do nothing but change their dressings, offer a quick cup of broth, and shuffle them onto the dock when we finally reach it. To top it off, the wind is not in our favor. It blows hard into our faces.

In the end, we stumble down the plank and assemble just as the second bell rings. My nose tips skyward to the Sanctuary, following the winding path up the mountain. The other candidates must be there already.

I look to Piper where she leans against the dock railing. She's expended all her energy healing the others and herself over the last two days. Samsen props himself against her, clutching his shoulder. Has it popped out of the socket again and he's not said? Marcus is on the ground, head bent forward, hands wrapped around his knees. This isn't good.

"Rise, savant." I give Marcus a shake, but he only groans.

We're not going to make it.

No. I will not allow myself to think like that. I will get Marcus and Belair through those gates if it is the last thing I do.

"Forgive me," I say under my breath and shake his shoulder, harder. He lifts his face and I slap it, stinging my hand like a hive of hornets. Belair gasps at my actions, but I have the Heir's full attention now. "You have to lead us to the Sanctuary, and you have to do it now."

He opens one eye. "How much time?"

"Not enough, unless we go *now*."

He straightens slowly, and in his deep brown eyes, I see the fear that echoes my own.

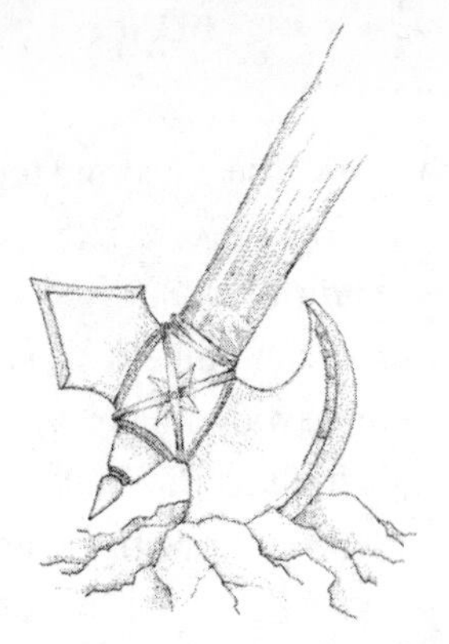

28

MARCUS

Ash and Kaylin pull me to my feet when I stumble for the tenth time. Why is the bosun's mate still here? That's a question for later, though. At least they're keeping me upright, but what I really wish is for Samsen to call a carriage to take us these last miles, or maybe turn the blasted headwind around. That's not going to happen. Initiates must enter the Sanctuary without phantom help, or horse and cart for that matter. It's part of the initiation which began the moment we left Baiseen. "Come on!"

The road to Aku Sanctuary is long, winding, and steep, a rocky terrain with trees bent by the wind. The fringing grass is dry as straw. I really thought it would be greener, from the stories I've heard. The ground rocks beneath me and my head spins. "I'm going to be sick."

"It's better if you don't." Ash presses the insides of my wrists until the nausea passes. She fusses over me, brushing mud from my clothes and pushing hair out of my face as we hurry up the mountainside. "You're a complete mess as it is. No need to stink of puke."

I glare back at her and push on. She's as red-faced and winded as any of us, though Belair is the worst. He took the arrow, after all.

We took a knife in the chest, De'ral reminds me.

I'd forgotten all about it, seems so long ago now.

Two days.

The pain is still there, when I think of it, but so much of me hurts that the individual injuries blur and my whole body aches as one.

Ash's touch is tender, even though her face is hard. "We've made it, Marcus. We're here." She squeezes my forearm. "Against all odds."

"Not. Through. Gates. Yet." I save my breath, which comes in gasps, trying to conserve strength. *I'm Marcus Adicio, Heir of Baiseen, here for my initiation training on the Isle of Aku.* I practice it in my head and keep my legs moving.

If Piper hadn't healed me—multiple times now—I'd be back at the headland, dead under an ironbark tree. I grit my teeth and keep moving forward until all I feel is the slap of my feet on the hard packed road and the rush of blood in my ears. And the pain.

"Marcus, look up," Belair says, stumbling to my side. He chokes out the words. His eyes are bloodshot and swimming in wet sockets. "The gates!"

Fifty yards away, they rise, high as the bell towers in Baiseen. It'd take an entire team of draft horses to draw those gates closed—or some powerful *callers*.

And then I hear a noise, like the pounding surf redoubled. No, it's cheers! The road ahead is lined with orange- and yellow-robes, yelling at us, yelling *for* us! They're whistling and hooting, shouting *Khu-laua, Khu-laua*, the ancient word for "initiation" on Aku. Their phantoms are up in a menagerie of shapes and sizes, some in the air, some on two legs, some four. In a rush of spirit, I believe we have made it, but Ash's voice goes up an octave.

"The gate. It's closing!"

At that moment, the fourth bell rings. We have three more tones in twice as many seconds, one for each hour since sunrise.

"Marcus, sprint for it!" Ash yells as she falls behind.

I look over my shoulder, my momentum paused mid-stride. Belair's stumbled to the ground. Ahead, the gap at the entrance shrinks. The debate in my mind lasts less than a second, and I turn back to Belair.

The bell rings a second time. Two more to go.

The crowd cheers their support.

Kaylin hoists Belair up, and I grab the Tangeen's arm and sling it over my shoulder. With a push from Samsen and Piper, I call on phantom strength.

Run! It's De'ral booming in my head. His strength surges through me in a rush.

Third ring of the bell...

My feet pound the earth. This is it. My realm, my future, my *everything* hinges on those two giant doors drawing closed.

Faster!

In a massive leap, Belair and I fly through the narrowing gap, falling headfirst onto the grounds of the Sanctuary proper. The others stream in behind and pick us up as the fourth and final ring fades away.

Behind us, the gates slam closed.

There is no time to savor this moment. I can scant draw a full breath and already Samsen is pushing me forward. "To the training field." He shoves me hard. "The first elimination trial has begun. Go!"

My mind spins. But there is no time to pause or think. He's right. Now the real test begins.

I vaguely see my way up the street, past the main courtyard. I catch a glimpse of the treasured fountain of Aku. It's larger than I imagined, a mist of cool water hitting my face, even from this distance away. No time to toss a coin now, but I do wish to reach the training field without passing out.

Cheers continue to well up, a choir of joy that seems almost out of place given all I've seen and done to get here. It's hard to imagine this joyous peace after all the violence we've faced. Faces smile and hands reach out to pat me as I stagger past. We're so tightly packed, it's the jostle and closeness of bodies that helps to keep me on my feet. Orange- and yellow-robes flow around us, guiding the way. I'm not sure if they know who we are, but clearly, they're glad we made it, the last of the initiates to arrive.

"Never seen it cut so close, lad." One claps me on the back and laughs. "Half a second to spare."

An orange-robe woman reaches up and roughs my hair. "That old wolf Adicio will be proud of this day."

I smile and keep stumbling forward. I guess they do know who I am.

We make it to the training field where dozens of green-robe candidates wait. They are clean, showered, shaved, bright robes wafting in the breeze. They stand with hands behind their backs, calm and easy. Belair and I, on the other hand… We stagger into line at the end, swaying like drunken sailors, lungs pumping in and out with each breath, filthy faces dripping with sweat, and our many wounds welling with fresh blood.

Several instructors give speeches—short ones, thank the skies—followed by cheers and applause. I hope Ash is taking notes because my head is swimming. I have no idea what's being said. The only way I stay upright is by bracing my hands on my knees. Belair has collapsed altogether. I look at Piper, who beams me an exhausted smile. I guess she's not that worried at this point. When the assembly breaks up, I straighten. "What now, recorder?" My heart throbs in my neck.

"Weren't you listening?"

"I was too busy trying to breathe."

She looks no better than the others, save that her smile is the brightest. "An orange-robe will come assign you to your bunks and explain the roster."

"There's a roster?" Belair groans from the ground.

"Oh yes, and it's not to be taken lightly." Samsen has recovered quickest from our run to the gates—well, quickest, if you exclude Kaylin. He never worked up a sweat. I give the training field a sweep and turn toward the cobbled courtyard in front of the temple steps.

"Now, we've made it." Ash takes her place between me and Belair, the proper position for our journey recorder. "Safe on Aku, at last," she says softly. "Steady now. Here she comes."

As my eyes focus, I realize the savant approaching is a child.

"Young for an orange-robe," Ash whispers. "But an orange-robe nonetheless."

"Well..." I choke. My voice is hoarse. "Well met," I try again, hoping not to scare the girl. Beside me, Belair staggers to his feet and croaks out the same.

"Well met." Her voice is light, as if ready to laugh. I think she's all of ten. Her long black hair is kept in a single braid, unadorned. Her round cheeks dimple when she smiles, which seems her constant expression when looking at me and Belair. Beside her is an equally composed phantom in the form of an impala. It has large, round eyes, floppy ears, and an incredibly long, slender neck. Its tiny cloven hooves tap an even rhythm on the ground. Behind her are two yellow-robes, hoods up. I can't see their faces.

"I'm Tyche." When I hesitate, still catching my breath, she pronounces it slowly, as if I'm thick. "TIE-key."

I clear my throat. "Tyche, please forgive our appearances." I use my most formal manner. "I am Marcus Adicio from the realm of Palrio, son of the Magistrate, Jacas Adicio, green-robe to a *warrior* phantom and Heir to the throne of Baiseen. My companion savants are—" I open out my arm and nearly lose my footing. Ash catches me, and I continue as if I hadn't almost fallen. "Samsen and Piper, yellow- and orange-robes, returning to Aku for the second and third time, also of Baiseen, and Belair Duquan from Pandom City in Tangeen, also green-robe to a *warrior* phantom. We've been—"

Belair drops to his knees and throws up.

"...drinking?" Tyche asks with a giggle.

Ash steps in. "I assure you, Tyche," she says, also speaking in formal Palrion. "There has been no drinking on this journey, but we did nearly drown in the Ferus River, among other calamities. Our travels have not been smooth."

"It's true," I say. "Please allow me to introduce to you Ash, my recorder, wordsmith of Baiseen, ward of High Savant Brogal."

"Robe?"

I hesitate. "Non-savant."

Tyche's brows jump. I can tell it's the first surprising thing I've said to her. But the impala leans forward, stretching its long neck out to Ash as if I'd introduced her to it specifically. I can imagine Ash will cause a stir with so many phantoms about. Like bees to honey they have always been with her.

Tyche clicks her tongue, calling her phantom back, her eyes wide. "I see the journey was hard for you." The girl keeps her hand on her phantom, who tries to inch toward Ash again.

"Excessively so, with little food or sleep for days. We lost our horses, travel documents, and most of our personal effects. The only thing I have to assure you of my claim is this." I pull my medallion from around my neck and show it to the girl. Ash gives a relieved sigh, and I nod a thanks to Kaylin, who fished it from the bottom of the river for me.

Tyche examines our family seal and dips her head.

"Marcus Adicio, welcome, and you as well, Belair Duquan." She claps her hands and the graceful phantom turns to her. Together they chant in clear, high-pitched voices. A moment later, she faces me again. "I've called the master healer. She may want you two in the infirmary."

"Unnecessary."

"Really?" She points to my chest. "You're bleeding, and so is Belair." She looks to Piper as if she's not been doing her job, then turns to the rest of my company. "There are guest rooms for you all." She glances at Ash. "One non-savant?"

"Two," Kaylin and Ash say at the same time.

Which reminds me, why is he still here?

We wouldn't be, without him. De'ral rumbles in the depths.

"True."

"This is Kaylin of Tutapa, our guide," Ash continues when I don't introduce him.

"Well met." Tyche grins. "My grandmother will want a word with you. She's quite fond of Tutapan cuisine."

I close my eyes while arrangements are made for everyone's lodging. Their voices blur into the background, and for a moment, I think I'll pass out. The steady pain in my head blooms brighter, while my phantom strength retreats like water down a drain. I jolt awake when the impala bleats at Ash, springs into the air, and bounds away, leaping and jumping through the crowd.

Tyche opens her arms. "On behalf of the High Savant of Aku, welcome. May your path here be successful."

As I'm led away, Tyche directs Kaylin and Ash toward the main temple. "You'll have quarters there, and the librarian will be alerted to accommodate you. I imagine you have much to record."

"Indeed, thank you." Ash smiles. "See you at supper, Marcus, Belair."

I've never heard her sound happier. Why not? She's one of the few non-savants to make it to these sacred halls of training. I'm just as happy for her as I am for myself. Or I would be, if I had any energy to feel happiness.

My lids close as we walk to the infirmary. My main wish is that it's not far, and I'm sure Belair feels the same. When we climb the steps and stop at the door, Tyche leans toward me before they take us in. "My grandmother worried you'd never hold your phantom to form, Marcus Adicio. We can't wait to see what took you so long."

I let out a groan. "Your grandmother?"

"Yuki, the High Savant of Aku."

29

ASH

The sound of the ocean lulls me as I float in a current of dreams, weightless, guileless, until the tide pulls me under. I thrash and flail, crying out for help as water pours down my throat, filling my lungs. I'm sinking deeper and deeper.

"Ash, wake up."

My eyes fly open and I gulp in a breath.

"You're safe." Piper leans over me, holding my arms. "You're in Aku."

I search her face, my heart pounding. A few more breaths and the nightmare slips down a dark hole, leaving only gurgling shadows behind. It is no wonder my sleep is haunted. Any one of the dozens of horrors that befell us on the way to Aku could be to blame.

"That was a bad one," Piper says, pushing her shiny black braids out of her face. They've been redone and are now secured with tiny orange beads that match her robes. She looks rested and as beautiful as ever.

"Marcus?" Fear floods my veins again.

"He's fine. Belair, too."

"But I have to record the—"

"They haven't started yet."

I expel a deep breath. Piper sits back on the other bed, adjusting the colorful pillows as if returning to her spot. The room is sunny and warm and the air smells sweet in a wintery way, like cinnamon apple pie baking in the kitchen. Gulls cry outside the large window. There are no treetops or branches to see—only pale blue sky and starch-white clouds.

"Samsen?" I stretch and yawn, forming my next question before she answers. *And Kaylin? Where is he?*

"Samsen's in the dining hall. Waiting for us."

I nod my head, not quite able to ask about Kaylin. I'll know soon enough if he's still here.

I try to remember going to bed. We were shown to our rooms, stripped out of filthy clothes, given towels and led to the most extraordinary communal bath. I touch my hair. It feels smooth and silky and smells of rosewater. At least that wasn't a dream. I remember being massaged, too, my cuts and scrapes treated. There was a large meal as well. "I think I fell asleep after dinner."

"You did, and it's now lunchtime the next day."

"I've been out that long?"

Piper nods.

I throw back the covers. "Toilet?"

"You have your own. Through that door." Piper hands me a dressing gown made of a soft, quilted fabric and I slip it on over my underthings.

"Thank you."

The gown is black with a magnificent blue peacock embroidered on the back. I tie the belt. "I won't be long."

A bell tolls three times and Piper calls out, "You missed morning ritual."

"Morning what?" I say from the toilet.

"Morning ritual. Everyone meets on the training field at first bell, and I mean *everyone*, from the High Savant to the groundskeeper's youngest child."

"For?"

"A moment's meditation followed by what they call *dynamics*."

"Sounds like exercise."

"That's putting it mildly. It makes my physical defense class look like a catnap." Piper gives a little laugh. "Samsen and I wanted to give a little warning on what to expect…but other things got in the way."

"Didn't they just?" I grumble.

Piper grins. "Meet us in the dining hall when you're dressed. I'll save you a place."

"Where's that?"

"Downstairs, west wing. Follow the aromas. There is much to discuss."

I find my travel clothes clean and folded on top of a chest at the foot of my bed. Next to them is a pale turquoise top made of the same quilted fabric as the robe, only more tailored. I hold it up to the full-length mirror. It's beautiful. The hem falls below my knees, covering the black drawstring pants that go with it. It must be what non-savant wordsmiths wear on Aku. I dress, but just as I pull the top over my head, I hear a loud tap at the window. Quickly shoving arms into sleeves, I turn to face it. "Hello?"

Is someone in the room? I look behind. "Kaylin?"

From the corner of my eye, I catch a shadow outside. On instinct, I freeze. "Who's there?" Inside me pressure rises in waves, welling from my feet to the top of my head. My fists ball and raise as a shadow moves across the sill. A second later, it disappears.

It takes a full minute before I can relax my hands to open the side pane and look out. I catch a faint scent. Unidentifiable, but a bit musty.

Two stories below is a narrow lane, empty save for an unhitched wagon and some garbage bins. Along one side is a wooden fence weighed down with honeysuckle vines. The leaves are late autumn gold. The trumpet-shaped flowers give off a sticky, sweet fragrance.

My forehead prickles with sweat. No one could climb the wall. It's flagstone, a dark red, hard-textured rock bonded in place with mortar. The window ledge is narrow and covered with bird droppings.

Am I imagining things?

My inner voice doesn't answer.

It's another moment before I can close and lock the window and go to brush out my hair, putting it in a ponytail. Most of it stays in place. The clothes fit perfectly. It's a new look for me, and I like it. The cuffs are narrow and held together with tiny hooks and eyes. They can be rolled up or left down—either way, they won't interfere with the business of scribing.

"The records," I say to myself in the mirror. I have to catch up. But first, breakfast, or rather, lunch. Next to the door, I find my boots, clean and dry. I slip them on and go in search of the dining hall.

The stairs run along a two-story-high wall decorated with murals. I want to breathe it all in, but I'm too close to the images to appreciate the full scope. Still, there are large cresting waves, the peaks taking the shape of swooping eagles, galloping horses, and leaping wolves. The smaller waves look like snowcapped hills, and in the background, tall ships sail past. The masts are hidden in the spray and clouds, but I can see a hint of black sail. Is that possible? The thought gives me shivers but stare as I might, I can't be sure.

And then I momentarily forget all else as I spot Aku's first whistle bone hanging above the mural. They call it the Crown of Er—one of the original twelve whistle bones from the skeleton of King Er, as the story goes. It's carved from the jaw and represents the first lot or "way" to An'awntia*:* strength in oneself alone. On it is etched a ram with long, curved horns, symbolizing the urge to charge forward into life. Stake one's claim. Stand one's ground. I take a deep breath and sigh.

"Powerful, isn't it?"

Oh yes.

I keep going until the stairwell joins another coming from the opposite end of the hall. They merge like a forked stream and spiral down to the portico below. With a hand resting lightly on the railing, I pause to take in the view.

The foyer ceiling towers high above my head. On one side, pillars hold up open archways with steps leading down to the main street. The trees lining it are bare, but I imagine the blossoms in spring. Savants stride into the building from the street, all in their colored robes. So many of them. And phantoms, too. It's like a festival down there!

A woman in yellow robes hurries up the steps. She's leading the way for two young green-robed students. One is a girl with her phantom up. It's in the form of a sprite—short legs, pointy ears, and a very large grin. Behind her is a pale-haired, pale-skinned boy. No phantom, but wait! On second glance, I see it, hovering like a shadow, undulating around the folds of his robe, emanating sparks of blue light.

I'm still marveling at the sights when out from the hall strides another green-robe boy carrying a satchel full of books. Beside him is a strange green mist that ripples in and out of every shape it touches, an *alter* for sure. One moment it's a stair step, then a banister, then a perfect replica of an orange-robe master heading in the other direction. Trotting behind the master is a doglike phantom that barks at the mist. A *caller,* I'm guessing. Too small for a *warrior* and it has quite strong vocals.

This is spectacular.

"Look up," my inner voice warns.

I do, and find myself gazing into the keen eyes of an elderly woman standing several steps above me. She wears a white robe with black trim on the hem and cuffs. It's quilted and close-fitting, with a flare from the waist to the floor. Her hair is white, and her handsome face crinkles as she smiles.

"Good day." I make a curtsy. "I'm newly arrived to Aku," I add when she doesn't speak.

"Are you surprised by what you see?" She nods to the savants and phantoms passing below us.

"I must say, I'm impressed. Such a mix of robes, and even the young ones keeping their phantoms up, for a time at least." She pauses so long

I add, "Being non-savant myself…"

"Nonsense," she says with a grin and steps down to my level. "We find on the Isle of Aku, the students learn best by keeping their phantoms up for longer and longer periods of time." She opens her arm to another group of students passing below. "Builds endurance."

"You won't want to do that with Marcus Adicio, I promise." I hold my hand out to the odd woman. "I'm Ash, wordsmith and recorder for the Heir of Baiseen, and also for Belair Duquan of Tangeen."

"You may call me Talus. Welcome to the Sanctuary of Aku."

Her hand feels quite cool to the touch. Talus? The name is familiar, but I can't place it. The only thing I know for certain is that this woman could be a savant of the highest order. When she speaks, it's like all of Aku belongs to her.

"Talus." I dip my head. "It is an honor to meet you."

Talus chuckles. "You might like this, for the fountain." She offers me a large coin of burnished copper.

"Thank you!" I stand for far too long, simply admiring it. Everyone knows about the ritual of students making a wish at Aku's sacred fountain. I didn't know non-savants could as well. "I do have a wish or two in me."

"My, you do, don't you?"

My head snaps up. She speaks in riddles, I think.

"I'll see you in the library, Ash?"

"I look forward to it."

She heads down the stairs and out into the busy thoroughfare where I spot more savants with raised phantoms heading for the training field.

I pocket the coin, wondering what kind of phantom Talus raises. Something powerful for sure, maybe even a *warrior*.

At the bottom of the stairs, the foyer is nearly empty except for an orange-robed woman with a phantom walking beside her, a twin, if not for the blue skin and green hair. I follow at a distance, passing by reading nooks set up with window seats and study tables. Most are recently vacated, pillows in disarray, teacups drained, and only crumbs left on the plates.

I hope the kitchen is still open.

"Hurry then."

I run-walk the rest of the way to the dining hall only to hesitate at the wide-open doors. The sheer noise rattles me, with at least a hundred students gathered around tables, all eating and talking at once. There are a few phantoms up, too, some in meditative poses, some clearly standing guard. No one notices me, not yet, and suddenly I don't want them to.

"You've every right to be here."

Indeed. But my feet don't budge.

"Ash, you are the recorder to the Heir of Baiseen. All give way before us."

I stifle a laugh. *All give way?* It's a ridiculous statement, but just the encouragement I need to enter the hall.

And what a hall! It's not just noisy but frantic as students seem blazes-bent on dispatching their food. Have they no manners? Some still line up to be served, but those in their seats shovel down fish, potatoes, and greens like there's no tomorrow. And boisterous? Between mouthfuls, they talk to one another, and over one another, without pause. Where is the "midday silence" we observe in Baiseen?

"Not here."

On tiptoe, I spot Piper and Samsen across the room, three rows up and one over. I weave my way to them. Samsen smiles, his mouth full. He looks a lot better than the last time I saw him. As a matter of fact, his fair hair positively shines. "Got all the mud out, I see."

"And you, too." Samsen's dressed in a quilted, yellow robe with the image of an albatross on the back. Quite fitting. "Sit down. The food is good."

He and Piper resume eating, but not frantically like the rest of the room. "What's their rush?"

"They have to be back at training by seventh bell," Piper says, taking a leisurely drink from her cup. "Five minutes, by my count."

"I miss noonday silence," I say, looking at the serving line.

Samsen shrugs. "They forego it because the training here is so intensive. Students need to let the steam out, as they say."

"And they don't have any other time to socialize," Piper adds. "It's all very competitive."

As I nod, a rush of air at the back of my neck distracts me. When I turn around, nothing stands out. "Where are Marcus and Belair?"

"In the infirmary. Still sleeping." Piper takes a bite of bread, smiles, and passes it to Samsen.

My face falls. "Don't they need to be at it now, if it's so competitive?"

"Their success depends on it. But they must recover on their own first. It's protocol."

That's news to me. "But what if they are injured here, while competing?"

"I'm sure they will be, and healers will see to them, if there are breaks or cuts," Piper says. "But a healer must not boost their stamina or endurance. That they have to gain on their own." She stands. "Fish and tubers?"

"Oh yes, thank you."

"Part of training is building strength with no help from elixirs or potions," Samsen says as Piper heads for the serving line.

It has thinned and there's no wait. When she returns, I take my bowl, savoring each bite. Samsen's right; the food *is* good.

"My question to you, Ash," Samsen goes on, "is why aren't you in a little more hurry? You're starting over with the recording, for both Marcus and Belair, right?"

"I'll catch up fast." It's the one thing I'm not worried about, however… "Do you think Marcus is all right? I mean, his phantom was so…" My voice drops away and I look down, concentrating on my food.

"So savage on Mount Bladon?" Piper keeps her voice low as well.

I nod. "It was the first time I saw it held to solid form."

"A shock, agreed," Samsen says. "But he saved us from capture, torture, and likely death. The beast is a *warrior*, after all."

I agree but internally wonder, *At what price to Marcus?* He hunts, of course, but has never killed a man, until yesterday. Even recounting the incident with his father and the Aturnian spies seemed to make him feel sick. And then, on Mount Bladon, he tossed two dozen scouts off the path in half as many minutes. I shudder. "It's not in his nature."

"I disagree," Samsen says. "If it's in the phantom, it's in the savant."

"Smart boy, that Samsen."

"Don't worry, Ash." Piper pats my hand. "We're safe on Aku, and he'll have all the support and training he needs."

"If he passes," Samsen says, a bit ominously.

"Passes what?" All the focus was on getting to Aku and, now that we are here, I realize I've yet to be told what happens next.

"The elimination trial. At the end of the first seven days is a culling. Some will be sent home, asked to return next year to try again."

"But next year is too late for Marcus." Panicked, I make to rise, ready to sprint off to tell him.

Samsen waves me down. "He's been informed by now. And really, the elimination trial is more about potential than skill. Once he passes the first week, he trains for the duration. Then he's awarded his yellow robes, or not."

I stare, my mouth open. "As recorder, I should have been aware of the elimination trials."

"And you are now."

I have an indignant retort ready but keep my mouth shut. It's all part of the initiation…but I think the secrecy surrounding the process leaves a lot to be desired.

"Finish your food," Piper says. "They're asleep. Healing."

Asleep, and falling behind, I think but don't say that aloud. Instead, I ask the other thing pressing on my mind. "And Kaylin?" Heat rises to my cheeks. "Is he about?" A casual question, is all.

Piper chuckles, seeing right through me. "They've given you a room together, haven't they? For non-savants, as is customary?" Her smile says it all.

Kaylin and I share a room? How did I miss *that?* "I've been sleeping, and I guess he's been…" What has he been doing?

"Fishing," Samsen says. "I think our sailor's uncomfortable around so many people."

"Around so many savants and their phantoms, you mean." Piper plays with the buttons on her orange cuffs. "I've not seen him today." She returns to her chat with Samsen, discussing their teaching schedule and then the advanced training they will undertake. I thought they would have some free time over the next few weeks but it doesn't sound like it.

When I finish my meal, I stand, ready to leave, noticing again I'm the only one in the hall not wearing savant robes. At the Sanctuary of Baiseen, there are plenty of us non-savants, but not here on Aku. No wonder Kaylin feels uncomfortable. I'm starting to myself.

As I turn from the table, I nearly bump into an agahpa, a treelike phantom with branchy arms and legs. They are *warriors*, very tall, and this one's leading the way in front of its green-robed savant. One of those endurance exercises, I guess. But as I step back, it hesitates, staring at me through black, knotty eyes. For a moment, I see a picture in my head of the savant going through an obstacle course on the training field. The image is so clear, I shiver, and the hair on the back of my neck stands on end.

"Ash? Are you all right?"

When I look up, both Samsen and Piper are frowning at me, faces creased.

"It's nothing. I just…I realized I have to ask for all new supplies."

And collect my wits. Because while I'd been unconvinced the mouse image from before actually came from Belair's leopard, I'm nearly positive this phantom just spoke to me. Marcus said that's how it can be for savants and their phantoms at first, pictures in the mind, a snippet of meaning, a word...

I need to find Marcus and talk to him about this. "Where's the infirmary?"

Piper still looks concerned. "Out the front doors, left along the main boulevard, past the fountain, three doors down from the library tower."

"The building with the high arches," Samsen adds. "You sure you're fine?"

"Yes, thanks." I excuse myself and head for the door, but as I weave around the tables, past those still finishing their meals, I feel eyes watching my back. And not in a friendly way.

30

ASH

I have every intent of rushing to see Marcus, but as I leave the hall and follow the main path, I come face-to-face with Aku's sacred fountain, and it sweeps my breath away.

Water mists my face as it falls from a great height, pouring in streams from the massive jugs held high by four, larger-than-life, savants. Folds of their robes seem to waft underwater, but the entire sculpture is bronze, so no telling the color. One thing is sure. There is joy on their faces and hope in their eyes. I feel it, too, just looking at them.

In the center of the fountain, rising up from the savants, are four magnificent phantoms, a horse, an eagle, a wolf, and a stag. All lunge into the sky. Water tumbles from their mouths, hooves, wingtips, and antlers, raining down to the pool below. It's spring fed, or so it says on the plaque, and fresh for all to fill their vessels. There is actually a list of the physical benefits from the trace elements of gold and copper. Below the brief history of its creation, and the artists involved, there is a single command.

MAKE A WISH

I stand, breathe in, and send the coin flipping end over end into the center of the pool. It disappears as I release my heart's desire.

Let me be better than any expect.

"Lofty goal." My inner voice seems impressed.

I turn to go and suddenly catch a sharp glance from a pelican-like phantom. It swoops by, flying low, and before I can blink, my mind fills with a dizzying panorama of the island, a bird's-eye view. I'm queasy from the undulating heights.

What's happening?

"I think you know."

But I don't, not entirely.

I sit back down and close my lids. I need a moment.

"You'll see more with your eyes open, lass."

I smile but keep my eyes closed. "Is that what I'm doing wrong?"

"You do nothing I would call wrong." Kaylin sits beside me, close, but not so close we touch.

"That's because you don't know me well enough."

He nudges my shoulder with his. "Nothing time won't cure."

My heart does a little gallop as my eyes pop open. It's a cure I wouldn't mind waiting for.

He's in his usual garb, drawstring pants, open-necked shirt, bare feet. "You look..." *Good*, I almost say. His curly hair smells newly washed, and it dances across his face in the breeze. His eyes, in this light, are amber-green. The fountain's mist leaves beads of water on his long, dark eyelashes...

"Staring again..."

I quickly pull my eyes away.

"You were saying? I look...?" he prompts.

"Clean," I blurt.

"Can you think of no better word?"

Seems not.

My breath catches when he leans in close. "Did you make a wish?"

All I can do is nod. "And you?"

"My wish was made days before we landed." His eyes are warm and dancing.

No. He doesn't mean what I think, surely. "Wishing wells don't work that way, silly."

"Silly?"

Shut up!

He laughs as if privy to my inner thoughts. "Have you seen Marcus and Belair?"

"Not yet," I say, gathering my composure. It's like trying to put puppies back in a box. "I'm actually on my way to the infirmary to check on them."

"Allow me?" He's on his feet, offering me his hands.

I take them, but he doesn't let go when I'm up. Instead, we just stand there, face-to-face, hand in hand, fountain mist dampening our cheeks. I have no idea what to say, but he doesn't seem to mind and, as I allow myself to savor the warmth, I don't mind one bit, either.

And then, Kaylin lifts my hands to his lips and kisses them lightly, as if I were a lady of the court.

My heart skips a beat or maybe ten, and my body shudders with a rush of feelings I can't name. Bless the bones, I may pass out on the spot.

He drops his gaze to my lips before raising his eyes to mine. It's enough to heat me from the inside out. What is he thinking? Is he recalling our kiss? Because I am.

Just when I think I'll tremble apart, he nods toward the end of the street. "The infirmary is this way."

I may need the infirmary at this rate. The thought makes me giggle inside, and I'm afraid if I open my mouth to answer, one will escape. I smile with my lips closed to save myself the embarrassment. Finally, I say, "Lead on," and manage to fall into step with him, one hand still tucked securely in his.

"Lead on? That's it? After such a gesture?"

Good point. "Er..." I frantically glance around for something to comment on, but I'm still too flustered to form a coherent thought. "Nice arches," I exclaim as we pass under them.

"Nice...arches?" my inner voice repeats, incredulous.

Help me, please!

But all I hear within is a lighthearted chuckle.

I retrieve my hand as we trot up the infirmary steps, knowing it's the only way I'll be able to focus on my surroundings. So far, the infirmary is much like our healers' hall at Baiseen, only smaller. They don't have use for a larger one, the savant at reception says when she overhears me explaining this to Kaylin.

"Not many serious injuries end up here," the woman goes on. "The healers usually deal with them in the field."

"That's handy." I guess, because Aku is neutral to the realms, there's no fear of attack, unlike the rest of us. The thought of the threat looming over Baiseen sends a cold jolt through my body. What if Gollnar *is* in league with Aturnia and war closer than we thought? Marcus's father has leveraged so many sanctions against those realms their hatred for us grows exponentially. I witnessed it firsthand over the last few days. While Marcus and I believe in peace, we'll need De'ral more than ever if we want to keep war from destroying our realm.

"What you'll need are more healers to clean up the mess."

My heart sinks at the thought of the Gollnar scouts, peace be their paths. Yes, they took us prisoner, but to see them all brutally killed in front of my eyes…

"This way." The woman shows us to the ward—a single room with three beds along each wall. Marcus and Belair, the only patients, are both fast asleep. I sit at the foot of Marcus's bed. Kaylin leans against the far wall, his hands clasped behind his back.

"They'll be released this evening," Tyche, the young orange-robe who met us on the training field yesterday, says softly as she enters the room. Her little impala is nowhere to be seen. I imagine even a highly trained phantom of that nature, particularly its spring-loaded hooves, is a liability indoors.

"Have they awakened at all?" I ask.

"Long enough to fall straight back to sleep. They're exhausted, even though your healer dealt directly with their wounds, they must regain strength on their own."

"So I've heard."

"Who are you?" A woman with short, curly gray hair and a strict face enters the room, her orange robes flowing around her. "No non-savants with the patients." She speaks in hushed tones, but the intention is clear. A large chameleon phantom follows her, nails clicking on the tile floor. It stops to change course and head toward me, until the orange-robe calls it back. Still, its protruding eyes watch as they rotate independent of each other. It's unnerving. Kaylin straightens away from the wall, alert.

"This is Ash, from the Heir's party," Tyche says quietly. "She's their recorder."

"A non-savant?"

Tyche shrugs and turns to me. "Let me present Bucheen, the master healer of Aku."

Bucheen nods briefly. "You can go. They'll be along in a few hours."

"But I'm Marcus's—" I almost say *best friend*. "His…"

"Recorder. I heard, but non-savant, nonetheless." She stares me up and down. "Have you finished recording the journey so far?"

"Oh, no, mistress. There is much to do. The scrolls and notes were lost, and I haven't even—"

"Then you're a recorder with no free time on her hands."

"Yes, Mistress."

"Off with you. And write fast before the Heir tries to influence your words."

My hackles go up. "Marcus wouldn't do such a thing."

Bucheen waves the thought away. "If he is anything like his father, he would." The healer's eyes are lakes in winter—slate blue, cold, and impenetrable.

I try to imagine the Magistrate as a young initiate and can't until a perfect image of Jacas Adicio pops into my head, so like Marcus but with dark hair. He's a green-robe with a wolf phantom by his side. The picture vanishes as quickly as it came, leaving me gasping in a breath. I rest my gaze on the chameleon. It cannot be.

"Can't it? Mouse pinned under the sun leopard's paw back on the headland? Agahpa's savant on an obstacle course? Bird's-eye view of the Isle? And now the boy magistrate and his wolf? Not to mention De'ral..."

It's a lot of mounting evidence, but it's also inexplicable, as far as I know. I wouldn't ever presume to broach the topic with a savant except Marcus, and he will need all of his focus to make it through the trials.

Bucheen frowns at me. "I presume he's with you?"

"Yes, Mistress." I straighten up fast. "This is Kaylin, the sailor who guided us from Clearwater."

The two exchange a nod, and her face softens. "Be sure to toss coins in the fountain. Non-savants aside, it's our tradition."

"Thank you." Kaylin is already out the door, but I turn to say, "Talus gave me a copper coin and I threw it already. It was burning a hole in my pocket."

The room goes palpably still. "What's that, young woman?" Bucheen's voice is cotton around broken glass.

"Um, Talus? We met on the stairs and—"

"*The* Talus?"

I try not to squirm under the scrutiny. "I-I don't know, Mistress. She introduced herself as Talus."

The woman's expression turns thunderous. "You dare to use our first Bone Thrower's name in jest? Explain yourself."

Kaylin is immediately at my side.

And then it hits, like I'm being tipped upside down. *The Talus* was an ancient title for the first Bone Thrower on Aku. How could I have forgotten?

I squeeze my eyes shut, trying to recall my history lessons. Talus raised a powerful phantom that seldom held to form. When the bones of Er were carved into whistles, she, as leader of Aku, copied the shapes and used them in divination. It is said that her elemental phantom sent wind through them, lifting them in song. From her, the first black-robes came into being and only she among them wore white. I rub the back of my neck. Why would the woman I met today tell me her name was Talus?

Bucheen smooths her robes down, waiting for me to explain.

I point vaguely back the way I'd come. "I met a white-robed savant in the temple proper. She introduced herself as Talus and gave me a coin."

Bucheen finally relaxes her shoulders. "You wordsmiths." She chuckles. "So gullible."

I frown. "Did someone play a trick on me?"

"You're non-savant. You'll find a bit of that here, I'm afraid. All in good fun, of course, but know this—The Talus's name is never to be taken lightly."

"Yes, Mistress." When I reach the door, I turn around. "There isn't anyone named Talus on Aku, I take it?"

"Ash, child, there hasn't been anyone named Talus on all of Amassia for thousands of years."

I give Bucheen a respectful bow, and Kaylin and I head back out.

"That was strange," he says when we're at the street.

"Very."

We walk in silence to the library tower and cross the courtyard that leads to the imposing doors. Already, my mind buzzes with lists, the materials I'll need, ways to present the facts, and of course, my long-standing orders from Master Brogal to search for stories about Mar.

Kaylin turns to me. "I'll leave you to your recording, lass."

"Don't you want to come in?"

"I do, but there are things I must tend to."

Normally, I'd love getting lost in a musty library on my own, but something about parting ways with Kaylin makes me linger. "Just a quick look?"

Kaylin lifts his face in the direction of the sea and closes his eyes. When he comes back to himself, he says, "A quick look then, if it pleases you."

"It *does* please me." So much so that I can't stop the smile from spreading across my face.

He leads the way up the flower-lined steps to the threshold. When we enter, a gasp escapes my lips. "Oh my."

"Yes…truly," Kaylin whispers.

The main entryway reaches two stories high with floor-to-ceiling bookshelves and as many scroll cases. There are ladders on wheels to reach them, and savants, mostly green-robes, studying at tables. Others relax in the reading area, a comfortable setting with dark red rugs, orange pillows, and a huge window seat. The lighting is perfect, direct sun from the skylights.

I take a deep breath, drawing it into my heart and letting it beat out through my body. The scent of inks and scrolls and leather bindings infuses me.

I've come home.

"May I help you?" a man with a thin face and shaggy white hair asks. He wears faded orange robes, the sign of an accomplished master, and has round spectacles on his long nose, his blue eyes and bushy brows enlarged behind them.

"I'm Ash, recorder for Marcus Adicio and Belair Duquan. We're newly arrived."

He looks at my empty arms. "Your records thus far?"

"At the bottom of the Ferus River," Kaylin says.

"Adventures, is it?" His brow lifts as if he's talking to small children on a teeter-totter. Before either of us can respond, the orange-robe rubs his hands together. "You'll have to start fresh, with not a moment to waste."

A phantom similar in looks to the lemurs on the Isle of Nonnova comes scampering down a ladder and right up to me, chittering, whiskers spanned wide.

"Ah, so you are a pet," the library master says, eyeing me up and down.

My face heats. "I didn't—"

"Nothing to be ashamed of." He claps twice, recalling his phantom as it sniffs my boots.

I'm hardly ashamed, but I would like to understand it. Especially since there's something, I don't know, a bit condescending in the way he says *pet.* Like I'm an object of amusement. Maybe I can find a reference to it here. My eyes drift over the tall bookshelves.

"Let's assemble fresh quills, inks, new scrolls, and translation guides," the master says to his phantom. Then, to me, "We'll supply you with all your needs." He opens his arms to include the entire building. "You and your friends may partake of our library to your heart's desire, provided you mind the rules."

I bow, and we follow after the phantom.

"Remember," he calls to us. "It is a privilege to record, no matter your station."

Everyone in the library turns to look at me, or so it feels, but I don't care. This is the most celebrated hall of learning in all the realms, and I've just been given access to everything.

Kaylin stayed only long enough to peruse the novel shelves and choose one to take with him, leaving me to my work. It's a good thing, too. As I outline what needs to be done, not just for Marcus but Belair as well, I think Bucheen is right. I'm a recorder with little free time on her hands, at least until I catch up. With a backpack full of supplies and reference books—including one titled *The Ways of Phantoms,* and weighing ten pounds if it's an ounce—I head back to my room in the late afternoon light. There's no sign of Talus on the steps, or any other trickery, and in moments, I'm turning the key in the lock.

"Kaylin!" I yelp as he swings open the door for me. Bones of Er, I forgot we share a room.

"I was just going out," he says but steps back, closing the door with a *snick.*

He hesitates and it hits me that we're completely alone. In our shared room. Together.

Neither of us moves and, though I try to think of something to say, all my thoughts scatter on the wind.

"Can I help with that?" He's looking at my heavy pack but not taking it.

"Maybe because you're gripping it for dear life."

Huh? Oh... I start to shrug out of the straps. "Thanks."

"All stocked up?" He puts the pack down by the low table and returns to stand there, staring at me.

My throat's so dry I can hardly swallow. When I do, it's a noisy sound. Great. Now my face is heating. "All stocked with tools, inks, yes. Some books, and a..."

"I don't think he needs an inventory."

My heart's racing and in the dead quiet of the room, I'm certain, and not for the first time, he can hear it pound. Just thinking that turns up the heat like a boiler. *Help!*

"You're on your own with this." The amusement in my inner voice does nothing to calm me.

I clear my throat. "You were going?"

"Not sure that came out as you meant it."

Oh! B'larkin squad! "Not because I'm in a hurry for you to leave, though it's fine if you do. Of course. Fishing, is it? Samsen, or was it Piper? They mentioned you have been fishing a lot."

"Ash." He puts both hands on my shoulders, no doubt trying to still the frenzy of words bubbling out of my mouth. "I'm off to the docks to see if there's a market for lures."

"Lures?" In my current state, with his face hovering above mine, it doesn't quite make sense.

He leans back and smiles. "I enjoy carving, and they bring a good bit of coin."

"Lures! Of course. For fishing!" Why am I talking so loudly?

He chuckles, hands sliding down to my arms and finally letting go at the cuffs. "I'll be back."

"Farewell," I say, formally. Ugh! "I mean, be well, while you walk to the docks…and back."

"Please stop talking, Ash."

I close my mouth and wave goodbye.

Kaylin's eyes dance and he gives me a see-you-later wink before closing the door behind him.

It's a moment before I can take a proper breath. When I do, I head straight for my bed and belly flop onto the pillows, groaning into them. Could I have been any more awkward?

"Probably not."

I wasn't asking you!

Part of me wants to crawl under the covers and never come out, but it's silly. I mean, could it have really been that bad? My inner voice starts to answer, but I hold up a finger in warning. "You just be quiet." I have to pull myself together.

I sit up, sliding my feet to the floor while running back through it all in my head. Not that bad, really, though my hands are still jittery. "Tea," I say to myself and stoke the fire. "Hot, calming tea, and the records." I make a pot of rosehips and chamomile, already steadying with a plan before me.

And, praise Gaveren's great sword, I have more tools of the trade in reach than ever before in my life. It's a veritable goldmine! A rush of warmth runs through me as I unpack the bulging satchel, laying out each item with the reverence it deserves. There are quills of no less than twelve assorted sizes, all from left primary feathers—perfect for a righthanded scribe like me. I recognize their origins, large flying birds, goose, hawk, sea eagle, and turkey. And oh, the inks! The glorious inks. Not only do I have the standard bottles of cuttlefish and carbon black, but an array of mineral powders to grind—cobalt, red ochre, yellow ochre, malachite, azurite, and copper. Some purple powder I don't even know the name of… And a perfect little mortar and pestle for mixing. The neat stack of papyruses are all accurately matched in length and width for binding later. I breathe in the familiar scents of feather, ink, reed, and pulp and exhale slowly. This is my dream come true.

I don't know how long I sit at the little table marveling, sipping my tea, but my lids grow heavy and my head nods. When I glance again, the fire in the hearth has turned to a bed of glowing embers. I force myself up, change into my nightdress, blow out the candles, and crawl under the covers. For a fleeting moment, I wonder if I locked the door but am too tired to check. And this is Aku—there's no safer place in all the realms. I turn my head, resting my cheek on the cool pillow. My days on this enchanted Isle are numbered, and I want to memorize every detail—the feel of these sheets, the look of this room, every sound and sensory detail.

"*Sleep.*"

My eyes close and I peacefully drift.

Tap. Tap, tap.

I was immersed in the path of sleep, cocooned in warmth and security, as safe as I've ever felt in my life, until now. That tapping. It tells me something's wrong. On a faraway hill in the landscapes of thought, my inner voice shouts a warning, "*Ash!*" There's more, and a sharp sense of urgency worms into the cocoon, but before I can act, the walls of awareness turn to dust and blow away, along with the lingering sound of my name…

Tap. Tap, tap.

I'm in the dark; I can't move. And I'm not alone.

A shadowy weight hunches over me, pressing close to my chest. It's drawn to my heartbeat, or my breath. The room smells of must and mildew, suffocating me. I swallow the dryness in my throat as the wind rushes outside and—I hear it more clearly now, or perhaps I'm just more conscious—a *tap...tap...tap* sounds at the window. I struggle again to move, but the darkness paralyzes me.

"Wake up!" My inner voice jolts through me. *"Wake up!"* It's blasting in my ears.

But all I can do is stare unblinking at the dark, hungry shape bending over me and listen to the fingernails tapping on the sill. My mouth opens, and I scream, throat vibrating, but no sound escapes.

Tap...tap...tap...

"Be gone!" my inner voice roars, molten lava spewing from the earth.

The sound shatters the world like glass and my eyes fly open. Heart in my throat, I take in the warm glowing embers, the quiet room, gentle wind outside.

I draw a breath and hold it, ears straining for the slightest whisper.

"We are safe now."

It takes quite some minutes of conscious breathing, in and out, slower and slower, before I can release my shoulders into the softness of the bed. *Just a dream, then?* I turn over, burrowing back down into the warm folds of sleep, but as I drop off, I hear my inner voice whispering.

"That was no dream."

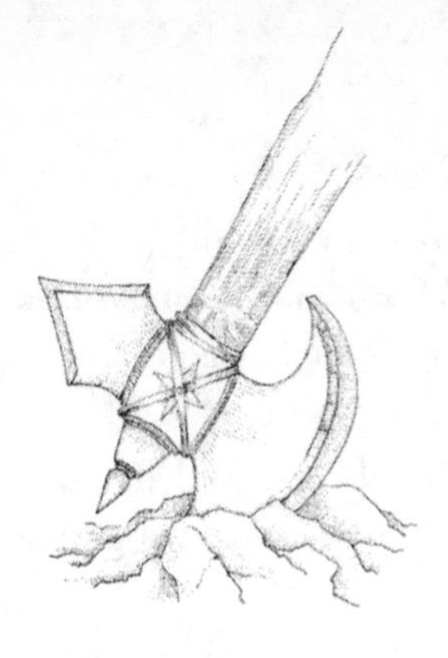

31

MARCUS

I wake with a start. Where am I?

I grab the water jug by the bed and drain it. As I swallow, the events of the last few days hit like a landslide. Aku. We're in Aku.

"We made it."

"We did," Belair answers, groggy, like he's just awakened, too.

I throw back my covers and find my feet. "Up, Belair. We can't afford to linger in the infirmary—not with the first trial to pass." I glance around, trying to get a sense of time. Afternoon? Evening? How many hours have we lost on the other candidates? As that thought surfaces, others rise, too—voices above me, *healer* phantoms descending, decrees not to leave our beds.

And then I remember the last time De'ral rose, and my stomach tightens. Mount Bladon. The bodies and blood. So much blood. My lack of control, and something worse I don't even admit to myself but know is there, like a shadow behind my eyes...

"All right!" A woman streams into the room. "Let's see if these young savants are ready to work." She tosses me a small purse without warning, and I catch it in a snap.

"Reflexes good." She marks something down on her chart.

I clear my throat. "I'm Marcus Adicio, and this is Belair Duquan of Tangeen. We could both be at our training, Mistress, but I believe our orders were to wait for release."

The savant smiles. "I'm Bucheen, and the orders are from me."

I brighten.

"*When* I deem fit."

My face falls.

She does little to test our health, but her phantom, a chameleon, studies us with roving eyes. Bucheen nods and says we are free to go. That's it?

He spoke to me, De'ral says.

"And I didn't hear?"

I don't even know what this means—phantoms conversing apart from their savants. It isn't something we learned of in Baiseen.

"There are Aku green robes in the closet for you both."

I hesitate, unsure if she will leave and give us privacy.

She claps her hands. "Get to it. You'll be in time for the evening meal if you hurry."

"Excellent," I say. "I feel as if I've missed ten meals, not just one."

Bucheen laughs. "You think it's been one?"

"More?" I raise my brows.

"You've slept for over fifty hours straight," Bucheen says. "*Called* to it by the chants of Tyche and her skillful phantom."

"She *called* us into unconsciousness?" Belair asks.

"Those two are expert at giving dreamless, restful sleeps…but why was it necessary? Clearly, you've been engaged in battle. Either that, or fell off a mountaintop, which would be very clumsy of you. I hope there is a sound reason."

Belair and I start talking over each other.

"Not my concern." Bucheen holds up both hands, unwilling to listen. "That will be for Yuki to address." Bucheen makes to leave, but she lets her gaze linger again on me. She's judging, I can tell. "So like him," she murmurs before rousing herself back to the present. "Go on. Dress and depart. I want at least a day to pass before my healers are mending you on the field."

Belair starts to protest, but I subtly shake my head. After what we've been through, I'm sure we can handle the training grounds, though I think it's best not to argue with the master healer.

De'ral grumbles in the depths.

"Don't worry. We'll show them what we're made of in the morning."

It's late afternoon when we walk outside, the sun near to setting. We head for the dining hall, but at the rate Belair comments on the architecture, it'll be midnight by the time we get there. He points at walls and roofs, quatrefoils this, cupolas that… I have no idea what he's talking about.

"Enough with the buildings," I finally say. "Look at the phantoms on the training field." I nod across the thoroughfare. "That small group of local blue-robes is doing well with their phantoms up." I can't take my eyes away. "Imagine growing up on Aku."

Belair stops to watch the group gathering in front of their orange-robe instructor. They jostle each other and laugh while a small herd of foggy shadows melt back into the ground. "They can't keep them up for long."

"True, but look." Back up they pop, so soon after going to ground. Brogal never worked with me this way. I should have held De'ral to form years ago and come here sooner where there are warrior instructors—ouster too. Most of those class are from Sierrak and the Aturnian realms. My eyes narrow. I'll train with those who will be my enemies if war breaks?

As I chew on that, I glance behind and see a green-robe savant with an armed phantom—a sword-carrying beast with huge eyes and protruding teeth—catching up to us.

"Good afternoon to you," Belair stops to say. "I trust we are headed toward the dining hall?"

I smile, trying not to be obvious about sizing him up. Every visiting green-robe is our competition, after all.

"Two green-robes coming from the infirmary?" He pushes back his sable hair and grins wide. "You must be the ones from Baiseen."

I nudge Belair before he starts babbling about me being the Heir to the throne. I may not be good at languages, but I know a Northern Aturnian accent when I hear one. That's the only realm currently banned from Aku, sanctioned until they sign peace treaties with Palrio and Tangeen. "I'm Marcus, and this is Belair." I state our first names only. Could he be a spy? In the halls of Aku? Surely not…

"I'm Destan, green-robe with a *warrior,* as you can see, from Southern Aturnia." He opens his hand out to his phantom. "And you raise?"

I smooth down my fine quilted green robe. "*Warrior*."

"Both of us," Belair adds.

"In Zarah's class?" Destan doesn't wait for an answer. "She's tough as Sierrak brown bears, I promise. Be ready."

"We are." I look him in the eyes. "The dining hall?"

"In the main temple, on the right. You're about there." He points the way. "It's Nonnova today."

"Pardon?" Belair asks.

"Oh, you'll know soon enough." He dips his head to us both, respectful. "I'm off for special training. See you on the field tomorrow." He smiles his very wide grin and jogs off with his phantom. In perfect sync. It's hard not to conclude that we're behind. Way behind.

"Friendly, wasn't he?" Belair says as we keep walking.

"Very. But did you hear the accent?"

"Aturnian. He said Southern, but I would have picked Northern, the way he said 'about' like it was *a boat*." Belair lowers his voice. "Which means he should be banned from Aku, am I right?"

"Unless something's changed in the last few days." I'm doubtful the sanctions have been recalled. It's long been a point of contention, the way Northern Aturnia occupies lands it does not rightfully possess.

"The others might know something," Belair says, then lets out a whoop and points. "Look! It's the fountain." He grabs my sleeve and pulls me toward it at a run.

And there it is, more spectacular than any rendition hanging in the Sanctuary halls, with water spouting from the launching phantoms, vessel-bearing savants in the midst. We rush to the edge and stand there, misted in spray, transfixed. It's huge. The sculpture's three times the height of grown men, and the water spouts double that distance into the air.

"Are you ready?" Belair asks.

I reach for my coin and Belair does the same. Together, on three, we toss our hopes high and make our wishes.

But as I watch the coin spin end over end, reaching its apex and plummeting into the churning pool, my stomach turns to rock and sinks with it. So much rests on my success, and we are already three days behind before we start.

Belair and I enter the maelstrom they call the dining room and eventually spot Ash. My shoulders relax at the sight of her. "Ash!" I shout across the room, but she doesn't hear me in the din. She's with Samsen and Piper at a middle table. Kaylin's not with them. I assume he's on his way to the other end of the world by now. That's a relief.

Is it?

De'ral's question makes me pause.

It's not exactly a relief. Kaylin protected Ash. He protected us all. I have to admit that, even if I don't fully trust him or enjoy his flirtations with her. I've never had to share Ash before, and if I'm honest, I'm worried they grew even closer while I slept. Worried might not be the best word—

I'm not the wordsmith that Ash is—but we're as close as any two people can be. And now, this sailor…

This sailor, what?

"That's the problem. I don't know."

As I weave my way to the table, it dawns that I haven't properly thanked Kaylin for getting us here on time, against all odds. I must make amends and put these rogue feelings aside.

"Ash!" I shout again from a few lengths away.

She spins around, then she's out of her seat and running.

"About time!" She kisses Belair on the cheek and turns to hug me. "And you!" She goes up on tiptoe and holds my face in her hands.

I wrap her in my arms and lift her off her feet. "Thanks for the visit," I say. "I heard you came but I didn't wake."

"You're up now," she says with a grin. She leads me to the table and I notice the glances we receive. No, not *we*. Just Ash, and they aren't friendly. Is that boy snickering? I stare him down, muscles in my arms tightening, and turn to my recorder. "Did you do something to upset everyone?"

"Yeah, actually. I was born non-savant."

They're prejudiced? I push up the sleeves of my robe, half a mind to go and give them a talking to. Aku is supposed to be the most enlightened realm in Amassia. They welcome all, um, savants… My stomach clenches. "This is unacceptable. I'm going to—"

"Calm down, Marcus." She sits and pulls me into the chair next to her. "It's nothing I'm not used to."

"In Baiseen? Surely not so pronounced as this."

"Surely?" She laughs outright. "Maybe not so *you* would notice, Marcus, but I live it."

"Mistress Yuki wants to see you both, and you, Belair," Samsen cuts in. "Tomorrow morning."

"Before classes start, I hope." I'm still frowning at Ash's revelation. She can't think I see her as inferior, can she?

"What will you say?" Samsen asks, pulling my attention back to him. I force a smile, unable to count how many rules we've broken on our way here. Raising untrained *warrior* phantoms. Killing with untrained *warrior* phantoms. Crossing Northern Aturnia territory with untrained *warrior* phantoms…

Maybe I *can* count them.

"We'll figure it out tonight." Ash answers for me while passing a serving platter. "Steamed rice with leaks and poached bass."

I sniff it.

"Delicious," Belair says and fills his bowl.

"Looks like Nonnova fare." I poke it with my fork.

"That's because it is," Ash says. "Each day's recipe comes from a different realm. Aku honors them all."

Belair turns to me and we say at the same time, "Nonnovan day."

Ash chuckles. "Yes, now eat up."

"When's it Palrion day?" I take a tentative bite.

"Don't be a baby." She punches my arm. "Eat."

When the others turn their attention to the food and conversations, I lean toward Ash. "Kaylin gone?" I say it lightly but really, it's still weighing on me.

"He's fishing."

"Still here, then?" *Neutral. Neutral. Neutral.*

"He is." She smiles, and her eyes shine.

Is that excitement for us being here? For him?

"Marcus, it's spectacular in the library. You've no idea the size of it."

Ah, for her books, of course. "I'll find out soon enough." There will be a lot of reading in my training schedule, on top of physical tests, endurance, fighting…

"Have you been on the field yet?" Piper asks.

"We came straight from the infirmary, passed the fountain, made a wish…" Ash's worried frown catches my eye. "What's that look for?"

"It's very demanding, from what I've seen. And, there's a lot of competition here," Ash says. "I hope you both pace yourselves."

Belair rubs his hands together. "Can't wait!"

"We're fit and ready," I say and take a big bite of rice. "There's nothing to worry about there." But a cloud gathers over me as I study my competition around the room. How many are Aturnian? Or from Gollnar? More to the point, how many raise *warriors,* and how advanced is their training?

Samsen and Piper outline the details of the week, details and protocols that I likely would've learned had I been more coherent at the first assembly. Week one is meant to be the hardest. Some will drop out of their own accord; others will fail and be asked to leave. Not that having to drop out is the worst thing for most savants. Humiliating, for sure, but the younger ones can try again next year. If they fail a second time, it just means they won't go on to teach at their sanctuary or take a higher-level role in service to their realm.

For me it's a death sentence. Failing the elimination trial will cost me the throne—and my father's favor, not that I've ever really been in his good graces. But what's more, failing will cost my realm their potentially greatest phantom, De'ral.

Again, the pressure strikes hard. Belair and I have only a few days to prove that untrained warrior savants from the south can stand and fight with the best of them.

"We can do it, right?" I reach out to De'ral for assurance, but maybe that's a mistake.

Under my skin, he roils, laughing in a way that chills me to the bone.

32

MARCUS

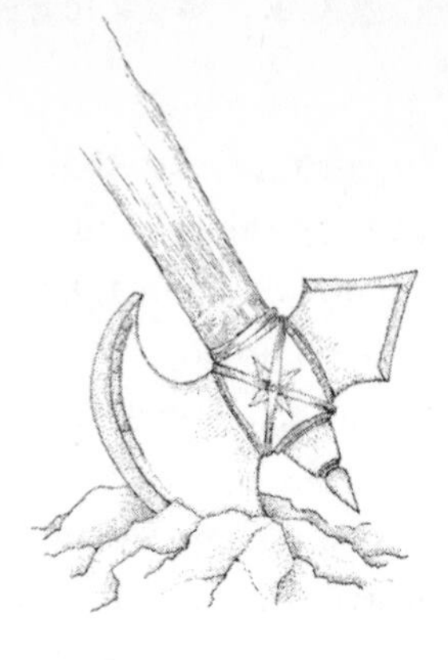

I stop halfway up the stairs, studying Aku's first whistle bone. Really, it's just an excuse to rest. I hate to admit it, but I'm dizzy. Plus, those Nonnovan greens were laced with pickled onions, which never sit well with me. After a few deep breaths, I continue up the stairs, reach the third level, and head down the hall. There are smoky mirrors on either side, and between the doors stand tables with colorful vases full of dried flowers. Aku doesn't skimp on the fine details. "Eight, ten, twelve." I stop at Ash's door and knock.

Kaylin opens.

My head jerks back as if slapped. "I thought you were fishing."

"I thought you were in the infirmary." He stands tall, not moving aside.

"Fully recovered, thank you." I try to peer around him. "Ash is expecting me."

Kaylin finally moves to let me in. "She's getting changed."

I frown at that, then focus on the room. It's large, well-appointed, and lit with colored lanterns hanging from the high ceiling. There are two double beds in an L-shape against the back and side wall.

"The swim was amazing, Kaylin." Ash comes out of the en suite in a black robe that brushes the floor. I fixate on the embroidered cuffs as she towels her hair dry.

Why are you angry? De'ral asks.

I don't know. The obvious seems preposterous to me. I am *not* jealous.

"And thanks for—" She stops mid-sentence when she sees me. "You're here! Perfect timing."

I look between her and Kaylin, a burning sensation growing in my chest. Ash needs to focus on her job as a recorder. She needs to focus on *me*. And Belair, of course. My hands ball into fists.

She is *focused.* De'ral defends her. *Look around.*

He's right. The table is covered with parchments, quills, and inks. I resist the urge to tilt my head and read the exposed pages.

So, there is no problem, De'ral says.

"*Except...Kaylin's a sailor. He could be gone with the next tide, leaving her heartbroken.*"

And that's your real concern?

I think I liked it better when De'ral and I didn't talk.

"Marcus?" Ash's brows are up.

I force my face into a pleasant expression. "You were saying something about swimming?"

She laughs. "In the tidepools!" She throws the towel over the back of a chair. "They're clear as crystal and full of brightly colored sea creatures. Kaylin's teaching me about them."

I look at him, wondering what his intentions are.

"*See? This* is *a problem.*"

"And the water's warm in the shallows." She seems to be purposefully averting her eyes before Kaylin can meet them. Strange. "We ran all the way back."

"Temperature drops when the sun goes down." Kaylin looks at Ash.

I can tell he's keen but guarded. What's he hiding?

"I didn't want her caught out with wet hair," he goes on.

"Very thoughtful." I make a show of glancing further about the room. Maybe I'm just jealous of how well-appointed hers is.

Theirs is.

"*Thank you, De'ral. I needed that reminder.*"

"This room is nice. Belair and I are crammed into bunks on the bottom floor with two other green-robes. It's nothing by comparison."

"These rooms are for visiting non-savants. They aren't used very often, I guess, and, trust me, it's not as—"

"No need to explain." I'm not sure why I'm being so childish about it all. At least there's one thing I can do to improve. I step toward Kaylin. "I've not had the chance to formally thank you for your assistance on Mount Bladon, the river, the farmhouse..." I pause, searching for a better word than appreciation. "Your bravery and skill... Compensation will be forthcoming. You can leave a forwarding address with Ash, and I will see to it upon my return to Baiseen." I give a slight bow.

"Compensation isn't necessary."

"You saved our lives and got us to Aku on time."

"And you're welcome, but I didn't do it for the coin." He sits at the little side table. "Cup of tea?"

"We have blackberry leaf," Ash says. "And Ochee! Has Belair noticed? It should make him happy."

"Or this." Kaylin picks up a small jar, unscrews the lid, and sniffs. "Smells like summer."

"Whatever's in the pot's fine." I feel the irritation creeping in again. They seem so…together. I'll have to ask Ash where this is heading.

Why? She's done nothing wrong.

I can't believe this. On the topic of Ash, my phantom has so much to say? "*Never mind.*"

"Come, sit down." Ash takes a seat and motions me to do the same while Kaylin makes the tea.

I lean toward Ash and speak under my breath. "Maybe we should talk in private?"

"Why? Kaylin's in this, too, remember?"

Since when?

Since he killed his crewmates, fought off the Aturnians, rescued you from the Ferus River, got us safely to Aku…as you just stated. De'ral speaks as if I have lost those memories. For a moment, maybe I had.

I rub my head. "You're both right, of course."

"Both?" Ash studies my face. "You feeling well?"

I wave the concern away. I'm not myself, it seems. Ash is my best friend, the person closest to me, the one I can always confide in. She'd laugh if she could hear my inner thoughts just now.

De'ral grunts.

Kaylin pours a mug of tea and makes himself comfortable on the settee under the window.

"So, sharing a room?" I'm stuck on this arrangement, it seems.

Ash lets her breath out in a little laugh. "As I was trying to tell you, Kaylin and I are the only visiting non-savants. It's customary to put us together."

"How together *is* that?" It's out before I can stop it. Internally, De'ral rolls his eyes.

Ash does the same thing. "I know the protocol, if that's what you're worried about. But I want someone here with me. This room, for all its finery, is full of tapping and shadows in the dark." She shudders.

The trip was traumatizing for everyone, I see. "We're all a little jumpy."

"Understandable, after what it took to get here." Kaylin's tone is serious.

I nod. Speaking of that… "Have either of you heard Aturnian accents here? Northern, specifically?"

"A green-robe, Northern for sure," Ash says. "And also there's an orange-robe instructor, but she's been teaching at Aku for years, according to Samsen."

"I met the green-robe on the way from the infirmary. Destan. He says he's from the south. I can't tell for sure, though." I tap the table with my fingertip, thinking. "Could the ban have been lifted?"

"I wondered, too, so I asked Master Huewin, the head library keeper, about it."

"And?"

"He said Aku keeps its doors open to all the realms *but* Northern Aturnia. It's being sanctioned right now, like we thought."

"Which doesn't explain why we're hearing the Northern Aturnian dialect." Kaylin tops up my tea even though I've had only a sip. "Drink."

"So it is Northern?" I pick up my mug. Holding it calms the storm in my head. "Then they've broken the ban."

"I don't think so," Ash says. "Not directly. Kaylin has a theory."

I give the sailor my full attention. I'm going to have to thank him for this as well, no doubt.

"What if the Northern Aturnians are shipping their green-robes south, sending them to Aku from Clearwater, or even Gleemarie?"

"Passing them off as Southern Aturnians?" It's a good strategy, from their side. Simple enough, too, I imagine. "But High Savant Yuki would know, wouldn't she?"

Kaylin walks to the window and stares into the night. "You'd think so. I'd be careful there."

"Agreed." I drink my tea down in a few glugs, admitting to myself that having Kaylin here isn't a bad idea. "We should avoid speaking fully of the incident on the headlands or the brush with the Aturnians' encampment when we report to her."

"Brush?" Kaylin toasts me with his mug.

"I'm trying to avoid words like 'massacre.'"

Ash's eyes go wide. "Are you saying for me not to record it?"

"I'm saying we need to be on guard with the savants here, Yuki included." I look to Kaylin for help.

"I think he's right, at least until we know who to trust," Kaylin says.

Funny, coming from him.

"Then what will we tell Yuki?" Ash looks unconvinced. "The alliance with Gollnar and Aturnia needs to be reported, even if those scouts were mercenaries. Your wounds and poor condition must be explained, too. Belair took an arrow, you a knife to the chest, all the bruising… I won't lie."

"I'm not asking you to. We say that we were put off at Clearwater, got lost in the woods, went the long way around, and had a mishap on the Ferus River. All true."

Kaylin snorts. "A mishap? That's even better than 'brush.'"

I manage to laugh with him. "We can say we slipped past an encampment sporting multiple realm flags. But we don't mention the details, including the theft at the Capper Point sheep farm. Not yet."

"We're going to compensate the farmer," Ash reminds me. She folds her hands together and closes her eyes, a habit she has when thinking deeply.

Kaylin's about to speak, and I signal him to wait.

Moments later, her eyes pop open and she gives us a nod. "For now, we say we evaded them, which is true. No one has access to what I'm recording, not even the High Savant, until I hand it all over for her seal at the end." She levels her gaze on mine. "I won't fabricate the records, Marcus, but this will give us time to get to the bottom of the Northern Aturnian mystery." She narrows her eyes at the window. "And my tapping shadow."

I rub my forehead to cover the cringe. "So, you will put everything in the records?"

Her eyes come back gleaming, and I know that look, too.

"Are you kidding? The most chac'n nang perilous initiation journey in the history of the realms and *I'm* the recorder. You bet your life it's all going in."

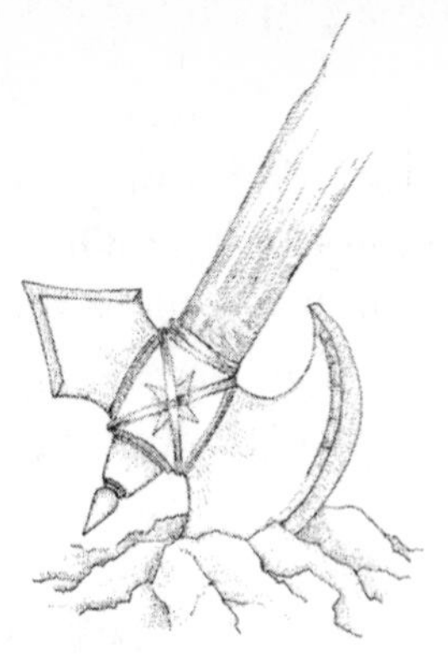

33

MARCUS

Yuki's reception room is larger than Brogal's, with wide east-facing windows overlooking a landscaped garden. The morning sun blasts in, and I drop my eyes to the floor, studying the knotty hardwood. I quickly correct my bad posture, straightening up, eyes forward to show respect, not that it matters. Yuki isn't paying attention to me in the slightest.

Belair stands on my right and Ash on the left. Kaylin's not here, and I actually miss his ability to make the ridiculous sound plausible. But again, it doesn't matter. The High Savant of Aku, a mature woman, both graceful and attractive, with golden skin and silver hair woven into a braid that falls past her waist, is completely preoccupied. With what—who knows? I'm ready with my rehearsed explanation for the raising of our phantoms and obvious wounds, but her mind seems realms away.

Meanwhile, Ash weaves a riveting story—one that has no mention of black sails, marauders, or our capture by Gollnars in league with an Aturnian horde. It does speak the truth, though, which means Father and the Tangeen Magistrate will be informed of the unexpected alliance of realms. The story also tells of our evasion and tumble over the falls.

She's a wordsmith, De'ral reminds me.

"A very good one."

But Yuki appears bored. While Ash talks, the High Savant's eyes remain on a scroll. Every so often she ticks something off that may or may not have anything to do with us. Beside her is a phantom that looks like a pyramid of rocks. It has no face but breathes, occasionally tilting its "head" or whatever that is that sits on top. A few pebbles roll down its side and spill across the floor toward Ash's foot.

She shoos them back and they retreat, but Yuki doesn't notice that odd exchange, either.

When Ash's narrative ends, the High Savant lifts her gaze. "And you came by ship from Toretta to Capper Point?"

The muscles in my neck cord. Is she not listening at all?

Ash stays serene and repeats herself, as if it were the first time. "The captain insisted we disembark at Clearwater, Mistress. But we had a guide with us, otherwise, I doubt we would have escaped the dangers on the road, made it through the woods, and down the river."

"Oh, yes, your guide. Kaylin, is it?" Yuki's face brightens for the first time since we walked through the door.

I frown. Bored with us, but the sailor sparks her interest?

"Kaylin's—"

"A remarkable young man." Yuki beams and her phantom quivers.

I clench my fists then force them to relax. How did Kaylin gain an audience before we did? And why?

"I met him in the kitchens at dawn." It's as if she heard my query. "I love a man who rises before the sun."

"Belair and I are up at dawn, ready to—"

"He's brought in quite a catch today. We'll be having trevally at my table tonight." Her expression is almost whimsical and the phantom hums. "Poached in coconut milk and cilantro, the traditional way of his mother's people in the islands."

Well, if Kaylin's made such a stellar first impression, maybe he'll put in a good word for us.

"Please, continue." Yuki waves at Ash. "From Clearwater you hired another ship..." Her eyes go back to the scroll.

I keep the groan from escaping my throat. Mother of all Bone Throwers, will she pay attention?

"Not another ship, Mistress." Ash describes again how we disembarked at Clearwater, moved the horses down the ramp, sought the apothecary. "From Clearwater we went through the woods, diverted to Mount Bladon to avoid a large troop of Northern Aturnians. Our travel documents were in order, but Marcus deemed it best to err on the side of caution."

Yuki glances at me for a moment, her expression doubtful. I'm counting the moments until this interview is over and we can get out on the training field. There's so much to catch up on. I understand now my father's impatience. If war is imminent, we *must* prepare, but not provoke.

Ash continues to regale Yuki with our journey. "Then it was straight down the Ferus River and on to Capper Point..."

Yuki's head lifts toward Ash, and the scroll she was studying so intently falls from her hand. It moves in slow motion, tumbling end over end until it hits the floor. Her phantom undulates in and out of various forms, and Yuki holds up her hand to stop even my breath. "What did you say?" Her eyes turn from Ash to Belair, to me.

I clear my throat. "It was a roundabout way to arrive, I know—"

"Say the route!" Her phantom fragments, large rocks falling down its sides only to reform again at the top.

My scalp prickles. Now that I have the High Savant's full attention, I wish she would go back to ignoring us. "It was through the woods to Mount Bladon, and down the Ferus River, Mistress. We survived the falls but lost our horses and gear. We hiked to Capper Point in the night, hired a sloop, and arrived at the docks of Aku after the first bell. We ran like fiends to make the gate."

Yuki says nothing, her brow creased as she studies each of us again.

When I can't stand the silence any longer, I add, "We had less than a second to spare."

"Over the falls?" the High Savant says. "All of you?"

We're back to this again?

"All but Belair, High Savant," Ash speaks up as I nod. "The rest of us were swept away."

"Sank like stones, I'm afraid." Suddenly I want her to smile again, talk about Kaylin's fishing, anything else. "Only Ash and Belair can swim. And Kaylin, of course."

"But I was injured." Belair finds his voice in the void. "Kaylin got me to the banks, and I hiked down."

"But Marcus? You actually went over the falls?"

"Yes, Mistress." I explain about the ferry and the rope Kaylin secured, how it went slack, but Yuki doesn't appear to be listening anymore. She sweeps the scroll up from the floor and calls out. Her assistant runs in, a panicky look on her face. They have a short, hushed conversation before the assistant hurries away, the door left swinging on its hinges. Yuki turns back to us. "You may go."

Wait, what? My mouth opens to speak but attendants come to escort us out.

"Thank you, Mistress," I say as the door closes behind us. Words she doesn't hear. When we reach the tree-lined boulevard, we stop.

"What just happened?" Ash's eyes are round.

"The mention of the Ferus River Falls caused quite a reaction." I keep my voice low.

"Strangest interview I've ever had." Belair stares toward the field, bouncing on his toes. "And now we're late for training."

"You go. I'll catch up." I turn to Ash. "You were perfect in there."

"I was— " Ash stops talking while a group of local, Aku blue-robes approach. Their instructor, a yellow-robe savant with a phantom like a sheepdog, is herding them along. When they are out of range, she continues. "I thought I would be backed into a corner, but she didn't ask for a single detail, except for the route and the Falls." Ash pushes hair out of her face and reties her ponytail. It stays in for once. "Is this her normal manner? Are we making too much of it?" She stops in front of the library. "Maybe she's like this all the time."

"Disinterested, abrupt, panicky? I don't think so." I give her a quick hug. "We'll talk about it later. I have training."

"You don't want me on the field after warm up?"

I shrug one shoulder. "They won't ask for much on my first day."

"I don't know, Marcus. It might be straight into it. The other recorders— "

"Give us a day to orient before you scrutinize our every move." My cheek quivers when I try to smile.

"Sounds good." Ash smooths the cowl of my robe and heads up the steps. "Luck of the bones be with you." She waves.

I wave back, but a cloud comes over me when I think of Yuki and the look on her face. For a moment, I could swear she was terrified, but by what?

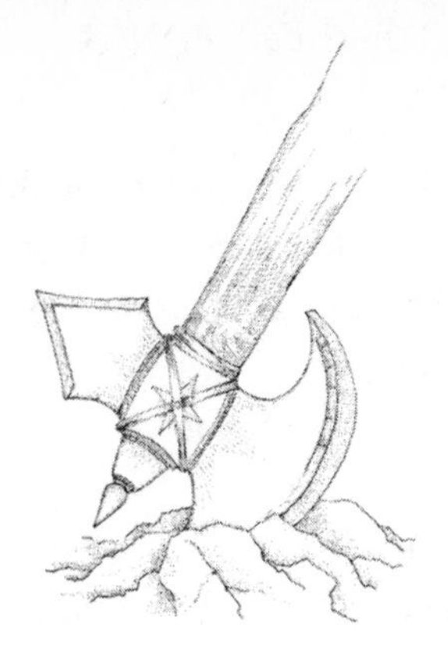

34

MARCUS

I exhale puffs of air as I run to the training field. Is there hope of getting there in time? I have to weave around spectators, jumping every so often to see over their heads and across the field. Students cluster in small groups, but I can't tell which instructor is Zarah. She's the orange-robe we're meant to report to. I search for Belair and his bright red locks. And Destan. He said he was with Zarah, too. But I don't spot either of them.

I stop to gape at two raptor phantoms in aerial combat. They dive and spiral, fighting hard, until one plummets to the ground. I shoulder my way to the edge of the field, dodging a free-for-all wrestling match, then jog past a group of sweet-voiced *callers*.

"Belair!" There he is. I sprint, feeling much stronger than last night.

The closer I get, the more I can tell Belair is struggling. The orange-robe instructor fires orders while the Tangeen tries to comply. Tries and… fails. He's doing push-ups while his phantom leaps over him but he ends up flat on his face after only a few. His vivid red hair hangs lank with sweat. The leopard pants, tongue nearly on the ground.

"Back into line!" Zarah shouts. She's one of the finest warrior savants on Aku and hard as Northern Aturnian granite, everyone says. Seems they're right.

I shoot Belair a compassionate look and turn to Zarah, ready to introduce myself. She doesn't give me the chance.

"And here is Marcus Adicio of Baiseen." All heads turn to me.

"Yes, Mistress." I know the tone she is taking. My father's quite fond of it. Brogal, too. "I can explain my tardiness."

While she studies me, her ropy, muscled *warrior* phantom with a keen blade and skin as deep brown as her own looks on. "Sleep in, did you?"

"No. I—"

"Don't want to hear it." Zarah rests her hands on her hips as spirals of black and gray hair sway across her shoulders. "You'll be told this once only, so listen well. On the Isle of Aku, field training begins at third bell. You either be here on time, or I get a message from the infirmary saying you're stone-cold dead. There are no other options."

"Uh…yes, Mistress."

"Seeing as you don't appear dead, you've nothing to say."

I stifle my next reply.

"Don't stand there, green-robe. Show us what you've got!"

I hesitate, heat reaching my cheeks. Her reference to the color of my robe is not complimentary. I can hardly believe my ears.

"Did you hear me? Raise. Your. Phantom!"

Straight into it, then. All right. I take a deep breath before dropping gracefully to one knee and then the other. I sit on the heels of my sandaled feet, straighten my robe in neat, pleated folds around me, and lace my hands in my lap. After a few deep breaths, I let my eyelids float shut.

"Stop!" Zarah jolts me with a shriek. "What do you think you're doing?"

"Preparing to raise my phantom, Mistress." Isn't it obvious?

Some of the students laugh and she silences them with a look. "And where did you learn to do that?"

"In the Sanctuary of Baiseen, Mistress." My chin lifts as I enunciate my home city. "The High Savant Brogal has us—" She cuts me off and I see my mistake too late.

"So, you do it that way in *Baiseen*, do you? *Master Brogal* knows best when it comes to *warriors*?"

I start to sweat. "Um…"

"Let me tell you something. He doesn't." She takes a breath. "And how do I know he doesn't? I trained by his side at our initiation rites, so many years ago. Do you know what they called him then?"

I have a feeling I don't want to hear this. "No, Mistress."

"Baiseen." Her mouth twists like she just licked the bottom of a stable hand's boot. "And he was called that until he could finally…" Her expression softens for an instant. "Never mind, Baiseen." The twisted face is back.

My nostrils flare. She dares to malign Palrio's capital city, the seat of my throne? "Mistress, I assure you, I meant—"

"I know what you meant but answer me this." She directs her question to the entire group. "In a real battle, how much time will you have to place yourself thus on the ground, making everything just so before you coax your phantom up?"

I bite my lower lip, my mind going back to the last time I raised my phantom—bound and battered at the bottom of a cliff. "In a real battle situation, none."

"Congratulations, Baiseen. You've given your first correct response of the day. We can only hope there will be more to follow. Observe." She holds out her hands and her phantom returns the sword with a bow.

The entire group scurries back. Even the recorders pick up their writing boards and retreat, leaving me alone at the front. I'm still sitting on my heels when Mistress Zarah takes a step forward and dips briefly so one knee touches the ground. Instantly, her phantom melts into the earth and she darts ten paces away in a blink.

"*This* is how you raise a *warrior*." Without another word, she leaps into the air, lets loose a battle cry, and comes down hard on both knees, skidding along the grass. The moment she contacts the ground her phantom erupts in front of her—a fountain of dirt and rocks exploding. Zarah unsheathes her twin blades and flips them, hilts held high. The phantom shoots up, somersaults, grabs the weapons, and continues the war cry in a deep, guttural tone. Before Zarah skids to a halt, she is back on her feet and running straight for me.

It takes all my strength not to flinch.

Zarah stops just short of plowing me under. She has a knife to my throat, and her phantom's swords are at my back. De'ral surges, making my head pound.

"Now, Baiseen," she says. "Your turn."

The phantom behind me steps back, and so does Zarah. They must have heard about the size of my *warrior*. I smile to myself. *"We'll show them."* I prepare mentally, without the props of position or meditation.

"Now!" Zarah shouts.

"Be ready," I say to De'ral.

And jump because that spindly phantom's savant says so?

My gut tightens. *"No, jump because I say so. Please?"*

I sprint several lengths away, turn and leap into the air. My war cry comes out a little high-pitched and strained to my ears, but I carry on, letting go my thoughts as I fall to my knees. I thud hard into the closely cropped grass and close my eyes. Nothing happens.

"Damn the bones, De'ral. Rise!"

"Does he have a phantom?" Someone from the group calls.

"Hand him a rope and he can haul it up," says another.

"Too weak to break through the ground?" a girl mocks.

I grind my teeth.

"Let it out," Zarah says evenly. "A timely fashion is preferable." Her words cut deep but the tone is actually supportive.

As my emotions well, the ground shakes.

"Eyes open," Zarah says. "You have to see the thing to control it."

I open my eyes as the ground rips apart. The group presses closer, all but Belair and his leopard. As the cracks lengthen, the faces of the students change. The teasing expressions turn to awe as a giant fist punches through the earth. They recede like a wave, and De'ral pulls himself up. He shakes like a wet dog, dirt flying, and stands to his full height, taller by three times anything on the field. Suddenly, Belair has company along the far edge of the grass.

"Stand up," Zarah shouts. As I gain my feet, she darts in and whispers, "You be ready to bring that monster to ground or my phantom will knock you unconscious, understand?"

"Yes, Mistress."

"What's everyone waiting for?" she hollers to the others. "Second lap, at the run."

I watch them take off, savants with phantoms beside or behind, running the perimeter of the field. I fall in after Belair, who gives me a sympathetic look.

At first, I think we'll make it, because De'ral and I are in sync, me running, him jogging with thunderous steps. We pace with Belair and his sun leopard but fall behind the others. I actually pass Belair at one point when the Tangeen stops to call his leopard down from a fringing tree. A bevy of doves launch skyward from the branches along with a chorus of laughter from onlooking students. Belair's face turns as red as his hair. We plow on, the gap between us and the next-to-last student in our group increasing. Near the end, we're lapped. *"Come on, De'ral. We're going around again."*

Destan, the Aturnian green-robe, overtakes us. He and his sword-wielding phantom fly along at a fast clip. I wonder if it has other skills besides fighting, with its huge eyes and long limbs. I pant and blow as Destan sprints by.

"Don't worry. You'll be up to speed soon," Destan calls over his shoulder. But his phantom makes unintelligible grunts and gurgles that sound a lot like laughter.

My shoulders hunch inward, hearing the laughter again in my head. Before I can control my emotion, De'ral takes two huge strides toward Destan's phantom. Suddenly, I'm fully in my phantom's perspective, staring down at the creature. It turns with its sword overhead.

My heart races. *"No, De'ral. He's not an enemy!"* Not here on Aku anyway, and not during the elimination trials.

De'ral isn't listening. He raises his fists, ready to bring them down and flatten the Aturnian's phantom like a pancake. My only recourse is to call De'ral in, but before I can, he trips over his own feet and smashes to the ground. The jolt snaps the perspective back into my own head. I stop, doubled over, desperate for air.

Belair and his leopard catch up, both panting as hard as I am.

"Did you see?" I ask.

"Your phantom fell flat on his face, Marcus. Everyone on the field saw."

"Not that," I grumble. "Before." I wipe sweat from my brow. "Did you see what he was about to do?"

Belair pulls at my sleeve. "No. Now come on, Marcus! Run."

I stagger after him. *"Keep up,"* I tell De'ral as he gains his feet. *"And no fighting."* I draw in deep breaths and try to catch up to Belair. *"No taking the bait. That goes for both of us."*

Students' faces blur as I run by. The footfalls of my phantom pound hard, and we are given plenty of room. At the home stretch, I start to smile to myself, until I glance over my shoulder. My phantom has fallen way behind.

"De'ral. What are you doing?"

He stops completely.

"Crack the bones, keep running!" I try to slip inside his perspective, but the way is closed. Could this go any worse?

Meanwhile, my phantom stares into the distance. He takes a few steps toward the main Sanctuary buildings, and the savants below scatter out of the way. The others in my group lap me again, running past us without taking much notice. *"Come on, De'ral. We look like idiots."*

But my phantom doesn't budge. I find a chink and push into his perspective, it's like sticking my head into a room but not being able to cross the threshold. From De'ral's sharp vision I see what is so damn fascinating. Across the field and over one street is the library with its high bell tower. A tiny figure stands in a second story window, watching the field. *"Ash?"*

De'ral points.

I swallow bile and catch my breath. This is just great. He's paying more attention to my recorder than to me. *"She's not the one to listen to."*

I like what she says.

"Stop it!" I shout at him. *"Run!"*

De'ral turns to me. *Ash is watching.*

"Of course, she's watching us. That's her job. Now please, let's give her something worth her time and quill."

Slowly, he breaks into a jog, then a sprint, gaining on me fast. Now I have to dash to stay ahead, overtaking Belair and his sun leopard, who are flagging as well.

By the time I reach the starting point, I drop to the ground, keeping my meditative position out of sheer willpower. I would much rather be sprawled on my back, gasping for air, but pride prevents it. Plus, Zarah's ridicule.

Maybe De'ral will step on me and put an end to the humiliation.

"Glad you could join us, Baiseen, Tangeen." Zarah bends over to peer down her nose at us. "You'd best build up your stamina fast. Those who aren't showing promise by the end of the week are out."

Like I need the reminder.

She straightens and addresses the group. "Obstacle course. Look sharp."

The students take off at a run, all but me and Belair. I stumble, face set forward, trusting that De'ral will follow. *"Please follow…"* Belair looks like he's going to cry. I know how he feels.

We trail the others to the far side of the training field to the series of physical tests—twin obstacle courses, side by side with climbing, swinging, jumping, hand-over-hand, running, crawling, balancing, and a water component. Belair and I exchange a look. It's not optimistic.

Zarah projects her voice over the field. "For the benefit of the southern realms"—she glances at me and Belair—"the obstacle course is used in my class to familiarize you with tactical movements, increase combat endurance, build physical strength, and most importantly, reinforce collaboration with your phantom. You must take the course together, side by side. Not all of you will be able to achieve each segment with your phantoms up, not at first." She turns again to me. "But I promise you, no one leaves the Isle of Aku as a yellow-robe until they can complete this exercise to my satisfaction."

Just knowing the number of savants at home who had journeyed to Aku and successfully earned their robes gives me courage. Then again, I'm the only one to raise a *warrior* among them, so they probably never had an instructor the likes of Zarah, but I prefer to think positively.

"Notice the mix of obstacles," Zarah continues. "There is a climb-over/crawl-under challenge. Do not skip the second step. Balance is demonstrated here." She points at the beam. "Don't forget the water on either side is head high. If you fall, you will have to swim out and go back to the start. If you can't swim..."

My ears prick.

"Learn how." Zarah cocks her head and smiles as if enjoying a memory. "After the rope-net climb and grapple wall, there is a 'no touch' tunnel. I promise you those barbs are razor sharp."

I study the situation and see a problem immediately, at least for Belair. I raise my hand. Zarah ignores it.

"Some of your phantoms may not be suited for every obstacle. In that case, you are to direct them to the side, off course, where they will perform a series of combat moves, rolls, and lunges, while you carry on. Those of you with mixed-class phantoms, I want to see both alternate. No favoring just because one comes easier. Have your phantom rejoin you at the next suitable obstacle. Don't worry about speed today. That will come with time. Destan, take the lead. Show us how it's done. Cyres is next. The rest of you can line up. Begin!"

It's good she doesn't make me go first, or second. It gives me a few moments to recover. De'ral sits down, looking over his shoulder toward the library.

"Can you at least pretend you're interested?"

He turns toward me, sulky.

I don't know how it can get worse. Maybe Zarah will have some advice for me. While I muse on that possibility, I watch Destan go through his paces. He and his small, agile, disciplined phantom are a tight team as they run the course with no faults.

When he returns he pats my back as he walks by. "Don't worry. You'll get it."

It gives me hope. It also gives me perspective. He may be Northern Aturnian, but he's not so different from me. We're both here to learn and train, to earn our robes. Ash has said many times that change comes from communication. Maybe it begins with me and Destan. With our generation.

"Cyres." Zarah points at the girl. "Next."

Cyres is a stocky young woman. I look at her and think strong. Like a tree. No coincidence, her phantom is an agahpa—gnarled tree-like joints, long fingers and toes. It's the height of Cyres, with skin like bark and black knots for eyes. The legs don't seem to separate much, and it moves about like a spider, darting and hesitating and darting again. "Hair" caps its head in tendrils similar to Larseen's ropey locks. I suspect De'ral and I will have troubles, but this phantom? I have no idea how it will make it over the first challenge.

"Go," Zarah tells the girl.

They take off, Cyres scrambling up the ladder to the platform, her phantom not far behind on its side. It turns out to be more flexible than I'd guessed. They make a promising team until Cyres loses her grip on the rope mid-swing and splashes into the pool, her head going under. The phantom immediately swings to her side of the course, wraps its long toes around the horizontal ladder, and drops a branchy arm down to the muddy pool to rescue the savant.

Cyres coughs and sputters while her phantom pats her on the back.

"Sit this round out, Cyres. You can try again when you recover." Zarah turns to the start line. "Baiseen, you're next."

The students give me plenty of room and there is no jeering this time, not within earshot of Zarah, anyway. "Direct your phantom to jog, keeping up with you on the sideline. That'll be enough of a challenge for today, I think."

I think so, too.

"Go."

I climb the ladder, grab the rope, and swing.

"Move him with you!" Zarah shouts.

I swing to the platform, but De'ral still sits on the grass like a sullen child. *"Run with me,"* I command. *"Don't make us look any worse than we already do."*

My phantom grudgingly rises, but the rope swings back toward him and he catches it in his hand. *"Wait! Let go of the rope!"*

He doesn't. Instead, he takes off. It pulls tight, and he uproots the horizontal bars on his side of the course.

"De'ral! Stop!"

He listens! Finally. But when he comes to a sudden halt, the broken bars slap his back, sending him careening forward. He smashes down into the mud pool, splashing everyone within a twenty-foot radius, which is me, the entire class, and plenty of onlookers. In water up to his waist, he thrashes, knocking the balance beam off its supports as he tries to wipe mud out of his eyes. He manages to pull himself out of the pool, but then slips, and plows straight into the rappel wall.

The entire structure creaks, teeters, and falls over, crushing the no-touch thorn-crawl flat.

"Look out!"

De'ral's hands come down on the springboard to regain balance, but he slips and grabs the large ring, which immediately breaks off. The weight of him falls full force onto the shimmy pole and snaps it in half like a toothpick. Finally, he gains his feet again and manages to stand upright. Before I can contain him, he takes off, dragging bits of the obstacle course behind him.

"Stop!" I shout aloud this time as he reaches the end. *"Wait there. I'll catch up."* Determined to finish, I go hand over hand to the beam. I don't hear a word from Zarah, so with my phantom standing quietly, the balancing test isn't too hard. I manage it, avoid near drowning in the deep water below—somehow, I don't think De'ral would be so quick to rescue me as Cyres's phantom had been—and rappel down the wall. What remains of the thorn obstacle isn't much of a challenge. Petén and I used to spend plenty of time in the brambles, searching for lost arrows behind the practice range when we were younger. I climb the rope ladder to a springboard, launch, miss the ring, and fall flat.

No one laughs. They are all staring through mud-covered faces at the ruined obstacle course. I struggle to my feet and climb back up to the springboard.

"Enough." Zarah strides over to me.

I can't see a scrap of orange fabric on the front of her robe that isn't spattered in mud.

"I think we have a fair bit of work cut out for us, wouldn't you say?" She doesn't let me answer. "Pair up for sparring," she orders the others.

When I drop to my knees and bring De'ral in, I'm not sure I'll ever stand again. But I manage and make to stagger back to the group. "Not you, Baiseen."

"Mistress?"

"You're with me."

35

ASH

"Oh, Marcus." It's a panoramic view from the library tower and what a mess. He and De'ral have singlehandedly demolished the obstacle course. Why didn't I stay at my desk? It's going in the record now, though as Brogal always says, when you sink to the bottom, there's only room to rise.

Marcus and Belair better rise fast.

I drag myself from the window, returning to the job of recording. The first step is to copy down the moon phases from the planetary ephemeris. In my original notes, I'd marked them from observation—up until the attack on the headland. With those records gone, the rise and set and "weight" of the moon is one of the many things to confirm and include in both Marcus's and Belair's records. I select a hawk quill and thumb over to the new moonrise, the day we left Baiseen.

"Interruption coming."

I startle and look up. "Talus?"

"Finding everything you need?"

The white-robe woman didn't make a sound coming up the stairs. Time to solve the mystery, though looking her in the eye makes me fidget.

"Yes, thank you." How to put this? "Mistress Talus…" Surely, if I misstate her name twice in as many breaths, she'll correct me.

Her calm expression doesn't change. "Something I can help with?"

My brow knits. No correction, which is odd. The last thing she looks like is a prankster.

"Actually, no. Master Huewin's supplied me with everything I need."

"Then why aren't you down there with the other recorders, taking in the events?"

I blow my bangs off my forehead. She's right. I *should* be there, recording, but happily, I've a valid excuse to be here instead, not on the field, noting every fall and stumble. "I thought I'd give Marcus and Belair a day to settle in."

"That bad?" Her lips twitch, like she's trying not to smile.

I admit, I'm a bit taken aback. "They're green-robes," I say in a rush. "They'll both be magnificent, given time." I choke on my words as a vision of Marcus's *warrior* crushing men and horses beneath him comes to mind.

Her eyes darken and she turns away. "Time is what they don't have."

I tilt my head to the side. "Pardon me, Mistress?"

Talus goes to the high arched window and I join her. "There they are."

I watch in silence. Marcus's phantom turns again toward the library, and I send a thought out to him. "*Can you pay attention to Marcus? This is a competition, remember?*"

When I turn around, I find myself alone. "Talus?"

Chills skitter down my spine as I look toward the stairwell and back up the rows of books. Nothing. If I didn't know better, I'd believe I imagined her.

What with the tapping at my window again last night, it's not a calming thought. Still, I go back to work. When I reach my desk, a book sits open on top of the stack. "Where did you come from?"

I glance around one last time for Talus. So odd.

I'm about to flip the book closed when the symbols in the middle of the page catch my eye. I trace them with my finger, exhaling long and slow. Two spirals, each spinning opposite directions, overlapping in a fancy knot. They look similar to the twin circles I've seen multiple times since the apothecary's notice in Clearwater. I frown, studying the image closer. The script looks much like what Master Brogal called Retreen, waving it off as a dead Tangeen language. Nothing but an auction list, he'd said, but in the margins of a song book about the Mar?

I check the title and see it's a Sierrak text on planets and stars; not where I'd expect to find a dead language from Tangeen. This passage actually looks like the ancient Sierrak script of the stargazers, Retoren. I don't speak it, but Kaylin pocketed the notice on the docks. I'll have to ask him.

"Ash?"

I jump. "Master Huewin."

Is everyone part cat here? The library keeper smiles down on me without showing any teeth. He's in a long orange robe, different from the quilted robes and pants the savants in training wear, but more like Yuki's. The hem brushes the floor and his cuffs cover all but his bony fingertips. "How's the recording going?" His brows rise. "Have everything you need?"

"I've made a start, thank you. The reference materials are very helpful." I smile warmly at the bookshelves surrounding me. "I'll enter my notes into the new record books next week. I so appreciate the ones you reserved for me. They're lovely."

"I know a sketch artist who might contribute to the Heir's record, and the Tangeen's as well, unless you have skills?"

My inner voice laughs, and I have to agree. "I draw like a toddler."

Master Huewin chuckles. "Then I will make the introduction."

"Appreciated. And what about maps? Since our route here was a bit off course, I would like to include one."

His smile turns brittle. "Naturally."

His uncomfortable expression makes me hesitate. Yuki reacted strongly to the Ferus River Falls. I decide to say nothing further on it, for now.

"Hali, the artist I have in mind, has cartography skills. She's well-versed in all the coastal terrain. I'll send her to you tomorrow."

"That sounds perfect."

"Is there anything else?"

I don't skip a beat. "May I trouble you with a query, Master Huewin?"

"No trouble at all. We expect recorders to use their time on Aku to the best of their advantage."

I smile with my mouth closed as well. "I'm confused about a language."

"Which one?"

"Retreen. I might have it confused with the old Sierrak Retoren."

He remains placid, save for a twitch above his right eye. "Though they sound similar, Retreen is a Tangeen tongue, used mostly for commerce. Retoren is a poetic and spiritual language of the Sierrak savants." His brow knits. "Why do you ask?"

"Is this Retreen?" I show him the script in the planetary text.

"Where did you find this book?"

"On my desk. I thought you put it there for me." My words tumble out. "It matches a bit of script Master Brogal identified for me as Retreen."

"What script?"

I cough to stall. Brogal mustn't be incriminated. He's done so much for me, but I'm not sure how to back out of this now. "I came across a scroll, a snippet really. It turned out to be a list, a manifest of cattle—"

"According to whom?"

"High Savant Brogal." What else can I say? "I thought he said it was Retreen but…" I am talking too much, unable to stop. "I guess I was confused and heard him wrong," I finish lamely.

Huewin taps his thumb on his temple, an odd gesture. "This is neither, but a tongue from Gollnar, no longer in use."

"Is it? My mistake." Except it's not.

"Don't worry. You have much to learn. For a student your age, you're doing well."

The hairs on the nape of my neck bristle. Why are these masters sending me around in circles? "And what would Retoren look like, exactly? You make it sound so interesting. I would love to see."

"What it looks like, exactly, you are not ranked high enough to know." He presses his lips together, no smile. "Keep studying, Ash, and on your next journey here you may be advanced far enough along the path to read such scripts." Huewin frowns at my turquoise robes. "Ah, but I forget. You're non-savant, and here only by the grace of the Baiseen Magistrate. It's doubtful you'll return to these halls in this lifetime."

"Charming man, this librarian."

Unlike my inner voice, I lack the patience for sarcasm. And I'm liking the master librarian less and less. "But would I be able to see the language script, for inspiration? I wouldn't read it—how could I—but just to know that I've viewed it would be such a motivation along the path." I pour it on thick like honey, though I'm so angry I could choke. *Only here by the grace of the Magistrate?* Well, it's true, but my skills are not what's lacking.

Huewin makes a great show of deliberating. "Very well. I can authorize a glimpse, under supervision, but it will mean nothing to you, except symbolically. Retoren takes much time and dedication to learn. There are seventy-two letters in its alphabet, and the conjugations are extensive, each verb having multiple aspects of gender, phantom, mood, color. As I said, it's for those much further along the path." Huewin walks to the other side of the bookcase and I follow, resisting the urge to stick my tongue out behind his back.

He takes a key from a ring on his pocket chain and opens a glass case. "This is Retoren as written by the savants of the High Sierrak Plains." He unrolls the parchment with great care. "I am not allowed to translate it for you, and please don't mention to anyone you had this glimpse." He holds his brittle smile in place. "It will be our secret."

Caterpillars crawl under my skin, but I turn my focus to the old scroll. Immediately, the edges catch my eye. What I'm looking at can't be Sierrak anything. "Beautiful," I say aloud while scrutinizing the papyrus.

It's from Gollnar, ancient Gollnar, hence it being under glass, I imagine. There is no way it can have fallen into Sierrak hands or originated there. I'm certain because, up until several hundred years ago, the Gollnarians took an extra step in the preparation of the pulp for their writings; they added a "secret" ingredient, chenopodia, a beet-like bulb growing only in the wild, now extinct from overharvesting. Chenopodia produced papyrus less prone to wrinkling.

It also left a faint mauve hue at the edges, like this one before me has.

My scroll-crafting instructor at Baiseen was from Gollnar, and she showed us just where to look to identify these antiquated texts. With the age of this scroll and the time periods involved in the use of chenopodia, it is not what Huewin claims. Sierrak and Gollnar didn't communicate in that era. By the time they did, chenopodia was no more.

"Now you have seen Retoren. Keep it to yourself."

"I will, but master, this is from a savant sect in Sierrak, correct?" I have to be sure I haven't misunderstood.

"Exactly. It is used only to teach the deepest of spiritual knowledge." He speaks as if the notion of "spiritual knowledge" is far beyond my comprehension.

And who knows? Maybe he's right, but if I had more of that "spiritual knowledge," I wouldn't use it to shame those who had less. "Hmmm," I say aloud, trying to sound reverent.

Huewin rolls up the scroll before I can take a second look, but I catch enough familiar words—flood, rain, famine—to make an educated guess. It reads like an account of the *Time of the Floods*, a story told by all the realms in slightly different ways. No secret spiritual mystery here. I'm guessing age is the only reason it's under lock and key.

"Now, Ash, with your curiosity sated, I will leave you to your work." He turns and retreats down the stairs.

I'm left standing alone on the second floor, completely mystified. After a long search through the library card filing system, I make my way to the very top level of the tower and into a room called "Ancient References." There I find the dictionary I'm after. It has a single mention of Retoren:

Reto-rene

1. of or pertaining to the ancient Retorie stargazers of northern Sierrak.

2. any obscure and seldom written language. Abbreviation: Rt, RT.

3. the language used by the founders of the Sierrak Planetary Guild including the Brothers of Anon. Abbreviations: BOA.

I blink and read again. "Brothers of Anon?" From the fabled Sanctuary of Avon Eyre? The one surrounded by ice at the top of the world? Could it be real?

The more I uncover, the more information I seem to need.

My mood brightens. There's a certain crafty someone who might join my cause, and I shall try to recruit him tonight. But the mirth fades when I gaze out the narrow tower window overlooking the field. Far below, the entire training grounds is in ruins. "Oh, Marcus. This isn't good."

36

MARCUS

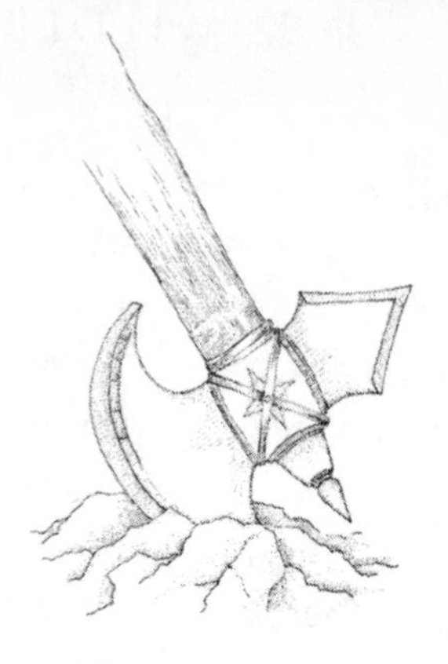

I face off again with Mistress Zarah. I'm worried for the woman. Orange-robe or no, De'ral is dangerous and, even though she and I understand perfectly well we are sparring for practice, I can't say the same for my phantom. "Mistress, I have little control, as you have seen. There might—"

"You think we can't outwit your brute?" Zarah brushes dried mud from her sleeves. "Relax, Marcus. This is training. If you keep that in mind, your phantom will, too."

"But that's just it. My—"

Zarah raises her brow. "You contradict me?"

"No, Mistress."

"Good. Let's continue."

She shows me a new sequence of moves in rapid succession—punch, block, kick, retreat, and then repeat, which I learn quickly, but when applied to De'ral, it's not so smooth. I raise my hand to say I'm not ready, but Zarah calls, "Attack."

Before I can gather my wits, Zarah flips me on my back and drops with an elbow strike to my chest. Her phantom runs circles around De'ral, keeping him contained, though there are some mighty fist blows as he pounds the ground, a giant swatting at a fly. No matter what the big *warrior* does, Zarah's phantom has no problem evading him. When it becomes comical, Zarah calls a halt. My face is hot to the touch, my teeth ready to crack with how tightly I'm clenching my jaw.

"Let's go over the basics again, shall we? Once they become routine for you, we'll work on him." She tilts her head toward De'ral.

And then her phantom runs up, executes a double somersault, and ends with a flying kick that stops just short of my face. "I've much to learn," I admit.

Not me.

De'ral snatches up Zarah's phantom by the nape of the neck, holding it out like a smelly sock.

"Stop! Put the instructor's phantom down." All eyes are on me, including Zarah's.

"Tell it to let go," she says, her voice vibrating through the air.

I push into De'ral's perspective with every intention of following our instructor's command, but the moment my eyes look down on the suspended thing that has taunted and teased, I realize De'ral isn't the only one who wants to squash the little *warrior* like a bug. It takes every drop of my willpower to detach and say, *"Put it down before you have us thrown out on the spot."*

De'ral lets go, from quite a height.

"Not like that," I say aloud.

Zarah's phantom falls but does a perfect roll and lands on its feet. It cuts back, pulls two spears from the weapons rack and charges, ready to launch toward De'ral's head.

Zarah ignores it. "If you can't gain better control than this, Baiseen, you'll be going home without your yellow robes."

I groan inside while De'ral catches up the spears and snaps them in half. "It's yours that's out of control now." I point to it, knowing I'm being childish. "Do something!"

She crosses her arms. "You may speak to your instructors in Baiseen like that, but you will not get away with it here."

My head pounds and I shout to hear myself over the throbbing. "In *Baiseen*, I am the Heir to the throne and command a measure of respect." Spittle flies from my mouth. "It's just common courtesy for my rank."

"Your rank?" Her face turns hard. "On the Isle of Aku, rank is earned, not handed down a line of succession. I assure you, it will not be earned by arguing with me."

My head explodes, and all reason flies away. Our phantoms brawl nearby, tearing up the grass, kicking and punching, pounding and snarling. De'ral swings and stomps, trying to mash Zarah's phantom like a potato and hers is dodging blows and jabbing with two new spears. The students flow around them like a tide, keeping a safe distance while cheering and whooping. I shout to Zarah, "I can't stop him!"

"Then bring him back in!"

"We didn't start this!" The words are out before I can bite my tongue, and in the heat of the moment, I don't care.

Zarah blasts me in her native tongue with what I can only guess is a string of obscenities. Ash would know. Some I recognize as curses my recorder has used, and though she's never translated them, I can imagine they're obscene.

When I catch a glimpse of the High Savant storming our way, her bloodred robes flaring around her, I close my mouth mid-sentence and freeze. Zarah's back is turned to Yuki's, and she carries on, shouting in her native Aturnian, our phantoms still brawling behind us. The students realize who approaches and go silent, bowing their heads. Zarah finally turns to see Yuki and drops to one knee, her phantom going to ground before she stands back up again.

She clears her throat. "High Savant."

Yuki looks over the group and out into the training field. She takes in the rents and tears in the grass, the ruined obstacle course, and the mud-covered students. She motions me forward. "Your phantom did all this?" She bends over to pick up a snapped spear and examines the tip.

"Not entirely all of it, High Savant. Some was..." My voice trails off. She is staring at me in the strangest way. "Yes, Mistress Yuki. We went a little out of control."

The High Savant surprises me with a thin smile. "Thank the Deep the black-robes never got their hands on you. I can only imagine what a *warrior* you will have by the end of your stay with us."

I blink.

"Can *you* imagine it, Marcus Adicio?" Yuki asks before I sputter a response.

"Yes, High Savant."

"Good then. That is where to begin." She leans in toward Zarah. "Walk with me?"

Zarah nods and addresses all of us. "You will help the gardeners rake this field back into order."

The groan from the students isn't audible, but the mood around me thickens.

Yuki speaks up. "Order the carpenters to rebuild the obstacle course. I want it twice as high on the phantoms' side and doubly reinforced." She eyes the whole group. "Aku will accommodate every student on Amassia, including the likes of Gaveren the Great."

Everyone gasps at her comparison, and I stand taller as she points at me. Likening De'ral to a phantom literally out of legends? I savor the compliment. By the bones, I've never heard such praise from Father or

Master Brogal. Although most don't think the stories of Gaveren are actually true. "But he will not be thumping up and down the boulevards and about our meditation paths just yet, will he?"

"No, High Savant," I say and bow my head.

"For now, raise him only on the field for your daily classes or on the beach when your group does special training." Her eyes go to Belair. "It's good to see Tangeen in our midst. What a magnificent sun leopard."

Belair beams. His phantom stretches, digging its claws into the grass, its long tail curling skyward.

High Savant Yuki claps her hands. "Hop to it, all of you. I want the field pristine by the noonday bell, before any of you eat." She touches Zarah's sleeve.

"You heard the High Savant!" Zarah shouts. "Rakes are in the toolroom by the stables, wheelbarrows and water carts in the wagon shed. Take your direction from the gardeners. And make sure you cleaned up before you go near the fountain or enter the dining hall." Her eyes drift to me and Belair. "Your phantoms have seen enough of the sun for one day. Call them in."

I don't need to hear it twice. Well, I guess I do, since Zarah had asked before, but this time I lower to the ground and energy rushes in. With my phantom down, a wave of weariness replaces the heat and exhilaration, but I force myself to stay alert. I stand and we all bow to Zarah and Yuki before fanning out over the field. Some of the looks I get are not friendly, but a few are, including Destan's. That's something.

"Quite a start to our training." Belair is at my side, patting me on the back.

"Not what I was expecting."

"Do you think we'll make it through the eliminations?"

Yuki hinted at it, didn't she? "By the toss of the bones, the black-robes foresaw it."

"What were their words, exactly?" He sounds worried.

I know the phrase by heart. I cling to it. "Out of Aku, the warriors triumph, and the southern realms are changed forever."

"Promising." Belair chews on it for a moment. "Unless, when they said *warriors*, they didn't mean us."

I laugh. "Who else would they mean?"

But my smile fades and suddenly, I'm not so sure.

37

ASH

I'm at my desk, absorbed in work, when someone clears their throat.

"Kaylin!" I look up. "How long have you been there?"

His smile warms me like the sun.

"Have lunch with me?" He turns side-on to show his brimming pack. "I found a beautiful cove. You have to see it."

"*That does sound nice,*" my inner voice says.

Focus. We have a lot to do. "You're just the one I wanted to see."

"Is that a *yes*?"

"I can't go now." I wave my hand over the books stacked high around me. "I was thinking more along the lines of—"

"Ash." He stops me mid-sentence. "From what I saw of Marcus and Belair's performances this morning…"

My stomach sinks. "You saw?"

"That I did."

They *will* pass the elimination trials. They have to. That is, Marcus has to at least. "It was their first try."

"So it was." Kaylin tilts his head. "Lunch with me?"

"I don't know…" Somehow going off to a lovely cove with Kaylin while Marcus and Belair struggle seems wrong. Like I'm abandoning them. And their records. I'm responsible for them both, which is twice the work.

"You have to eat," Kaylin argues.

"True, but there's another problem. Maybe you can help?"

"Tell me." He takes a seat by my side. "Is there a conspiracy?" He lowers his voice and leans in, making me more flustered. "I would love a conspiracy, unless this is about the sounds you've been hearing at night."

"It's not that." I brush my hair back with both hands, trying to sound calm. Meanwhile, the heat in my face spreads across my chest. I want to fan myself but don't. "I need help, um…finding some reference material."

"Isn't that what the index scrolls are for?" He raises his eyes to the ceiling-high shelves of books.

"Strangely, not in this case."

He looks intrigued. "What then?"

"Remember the notice at the Capper Point harbor?"

"Aye, lass."

I clear my throat. His proximity is very distracting.

"I found the same script in a Sierrak book," I manage, "but when I asked Huewin, he led me astray, rather elaborately. Brogal did, too, in hindsight, though, in a different direction."

He folds his hands together, brows narrowing. "I don't understand."

I take a deep breath and let it out. "Before the journey, I came across a script I think might be Retoren. When I asked Brogal, he called it Retreen."

"They do sound similar."

"But in fact, they're very different. I asked Huewin to clarify, and he misled me further. Might as well have fanned smoke in my eyes. Both masters seem to be concealing something. I want to figure out what, and I want to translate this passage." I show him the Sierrak planetary text.

He glances at it briefly. "Recording the journey isn't engaging enough?"

"It's fully engaging, but this could be part of it, don't you see?" I clasp his forearm. "The tattoos on the scouts. The messages about Amassia's dark sun. This script. It could be Retoren, and if so, with a dictionary, we can translate it. Doesn't that spike your interest?"

He slides his hand over mine. "If it involves working with you, lass, I'm in. The flyer's in our room."

A different kind of warmth spreads through me. Gratitude. Excitement. Maybe both. I smile until my cheeks hurt. "We need a dictionary, and Huewin made it clear that Retoren is far too advanced for me to lay eyes on, let alone read."

Kaylin outright laughs. "Well now I'm definitely helping, if for nothing else but to prove him wrong. Though I can't believe you'd rather hunt down a lost language than eat oysters on the beach, under the autumn sun." His eyebrows dance. "Berry tarts, as well."

My mouth waters at the thought. "We can do both?"

"Aye." He turns my hand over and laces our fingers together. "Where do you think they would keep a reference book on Retoren?"

My heart stutters as his thumb strokes the back of my hand. "I don't know; that's the problem."

"How about we ask?"

"Bit of a giveaway, isn't it?"

"We don't ask about Retoren, specifically," he says. "But something similarly obscure, a dead language, or one not in common use on Aku?"

One comes quickly to mind. "Northern Aturnian?"

He nods. "With their rights to Aku suspended, the materials in that language could be archived. The library keeper may wonder what you're up to, asking for a Northern Aturnian dictionary, though."

"Not if I record it being spoken in Clearwater, on the wharf when we disembarked. I would need it for the correct translations. The records must be as accurate as possible." I squeeze his hand. "I'll wager it was spoken on the *Sea Eagle*, am I right? Let's go ask."

The main desk downstairs is busy, and we have to wait in line. When it's my turn, I step up, recognizing the girl in charge. "Mia, I'm after a Northern Aturnian dictionary."

She puts down her quill, her nose wrinkling when she lays eyes on me. "Do I know you?"

I exhale, but inwardly, I roll my eyes. "Yes. My name is Ash, recording for Marcus of Baiseen and Belair of Tangeen."

"That's right. You're the non-savant."

Kaylin raises a brow.

I hold my smile in place as her possum-like phantom jumps up to the desk and clicks toward me, nails tapping on the polished wood. Mia pulls it back but not before I receive an image of it stealing bread out of Kaylin's pack. It gives me chills, but by now I'm less surprised and less quick to call it a *coincidence*. "Northern Aturnian dictionary?" I repeat.

"Sorry." Mia shakes her head, curly hair dancing around her face.

She doesn't look sorry at all.

"You'll need to speak to Master Huewin about it. Anything else?" She returns to her work as if I've already walked on.

"Are they archived?" Kaylin steps up to the desk. He puts both palms on the surface and leans in.

Mia's face softens. "I can't say more."

"No?" He moves closer, keeping his eyes intent on hers.

He's going to *charm* her? I press my lips together and cross my arms. Does he go around charming everyone like this?

But as I watch, Kaylin's tactics work. Why wouldn't they? I've fallen for the same things every day since we met. Hopefully our interactions are more...genuine? I frown at the thought.

The quill slips out of Mia's grip as she returns his gaze. Apparently, she can say more after all. "They're in the basement, first door on the left. All restricted texts are kept there."

"Under lock and key?"

She nods stupidly.

I gaze at the ceiling and let out a sigh, but neither hear. Mia smiles. "I'm sure if you petition Master Huewin, he will supply the reference. He knows every book, script, and scroll down there."

"In the basement?" I ask to confirm.

"Yes, there." The girl answers me, but her eyes don't leave Kaylin. "I could take you to Huewin right now if you like."

"Not necessary. You've been more than helpful." He steps away from the desk, grin still in place, and leads me out.

We descend the library steps, a bright autumn sun warming my shoulders. "That girl was not helpful," I grumble. "All she did was…was… *swoon* over you."

He nods toward savants within earshot, but I can see the smile trying to escape. "This way."

Once we're around the corner, he lets out a laugh, and without thinking, I punch him in the arm.

He laughs harder. "At last, I'm worthy of the Heir's treatment. You have quite a swing."

My face heats and I quickly grab the straps of my satchel to prevent any more spontaneously stupid moves.

We walk down the heavily trafficked boulevard, past the stables and out the main gate.

When the traffic thins, I repeat the question. "Well?"

He grins. "You were jealous."

I lift my chin. "Was not."

"Liar."

I didn't ask for your opinion.

His grin only widens. "Mia was more helpful than you think."

"How?" At least the change in subject allows me to redirect my irritation. "We can't ask Huewin to let us in without giving him an explanation, and we can't steal a key."

He looks at me with his dreamy sea-green eyes and winks.

It takes a moment to sink in. "Oh no." I stop, hands going to my hips. "You aren't thinking… Kaylin, no."

"Just borrow it, for a time, so I can make a skeleton key to match."

"You're a blacksmith now?"

"I'm many things, lass."

That is true. I cross my arms as we walk along the side path to the headland. Finally, I say, "What's your plan?"

"We go to the basement in the wee hours of the night, use my skeleton key to unlock the storage room—first door on the left—and find the answers you're looking for. Unless, of course, you want to give up?" He lifts an eyebrow.

I stare at him for a long moment, wondering how he can know that when it comes to wordsmithing, I'll do anything to solve a mystery. "I don't want to give up."

"Then we won't."

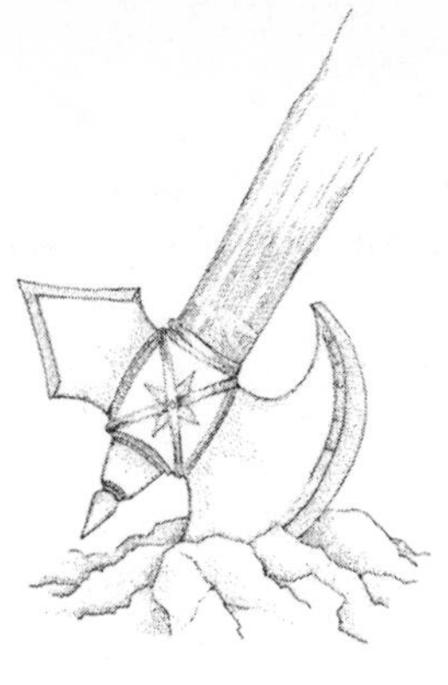

38

MARCUS

"This is the best K'mai I've ever had."

It's not really. Traditional Gollnar dishes of vegetables and roots braised in spices aren't that appealing. Too many chili peppers for me. But I'll say anything to keep from talking about events on the field this morning.

"Agreed," Belair says. "The yams are so sweet." He takes a massive bite from his bowl.

I blink and keep eating. Belair and I managed to make it in from the training field, clean up—with only cold water left after waiting in a long line of grumbling students—and reach the dining hall before the midday meal finished. Piper and Samsen waited for us, their bowls empty, expressions curious as they lean in to each other like a couple of slanting bookends. I can tell they know, or perhaps even saw, what happened on the field.

"Listen, you two," Piper begins, her arm draped around Samsen's shoulders. "First week's the most challenging. Just stay focused and you'll pass. They aren't necessarily testing for the obvious things."

Like control and ability? "Really?" I ask without looking up from my food. "Did you have *warrior* training?"

"You know I didn't, but everyone goes through physical workouts with their phantom, and it's grueling, I promise. You did well; you're still on your feet."

"Unfortunately, the obstacle course isn't," Belair says.

Samsen chuckles.

Piper refills my bowl from the central tureen. "Eat up. You'll need your strength for the afternoon."

I sigh, not sure I can face more of this fare. "You saw what happened?"

"To the obstacle course?" Piper tries to keep a straight face. "Everyone on Aku has heard the story by now."

Samsen leans in. "It's just the beginning for you and that house-sized phantom of yours. No one's expecting you to perform like an orange-robe on your first day."

"I don't think they were expecting the training field to be destroyed on my first day, either."

Samsen pats me on the back. "Great job re-turfing, by the way, and the obstacle course will be better for the new construction."

"There's that." I notice the empty place beside Piper. "Where's Ash?"

"Didn't she record your first session?" Piper raises her brows.

"No, thank the bones. I don't need an up-close account of this day bound into a book for all generations to come." Although I know she saw some of our debacle from the library tower. What she didn't see firsthand, she'd have heard about by now.

"Pity. She'd be in the library, though, no doubt."

"And our friend Kaylin?"

"Haven't seen him." Samsen and Piper speak at the same time.

I frown and return to my bowl. Among the background noises of the hall, I catch the words *Baiseen* and *stumbling fool.* I make to push out of my seat, but I hear my name called in that Aturnian accent.

Destan, sitting opposite a few seats down the row, leans across the table. "It's just Macor, from Sierrak, an inept ouster who can't stir a wind to save his life."

"Ouster?"

"Pay him no mind, I'm saying. With his gopher of a phantom, he won't last the week."

"Marcus." Samsen grabs my shoulder. "Leave it alone. You'll not serve Palrio by scrapping in the halls of Aku."

I grimace but stay seated. Samsen's right. Fighting in the dining hall would not earn me respect. It could even see us all booted out on the spot. For all that I've focused on reaching Aku, I must keep my eye on the prize. On honing my *warrior*. On serving and protecting my realm.

When I turn to thank Destan, he's gone. Odd.

Piper frowns at the seat Destan abandoned. "Is his accent Northern Aturnian?"

"Maybe, but he says he's from the Southern realm."

"Quite friendly," Belair adds. "He's in Zarah's group with us."

"He's been helpful." Which is true, but Samsen and Piper don't look convinced. I lean in close. "Kaylin has a theory. About Northern Aturnia sending their initiates to Aku from the south to bypass the ban."

Samsen's eyes widen. "Surely Yuki would know of this deception."

"Which is why we need to be careful."

Belair frowns. "You think Destan's here for more than training?"

I draw in a breath. "If he is, it will be up to us to find out."

Because protecting Aku from Northern Aturnian spies is exactly the complication we need while trying to earn our yellow robes.

39

ASH

The cove is every bit as beautiful as Kaylin promised.

The water sparkles beneath the noonday sun. I can't get my boots off fast enough, roll up my pants above my knees, and let the sand caress my feet. I cut quickly across the beach and let the gentle waves lap at my toes. It's wonderful, but cold. *Really* cold.

"Aren't you going to freeze to death out…there?" My voice squeaks to a halt when I look up because Kaylin is *undressing*. He's utterly comfortable in his body. Tutapa upbringing, I guess.

Wish I had some of that…

He flashes me a grin.

I harrumph. "There will be no rescue from me if you run into trouble," I say, backing up when a larger wave rolls in. "And I don't think they will help, either." I indicate the barking sea lions at the end of the breakwater. "They bite, you know."

"*Of course, he knows. He's island raised.*"

Here I am, talking too much again, but can't stop. The butterflies in my belly have to go somewhere, and it seems they see fit to escape through my mouth, carrying as many words with them as they possibly can. With Kaylin so close, and currently wearing so little clothing, there is an endless supply.

He takes a small medallion off from around his neck and hands it to me. "I'll be right back." He picks up his knife and a net bag.

"I'll be here." I study the medallion to keep from staring after him. He always wears it, as far as I recall, in or out of the water. Odd that it's in my hands now. I rub my thumb across the surface. The copper, tinged green, is shaped like a trident and etched very finely. I've seen the image somewhere before but can't place it. I must remember to ask.

Kaylin climbs onto the breakwater, the wall of rocks creating this natural horseshoe cove. Across the turquoise waters, kelp gardens fan out like golden threads. The fronds drift on the surface, held up by floating bladders. Halfway out to the pod of sea lions, Kaylin gives me a wave and dives in.

I hold my breath, just for fun, to see if I can stay under as long as he does, but soon I must breathe. I let it out, as slowly as I can, take another breath, hold it, let it out, and another, and another…

"What is he, a f'qadin *fish*?"

40

KAYLIN

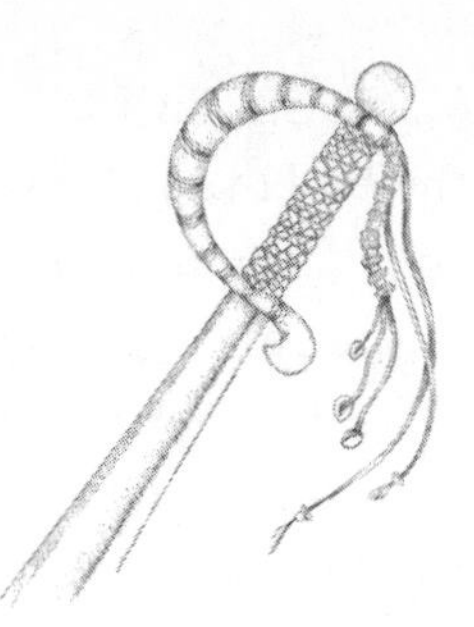

Blessed seawater rushes over me. My skin comes alive and every cell in my body tingles. I miss this feeling each moment I spend on land, except for when I'm with Ash. Those moments have their own form of pleasure and quickening of the heart. Still, a stalemate is nigh. Soon there will be no moving forward or going back, not without making a terrible choice. I dive deeper, swimming faster, a blur in the dark green currents, as if the answer to all my troubles lay at the bottom of the sea.

The sunken ship lists hard on her side, ringed with swaying kelp. The hull is partially intact, and a tall mast shoots up from the rotting deck. The crow's nest pokes out of the water at low tide, though on a slant. Oysters and barnacles cluster on both masts, fore and aft, and it doesn't take long to fill the bag.

The world's on the brink, and I gather oysters. What black-robe foresaw this?

"Having a picnic are you, brother?"

Curse the bones and throwers, where did she come from? *"Salila, what a pleasant surprise. Teern let you off the leash?"* I break the surface and make a show of taking a breath before diving again. *"Or perhaps you have lost your way?"*

"Me? Lost?" Salila sweeps by, a rush of water knocking me back. *"I'm hardly lost."*

"Good, then. Be a help and gather more oysters, will you?"

She swims back over the ship, kelp dragging along in her wake. Finally, she stops in front of me, arms crossed, hair fanning out in all directions. *"You have nerve, asking me for more help."*

"Taxed, are you, sister?"

Her lower lip sticks out. *"I did everything you wanted, Kaylin. Followed the Heir on his little detour. Brought the fish run to empty the harbors, both Cabazon and Toretta. Made sure you knew to be there at precisely the right moment for the party of five. And for what?"*

"To accomplish Teern's will, what else?" When she doesn't answer, I soften a bit. *"Sounds like you're free now, the price for breaking Teern's law paid?"*

"I wish, but no." Her voice turns conspiratorial. *"He sent me to watch* you. *Thinks you're mucking things up."*

"You can tell Father I have it under control." I keep my mental voice calm, but it's not easy.

She snorts. *"Then you're the worst assassin in the history of the profession."*

"What makes you say that?"

"Oh, I don't know. The Heir and his party are still alive?"

"I have my reasons." Ash's face flashes in front of me. *"Good reasons."* I surface again and dive. Salila follows but doesn't break the water.

"I will report this. Don't think I won't." She swims past me in a shot.

"By all means, do." I catch up, my fists tight. *"Just know, I plan to tell Teern myself."*

She stops dead in the water and I stream right by. It takes her a moment to fire off her next retort. *"You do that, Kaylin, and be sure to mention the Heir, alive and well on the training field of Aku. I imagine that will stir him."*

I force a smile. *"Are you done?"*

"Not quite." She spins like a whirlpool, tangling my hair in front of my eyes. *"Tann's on the move."*

My stomach drops to the ocean floor. *"High Savant Tann? Are you sure?"*

"The one and only, gathering a large Aturnian fleet while he's at it, too."

I think of the flags bearing the twin suns. The tattoos. The notice. *"Is he—"*

"Seeking the first whistle bones?" Her hair floats around her face as she nods. *"What else?"*

"The crown is once again to be formed?"

"Not by him, if Teern can stop it."

So…it has begun.

She rolls onto her back, gazing up at the surface, hands pillowing her head. *"You're welcome."*

I shake myself back to the present. *"Thanks."*

I mean it until she adds, *"Chop-chop with the murdering, brother. There's no time to lose."*

No time, indeed.

41

ASH

I sit on the beach and hug my knees. “Sailors…”

Kaylin has surfaced a few times, but now he’s been under for several minutes longer than I imagine a whale could hold its breath. It has me jittery, but after watching him swim across the raging Ferus River and rescue us from the falls, I shouldn’t be overly concerned. But I am. The beach has become quiet, the waves lulling and the barking sea lions blurring into the background.

“I’m really not going in there to rescue you,” I say aloud.

“*Even if he’s drowned?”* my inner voice asks.

As if that could happen. But I wring my hands as I scan the surface again.

Finally, Kaylin appears in the shore break with a net full of oysters, knife in his teeth. He tosses long hair out of his face, water spraying in an arc, the dark lengths clinging to his back and shoulders. I throw him a towel when he reaches me and busy myself with plates, cups, and blanket while he pulls on his pants. When I look up, he’s roughly drying his hair.

“Good catch,” I say and quickly look down again, slicing lemons, putting out a small loaf of bread and a round of cheese. He does know how to pack a picnic, that’s certain. “Tell me you didn’t steal these.”

He laughs. “They were offered freely.”

“That’s a relief.” I shoot him a playful smile and we share a laugh. One by one he shucks the oysters, slipping his knife into the hinge, prying it open, and removing one half of the shell. With an expert touch, he runs the blade along the inside of the remaining shell, freeing the oyster. Soon, he has a dozen half shells on a plate.

I squeeze lemon onto one and tip it to my lips. It slips down my throat with a smooth, salty tang. “Delicious.”

He does the same, minus the lemon.

“You like it simple,” I say, offering a piece of bread.

"Sometimes."

The look in his eyes… I can't help but lean forward, my lips parting slightly.

"Ash."

I look at him, a bit startled. It's as if he spoke directly into my head.

He leans toward me, saying aloud, "Ash?"

My pulse races as his sea-green eyes close. Unbelievably slowly, he leans in until our lips touch. His lips feel cool and salty, his hands strong on either side of my face. I close my eyes, too, while the ocean taste of him mixes with the lemon still on my tongue. There is only one thought in my head.

Kiss him back.

And as I do, warmth blooms, dispelling all doubt, all reluctance, and I let go, savoring the closeness. I reach for him. Touch his hair. Encircle his broad shoulders, his back. He gives a little groan and pulls me in tighter. My whole body goes weak and all I can do is fall, trusting that he will catch me. Or am I catching him?

But even as we melt into each other, warnings ring in my head. What am I doing kissing on the beach? I'm behind with my work, and I've not even been to the field with Marcus and Belair yet. Who are, I might add, making a terrible show of it. And where am I, their recorder? Picnicking at a cove, eating oysters. Tangled up with a boy? I have to get my mind where it's supposed to be, and fast, because the dak'n bones know as a non-savant, I'm lucky to even be on the sacred Isle of Aku.

When we pull apart, I swallow with difficulty. "Kaylin." I reclaim my hands and straighten. "I can't do this."

He leans back, and I miss his closeness already.

I reach for an oyster, to make it more normal and not a momentous declaration, but my hands shake. "On this journey, I'm the official recorder for the Heir of Baiseen, and Belair. The focus must be on the initiates, the journey. Then there's the training and recording. The—"

"Protocols?"

"Yes, that's it."

"But when the journey's over? What then?"

My heart skips a beat. It's not at all what I expected to hear. "I'll be back in Baiseen."

"And?"

"Not quite so constrained."

He exhales long and slow, then gives me a small smile. "A month or two is nothing to the sea."

My whole body stills.

Did I hear right? He'll wait for me?

We quickly finish the oysters in silence. I'm still working up the nerve to say something, anything, to break the tension when he abruptly stands. "Let's swim," he says. "The water calls. Can't you hear it?"

No, but suddenly it seems like the only thing in the world I want to do.

"I daresay you could use some cooling off."

Ha! I shrug out of my robe and undo my drawstring pants, stripping down to my underthings. Time is fleeting, I've learned. And we will never have these moments again. I will not waste them.

He extends his hand. "Ready?"

"Always."

He takes my hand and leads me to the surf.

Goose bumps rise over my flesh as the water laps around my knees. "It's so cold!" But I'm laughing as I wade out into the little crystal bay. He waits for me farther out, laughing back. When I push off the bottom and swim by his side, the temperature shocks me, then warms as I acclimate.

Out in the middle of the cove, among the slippery bull kelp, Kaylin pulls me against him and we bob in the gently swaying water. I rest my head against his chest and smile. My heartbeat is so strong, I wonder if all the creatures in the sea can hear it.

We stay that way for a long moment before he pulls back, winks, and dives beneath the water. I follow after him, and he reaches back for my hand. Together we wind through the kelp beds, their slippery blades skimming against my skin. Below us, I make out the sunken ship, a dark outline in the blurry blue water with silver fish darting in and out of the hull. Streams of green moss float from the mast like tattered flags, and I follow it down to the deck with my eyes.

There's something there.

I let go of Kaylin's hand and give a few strong kicks toward it, clearing my ears as I go.

It looks like a woman clinging to the bow of the rotting ship, her long hair waving in the current.

Before I can get closer, Kaylin has my hand again and is pulling me to the surface. Air escapes my lips as I scissor kick toward the sky. When I break the surface, I whip hair out of my eyes. "Did you see her?"

"Pardon?" Kaylin bobs beside me, looking anywhere but at me.

"I swear it was a woman with very long hair. She was clinging to the hull." I'm about to say I know how impossible it sounds, since we saw no one else on the beach or in the water, but he's gone in a flash, diving under to investigate, I assume.

I take a breath and dunk my head, watching from the surface, but all I see is a blur of green and blue water and the golden, swaying bull kelp.

When Kaylin returns, he's laughing. "Come on, the tide's changing. We should go in."

We swim side by side toward shore. "What's so funny?" My feet touch the sand bottom and I stand. "I'm sure I saw something down there."

"Aye, you did. The ship's figurehead sculpted as a Mar, fixed to the prow."

"That must be embarrassing."

My inner voice couldn't be drier.

"Figurehead?" I consider it. "I was sure she moved. Pushing incredibly long hair back from her face."

"Easy to mistake in the kelp garden, and without a mask."

"A mask?" We walk out of the surf to the beach.

"You don't know? They're made of glass set in soft leather." He cups his face with his hands, demonstrating. "You can see clearly under the waves with them."

I think of my blurred vision, the rippling current, kelp floating by. "Maybe we can find one of these masks on the island and have another look. I would love to explore the wreck that way."

"And I would love to show you more of the sea." Then his eyes lose focus, almost like a savant's does when speaking to their phantom.

We stop just short of our picnic spot. "Kaylin? What is it?"

He comes back to himself. "You're shivering." He runs to retrieve my towel and drapes it around my shoulders, rubbing warmth back into my arms. I find myself huddling against him, though he is as cool as me.

I close my eyes, reliving the kiss, melting in to what we started but can't finish. I tell myself to take a step back, but my feet don't listen. When he tips my chin up, bringing our faces a short breath away, I force my eyes to pop open. "Berry tarts! Are they still warm?"

He lets out a breath. "Should be."

"Come on, then." I lead us back to our picnic, determined not to let my heart get in the way of my duties. "We've dessert to eat and a break-in to plan."

42

MARCUS

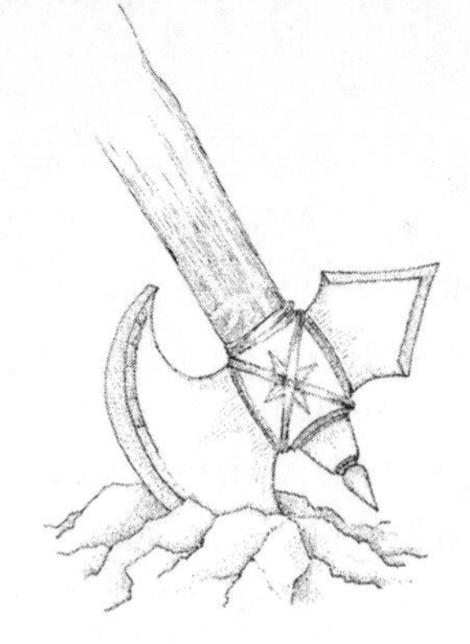

Rain pours onto the field as we line up in front of Zarah. It's the end of our first full week on Aku, and she's about to announce the results of the elimination trials.

These days have been the most treacherous of my life.

On the first day—which was the third day of training for everyone else, bones be damned—I thought the training so hard it would boot me off the path, but that was only the start. Each day since has compounded the feeling, beginning with Morning Ritual, which is not nearly as sedate as it sounds.

I groan at the thought. We warm up by sprinting to the highest lookout and back, then meet on the field for a series of hand-to-hand and weapons exercises. Then, with phantoms still down, we fly through the obstacle course and race to the hall for breakfast. For an hour after, we're in classrooms taking oral and written exams, firing off answers to questions we studied the night before. Belair is very good at those, and I excel at the additional sword work we practice after lunch, but everything else—the classes with Zarah, phantoms raised and running the perimeter, tackling the obstacle course side by side, then sparring until dark—nine times out of ten, De'ral and I are left looking like fools.

Eight times out of ten, De'ral growls.

Maybe there has been a small improvement, but we'd need a Sierrak reading glass to spot it. My heart sinks at the thought, and I have to force my shoulders back to stand tall. Of course, each day, who is on the sidelines, writing board in her lap, recording every slip and mishap? My recorder, of course. Ash's face is hopeful, always encouraging, but today I see my own worry mirrored in her eyes.

Zarah claps her hands, bringing me back from my rambling thoughts.

The tension weighs like an anvil on all of us. Pass or fail, stay or go, this is it.

If we pass, we continue on with the training. We'll be judged at the end as to whether we're fit to advance to yellow-robe or not. Fail and we're out. I think I understand now why my father called for the second throw of the bones. Better that I never tried, that I never reached this sacred Isle, than to raise a phantom and fail so spectacularly to master him.

Belair casts me a nervous glance. I don't want to consider one of us passing and the other not. Belair and I are in this together now. We've been through so much.

Zarah glances at a list and tucks it back into her pocket before it gets soaked. Her face is a mask. Unreadable.

My guts tighten and I think I may be sick. Belair looks much the same. I imagine the results in my head. Fail. Fail. What else could it be?

She clears her throat to get our attention. As if she needs to. We're all hanging on her next words. "Macor of Sierrak and Brigit of Goll. Dismissed. You both show promise, just not enough yet. Maybe next year. Come by my chambers for a full report for your High Savants before you leave."

I look to them both feeling pity. But is Zarah done? Are there more names on her list? I thought Brigit was stronger than me and Belair, but no one will tell us the criteria for the eliminations, so we're in the dark.

"And..." She pauses, torturing us to the core. "The rest of you pass."

Cheers well up. Backs are slapped. Swords point to the sky while Belair and I stand like stumps. I never knew relief could nail me so completely to the spot.

Zarah whistles for attention. "Hit the books! There's a written test tomorrow at second bell. I will be looking for improvement from all of you—among other things."

I struggle out of my stupor and turn to Belair. "We made it."

"And now the pressure starts all over again." He's just as weary as me, the stress of the training taking a toll.

But what else is there to say? Certainly not, "great session today" or "amazing work." My eyes are on the mucky ground as we follow the others back to the main hall. We need to improve. Fast.

"Congratulations, both of you." Samsen claps me on the back, the wetness making it sting. He's as soaked as we are.

"Your sword work was excellent." Piper trots up beside me. "Especially in such bad footing."

"Swordsmanship was never my problem." I feel like my whole body is wading through mud.

"Marcus, take this win. You did it." Ash sounds genuinely cheered. "I knew you would, both of you."

I think I'm still in shock. From the moment I left Baiseen, nothing has gone to plan, and now that one thing has, I can't let it in. If only I were further along the path, I'd be able to appreciate this experience of accomplishment. But I skip over it, too focused on what comes next. And next beyond that. Time is not on my side. I have to show more than potential now. I have to succeed.

"Marcus?" Samsen purposely slows the pace until the other students are far ahead. "I hate to bring this up now when we should be celebrating, but I have an oddity to report."

I don't feel capable of celebrating anyway. "Tell me."

He describes Destan sitting in the highest ocean lookout, in the pouring rain, phantom set to guard while he...just sat there.

"Doing nothing?"

Piper leans in. "He held a medallion."

"What do you make of it?" I'm shuffling through my memory of all forms of meditation. Nothing stands out as similar.

"No idea."

Ash frowns like she's trying to recall something, too. "Medallion, did you say?"

Samsen nods. "But the Aturnian was on the lookout for some time before pulling it out from under his robe. He watched the road down to the pier, the track that leads off to the leeward beaches and far out to sea. He also paid close attention to you and Kaylin, Ash, when you came back from the beach."

I turn to Ash. "Beach?"

"A cove Kaylin discovered," she says.

"In the rain?"

"It wasn't raining at the start. It was low tide and the rockpools—"

I stop listening, unwilling to be pulled off track. "Piper, did you send your serpent in to get a closer look at Destan?"

"I tried, but his phantom sensed it. I brought it straight to ground."

"He has skills." I have to admit the truth. "More than most green-robes."

"It's his second attempt," Ash says. "I meant to mention, and I think I know why he would love the rain."

I turn to her, brows raised.

"I heard Cyres's recorder chatting with the others." She rubs her brow. "You know, sometimes I think I'm invisible to them, being non-savant."

I avert my eyes for a moment, not knowing what to say about the prejudice here. "But you heard talk?"

"They remember Destan from last year."

"I guess that explains why he's so good at everything."

"But it doesn't explain why he doesn't have a recorder."

"That's odd." My brows go up. "Hadn't noticed."

Ash shakes her head. "I honestly don't think he can afford one, Marcus. His family… Northern or Southern, they didn't confirm, but his family were farmers. The drought hit them hard, and harder still were Palrio's trade sanctions. I know the sanctions are in place to forestall war, but Marcus, they lost everything."

"Because of my father." I bow my head.

Ash rests her hand on my shoulder. "Can you describe the medallion?" she asks Samsen.

"Aturnian design, silver, horses on it, I think." Samsen shakes his head. "*That* I could have my phantom *call*, but it might have tipped him off, suddenly jumping out of his hands."

When she doesn't respond, we all turn her way.

"Ash?"

Her brow knits. "It's just that some medallions are used by red-robes to communicate over long distances."

I rub my neck and frown. "He's good, but he's no red-robe." I look to the others to confirm it, and they all nod. "You haven't seen him meeting anyone, talking in hushed tones?"

"Nothing like that." Samsen's eyes study the distance before returning to me. "But if he is Northern Aturnian, he might be spying. Gathering information about us."

"Or about Aku," Belair says.

"When he's here at Yuki's behest, or at least, consent?" Ash asks.

"Good point." I feel a plan forming. "Ash, find out what you can about the medallion. Where is it from? What other realms wear such ornaments? How are they used?"

"I'll see what I can uncover," she says.

I turn to Samsen and Piper. "Continue keeping watch over him, just in case." It's an overreaction, I am sure, and I don't want to be like my father but—

If you were like your father, Destan would already be dead.

De'ral's words chill me to the core, because he's right. By the path, I will not follow in that man's wake.

43

ASH

I wake with a start, pulling my face out of the book I was studying before I fell asleep. The room is quiet. The fire burns low and there's a chill in the air. It's nothing like the toasty bright space it was a few hours ago when Kaylin and I were laughing and planning our break-in.

Retrieval, I correct myself. I mean, information gathering is part of my job, and nothing is actually going to be broken.

"*Who are you trying to convince?*"

I don't answer but reach for my sweater from the back of the chair and pull it on, and add a log to the fire. Kaylin left me to my studies, as he does. Fishing? Selling lures? I'm never sure. I start to stack our dinner dishes from the table when it happens.

Tap. Tap. Tap.

It makes me jump, and one of the plates slips from my hand, clattering to the ground.

Did you hear that?

The heat from the fire stops me as I back away, eyes glued on the window. *My imagination?*

"*Definitely not.*"

Without looking, I reach behind, fumbling for the hilt of the poker. I grip it tight and shove it into the fire, sparks flying up the chimney. I may not have master-level sword skills, but a molten shaft will make anyone think twice, won't it?

"*Anyone or any*thing*?*" My inner voice isn't panicked like me; but it's not saying I'm being silly, either.

Tap. Tap. Tap.

I brandish the red-hot poker in front of me, keeping my back to the fire. As my arm begins to shake, the door opens.

"Ash?"

"Kaylin!" I spin toward him, then return to my guard position, weapon pointing at the window. His casual smile evaporates and he's at my side, sword out of the scabbard in a split second. How does he move so fast?

"It's here again," I say in a hoarse whisper. "I think it's watching me."

"Did you see?"

"No, but I heard it. Outside on the ledge. Tapping."

He exhales a hissing breath. "I'll check the room."

Kaylin keeps his sword raised toward the window while he backs to the en suite and glances in. He scans every corner, eyes like a cat's, then advances to the curtains, opening them wide in a flourish. Nothing.

"It's gone."

"But it *was* here."

"I don't doubt you, lass." He sheaths his sword and puts more wood on the fire, lights a few candles. "Gone now," he says again in his comforting accent.

Slowly, I return the poker to its stand, the foreboding still hanging around the edges of my mind. "It woke me up." Somehow that doesn't cover the terror I still feel.

"Aye, lass." Kaylin rinses the teapot and fills it with chamomile, lavender, and lemon balm, a healer's potion for sleep. The steam wafts over the room while it steeps, but I'm tense as lute strings anyway.

He chats about his day, asks me about mine. I'm still so anxious I can hardly follow the conversation. I know he's trying to make me feel better, but in the end, nothing does. I'm scared out of my wits and ashamed to admit it.

"There's no shame in it at all, lass. Your mind is trying to protect you." And then Kaylin sighs. "Sleep is the only thing that will help."

I stare at him, unblinking. "I can't possibly sleep."

"You can, Ash."

"Why do you think that?"

"Because I will stand guard over you."

Oh.

When I think about it, the headlands, the Aturnian attack, it's true. Whatever's doing the tapping, having Kaylin between me and it is comforting.

He pulls down the bedcovers, holding them open for me to climb in. "Come. Sleep."

I keep my sweater on, and my pants, slipping out of my sheepskin-lined house boots. I am tired. But still, it's another moment before I can climb into my bed. "Are you going to watch over me for the rest of the night?"

"That I am." He blows out the candles.

In the dark, I hear his sword belt undo and the weapon being set against the nightstand. The rustle of fabric comes next.

Fear of the unknown hasn't left me; it's just being replaced by a whole new set of things to think about.

Such as the fact he's climbing into bed. *My* bed.

"He did *say he would stand guard over you for the rest of the night."*

Yes, but this is not the same thing!

Body flushed with something that feels a lot like excitement, I roll away, onto my side. When he says sleep, I know he means just that—sleep. But that doesn't stop the swarm of butterflies battering my insides. Especially not when Kaylin's bare arms wrap around me, holding me tight against his chest.

And this is supposed to make it easier to nod off? After forcing my lungs through the motion of a few deep breaths I manage, "Thank you."

"It's no trouble at all, lass."

My fingers and toes are tingling, a smile on my lips.

And amid that warmth and comfort, my lids grow heavy and I let them close.

I stir the next morning, perfectly rested even though it's barely past dawn, the daylight filtering honey gold through the lightly draped window. I stretch, long and satisfying, until remembering the events of the night before—the tapping, brandishing my poker, Kaylin sleeping next to me—and freeze.

I swallow noisily and peer over the pillow. He's still here, asleep beside me. At least, his eyes are closed, and his chest rises and falls in a slow, steady rhythm. I've never seen him so still.

As if he hears that thought, Kaylin shifts, and the covers slide down, exposing his broad shoulders and chest. I prop myself up on an elbow and study him. His body is flawless, surprising for someone who fights as much as he does. His hands aren't hatched with scars, and his chest and abdomen have neither scab nor blemish from the fight on the headlands or with the Aturnian scouts. I frown, looking closer. *Surely a mark somewhere?*

He opens his eyes. "You would prefer me marred?"

I jump. Had I spoken aloud? "I prefer you just as you are." I pull the covers up to my neck as I speak, which I know is silly, since I'm wearing day clothes and a sweater over the top. Plus, we swam together with me much more exposed. Nothing about my form can surprise him. Still…

He frowns. "That remains to be seen."

I puzzle for a moment, not understanding his meaning. "Cryptic this morning, aren't you?"

He changes the subject. "You slept well?"

"I did. Thank you for the comfort."

"Tonight's the night."

I give him a shaky smile. "We'll either find the text we need or get caught with a whole lot of explaining to do. What could go wrong?"

Kaylin chuckles. "It won't go so bad as that."

My smile fades and we go silent without a note of awkwardness for once, just a mutual gaze, a communion of sorts.

He reaches up and tucks a strand of hair behind my ear. "Beautiful," he whispers.

As is he, not that I can manage to grasp any of the many words I know to express this. Not with the way his eyes hold me captive.

A smile tugs at the corner of his mouth, as if he can hear my inner struggle.

Before I can embarrass myself further, the moment breaks with a start and we both sit up, listening.

Was that a scratching at the window? My eyes go wide. Is the tapping back?

Kaylin motions for me to stay put while he leaps soundlessly from the bed and finds his sword, slowly drawing it from the scabbard. I creep from the bed and pick up the fire poker. Kaylin checks, but there's nothing at the window. We listen intently until someone bangs on the door and I jump out of my skin.

Kaylin is there in an instant, shirtless in his drawstring pants, brandishing his curved blade. I follow him, gripping the poker. He throws open the door wide and his shoulders relax, sword lowers.

I peek around him to see who it is.

"Marcus?" I finger-comb my hair, wondering if he will start lecturing me about the protocols what with Kaylin's bed neatly made and mine rumpled, but Marcus isn't noticing anything of the kind. He's completely preoccupied.

"I have to talk to Ash." Marcus waves aside Kaylin's sword and strides into the room, wild eyed, not asking why we have weapons in hand. He sits at the table and lifts the lid on the cold teapot.

"You look awful," I say. "Have you not slept?"

"How can I?" Marcus scrubs his face. "Is there hot water? Tea?"

I pick up the empty jug. "I'll get it."

"Let me." Kaylin takes it and slips out the door, leaving us alone to talk.

"What's happened, Marcus?"

He stares at me, his eyes red, expression strained. "I can't do it."

I sit opposite him and push the plate of leftover bread and cheese in his direction. "Nonsense. What can't you do?"

"I can't control my phantom or glean an iota of respect from him, or Zarah for that matter. At this rate, I'll never receive my yellow robes."

"You've been at it only a week, Marcus. You passed the eliminations, and you'll continue with your training every day. That's why we are here." I pull my hair back into a neat ponytail. "There's plenty of time."

"That's just it. Yuki herself gave us a new deadline. Just under three weeks and we have to leave, with or without yellow robes."

My mouth drops open. "I thought we had another month at least."

"So did I. The freeze is predicted to come early. Bone Throwers called the deadline." He pulls at his tangled hair. "He's like a petulant child, Ash."

"De'ral?" I whisper the phantom's name, expecting to be admonished for using it.

Marcus only nods. "Whatever I do has no effect. When I ask for help, Zarah all but laughs. She still calls me *Baiseen*, and not in a flattering way."

"I've heard her." And I've felt the sting on Marcus's behalf every time.

"I'm the joke of the class." Marcus lets his face fall forward onto the table and leaves it there, golden hair spilling over the placemat. "You can't deny it." His voice is muffled. "You've been there for almost all of it."

"*Warrior* phantoms take the most work. You have to give the relationship time to develop, and if there isn't enough time, you'll just have to work harder." I get out of my seat and haul him up. On this journey, I'm both recorder and his best friend. "This is why you're here, Marcus. To train. To compete. To accomplish."

He frowns but gives a small nod.

"Baiseen needs *you,* Marcus. And your phantom." Strength comes out of my depths and into my voice. "Don't speak another word about failure or compare yourself to anyone else. Talk only about what *you* will achieve." I rub his back as I speak. "And relax. If you're this tense, your phantom will be, too."

Kaylin returns with freshly boiled water, and I make a strong pot of Ochee. The scent of spices fills the room.

"Maybe today, Marcus. Tomorrow or the next day at the latest. Things will start to look up. You've just had a tough beginning, and he is a very strong phantom." I look at Kaylin, thinking he might add something, strange as it is, us non-savants in the role of mentors.

He joins us at the table and surprises me with his insight. "At the core of your being, the phantom and you are one. That's where you will find communion"—he sets out mugs in front of us—"and build the relationship from a shared heart."

Marcus lifts his head and studies him carefully. "Odd that you know this."

They have a moment where neither of them blink or turn away. I don't know what passes between them, but eventually Marcus says, "It makes sense."

Kaylin shrugs, handing him a plate of fresh bread.

Marcus tears off a piece and layers on the butter. His eyes glance over the room and back to us both. "I didn't see either of you at dinner last night."

"We had it up here." Kaylin brightens. "We're planning a—"

"Map!" I cut in before he spills our plot to break into the library. "For the records."

Marcus nods. "You're doing great work, Ash. I only wish I was doing better."

"And you will be soon."

"Tell him of the shadow? The tapping?"

My inner voice seems fine either way, but I don't know if I should burden Marcus with the updates.

"If such a burden throws him, how will he ever hold the throne of Baiseen?"

Point. But no, Marcus doesn't need to worry about this now. Not on top of everything else.

Marcus stops chewing and looks to Kaylin. "The phantom and I are one?"

"At the core," Kaylin says.

Marcus downs his tea and rises. "You're right, the both of you. I need to work harder, connect deeper. That's all there is to it." He's at the door before I can stand. "First bell's in an hour. I'll see you on the training field." He nods to Kaylin and then he's gone.

The door shuts, leaving us in a moment of silence.

"Marcus isn't usually so abrupt," I say eventually.

"I know."

We finish our breakfast, putting the final touches on our secret plan. Next thing I know, Kaylin is pulling on his shirt and threading his sword belt through the loops in his pants.

"You're off?"

"Aye, off a-hunting." He leans close but doesn't touch me. "Could take a while. I'll see you tonight."

I wonder if he's going to track down the shadow that haunts my room. And I'm not sure which I'm hoping for more—a successful hunt that rids me of the danger, or an excuse to keep him close another night, with his arms protectively around me.

44

ASH

The late morning sun hits the training field with pale golden rays but offers no warmth. If it weren't for morning ritual followed by hot porridge, and the anticipation of our library break-in, my teeth would be chattering, quill hand shaking.

As it is, my blood's running hot and I'm content on the sidelines, writing board in my lap, noting the highlights of Marcus's and Belair's class right along with half a dozen other recorders. The students have come in from running the perimeter, and steam rises from their robes.

I note how Belair is improving, his link to the red cat progressing quite naturally. But I also see him holding back in subtle ways, allowing Marcus to, if not shine, then at least appear to keep up.

I think our carefree Tangeen is more loyal to the Heir than he first appeared.

"Loyal, or prudent?" my inner voice asks.

It's a fair question. Are Marcus and Belair becoming fast friends, or is the Tangeen thinking ahead, fortifying the relationship between our realms? A bit of both? I finish my entry and look up at the head of the class.

Bucheen is there, arms wide, keeping the students' attention as she talks about the ins and outs of phantoms, literally.

"It's always a push in. Don't expect the resistance to diminish until you've had years of practice. Instead, expect your ability and sensitivity to improve gradually. You will become proficient over time, I promise." Bucheen rolls up her sleeves. "Two things to know." She holds up her first finger. "The longer you stay in your phantom's perspective, the more of it remains *with* you. This can be beneficial, and it can also be dangerous. If you lose your sense of self, you will not be able to bring it to ground." She pops up her second finger and narrows her eyes. "Secondly, getting in is easy compared to getting out. You can find yourself…"

She pauses, searching for the right word. In my mind, I think, *hesitant, reluctant, resistant?*

"*Attached*," she finally says, "especially in battle. This is a great asset, as long as you stay in control. Lose it and you could lose your life."

The students stay silent while they nod for more.

"Make no mistake. If your phantom is overcome, sent to ground when you are fully immersed in their perspective, then peace be your path." She holds us all with her fierce gaze. "When your phantom is injured and starts to succumb, there is only one thing you can do." She crosses her arms. "Anyone?"

Cyres raises her hand and Bucheen nods at her.

"You get out," the girl says with just the right amount of conviction. "Before your phantom's wounds disable you."

"That's right. You move out of phantom perspective as if your life depends on it, because it does. Questions?"

The class stirs, but no one raises their hand.

Bucheen bows to Zarah. "I hope to never see any of you in the infirmary." She looks at Marcus and Belair. "Again."

I rest my eyes on Marcus. *You better be soaking this up.* He doesn't give me so much as a glance, but I know he appreciates my support. Marcus has sworn to train twice as hard as the others, get up before first bell, study late into the night, and that's definitely going in the records. Belair's, too. He's working hard right beside Marcus, but I know it's Marcus who leads. I tap my chin. The results may take the scant number of days they have left, but I have faith. His newfound resolve will make all the difference, and the instructors see promise or he wouldn't still be here.

Mistress Zarah claps her hands and off they go to do two more laps. Marcus, as usual, struggles with De'ral. He's going red in the face, yet again taking the brunt of Zarah's reprimands. I don't blame him for being furious. She is not kind. Belair and his beautiful leopard move off last, then slow to give Marcus a chance to catch up. But De'ral stays seated and crosses his arms. I've never seen a phantom sulk like this. "*What is the matter with you, De'ral?*"

My mind fills with an image of a raven in a small gold cage. It's overwhelming, my body feeling caged, just as the black bird. I have to take a few breaths to calm down. Whatever's happening, I need to accept it. And, use it. *"You're feeling imprisoned? By Marcus?"* I ask De'ral.

The raven beats his wings against the bars.

"It would seem he is," my inner voice observes.

I look over my shoulder to see if anyone else is seeing what I see, but they all have their heads down as they write and sketch. The only others here are Marcus, who jogs off, and his lump-of-a-grump phantom who stares straight at me.

"*Go on, De'ral.*" I send an image of a horse cantering proudly around a large field. *"Do as Marcus asks. If you work together, you won't feel so trapped."*

There's a faint spark in the *warrior*'s eye, and I know defiance when I see it. Maybe he hears me, or maybe not, but vez venom be damned, I will hold my peace no longer. "*Shame on you, De'ral. You are the* warrior *phantom of Marcus Adicio, Heir to the throne of Baiseen. Behave like it!"*

In my mind, I see a flock of birds startle and take flight, shock reflected in De'ral's eyes.

An answering shudder reverberates through me. I'm really communicating with Marcus's phantom? I pull my shoulders back and arrow the thoughts straight at him. "*You think this feels trapped? Let me educate you. Trapped will be if Marcus remains a green-robe, if he can't take the throne, join the council, and have a voice at the Council Summit meetings. Do you know what will happen if his father calls war down upon us? If you and Marcus cannot help defend the realm?"*

I receive the image of a horse slamming to a halt and turning to look back at me.

"De'ral, move it!"

The phantom jumps to his feet, sending a tremor through the ground that shakes from my sit bones all the way to the back of my skull. The other recorders glance up at once as the *warrior* takes off at a run toward Marcus.

Zarah smiles and cups her hands around her mouth to shout. "Finally, Baiseen." She pumps her fist in the air. "Now keep up and stay in control."

"*Well done!*" I send an image of a cheering crowd and he looks back, slamming his giant fist to his chest in salute before running on.

My hands shake and ink spatters off the end of the quill, leaving black speckles over the page. So...it *was* me?

"It was you," my inner voice confirms.

I grip the sides of the writing board until my knuckles turn white. "It was me," I whisper the words again.

"*We've established that...*"

True. But it's a long time before I can settle back into my work.

45

ASH

"Shh." Kaylin's breath tickles my neck as he hushes me from a few inches away.

"Going as quietly as I can," I whisper back.

The steps to the basement are dark as pitch, the library all but shut down for the night. A few students study in the main room of the first floor, noses in their books, not noticing us slip past. So far, everything's going to plan.

I've even managed to stop shaking after what happened on the training field. Questions still swim in my head, but who would I ask? Marcus? I don't think he would appreciate knowing it was me, not him, who got De'ral moving today.

I force myself to focus on the task at hand. Namely, not getting caught. I keep a hand on Kaylin's shoulder as we work our way down toward the archives. If there are any references to the Retoren language, they *should* be in there, under lock and key. We hope. "First door on the left," I say, even though Kaylin already knows.

He suppresses a chuckle. I can't see his face in the dark, but I sense the mirth. He takes my hand as he feels his way along the wall. We've been doing a lot of this lately—not breaking into archived rooms—but spending time together, more than I anticipated, though I'm not complaining. When he's not trying to convince me to come back to the cove, he helps me in the library, adding sketches to the journey records. They're quite good, but some are comical, and I can't allow them in. After dinner, he carves fishing lures while I work.

And then there was last night.

A shiver of happiness flits through me.

We share much of our personal philosophies about the heating realm wars, phantoms, the Bone Throwers, and the many paths to An'awntia. We pore over the notice from the docks at Capper Point, too. It doesn't make sense without translating the symbols. All I can surmise is a *dark sun,* or in some translations, a *second sun,* is rising and those who want to survive best heed the warning, which is given, presumably, in the Retoren symbols we can't read. I'm guessing Dark Sun might be the name of a Sierrak warlord, perhaps a mistranslation for Dark Son. Kaylin leans toward a more literal translation, as in an actual binary star. I've heard of them. The Sierraks note several stars by that name, plotting them with their giant distant viewers, but it's so unlikely, isn't it?

There's been no talk, however, of "us" or the protocol we agreed to keep.

"*Does it matter?*" my inner voice asks. "*Nothing changes whether you talk of it or not.*"

True, I guess, but one thing's sure. Being around Kaylin sends my mood to the heavens, and I think it's the same for him when he's around me. But whether it will be easier to spend time together or not after Aku, I don't know. I wish we could just—

"Here's the door," Kaylin says, interrupting my thoughts. He lets go of my hand and I reach for the wall, leaning against the foundations of the library.

"Will it open?" I whisper as he slides the key into the lock.

There's a soft *snick.*

"That it will, lass."

The door has to be shoved hard, and it protests with creaks and groans. I glance behind, into the blackness, half expecting to see a light descending the stairwell, and shouts of "Who's down there?" But it doesn't happen, and Kaylin, with his catlike, see-in-the-dark senses, leads me into the storeroom. The door thuds closed behind us.

It's stuffy in here and smells of musk, ink, and leather.

"Now, Ash, your light?"

I pull a small covered lantern out of my satchel. The flint strikes and flares, the wick catching. The little glass hood slides over the top, and the room comes alive with rows of high bookcases and long flickering shadows.

"No one gets down here too often." Kaylin wipes a layer of dust off the top of a desk.

"Not with a rag and broom, anyway." The corners of the room drip with cobwebs and the tables and shelves all could use a good wiping. It's a big storage space with shelves only an arm's span apart and double that overhead. Also cluttered around our feet are boxes, stacks of books, scrolls, and even some very old clay tablets that have yet to be filed away.

"How do we go about this?" Kaylin picks up a scroll off the main table stack and taps it into his palm.

I cough from the dust. "That might be a starting place." I point to the scroll. "There must be a ledger at least."

"Unless, as the girl said, he keeps it all in his head."

"Let's hope not."

He unrolls the scroll and smiles. "A ledger it is."

I lean in, reading, the text blurring for a moment as our arms touch. "It's in Aturnian, which is odd. I thought Huewin was from Nonnova."

"It's in his hand, I take it?"

"I think so, but this is good, a list of shelving order." I run my thumb down the scroll to the *R*s, looking for Retoren. Nothing.

"They don't seem to be listed by language," Kaylin says.

"No surprise there. Huewin's very guarded on that topic."

We both look around and sigh. There are hundreds of books and we have only the night, unless we come back—not something I want to risk. "Start with the reference books?" I hold the lantern over the scroll. "Left wall, it looks like." I'm about to go, but Kaylin's still reading.

"There are categories." He holds down the right-hand corner of the scroll. "Animal classifications, insects, plants, weather…"

"Any for planets and stars?"

"Here." His finger stops on a row. "Planets, suns, and moons, right wall, shelf twenty."

"Suns and moons, plural?"

"That's what it says."

"I'll look. If that's Retoren script in the planetary guide, there could be related texts in the same category." The lantern flickers as I weave my way through the stacks to find shelf twenty.

Kaylin remains at the table, untroubled by the dim light. "What about this one? *Amassia's Second Sun*."

I gape at him. Surely it can't be that easy. "Where?"

I feel his smile. "Shelf twenty-three, row five, number one thousand nine hundred and fifty-four. It even notes the authors. All Sierrak names." Kaylin comes to join me. "How about I'll start at this end, you at the other, and we'll meet in the middle?"

We scan along the row, pulling each book out and checking the title. Most of the older texts don't have names branded into the leather binding.

It requires opening each one to the title page, which is slowgoing, but also fascinating.

Kaylin and I are a handspan apart when I find it. "Here." I check the text, pulling the notice out of my pocket. Sure as old Bone Throwers, it's a match.

"Does it mention a second sun?" he asks.

"No idea. I can't translate it." I turn to him. "Now, all we need is a dictionary."

"And more light."

As he tucks the book into my satchel, the wick sizzles and fades out. The darkness that follows is complete, and I see no different with my eyes open or closed. Suddenly I'm aware of how close Kaylin is standing. I can feel the rise and fall of his chest, the press of him along my side, his body turning to face me… "Kaylin?"

He cups my face in his big hands. "Damn the protocols to the Drop."

I lift my chin, and it's all the invitation he needs. He bends down until his lips brush mine. Fire flushes through me, and my mouth opens as if about to taste a sweet, ripe fruit.

"Ash," he whispers against my lips and kisses me deeply.

I surrender, eyes floating closed, arms going around his neck, pulling him in to me.

"Someone's coming."

My inner voice startles me, and I jump back.

"Someone's coming," I repeat aloud.

Kaylin straightens as footsteps shuffle outside the door. A key goes into the lock. Kaylin silently pulls me toward the far wall. I bump my knee into a table leg and stifle a cry. The door opens and light floods the room. They must have a dozen lamps. But I hear only two people, chatting away, mid-conversation.

"…more than I thought." There's a pause. "Do you smell smoke?"

There's a fair bit of sniffing and I am sure we are caught.

"No, but it's musty down here. What a mess."

I recognize Hali's voice, the artist doing portraits of Marcus and Belair, their phantoms, and maps for our peculiar route to Aku. I like her work, so far, but don't want to trust her with our unauthorized research.

"Are you going to complain or help me?" the other voice asks.

It sounds like Mia, the library attendant Kaylin charmed into telling us about this room, the girl with the possum phantom. Sweat prickles the small of my back. Every time I see that saucer-eyed creature, it turns toward me and chitters. *Not tonight!* I say to it directly.

"Secrets?" I hear a high-pitched voice and see a picture of apples stored in a dark cellar.

Mia's phantom is talking to me? In my head?

Kaylin's lips are against my ear again. "Try not to attract the phantom's attention."

"Little late for that."

"I'm here to help," Hali says to Mia. "Where do these go?"

They scuttle about while Mia's phantom sniffs up and down rows. It finds us and stares. At me.

I stare back, my finger to my lips. *"Do not tell Mia you see us."* But I'm not liking the chances it will obey me.

"Do not." My inner voice repeats the command with a rumble of authority. To my amazement, the little phantom lowers its head and moves on.

Then Hali's phantom, called a *willy-wisp*—an *alter* that glows like a tiny sun—hovers above the top shelves. That explains their illumination. I hope it's not drawn to us as well.

"The dictionaries go on the back wall, shelf eighteen," Mia says.

Kaylin nudges me, and I nod at the helpful information Mia unknowingly gave us, but we still have to avoid being caught.

"Put them in any order. Master Huewin said he'll come sort them this week." Mia makes a disgruntled sound. "Which means I will be the one doing the sorting, no doubt."

I close my eyes, thinking of what to say when they catch us. *We're working on the journey map and I had a hunch, so we…* What? Broke into the archives in the middle of the night? Maybe Kaylin will have a better excuse. He charmed her once before.

"Take these first and come back for more." Mia is bossy with everyone, it seems.

Hali puts the books away while the girls' conversation takes a new turn.

"I do agree. He is dreamy…" Hali sighs.

"And you get to sketch him, lucky!" Mia says. "But what about *her*?"

"She's nothing. Non-savant."

My shoulders tighten, and I feel Kaylin's do the same.

"They must be involved in some way, obviously, or why would she be his recorder? Is she even any good?"

There is no confusion who they are talking about. I wish I could be anywhere but here, listening.

"She must be good at *something*." Laughter rings like chimes.

I bristle, ready to lunge.

Kaylin holds me back with a touch of his hand and a shake of his head.

"It can't be serious." Hali clicks her tongue. "He must do better than a non-savant, Brogal's ward or not. He's the Heir of Baiseen."

"Truth! He's causing quite some stir with the High Savant."

"How so?" Hali asks.

My stomach tightens, and I still myself to listen.

"Nothing's been said to me directly." Mia lowers her voice like it's a conspiracy. "But I know for a fact *five* messengers were sent across the channel not an hour after his first meeting with her."

"Five?" Hali nearly gasps. "One messenger is traditional."

"They each sailed in a different direction," Mia says.

"Are you sure?"

"Truth. And I overheard other things."

"Tell me." Hali's eager, that's for certain.

"Keep it to yourself, though. There's lore in some ancient text. Everyone in Yuki's inner circle is reading it."

"What lore?"

"I didn't quite follow, but they were talking to several Bone Throwers who mentioned a Crown of Bones."

"Is it about King Er? That's pretty ancient."

"Maybe." Mia's footfalls head down another aisle. "So, have you talked much to *her*?"

She steered the conversation back to me? Great.

"No," Hali huffs. "That lynx may be non-savant, but she's got something to keep them both enthralled."

"Both?"

"The sailor follows her around like a puppy." She laughs. "Now there's a catch."

I can't meet Kaylin's eyes but feel him staring at me. I want to see his expression, or maybe just dissolve on the spot.

Hali and Mia's conversation trails away as they finish their task and file out the door. It closes behind them and the room falls into darkness. We remain silent for a few moments, just to be sure they don't return, and also because I don't know how to break it.

Finally, Kaylin chuckles. "Apparently, I'm quite a catch."

"Really? I hadn't noticed." I bark a laugh as the embarrassment vanishes. "Let's find the dictionary and go."

With a fresh candle lit, we head for the back wall where the dictionaries patiently wait for us. It doesn't take long to find the one we need. "Here!" I hand Kaylin the Retoren-to-Aturnian tome and he pops it into my satchel.

Once in the total darkness of the stairs, door locked behind us, I whisper, "That was worth it."

"The kiss as well as the books," Kaylin says.

I smile shyly. "I have to agree."

"Agree with what, lass?" he asks.

That stops me mid-step. "Didn't you just say…?"

"Hm?" I sense him turning around but can't see more than an outline in the dark.

My thoughts spin. It's late. I'm exhausted. I'm losing my mind.

"Or your hearing's improved?" My inner voice acts like this is as normal as toast.

I can't stop thinking about it, though. Going back in my mind, I call up moments from the escape from Mount Bladon, hiking through the sheep farm to Capper Point, our time at the cove… I have to know if it's real. "Kaylin?" I say when we reach the top of the steps.

He holds his finger to his lips, shushing me.

"Can I ask you something?" I whisper.

"Here?"

"No, you're right, not here." Not where we might be caught, but as soon as we get back to our room. I take his hand and hurry through the entranceway and out the library doors.

46

ASH

Back in our room, I unpack the books we've *borrowed* from the library. The old leather feels rough in my hands and smells musty in a way I quite like. Now that we're here, face-to-face in the golden firelight, uncertainty rises up to my chin and I'm not sure I can speak.

"You said there was something important to ask?"

"I did." And now I wish I hadn't.

"Something urgent."

I bite my lower lip. "I'm not sure where to begin."

"At the start?" Kaylin swings the kettle over the embers and adds a dry log beneath it. Sparks rise quickly and crackle. "Hot drink?"

"Please." I fold my legs under me on the edge of the bed, losing my nerve. How to warm up to this? I mean, I might be completely wrong. "The phantoms here…"

He gives me a half smile for encouragement.

"They stare at me."

He continues to prepare the tea. "I've noticed, but is it new?"

"No. They always do. In Baiseen, ever since I came to the Sanctuary to trial, they have a kind of curiosity toward me."

"They call non-savants with that gift 'hotu-pele' in Tutapa. It means the favorite one."

I like his definition but I'm not so sure it's a gift. "They say 'pet' here, but…" My face pinches. "Most savants are annoyed by it."

"Idiots," he says under his breath.

"I don't know." I put the books down and cross my arms. "But the link has expanded."

"How so?"

"Now they talk to me as well."

"Talk?" Kaylin looks surprised at that. "In words?"

"Sometimes, but mostly images. The pictures come into my mind with a clear meaning—at least, I think I know what they mean. The first few times, I startled, then brushed it off as my own confused ramblings…"

"Since when do you have confused ramblings?" He laughs and fills the teapot with fragrant herbs, lemongrass, apple mint, orange peel, and spices, a Tutapan version of Ochee.

I laugh back. "You'd be surprised what goes through my head. But it actually began even before we arrived at Aku."

"With Marcus's phantom?"

"It was a glimpse, initially. He'd catch my eye, and then it turned into a longer look and a feeling, then whole conversations."

He whistles through his teeth. "What does Marcus make of it?"

I'm back to biting my lip. "Haven't mentioned this to him yet."

He thinks about that for a moment. "Then what made it so urgent, there on the library steps?"

This is the time to get to the point, tell him that I'm picking up his thoughts, maybe, but I already feel myself falter. "In the archives room, Mia's phantom spotted us, and I told it to go away."

"That's why it backed off? You gave her phantom an order and it obeyed?"

"I think so, unless it was another coincidence." I already know he doesn't think much of coincidence, at least not philosophically.

He takes my hands and kisses my fingers. "There's nothing to fear."

"Nothing to fear?" I pull back. "Maybe for you, who can stare down enemies on any b'larkin day of the week, but I'm not like that. This cross communication from phantom to non-savant, it's not possible. I'm not even trained, and I'm…"

"Ash, slow down."

I guess this topic bothers me a lot more than I'd thought. "It doesn't make sense," I finish lamely.

He pours the tea, minty steam rising from our cups. "Maybe the phantoms find you attractive in an inexplicable way, and they're all trying to understand why."

"That's ridiculous."

He pins me with a look that makes my face heat. "Attraction comes in many forms, for many reasons."

"Maybe."

"There's nothing to fear," he says again.

We finish our drinks in a contemplative silence. When he takes the empty cups away, I retrieve the books. "For now, let's explore the treasures we've found."

"Not sleeping tonight?"

My eyes go to the window. "Not yet."

"Then I'll read with you." Kaylin returns to his place beside me and opens the tome.

"That's it?" my inner voice asks, sounding more than a little perturbed.

Pardon?

"You're not going to ask the burning question?"

I can hear it now. *Oh Kaylin, I meant to say, as well as phantoms talking to me, I also think I hear your thoughts. Do you hear mine?* Sure, I'll tell him that straightaway. Just what he needs, a good reason to question my sanity.

"Look at this," Kaylin points at a sketching in the book.

"Solar system?"

"Read the title."

I squint at the fine lettering. "Amassia's binary suns," I whisper, and all other thoughts disappear.

47

MARCUS

It's working! I hit the training field before dawn. Belair soon joins me, and by the time the bell rings for morning ritual, we're already sweating. When everyone else goes into the dining hall, we sit cross-legged on the sidelines and share bread, cheese, and apples from the kitchen. It's quickly dispatched, then back to it. By the time Zarah arrives, shouting for the class to do laps, I take the lead, Belair right beside me. My training must be inspiring him, too. And the best part is, Zarah notices.

"If you're trying to impress us, Baiseen, you'll have to do better than this," she says, but I see approval in her eyes. That afternoon, she is still sharp as knives on me, but she takes more time with us both, giving extra instruction. It means more work, especially when she assigns us special training, nothing less than ten times the workout, up and down the long steps to the leeward side of the island. And even better, Ash is always there to note it. Of course, she has *said* she's proud of me all along, but now the truth shines in her eyes. And I believe her. Belair and I won't leave the Isle empty-handed.

"I'm not sure I should thank you." Belair keeps pace with me as we run up to the top lookout, his chest heaving and hair sticking to his face.

"You'll thank me when you win all your matches."

De'ral surprises me with a war cry so loud, long, and guttural that it raises the hair on my neck. I holler a challenge as well, Belair and the sun leopard joining in.

"We'll be awarded our yellow robes. There is no doubt."

My new training schedule has made meeting up with Ash nigh impossible. Sure, she's on the sidelines, recording my classes with Zarah, but that's not when we can talk. When she's in the library, I'm taking extra training sessions with Belair on the beach. In the evening, I pass out in bed as soon as my studies are done.

It's been a week since Ash told me she and Kaylin discovered something interesting. *Extremely interesting*, were her exact words. She insists that Samsen, Piper, and Belair hear it as well, so finally, here we are, in her room, waiting on this "extremely interesting" report.

And waiting...and waiting...

Belair, who's finishing up writing his summary on the history of *warrior* phantoms throughout the realms, has yet to arrive.

"Why aren't you working on your report, Marcus?" Piper asks, glancing at my empty hands.

"Because I handed mine in this morning." My smile is smug, but bless the bones, I earned it.

The tide is starting to turn.

I'm no longer lagging behind my classmates, taking the brunt of oversized phantom jokes and withstanding thoughtless jeers. De'ral and I are neck and neck with the best of them, Destan included, though I've yet to beat him in a sparring match. Still, we are not the witless savant-phantom pair that stumbled through the gates of Aku scant weeks ago. Neither are Belair and his sun leopard.

I take a deep, expansive breath. No accomplishment in my life has ever felt this good. Or more meaningful. "Raw salmon and chile flakes?" Kaylin offers the plate of fillets surrounded by lemon wedges. My stomach growls and he laughs. Seems my taste buds have matured as well, thanks to the dish-of-the-realm custom here on Aku.

Ash, Samsen, and Piper join me at the table to slice off bits of the fine pink fish, while Kaylin takes his seat by the window and continues sculpting a lure. I've already put in a request for half a dozen of various sizes. Finest craftsmanship I've ever seen. I can't wait to try them when we get back home.

When Belair arrives, we brew another pot of Ochee and Ash calls the meeting to order. She has us in a semicircle, like a proper class, and proceeds to launch into a topic I don't quite follow.

Honestly, I have no idea what she's talking about.

"Can you repeat that please?" The cycle of the Great Dying? I vaguely recall the palace tutor mentioning it, but that's all. "How is this relevant?"

Ash blows hair off her forehead. "Are you paying attention?"

She sounds like my old tutor as well.

This is all very instructional if we ignore the fact that she broke into a storeroom and stole these "extremely interesting" books from the library archives. The sailor's light fingers are rubbing off. I plan to have a talk with her about it when we're alone. The last thing I need is to justify theft to the High Savant. "Tell me again?"

"This is written in a language called Retoren," Ash says. "I haven't translated much yet, but what we see here concerns all of Amassia and her leaders." She looks poignantly at me and Belair while holding up the page for us to see.

I recognize the drawing. It's the solar system, Amassia and her moon, the third planet from the sun, and seven others expanding farther and farther outward. But there's something else. A red dot with an orbit that goes right off the page. "You're saying this is written in the same script as the tattoos you saw on the Gollnar scouts?"

"Exactly, and the same as the notices at the Clearwater apothecary and Capper Point harbor, too."

Kaylin holds up the flyer and points to the overlapping circle symbols. "Recognize these?"

"The flags flying over the Aturnian camp?" They're more elaborate but definitely the same shapes. "Whatever this is, you've linked it to them?"

"Yes, though we aren't sure in what way."

"And the red dot?" I indicate that solar system image.

"Amassia's second sun." Ash's eyes brighten as she taps it.

"Second, as in there are two?" I ask.

"That's right."

Sounds farfetched to me. "Don't you think if Amassia had two suns we'd know about it?" I say. "See the other rise and set? Have endless daylight?"

"Not when the second sun is so far away. Only a bright star, until—"

"It draws nearer." Kaylin seems as excited as her by this discovery.

"It orbits our sun?" Piper asks. "Like a comet? Is that what the image shows?"

"Sort of." Ash lowers the book. "The Sierraks say they are twins—binary stars—that travel around a central mass. In our case, Amassia's second sun—and I daresay the translation *could* mean a 'dark comet'—has a much, much wider eccentricity in its path. This dark sun, or second sun, syncs with our bright sun only once in a great while, and even then, they don't show it getting very close."

"How great a while?" Samsen asks.

"Every twenty-five-million years, give or take."

No one speaks for a few breaths, the silence heavy.

"How can this knowledge have been passed down for twenty-five-million years?" Samsen asks. "Especially if there was a Great Dying. I assume everything dies?"

"The reference is the ancient sea scrolls." Kaylin lifts his brow. "The fossil records preserved in the thousands of petrified tablets found in the last centuries. Some predate several Great Dyings."

Ash turns the book to another page and passes it around. It's a more detailed representation of the planets, including Amassia. All are in orbit around our central yellow star, but out in the far distance is a second, dark red sun, so red it's almost black. "According to this, the dark sun's approach heralds the next Great Dying."

"Maybe it causes it," Kaylin says. "Some say as it comes closer, it drags debris behind it."

"What debris?" I ask.

"Stardust, ice, rocks, the crumbs of broken planets and exploded comets. It brings it to our inner solar system, and it falls on Amassia like rain. It..."

"It causes change," Ash says. She looks at Kaylin for support and he nods, though where the sailor learned this cosmology, I don't know. I plan to ask.

"Changes?" Samsen asks.

"Ice caps melt, the seas rise, the land heats and then freezes," he says. "The climate changes as Amassia is bombarded with solar dust that lasts for centuries. Everything dies. So it says."

"Everything?" I cross my arms. "How are we still here, if everything dies?" I'm not trying to disparage Kaylin or Ash, but what they're suggesting seems too far from logic.

"Not *every* single thing," Ash says.

"What then?" I ask.

"For each hundred species that die, five will live on, but in a different way. All must adapt to survive, or they perish from the path forever."

I stare out the window. It's a lot to consider, be it true or false.

"The stargazers of Sierrak plotted the course of the second sun," Ash goes on.

I rub my forehead. "Let me see if I have this right. Amassia has two suns, and the second, dark one, has an extreme orbit, returning into view only once every twenty-five-million years, dragging space dust behind it, which rains down on us and triggers the next Great Dying."

"Correct." Ash beams at me.

"And you gathered us for this discussion because…?"

"There's more, about a Crown of Bones." Ash turns to another page.

Belair leans in for a better view. "Whistle bones?"

"Not just any whistle bones," she explains, "but the original twelve carved from the skeleton of Er. Apparently, long ago, when under threat of war, the black-robes took apart the crown and sent each piece to one of the Sanctuaries for safekeeping."

"The honored whistle bones that hang in the Sanctuaries? They form a crown?" I smile. "Must be for a huge head."

Ash *tsks* me. "The crown could be a metaphor, Marcus."

"Fine, fine." I mull it over. "So now the *crown* is dismantled, one whistle bone in each sanctuary?" Well, I know that part is true.

"If we're translating right, yes, but for now, we need to decide what to do with the knowledge."

"Tell Yuki," I suggest, rising. "Or Brogal, when we return."

"But can we trust our High Savant?" Ash reaches for my sleeve to hold me back. "Brogal put me off the path when I asked him about this language. And Yuki's orange-robes would have seen the notices at Capper Point, and these texts are in her archives. She must know about the Great Dying and the Aturnians' sudden interest. Huewin tried to hide it from me, too."

"If they know or not, what does it matter?" I pull away and head for the door. "I mean, it's an interesting discovery, Ash. Maybe even extremely interesting. But once every twenty-five-million years?" I shrug. "You can spend the rest of your life working it out."

"That's just it, Marcus. I can't."

"Why not?"

"According to the notices, Amassia's second sun is nigh."

48

ASH

The fire blazes in the hearth, sparking as I grip the long poker in the palm of my hand. The logs burn hot, and sweat prickles my skin, and not just from the heat. How dak'n long does it take to dash to the kitchen and back with dinner?

My mind has been whirling all evening. Marcus and the others didn't share the enthusiasm Kaylin and I have for our discoveries about the second sun. Maybe it is all myth? But no. It's documented, spread across the pages of multiple books and images for anyone to see.

The Great Dying is coming. Soon, if the notices are to be believed.

But that isn't the only troubling thing… I tighten my grip on the poker.

When Kaylin finally sweeps into the room with a tray full of food, my body relaxes. "You're back." I try to keep the strain out of my voice.

"Did you miss me?" He closes the door then sees my face. "What happened?"

I swallow, my throat still constricted. "The shadow thing…tapping at the window."

"Again?" Kaylin puts the tray on the low table. The scent of cornbread and stew fills the room. Southern Gollnar fare tonight.

"Didn't see, but I feel it, like someone's constantly watching me." My shoulders tighten back up again. "Especially when you aren't here."

"I'm here now."

I'm glad for it, but it's not just that. I hang the poker next to the hearth broom and join him at the table. "Things aren't adding up."

He gives me his full attention, something I like very much about him.

"Did you notice? Aku's first whistle bone isn't displayed over the mural anymore."

He goes back to dishing up the food. "Maybe they take it down to polish it?"

"Then why not say so? I've asked everyone I can, and no one knows what's happened."

"You're worried?"

I can tell he isn't. "Finding out the original whistle bones once formed a crown, and knowing crowns denote power and control, honor and wealth—"

"And sometimes immortality."

I suck in my breath. "You mean, the old gods?"

He shrugs. "Why not?"

"Well, given all that, yes, my curiosity is piqued, and maybe some worry, too." The first whistle bone's disappearance is yet another thing to add to our growing list of oddities: the tapping, the warnings about the Dark Sun, the next Great Dying, Yuki purportedly sending out five messengers when we arrived, not the usual one, then pretending Destan is from Southern Aturnia when we all know he's from the banned North, the seemingly unified Aturnian and Gollnarian troops...

Kaylin serves me a bowl with a large square of cornbread in the center and rich meat stew ladled over it. In spite of all the questions, my stomach growls, very loudly, and we laugh.

"Thank you." I pick up my fork and attack my food. When I turn back to him, he's staring at me and I'm lost in the depths of his eyes. They are a deep violet in the candlelight—all traces of sea-green gone. As I draw breath to speak, there is a *snick* at the door. Kaylin leaps to the side and I find my feet.

He throws open the door so fast I half expect an eavesdropper to stumble into the room, but no one is there.

"Lock this behind me." Kaylin shuts the door and is gone.

I blow out a shaky breath, glancing over at the window. "Or *maybe*," I say to no one, "it was just the wind."

Not even I believe myself.

I finish my meal alone, have a cup of soporific tea to help me sleep, and dive back into the translation work while I wait for it to take, keeping the fire poker handy. In no time, my eyelids are heavy. I go to the door and check up and down the hall. Empty. I close and lock it again, have a wash, and put on a warm winter sleeping gown. As I crawl into bed, my thoughts turn to Baiseen. We'll be traveling home again soon, Marcus and Belair wearing yellow robes, I am certain. They have both come so far. But what then of Kaylin? Will he come, too? We haven't talked about it for weeks.

I have no answers, so I blow out the bedside candles and snuggle under the covers, the room bright from the fire.

Outside, the wind howls. I try not to think of long fingers on the sill and hollow eyes peering in, but there they are, in my imagination, rising to the surface to fill my mind. I close my eyes and shut them out. Slowly, the images fade away, but the wind rages on.

49

KAYLIN

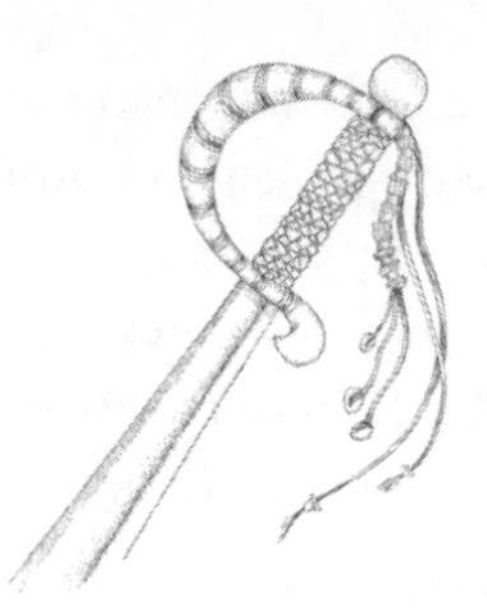

The snow swirls like doves taking flight, my feet sinking ankle-deep into the frost-white powder on the rooftop. Howling wind drowns everything but the barest whisper of waves hitting the coastline far below. I gaze south into the storm, toward Baiseen. Will I see it soon, with Ash? We've not been a day apart since that late afternoon when the *Sea Eagle* was the only ship left in the harbor. Whatever the cost, I can't let them know…

"Let who know what, brother?"

My mind slams shut. *"Salila."* There's a flash in the shadows on the other side of the roof and I am there in a bound, her pale wrists locked in my hands. "Are you the one haunting Ash?"

"Hello to you, too, and ouch!"

"Tell me the truth."

"I'm not haunting her!" She pulls out of my grip. "I came to help."

"Don't need it."

"Really? Then you already know High Savant Tann is south of Lepsea? Perfect time to get your job done, if you ask me, under the cover of his arrival." She crosses her arms. "You're welcome, again."

"Stay out of it."

"Spoilsport."

"Go, Salila, before you're seen."

"Don't you think I blend in?" She lifts one shoulder and turns from side to side.

I bark out a laugh. "A six-foot-tall woman leaping rooftops in the dead of a stormy night? You know you don't."

"As a phantom, though? Couldn't I get away with it?"

I lean in to her face and growl. "Stop your games and go, or I'll toss you off this roof from where you stand."

"You used to be fun." She flips her hair and walks away. When she reaches the edge, she looks over her shoulder at me, smiles a little too wide, and jumps. A moment later, I hear her laughter in my head. *"It's a phantom, by the way, the shadowy, tap-tap thing you are after."*

"Who does it belong to?"

"I'm supposed to do all the work? Find out for yourself."

I press my lips into a tight line. The snow continues to fall around me, a white blanket covering my shoulders. If she's right, it could make sense. Phantoms are drawn to Ash, but could it really be acting without its savant's knowledge? I doubt it, so what is their motive? I check the other three directions from the rooftop and return down the stairs. Instead of going back to Ash, I retrace my steps to the empty foyer and back out into the storm. I will keep vigil from now on. Around the Isle, around the sanctuary. Around my beautiful Ash.

50

ASH

"*Wake! You were meant to be up!*" my inner voice cuts through my dreams.

I'm jolted by a knock at the door that quickly turns into pounding. My eyes don't open, and my arms and legs are dead weights. "Come in," I speak into my pillow.

The pounding continues.

I lift my head. "Come in!"

"It's locked."

B'rack the bones, it is. "Hang on." I swing my legs over the side of the bed and wiggle into sheepskin-lined boots. It's freezing in here. Over my nightdress goes my winter coat and I head for the door, glancing at the window. There hasn't been a hint of the shadow all week and thank the old gods for that. My recording duties, with the shortened time on Aku, have accelerated, and so has the research. I was up late last night, delving deeper and deeper, but hit a wall. It's exhausting. Kaylin's been gone every night—I'm not sure he ever sleeps—which has been disappointing, but still, no nightmares, no tapping.

I swing the door wide.

"You aren't ready?" Marcus strides in. "We're late."

I yawn. "For what?"

"Festival day? Don't tell me you forgot."

I most definitely *did* forget.

Marcus groans. "Hurry up, Ash. The best spots are already gone."

I sweep my clothes off the back of a chair, shuck my coat, and dash to the en suite. "Get my pack, will you?" I come tearing out a moment later, face wet, buttons undone.

He throws me a towel.

"Where's my hairbrush?"

"Use your fingers. Let's go."

I thump down the steps with only one hand in my coat sleeve, a piece of last night's bread in the other. "Has it started?"

"Not yet." We burst out of the hall and into the crowded street. All of Aku is gathered on the training field, leaving clear a large, raised platform in the center and five wide "spokes" leading to it through the crowd. Most of the audience sits cross-legged on blankets, or lie propped on elbows, chatting to their neighbors, cheering for it all to begin. Food vendors circle the grounds offering all kinds of divine-smelling drinks and snacks, but Marcus won't slow down.

I spot Belair's red hair as he scans our way and waves.

"He's saved us places." Marcus pulls me along.

I hurry to keep up as a huge gong sounds, followed by clacking bone sticks, warning us that it's about to start. Every year on Aku, when training is in full swing, they declare a festival, a day of performances called the Spectacle of Realms. For the initiates, it's mostly about eating way too many sweet cakes, dancing in the drum circles, and playing games of chance and wit, but also, each realm shares their traditional dances, stories, and songs at set times throughout the day and night. How could I have lost track?

"Perhaps your mounting workload explains it?"

I guess it does.

I look around for Kaylin, wondering if he's watching, but all I see is a mass of colored robes and cowls.

Yuki steps up to a thunder of cheers, gives a short speech, and instructs us to have fun. Whatever cloud of concern she had when we met isn't showing in the slightest. I find myself cheering along with the best of them, until Marcus interrupts me.

"I learned something about her last night," he says, leaning in.

"Go on."

"The Nonnovan war dance!" Belair points as the performers make their way up the spokes to the raised platform in stylized, exaggerated movements. The only music comes from the women chanting in the background, a fiery chorus. They all wear leather armor breastplates and split skirts of leather and chain, with red and black snakes painted around their bare arms. I startle, pulling on Marcus's sleeve. Some of the snakes are live, phantom or not, I can't tell from here.

Soon bells, whistles, and drums join the chorus, creating a staccato beat that rises to the sky. Even if I was savant, I wouldn't want to face such ferocity, spears thrusting and stabbing in mock battle.

I lean against Marcus and whisper in his ear. "Tell me more about Yuki."

"You know how you overheard that five messengers were sent when we arrived, not just one?"

I nod, eyes on the performance.

"Those ships are missing. Sunk, they think."

"Deliberately?"

"Five separate ships accidentally sinking within days of one another? Has to be an attack."

"By whom?"

His face darkens. "Don't know, but Yuki was going to inform the realms of the Gollnar and Aturnian alliance. Now Father doesn't know anything about it."

I let my breath out in a rush. "Worse, Marcus. It means your father doesn't even know we arrived."

The dance finishes and I look over my shoulder toward the harbor. There, far away, a figure stands on the stable rooftop, watching. I know by the regal posture it's Kaylin. "Always in the crow's nest."

Marcus sees him, too. "What's he doing up there?"

"Watching the performance?"

"Looks to me like he's watching you."

"Hardly." I let slip a nervous laugh as my face heats.

"The Gollnar hunting dance!" Belair waves at the performers running and tumbling with their colorful silk robes and streamers. The music shifts in tempo and sound, the field filled with rhythmic tambourines and lilting reed pipes. Their movements are like bouquets of flowers bursting into the sky and raining down on us.

Marcus is back in my ear again. "Ash, don't get me wrong. I'm glad Kaylin is here, especially when I can't be, and I know you're friends…"

"But?"

He hesitates.

"There's been no breaking of the initiate journey rules of conduct, if that's what has you worried." I think about the kissing and clear my throat. "We did, um. I mean, there was a moment, or two…in the library."

He waves it away. "I don't care that you broke in. The information you gained is important, and you'll put it back, right?"

"We're going to, yes, but what I wanted to say is, we kissed." I wait, but he doesn't speak. "It will not happen again. Nothing in all of Amassia would keep me from my task as your and Belair's recorder."

"I'm a task, am I?" The audience applauds the dancers on stage like a thunderstorm.

I punch him in the arm, and he grunts. "Marcus, I promise you, I am pledged to my—"

"Duty?"

"Privilege!" My eyes well. "Your friendship has always been that to me, ever since our first day on the training field. You're my champion."

He nods like an overlord. "And don't you forget it."

I'm about to cry when I see it. His eyes, they sparkle. He's laughing at me! I laugh back and punch him again just for making me worry. We chuckle until a hush comes over the training ground. Extraordinary music strikes up, slow at first but building until every hair on my body stands out.

I close my eyes and drink in the harmonies. "They're playing the whistle bones."

When I look again, black-robes advance up the spokes. The novices with shaved heads beat bone drums and the elders with long, decorated locks play the whistle bones. They float to the stage in a dance that has the whole crowd enthralled. In their long robes, it appears their feet never touch the ground. They play and chant, their phantoms undulating around them like curtains of light, evoking the distant stars, the folds in the sea before sunrise, and the secrets hidden in the deepest parts of the forests. I can't pull my eyes away.

There's a breath-holding silence when they finish, followed by deafening applause. I look down, realizing I've gripped Marcus's arm like a vise. The Baiseen Bone Throwers seldom perform in public, at least not in any events I can attend. It's extraordinary. I hope they will do it again tonight.

They exit down the spokes with a livelier tune and the Sierraks take their place on stage, brassy horns blaring as they perform the Dance of the Four Elements. I know this one and cheer. The performers for each element wear brilliant colors—red for Fire, green for Earth, yellow for Air, and blue for Water. When they enact the water story, a romance between the sea and a river nymph, I lean forward, taking in every sound and nuance.

"This is better than I even thought it would be." Belair cheers with us when it's over. "What next?"

"Breakfast!" I beam a smile. "As your dutiful recorder, I think you two should buy a big one for me. There are pancakes today, I hear."

"I'll get you a stack two miles high," Belair says.

"And apple butter? Melted on top?"

"Anything you like." Marcus stands first and helps me up.

I smile and squeeze his arm again. But we hold each other's gaze and slowly the corners of my mouth turn down.

Five ships lost. Messages not delivered. One more week for us here on Aku, and much still to be done. What more could possibly go wrong?

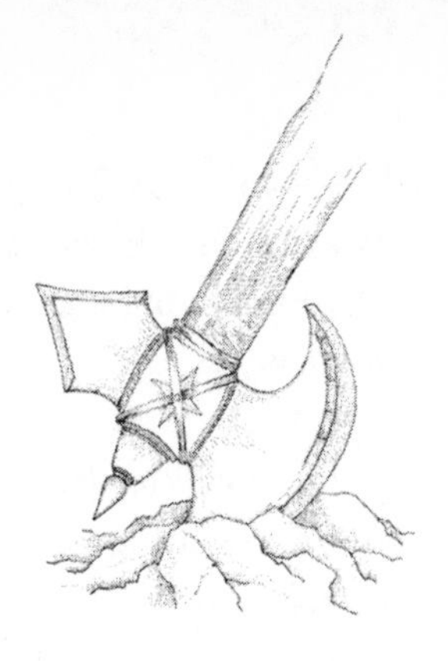

51

MARCUS

This is it. We've made it. At least, I hope we have. There's nothing more to study. No new exercise to learn. No more laps or drills to perfect. Not after today. We'll be awarded our yellow robes at the ceremony tonight, if we earned them, or not. I'll know soon enough. Zarah said she'd announce it at the end of this final morning class.

I think I might be sick.

The newly laid grass crunches underfoot as I stand at attention between Destan and Belair. In moments, I'll be hot and sweating, but for now, gooseflesh rises on my arms. I glance at Belair and he gives me a smart nod. We're ready, and this time, I know it's true.

Destan salutes us both. "May the best savant win."

He means the High Initiate award, yet another part of training we hadn't known about, but one I'd move mountains to win, if only to see Petén's face when I tell him. I don't know if Belair and I are even in the running, though, but I'm sure Destan is. We tap our fists to our chests and repeat his words. "May the best savant win."

The rim of the training field is packed with cheering support. Everyone on the island must be watching. The recorders sit farther into the field from the sidelines. Ash smiles and waves. She's bundled in a knee-length sheepskin coat, knit cap, and high, fur-lined boots, ready with her writing board in her lap.

"*Today we will give her something worthy of the records,*" I say to De'ral.

"Raise your phantoms!" Zarah's breath turns to fog as her voice carries over our heads.

I lunge forward and drop to my knees, touching the hard ground for less than a breath before I'm up again, running. In front of me, De'ral erupts from the earth, dirt and turf flying, but not in my face. Not anymore. It all happens too fast for that now.

"Perimeter," Zarah shouts. "Four laps."

I take the lead, knowing the execution is flawless. That Zarah doesn't find fault is the highest praise. She's like Father that way. The closest the Magistrate ever comes to a compliment is a momentary absence of criticism, which used to get under my skin. Today, it doesn't bother me at all. I can feel my worth.

I set a strong pace, De'ral pounding along by my side. At the first lap, my breath blasts out in white puffs, the biting cold in my limbs replaced with hot, rushing blood. I catch the grin on Ash's face and shoot her a quick wink. De'ral turns to Ash as well and pumps his fist.

"Please stay focused."

He turns back to me and keeps running.

"Line up!" Zarah makes a note as I finish the final lap in first place.

Destan runs in on my heels, his phantom like a black shadow with a carnivorous face, its tongue rolling out. Following him is Belair and the red sun leopard everyone has grown to admire. I suspect Belair can outrun us both, but the most he's ever done with me is tie. The redheaded Tangeen, who annoyed me to the bone when first taking Larseen's place, has become a friend and ally. No doubt what the Magistrate had in mind all along with the substitution. It looks like we'll both have a powerful position in our realms someday. Unless the next Great Dying comes beforehand.

I frown. It's no disrespect to Ash, but a second sun bringing mass devastation? Next thing she'll tell me Mar are real.

"Face your partners for battle moves." Zarah waves us into lines.

In three rows of three, we go through a series of punches, lunges, and kicks. Our group performs as one, in sync, phantoms mirroring savants in the way most appropriate for their form. De'ral punches and lunges in unison with me, as does Destan's phantom. Belair's leopard jumps and snarls and swipes the air, not randomly anymore but in full focus and control. We all march forward then turn around and repeat the moves back to the start. Ash watches me intently, and my chest expands.

"Marcus, Destan, Belair, and Cyres." Zarah calls the names of each contestant, and I want to shout my victory. I'm in the first group! "Choose your swords, spears, and shields." She points at the weapons rack. "Take the north end of the field and prepare to spar. The rest of you, to the obstacle course."

The four of us jog to the far side of the field, phantoms by our sides. Out of the corner of my eye, I see Ash pick up her things, along with one other recorder, a young man who's here with Cyres, and follow along.

Again, I wonder why Destan doesn't have a recorder following him; is it a matter of coin as Ash suggested? It must be nice not to have every single mistake put down in a book, but the records hold our triumphs, too, and I'm finally feeling like my good days now outweigh the bad ones at the start.

Our group squares off, ready to go through basic battle tactics while we wait for Zarah to referee the matches. Destan steps up and shouts out the commands and we alternately attack and defend in the prescribed moves. It doesn't take Zarah long to appear, and she actually smiles at us. "Well done." She moves to the center of our group. "Now let's see what you've really got."

I stand tall, shoulders back, chin up, warmth rushing through me. *"Be ready, De'ral."*

"You'll have one minute to disable your opponent by putting their phantom to ground."

It's all I can do to keep from thrusting my fist in the air. Full contact! This is it, but suddenly the air goes out of my lungs as the images of smashed scouts rise up from their graves. Will I be able to keep control or will this end in another massacre?

"First up, Belair and Cyres."

"You better be listening, De'ral."

Ash and the other recorder settle at a distance as Zarah drops her arm, signaling them to begin. The orange-robe upends the sandglass and steps back.

Belair sends his phantom straight in. It circles the agahpa, stalking, while Belair clangs his spear on his shield to harry Cyres. She darts and dashes about, keeping Belair preoccupied. Neither phantom lands a blow.

"Thirty seconds," shouts Zarah. "You can do better than this!"

The crowd presses closer, cheering them both on. There can be multiple winners in these final competitions, but only one High Initiate.

A second later, the sun leopard jumps onto the agahpa and sinks fangs into its back. The treelike phantom responds by reaching over its head and throttling the big cat. It tightens its branchy fingers until the sun leopard lets go and is lifted high into the air. Belair sends his spear sailing over Cyres's head. Out of reflex, she ducks, giving Belair time to run in and grab her arm. He flips her over his back and slams her into the ground. At the same time, Belair's phantom twists around, latches onto the agahpa's throat, and shakes it till it cracks. The agahpa goes to ground, leaving the sun leopard rolling woodchips off its tongue.

"Time!" Zarah calls and Belair releases Cyres.

Hollers roar up from all around, including the students at the obstacle course who have turned to watch. Ash stands, banging her hands together before writing in the records, a huge smile on her face.

"Good show." I slap Belair on the back as he leaves the circle.

"Baiseen, you're up with Destan," Zarah calls from the sideline.

When I step into the fight circle, my heart beats double-time. Destan gives me a respectful nod, but I catch a look behind his eyes and something in me runs cold. Or is that De'ral's reaction?

We fight! my phantom says.

The pale winter sun flares as it reflects off Destan's twin blades. He holds one in each hand as is the way of the Northern Aturnian warriors. He doesn't seem to be trying to hide his origins today, which is worrisome. I glance to Ash, to see if she notices, but her eyes are on De'ral.

When in position, Zarah shouts, "Fight!" and my head snaps back to my opponent.

Destan charges straight at me while his phantom flips in the air and takes one of the blades for himself. I raise my shield and spear but Destan darts out of the way, harassing again and again with his double-edged blade. It's all I can do to evade the strikes, which are dangerously close. But inside I hold onto a secret smile. Destan is flamboyant, making a fatal mistake. He hasn't taken our improvements seriously—particularly that of my control.

De'ral towers over Destan's phantom, but still the other *warrior* runs fearlessly toward us. Without breaking stride, it leaps, trying to sink its blade straight into De'ral's neck. Far from clumsy, De'ral blocks with his left hand, spins the other phantom up in the air, and sends it flying with a front kick. It sails over the field and lands smack in the middle of the obstacle course, knocking a student off the balance beam. My chest expands as I take a deep breath, and a wave of cheers wash over the field. Our win!

"He's up," Belair shouts just as I'm about to claim the victory. How could it not have gone to ground?

"Ten seconds," Zarah calls.

Destan's phantom runs back to the circle and fakes left, then leaps right, the movements so fleeting he ends up impaling De'ral in the forehead. It's a direct blow and puts my phantom to ground instantly. I square my shoulders and give a quick bow to Destan, who isn't looking, and then to Zarah, who is.

"Well done, all of you," she says, and announces the winners. "Destan of Southern Aturnia and Belair of Tangeen. We honor your achievement today."

Belair and Cyres bow to each other, but when I turn to Destan, he bows imperceptibly and with a smirk on his face.

I keep my expression bland and return the recognition, while inside my heartbeat steadies. "Now." Zarah claps her hands, bringing me out of the daze. "You four will officiate the other matches."

The command rings in my head. Us four? Did I hear her right? I look to Ash, who pumps her fist in the air. Those asked to officiate are in the running for High Initiate, surely. As I think it, Yuki appears. She's making the rounds, checking in with each group on the field. She and Zarah confer over a manuscript. A list of names? Quickly they nod agreement and Yuki moves on, across the field to the next class.

"Carry on," Zarah says.

I take charge before anyone else can, call the sparring partners, and referee disputes. Soon each of us four are beaming as we run our classmates through the trials. At the end, the entire class lines up in front of her. This is it. The moment of reckoning.

"Every one of you has worked hard," Zarah says. "Though some harder than others." Her eyes go to a few students in the back then rest on me and Belair.

My throat constricts. It's a good thing, right?

"We acknowledge you, and your efforts, whether you leave Aku with your yellow robes or not."

No one breathes.

Zarah scans the manuscript in front of her and clears her throat. "Trin, green-robe of Gollnar, it is not yet your time. You may return next year and try again."

We all clap for her and salute fists to chests. She's young and, as I recall, showed strong potential, just weak on focus.

"Ren, green-robe of Nonnova."

The young man steps forward.

"This was your third try. It's time for you to discuss with your High Savant a new role at the Sanctuary of Nonnova."

We all know what that means. We clap and salute him as well, though his expression looks more like relief than disappointment.

"Belair of Tangeen..." She pauses and my guts knot. "Yellow-robe warrior."

We all whoop and cheer until she calls the next name. "Cyres of Sierrak, yellow-robe warrior."

Thunderous applause.

"Destan of Aturnia, yellow-robe warrior."

Could anyone have doubted it?

She goes through the entire class, leaving me to dead last. By now sweat runs down my temples and I can hardly breathe.

"Marcus Adicio of Baiseen..."

My heart stops and won't beat again until I hear her next words.

"Yellow-robe warrior."

We all explode, students, recorders, the crowd. It's a while before Zarah can be heard again.

It's also a while before I can clear my eyes of the tears.

"Your robes will be awarded tonight in the great hall. Congratulations. You've all earned it."

We cheer again until Zarah waves us down. "Break for lunch, the lot of you. Then back here at eighth bell for the final trial for High Initiate." She pauses to smile down on us. "If you aren't familiar with rigg-tackle-stuggs, learn the rules."

My brows slam down as Ash gasps. Rigg-tackle-stuggs? Is she kidding? High Initiate will be decided by a bones-be-cracked *ball* game?

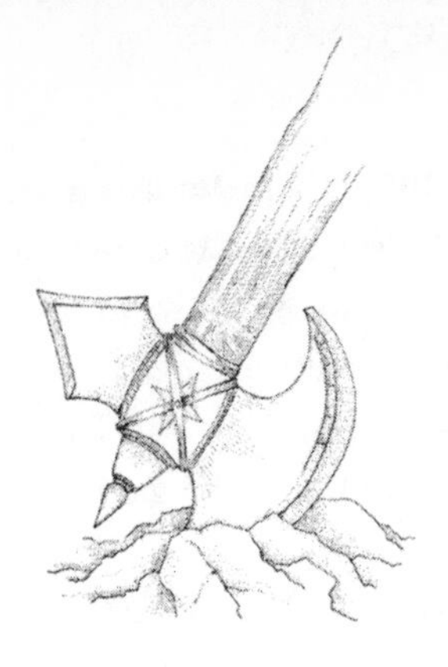

52

MARCUS

I still can't believe the final trial's a ball game. Yet another surprise of the trials, though I suppose it could be worse. I've won my yellow robes, bones be praised. I'll go home and take my rightful place on the Council. *"We did it, De'ral."*

You keep mentioning.

"And you don't seem to realize what we would have lost if we'd failed."

What you'd *have lost. I am De'ral, warrior of Baiseen, either way.*

This is no time to argue with my phantom or try to explain the realm politics involved in robe hierarchy. We have a game to play, and it's no ordinary ball sport. Crazy rules, rigg-tackle-stuggs. I don't know how the Sierraks thought it up.

"Baiseen, third down. Pick up the ball!" Zarah shouts then blows her whistle. It echoes through the air, piercing the afternoon fog rising up the road.

This stuggs game has two balls in play at any given time, and only three savants on each team, which makes six a side, counting phantoms. There are four goalposts, one at every point of the compass. I've only just learned the rules. Make that *lack* of rules. You raise your phantom, score a goal, or prevent the opponents from doing so. It's all about possession of the ball, and practically anything goes.

The mood is tense, the game tied, twenty-four all, but I'm smiling inside. Win or lose, we've made it, mere green-robes no longer.

De'ral grumbles.

"I'm happy, all right?"

I search the crowded sideline for Ash and then remember. She had to hurry back to the library at halftime to put the finishing touches on the records. Yuki must approve them before we leave the island. I picture myself boarding a sloop for the journey home, yellow robes flapping in the sea breeze…

"Huddle up," Belair shouts. We put our heads together while he relays an elaborate play I barely follow. The Tangeen knows the game and isn't shy about being captain. The whistle blows again, Belair tosses the ball to me, and I maneuver for position in the center of the field, dead set in front of Destan, a block-and-tackler who has decked me repeatedly so far, hard. In these final minutes of the game, I intend to reverse that experience. Seems only fair.

We square off and the whistle blows three times. Belair runs wide, and I pass to him as Destan tackles me high. I hit the ground backward, head slamming the grass, but not before getting off a perfect throw. Destan turns to plow after Belair, his phantom already on him, but Belair jumps high and catches the ball. Behind us, another play is in motion and I see through De'ral's eyes that Cyres, on Destan's team, has the second ball and is coursing for a goal.

On our side of the field, Belair throws a high arcing pass to his phantom just as Destan's *warrior* slides in front of him, tripping him up. The ball's already in the air, though, and the sun leopard catches it mid-leap and thunders twenty yards at unstoppable speed to score. We run back to the center and slap each other hard on the back.

"Chew on that one, Destan," I call out, taunting. Unlike Palrion football, this game of stuggs has no etiquette. Quite the opposite, we're expected to harry and harass one another, and apparently, a good game isn't complete without a few players ending up in the infirmary. I'm actually starting to enjoy the barbarism, or maybe that's De'ral.

"*You* chew on it," Destan shouts back as the second ball in play on the other side of the field scores, his phantom making a touchdown.

"Tied at thirty-two," Zarah shouts.

A new savant to our group, a girl named Jain, leans in close in the huddle. "Pass to me, Baiseen. I can score." She has a large condor phantom that appears docile at first glance, a big bird with a comical head that turns sideways to see to the front. But it's no clown. The lithe, dark-eyed phantom is a *warrior/alter* combo and can turn its wings into knife blades and its beak into a dagger. It also knows how to catch a ball and drop it behind the goal posts.

"I will if you're free."

Jain winks. "Count on it."

"Phantoms to ground. This is your fourth and final down. You have fifteen seconds to break the tie," Zarah says. "Or we go into overtime."

We all drop a knee to the ground and bring our phantoms in before standing back up. I shuffle side to side around our lineup, as does the opposing team, finding the best position, but Destan always ends up in front of me.

I huff. Just let him try to block De'ral.

The whistle sounds three times in quick succession, and the game's in play.

We charge toward one another, then drop to our knees. In front of us, the grass erupts, rocks and earth exploding skyward. De'ral is up first and he somersaults high in the air to grab the ball as I hurl it toward him. Quickly, I lower a shoulder and slam hard into Destan before he can change course. The wind's knocked out of him this time and he lies there gasping for it back. Yep, seems fair.

Meanwhile, De'ral lands on his feet in time to dodge a blow from Destan's *warrior*. The second ball fumbles and bounces out of bounds.

"Only one ball in play," Zarah shouts.

I'm up fast and De'ral tosses back to me on the sprint. Cyres intercepts the catch and doubles back, heading the other way. De'ral slams her off her feet, the ball goes high, and Belair catches it on the bounce. Still in play. He feigns left-right-left to distract Destan, who's charging after him. We run on opposite sidelines, the crowd going wild, and when he's about to go down, he passes to me.

"Baiseen!" Jain shouts. She's wide open.

The afternoon fog grows thicker. It's going to make it hard to see to the goals soon, but no one is going to give up. Not with High Initiate at stake. I cock my arm, looking for Jain, who was there a second ago. I blink moisture from my eyelashes. Where is she?

Zarah calls, "Ten seconds."

Destan slices toward me. The sun leopard charges and bowls the savant over, his foot clipping my ankle. I stagger, but there is Jain waving as I stumble to a halt. I turn sideways to throw the ball as Destan jumps up, coming at me with a lunge punch. I change tactics, gripping the ball to my side with one hand and blocking with the other, shouldering him full in the chest. With Destan down, his phantom hesitates, a chance for De'ral to knock it flat. I look again for Jain. She's covered, but Belair's free. I cock my arm, ready to let loose, but check myself again.

"Marcus!" Belair shouts.

My ears prick and I look up at the sky. I thought I heard something but there's nothing there but gathering clouds.

"Five seconds!" Zarah shouts as she watches the sandglass. "You won't find help up there, Baiseen."

Everything turns to slow motion in the final moments of the game. I do a front roll, hitting the grass and coming up in a clear zone, arrowing the ball to Belair. A boom sounds in the distance, like waves crashing into the seawall. At the same time, Belair jumps, catching the ball as it hits him hard in the belly. He flies, running it between the goalposts a half a second before Zarah calls time.

"Goal!" Belair cries. He holds the ball high over his head and prances back to me, leopard bounding by his side.

I take the ball and slam it hard, sending it into the air. "We did it! We won!" De'ral and I lets loose a war cry as Belair and I slap each other on the back.

"Baiseen! Baiseen! Tangeen! Tangeen!"

I spin to find Zarah and her phantom cheering for us at the top of their voices. Her eyes lock onto mine, and I see it all in the depths of her regard. It's what she's never given me before—full, unreserved, wholehearted approval. Grinning, I turn to the opposing team to show respect. With Belair at my side, we bow to all save Destan. He's nowhere to be seen. "Sore loser?" I say to Belair.

"Appears that way," he replies.

Another boom cracks across the field, shaking the ground.

I tense, hand going to the hilt of my sword, which isn't there. All around me, the celebration sputters out as my teammates brace, searching for the source of the sound. Is it thunder? I look to the sky again. The phantoms are as confused as us, but they return to their savants, alert and at the ready.

"De'ral?"

He cocks his head, listening.

Zarah shields her eyes, focused toward the sea, the game forgotten. She looks back at us, her expression darkening. "Everyone down!" she commands.

Another boom echoes through the Sanctuary, and the whole Isle of Aku trembles. People gasp around us, stumbling, falling to the ground with hands over their ears.

My muscles bunch, ready to fight, but there's no sign of an enemy. I slip into phantom perspective. From a greater height, I see rocks hurling toward us. A few fall on the slopes just short of the stables, but others find their marks in the buildings and streets. The Sanctuary erupts into chaos. Cries rise up. The tower bells clang. Savants and phantoms rush from the buildings and scatter like ants.

Cold dread grips me as the truth slaps my face. "Aku is under attack!" I shout and leap to my feet.

But before I can stand, a boulder sails through the air and hits the library, cracking the top half of the tower. The steeple leans over, snaps off, and crashes to the ground. Debris billows up out of the eerie fog, and papers and bits of books and wood chips rain like confetti.

My heart plummets, and the air is punched from my lungs. "Ash!" I cry and sprint toward the toppled building, De'ral ahead of me.

"Marcus!" Zarah shouts.

I look over my shoulder at Zarah. A low-pitched whistle sings as a boulder flies straight toward her. De'ral responds before I can direct him, throwing a punch into the air. He hits the catapulting boulder, shattering it into a thousand pieces. They fall like hot sparks around Zarah, who barely has time to cover her face.

When she looks up, she salutes me and De'ral. "Thanks, Marcus. Fast thinking."

"Orders?" I blink back tears, my heart torn from my chest. There's no time to rummage through the ruined library, searching for Ash's remains, not while we're under attack.

"You and Belair, send your phantoms to the first outlook. Cyres and Jain, to the second level. Report to me everything they see. Go." She turns to dole out orders to the others pressed around her.

Our four phantoms take off, sun leopard, *warrior*, agahpa, and the condor in the lead overhead. Zarah's phantom races to the High Savant's hall. "All of you. Keep your phantoms up. Stick to me. Close in."

We circle her, savants and phantoms alike, while more alarms rise. The shower of rocks continues.

It doesn't take De'ral long to reach the first lookout, overtaking the others with his giant strides as he climbs to the top of the cliff. At first, there is nothing but a thick, gray wall of fog in the harbor below, but slowly, the wind blows across the sea, pushing some of the fog away. "Ships," I say to Zarah.

"Realm?"

"Northern Aturnia flags and…" I should have told Yuki about the encampment under Mount Bladen, specifically about the twin sun flags they sported. Because here they are again, one atop every ship, beating down our door. "Twin suns."

"How many ships?"

"A hundred or more, if there's one."

"All with catapults," Belair adds.

"The docks are taken. The enemy's landing." Cyres's voice is shrill, her face streaked as she watches through her phantom's eyes.

"The nearest catapults are lighting pitch." There is a thud, and Jain staggers backward. Her face goes slack and she falls to the ground.

"Jain!" Cyres shouts. "Her phantom was hit."

Zarah checks the girl's pulse and shakes her head. "It's too late. Hear me," she says, shouting over the frantic cries in the streets. "We must block the main road. That's our first line of defense." She points to the yards and paddocks near the stables where the equestrians are mounting up. "Warriors, take weapons from the racks. I want you there with your phantoms. Others will join you soon." The students race off and Zarah turns to me. "How many have reached the shore?"

"Dozens are landing with at least fifty rowboats coming up behind."

Zarah nods. "Bring your phantom back, get your weapons. Belair, you too. Defend the road below the stables. Don't let them into our temple grounds."

Belair and I drop to our knees and bring our phantoms back. A second later they roar out of the ground in front of us. When my eye catches the ruined library, I hesitate again.

"Marcus, to the stables," Zarah says firmly. "If we can't defend the Sanctuary, it will matter little if your recorder is dead or alive."

She lives, De'ral rumbles in my mind.

Nausea rises to the back of my throat and my eyes burn. *"You can't know that."*

"Marcus Adicio!" Zarah cries. "Go!"

I clap sword on shield and take off at a run.

53

ASH

Kaylin holds me under the archway, the only structure around us that hasn't crumbled. Fog and dust obscure the entire boulevard, and all I can think is, *What in all the B'dakin blazes just happened?*

Only moments ago, I sat at my library desk, putting the last touch on the records. Yellow-robe savants, the both of them! I nearly gushed with pride, recording that. And then my inner voice blasted in my head "*Get out!*" the same instant Kaylin thundered up the second-story steps and into the room. The look on his face launched me from my seat. He threw the records into my bag and raced me out of there so fast I thought there was a fire. The whole time, he shouted at everyone else in the library to run.

I literally flew out the door and across the street, he moved so quickly. We ducked under this very arch as a massive rock smashed into the library tower, toppling it to the ground.

I cover my head with my hands as more rocks plummet down. Kaylin does the same, leaning over me. When the dust clears, I see the temple proper, farther up the broken street. The doors are crushed and the courtyard fountain… It's gone. My eyes fill with tears at the rush of muddy water bubbling over piles of rubble. That's when it hits.

"Marcus!" I cry and try to run to the training field. I whimper when Kaylin pulls me back.

"Not that way." For the first time, my sailor looks shaken. "We have to get off the island. An Aturnian fleet attacks."

"Aturnians? Attack?"

"Aye. A hundred ships strong."

"We're under attack?" I say it again but still don't comprehend.

"Let's go." He makes to pull me along.

I dig in my feet. "We can't leave without the others."

"Why not? They're warriors."

"So are you."

"Aye, and I'm using my skills to get you to safety." He tries to shuffle me along again, but I won't budge.

"No," I insist. "They're *our people*."

He looks confused.

I grip his forearms so tight his hands must be losing circulation. "Kaylin, we don't leave our people behind."

He stares at me for a long moment. With how protective he is, I'm afraid he'll just toss me over his shoulder and flee the island. Maybe he sees my desperation, because finally, he relents. "Where're Piper and Samsen?"

Thank the bones. I release his arm and pull on my coat, then secure the satchel straps onto my back. "They were watching the game, I think."

"Marcus and Belair?"

I close my eyes and try calling to De'ral.

He doesn't answer in words, but I receive a clear picture in my mind of where he is, high on the lookout, gazing back toward his class, still on the field.

"Near the stables, with Zarah," I say.

"All right." He takes my hand and leads me into the chaos. "Let's go get our people."

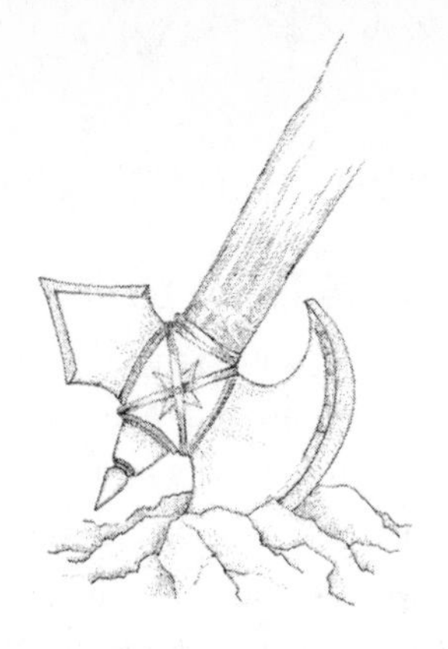

54

MARCUS

I'm numb inside, my heart frozen solid, yet somehow, I move. How did this happen? Aturnians bombard the sacred Isle of Aku? For what possible aim? There are no answers on offer and only Zarah's command to follow. "Defend the road. Let none pass." I go through the motions knowing I will either succeed or die trying.

Belair and I take cover among tall hedges beyond the stables. The gate and the road beyond are nearly invisible in the fog as I split my vision between De'ral's perspective and my own. Nothing moves in either direction but the rolling, silent mist.

"It doesn't make sense," I whisper to Belair. "We saw them land."

Belair nods, keeping his eyes fixed between parted leaves. "They should be here by now."

The High Savant's phantom is nearby, taking the form of tumbleweed and wedged in the low fork of a tree. The members of the Aku High Council, those who are left after the first air attack, position their phantoms around the perimeter of the Sanctuary to keep watch on all borders. Some of the students' phantoms are also manning the lookouts, their savants' perspective in them as well. We have a panorama of the siege if nothing else.

Siege? Is that what this is?

"Have you seen Samsen and Piper?"

"They waved to us from the sidelines before the last play." Belair wipes his brow. "I think they had young students with them."

I can only hope they made it to safety, but as I look skyward, I'm not sure where that safety would be.

"It was Destan, wasn't it." Belair isn't asking.

"If so, may his path be snapped in two like a stick." I spit as I say the words. "Was he communicating with the Aturnian fleet somehow?"

"What red-robe leads them?"

"I don't know." I move more into De'ral's perspective. "They can't stay in the harbor forever."

"Maybe they have an endless supply of boulders." Belair lets the shrub go. Like me, he holds a war sword and keeps the tip low. I can just make out the orange and red glint of his sun leopard stalking down the far side of the road, fog rippling over it like a gray stream.

"It's not a bad tactic, for them." I send De'ral to the middle of the road. He puts one knee down and presses both hands into the packed dirt, like a sprinter ready to take off, feeling for vibrations. The *warrior*'s muscles twitch, a response mirrored in my body involuntarily. We walk a razor edge, ready to smash the first enemy wave, and the second, and the third.

Nothing coming this way. The words echo in my head, but I don't know if it's me or De'ral who speaks, our senses are that entwined. With each word, my head throbs.

"Listen." Belair points skyward. "I think they've stopped firing."

He's right. I hear the rhythmic crash of waves onto the rocks below and the crumble of wreckage and cries behind me, but no more boulders whistle through the sky. I look over my shoulder, watching the dark coils of smoke rise from the fallen buildings, chased by tongues of bright orange flames. The fires look tiny from a distance, like candles set around the rubble.

I pull my focus back to the road, imagining the path from the harbor up to the heart of the Sanctuary. "They have to come this way." Sheer cliffs on either side of the island guarantee it unless they send phantoms flying over the tall headlands. The only way in for this horde is up the road and through the gates, which are locked tight.

"Should I send my phantom farther down?" Belair asks. "Have a better look?"

I nod. "Do it."

He moves off in a crouch, swallowed up by the fog in three steps.

I wait, rolling the hilt of my sword back and forth in my hand. When sunlight breaks through the fog, the blade mirrors a stream of refractions that pierce the gray-washed world. The light glances off a form coming up the road. I narrow my eyes and peer through De'ral's gaze. It's Belair, his shoulders hunched and limbs jerky. He's scared, like all of us.

"Anything?" I call to him.

He signals negative.

"Come back." I motion with my hand and direct De'ral to check the rest of my classmates. They are watching, like us, determined, ready for battle, though their eyes are wide, bodies taut. A small part of me hopes this is our final examination before gaining yellow-robe level, some grad test for High Initiate. But it can't be. The catapults were not an illusion. The library fell. Halls and buildings were crushed with savants inside them. Aku is meant to be invincible, as old as the ocean and stronger than the rock that supports it. But I saw the buildings crack, smashed to the ground before anyone escaped, people buried beneath stones… Ash gone…

De'ral sends me an image of an ancient tree whose roots cover all of Amassia. *She's stronger than you imagine.*

A sliver of hope that she might have survived finds its way in, but before I can ask more, Belair nudges my side.

"Did you see that?"

"Where?"

"Phantom eyes." He nods toward the sun leopard. "Movement. Middle of the road."

I put my thoughts of Ash away and move further into De'ral's perspective as he stands up to his full height. "What is it?"

"There," Belair whispers.

Then I see. Not a stone's throw from my *warrior*, the mist flickers and plumes. It's subtle at first, but growing, expanding up and down the road. To see better, I take full phantom perspective, leaving nothing behind. I'm deeper than I've ever gone into De'ral's view, even though part of me screams a warning against it.

"*A savant must keep ever present in their own body. A savant must always stay in control.*"

My lectures are not forgotten. But I ignore the tenet, shouldering my way in until I hear a snap, like a door slamming shut. And through De'ral's eyes I finally have a full view of the mist coursing over the road and around my legs. It picks up like a storm at sea, rising and falling in violent waves. Frothy streams blow off the crests until the ground fog takes form, congeals, and shoots straight toward me.

"Defense!" I shout, but the sound roars out of De'ral's mouth, booming up the road to the other students. "Attack on the road!"

I'm inside my phantom completely when he, when *I,* am struck full force. I raise a phantom fist to ward off the blow, but searing pain smashes me out of De'ral and back into my own body. I gasp, and De'ral roars, echoing my agony.

"To the stables!" I order De'ral and the others, grabbing Belair's shoulder. We must regroup to assess and warn Zarah. I turn to Yuki's phantom and shout, stealth no longer important. "The enemy approaches, hidden in the fog."

We have to form a blockade, keep them from winning through to the Sanctuary. But I am running *toward* shrieks and chaos. Impossible! They have not yet passed.

A girl's voice cries out above the others. The sound arcs overhead as her body comes into view like an awkward, flapping bird. Cyres flies above the mist and snaps to a stop midair as if an invisible rope around her reaches its length. Her neck cracks and she falls to the ground. I struggle to comprehend until the realization roots me to the spot. *"The enemy* is *the fog,"* I tell De'ral. "Phantom fog!" I shout to the others. "The gates are breached! We're surrounded!"

At the same moment, outlines emerge all around us, hundreds of them. They form into crouched figures with armor and swords, teeth and claws, all advancing.

"To Zarah!" I yell as I face the High Savant's phantom. "Yuki! See this. *Alter* phantoms breach the Sanctuary." They continue to materialize in multiple forms—gaping maws, giant insects, bears without fur, gruesome winged predators leaping to the sky, and ghostly forms, each controlled by the marching savants suddenly appearing on the road unchallenged.

Defense! De'ral hollers in my mind.

I push back into my phantom and survey the enemy phantoms and savants. Behind them, a long line of foot soldiers march, rank upon rank all the way from the docks, their vibrations through the ground now palpable. But De'ral isn't cowered. He's fighting hard, surrounded by dozens of their fallen, broken bodies, but for every soldier he puts down, another ten rise out of the fog to take its place. The phantoms come at De'ral like ants crawling past their dead, swarming over us, pinning us down, taking us apart, limb by limb.

Belair gasps for air. "Their phantoms have been here the whole time."

Part of me is aware of him by my side. My body is safe, but De'ral is falling to the ground. When Belair asks what to do next, I can't answer.

"Marcus, you're bleeding."

Phantom wounds rip through me as each of De'ral's gashes bloom blood-red through my robe. I try to bring De'ral in, but there's too much pain. I can't focus. My phantom has fallen to all fours, his powerful hands pinned to the ground, pierced by a dozen spears. Huge ripples of rage flow over his massive body. The *warrior* shrieks, trying to tear his hands free. His feet dig up piles of dirt from the road, pushing hard, seeking purchase. Slowly, De'ral's hands slide up the spear shafts as mine curl in on themselves, dripping blood, but the weapons penetrate at different angles.

Still trapped! my phantom roars. *Cut me free!* The last is directed straight at me.

Blood flows from his wounds, sending dark rivulets down the road. I watch, horrified, as my own hands are rendered useless, my sword clattering to the ground. "No!"

De'ral responds, defiant, rage spiking like hackles down his back.

My awareness lurches from him to me, back and forth in excruciating bursts. Fractured. Searing pain. I'm anchored in both bodies, his torture mine, too.

And still, the enemy advances. *Weapons!* I see my sword lying on the ground and try to grasp it.

Before I can open my wounded hand, Belair lets out a war cry and sprints toward De'ral. His sun leopard runs from the other side of the road, same destination. Chunks of dirt and rock fly up behind him. Belair's assault takes the enemy's attention as the sun leopard rears back on its haunches and swipes the air. Its fully extended claws slice the spears between the ground and De'ral's huge palms. One hand free! Blood and wood chips spray the road as my phantom pulls his hand back. But the soldiers circle, nets flying over him. Pinning him down. Driving the big cat back.

"Retreat!" I yell to Belair before he is taken, too.

De'ral tries to gain his feet, crushing the enemy beneath him like bugs, but a ring of soldiers hem him in. Belair darts to the rear to attack again where a giant dragonfly phantom awaits him.

"Not that way!" I yell, my throat on fire.

The Tangeen warrior lops off its wings and limbs as the insect spits corrosive liquid at his face. I fall to my knees, powerless to help, the cold inside me growing deeper.

More spears impale De'ral, the backs of his hands and forearms skewered to the earth. I feel the slice and drive of each one, unable to close the door to my phantom's perspective. Unable to get out.

"*Ousters*!" Belair shouts as the enemy advances up the road, blasting open the gates.

Curse the bones… I redouble my efforts to arm myself. To free De'ral.

The *ousters* whirl their long, thin arms, sending an invisible wind that burns flesh like lava. It leaves great rents in De'ral, each strip and cut shared with me. But my *warrior* phantom doesn't struggle. Instead, he locks eyes with me.

I gasp at the sheer intensity, the agony forgotten. Heat builds up in my chest, melting my frozen core, feeling as if my heart will explode through my ribs. A current pulls me like a raging torrent. It grows stronger and stronger as De'ral continues to stare.

Stop fighting me! We speak at the same time.

Severed bodies rain from the sky. The sun leopard slings soldiers high into the air, blood spraying in a sparkling red shower as the rest of my classmates rise to the defense. I barely notice, as in me a terrible rage builds. A force uncontrollable. It emanates from the depths and shoots out through my eyes, my mouth, ears, taking the pain away with it.

I laugh to myself.

Or is De'ral laughing at me?

It's the sound of madness, my mind snapped in two. I have enough awareness to know that. Ash is dead; Aku invaded. There is nothing left to lose. I slam the rest of my being into my phantom, leaving my own body falling to the ground. The union complete, I, Marcus-De'ral, open my mouth and thunder a war cry. Through wild phantom eyes, through burning ropes and torn flesh, I spot my true enemy, Destan. The challenge we send cracks through the sky and rains over the entire Sanctuary.

55

ASH

Kaylin grips my hand painfully as we scramble up the stairs. I don't want him to loosen the hold, though, not one little bit.

With the field impossible to cross, we're working our way down the street, hiding in buildings and behind rubble while flaming boulders scorch rain from the sky and Aturnians search for survivors. Their phantoms and savants attack without warning, capturing and questioning anyone they find. The gruesome truth is they are looking for *callers*. If they find one, they take them prisoner. Any other kind of phantom they kill on the spot.

Plenty of our savants fight back. Kaylin and I certainly fight back, but Aku is shattered, outnumbered, and falling. Most who survived the first round of catapults are students, not fully trained or ready for battle. They've never had to fight for their lives before.

With no quick way to Marcus and the others, Kaylin and I retreat to our room in the main temple for supplies. He goes in first, and when he gives the all clear, I slip in behind him.

"Food, boots, your other satchel?" He edges to the window, peeks around the curtain, and checks below. "We'll try to cross the field from here."

I run to the bed and pull out my satchel stowed underneath. With the library completely destroyed, the only text on the next Great Dying and Amassia's second sun might now be in my possession. The realization is like a punch to the gut, and my hands shake. Or maybe that's fear from the last dozen brushes with death.

I kick off my fluffy sheepskin shoes and put on a pair of wool socks and my winter boots, lacing them tight. Kaylin grabs his pack and tosses in a compass, the waterskin, and a sack of gold. I have no idea where that came from. It would take a lot of hand-carved lures to fill that bag, but I don't ask. I wrap up bread and dried fruit left from breakfast and pack it with another waterskin and a skein of nuts, the knives that are on the table, two pens, a blank scroll, and a bottle of ink.

"Wear this," Kaylin says as he tosses me a knit cap.

I plunk it on my head, tucking my hair back behind my ears, and crisscross the satchels over my back.

Kaylin is at the door, eyeing both ways. I turn around and take a final look at the room. It held so much promise until today. Mystery and fear, too. My eyes go to the window, the tapping sound's haunt, the table where our discoveries were made and where Kaylin and I shared so many meals. My bed… "Let's go." I turn away quickly and we slip out, footfalls silent.

After climbing down to the second-floor landing, I glimpse the foyer, gape for a second, and pull back, flattening myself against the wall. There is no way to erase what I've just seen as the image brands the backs of my eyes—three blue-robe savants cornered by a reptile *ouster* walking on hind legs. It twirled its clawed fingers, gathering air, and blasted it outward. The robes were torn away, followed quickly by skin, muscle, and guts until the bloody bones of the three students collapsed in a heap.

Nausea rises up the back of my throat.

"We can't go that way," Kaylin says needlessly.

The enemy savants swarm through the lower levels, taking savants prisoner, questioning them, asking if they raise *callers*. I hear their interrogations, and it's a wonder I can make any sense of the madness surrounding me. Why do they want *callers?* "I don't understand—"

Kaylin puts his finger to his lips and motions me back up the stairs.

When we are on the third floor, I ask, "What now?" As far as I know, the only other exit leads to the roof.

Sure enough, he points at the ceiling.

My knees go weak and I shake my head. "F'qadin demons, *no*."

He nods a yes and leads the way. We climb a narrow ladder at the end of the hall to a hatch. Kaylin opens it a crack and looks out before he pushes it wide, snow from a few nights ago falling around our feet. "Wait here."

This time, maybe for the first time in my life, I do what I'm told without question. The sounds of screams and clashing weapons ring in the distance and the wind slaps my face. It has lost its fresh sea scent and is laden with smoke, debris, and the taste of burnt metal.

When Kaylin returns, he sheathes his sword and scans me up and down. "Are you all right?"

I palm the tears from my eyes, wondering if I'll ever be all right again.

"I'm fine." I climb out onto the roof and see a trail of red spatters in his prints. "Are *you*?"

"Aye, lass." He smiles. "I'm well, but the guards on the roof will need more than a light healing."

I draw in a breath. Death comes so easy to him. *Peace be their paths,* I say silently.

"Peace be their paths," he says aloud and leads the way toward the eastern corner of the rooftop.

When we reach the edge, I gaze down three stories, hand going to my throat. "Kaylin, I don't know how to break this to you."

"What's that, lass?"

"I can't fly."

His eyes crinkle with his smile, and the wind blows his curly hair back from his face. For a moment, the battle cries and urgency disappear. I take a step closer. Kaylin bends toward me and touches my cheek. I close my eyes as his lips brush across my mouth. *"I'll let no harm come to you."*

I peer over the edge. "How?"

"There are steps laid into the stone."

I squint. "For ants?"

"They're chinks, really."

My stomach drops. "Chinks?" I give him an incredulous look. "I'm going down the wall holding onto *chinks*?"

"I'll guide you."

"If I fall…"

"You won't. Trust me." He smiles again. *"Have a little faith."*

56

MARCUS

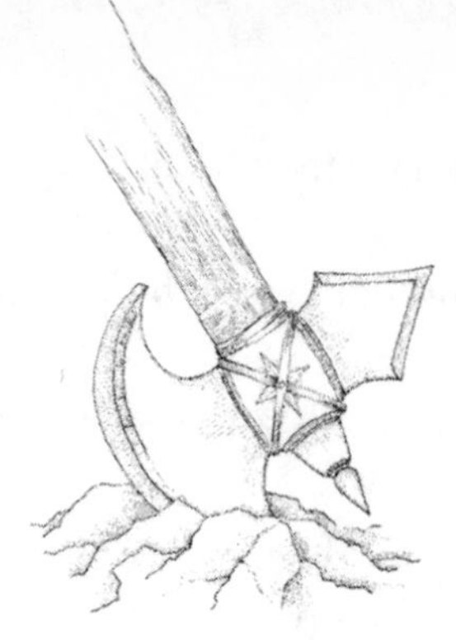

Pain wracks me from head to toe, but De'ral's strength helps me ignore it.

I follow Destan with phantom eyes, sending a small kernel of awareness back to my tortured body. The traitor runs catlike across the stable roof then jumps, free-falling to the ground. The downward force as he hits launches his phantom high into the air. Together, they burst into the fray, his phantom sweeping up a sword from one of the corpses on the road and locking onto the sun leopard. Destan heads straight for Belair.

I roar a warning, but it comes out as an unformed cry from De'ral's mouth. Just before impact, Belair turns toward Destan. In my phantom's body, I struggle against the restraints that pin me to the road. From my own flesh and blood, I watch on, helpless to save my friend. Destan's momentum thrusts him forward, an unstoppable surge. The redhead's free hand comes up to his chest. For a split second, a smile crosses Destan's face. Belair drops, twisting his shoulders into Destan's legs as he bends to throw him.

But the move is predictable, seen dozens of times on the training field. Before Destan flips off his feet, his knife hand comes up. In one clean sweep, he slashes out at Belair. The blade rakes from ribs to shoulder, carving a path through cloth and flesh, taking a chunk from his right ear. Destan slams hard into the ground, an arc of dark liquid sailing off his blade. From the tip flies a mat of wet hair.

Belair hits the dirt face-first as Destan rolls and then springs to his feet. I roar a challenge again. Out of the corner of my eye, I can see the leopard trying to fend off Destan's phantom. The *warrior* is harrying the cat from every angle. Belair has found his blade and is trying desperately to defend himself. A kick to the chin knocks him out.

Even so, his leopard fights on.

Destan's phantom has a hold of the sun leopard's neck, but the big cat twists around to bite and slash, its hind legs raking to disembowel. More *ousters* come, whipping up the air. The cat is thrown on its side by the invisible winds, pinned to the ground, legs scrambling against the gale. It tears up dirt and fallen bodies but can't break free. Destan's phantom raises his sword high. As it comes down, the whistling blade slices through paw and neck, forcing the sun leopard to ground. Belair's body shudders as the phantom finds its home.

Rage fills me and I curl my hands into fists, splintering some of the spears that impaled De'ral as he emulates my actions.

Destan gives a rebellious cheer. Warriors of his realm are everywhere, snaking up the road, swarming the Sanctuary in the hundreds through the toppled gates. "Victory!" the traitor shouts, and beats his chest like a beast. He stands tall, basking in the rallying crowd until he turns, searching.

He's coming for us next.

And I see him, heading for me, not De'ral.

In panic, I rip a fraction more of my awareness from De'ral and snap it back into my body. I'm weaker than I thought, basically a lump of wounded flesh and blood. But I don't feel pain. Not yet. All I know is the rapidly building wall of blind, voracious hunger within. I struggle to stand and fail, my frustration adding to the rage. Dirt and saliva run from my mouth, and a strange gurgling wells up. It's coming from me, from my throat.

My head hangs like a door off its hinge, but still the sound grows. I surge to my knees, my body a reflection of De'ral's. Tags of flesh hang with torn strips of my quilted green robe, wet hair slapping my eyes. I raise my arms wide and strands of blood fling from my crippled hands. Destan stops short, and I slowly lift my head and grin right in the traitor's face.

"I've been watching you, Baiseen," Destan says. He would sound arrogant, which I think is his intent, but his voice cracks at the end. His eyes travel my ruined form.

"Have you?" I answer.

"There's someone who wants to see you," Destan goes on. He's not as sure of himself, though. I can see it in the unease flickering in his eyes.

"Do tell."

The traitor hesitates. Is he surprised by my composure in the face of overwhelming defeat?

He quickly gathers himself. "I had hoped you would be more reluctant," he says, "but judging by the lack of fight, you're all too eager to meet him, too."

The building storm inside my skull roils. I laugh as wisps of rage escape through my mouth and nose like invisible smoke.

Destan sneers, then turns to the Aturnian soldiers joining him. "Take the Heir to Master Tann. He wants him alive for questioning."

Tann? The High Savant of Lepsea? Lightning cracks through my veins at the thought of that Sierrak red-robe being behind all this. "It is I who will question him." I grind out the words and spit blood on Destan's boots.

He responds instantly, smashing his fist into my forehead without warning. My head snaps back, and fresh blood spatters the ground. Two of the soldiers grab me, one on each side, and haul me up. My chin drops to my chest as they drag me away, but the gurgling laughter returns.

Destan yells, the fear in his voice more apparent this time. "You want more? I've got plenty." He stops his men and catches up.

From my throat comes a long, thin howl. Not pain. My body begins to shudder with it, yes, but this siren sound is from a stronger place than flesh and bone. I lift my head and stare Destan straight in the eyes. Power flows into me from De'ral, filling my core with red-hot fire. My limbs tingle. The agony retreats, replaced by something unfathomable. The rage and madness of us together, De'ral and I, hits the surface and explodes to life.

Destan glances at my *warrior* phantom struggling to break his restraint and hesitates. "Put that thing to ground," he commands, and more *ousters* turn toward De'ral, their arms spinning, creating funnels of wind.

While Destan focuses his attention away from me, I launch. The soldiers hold tight, but I manage to spit blood straight into the Aturnian's face this time.

Destan throws his blade down, his fists windmilling in a flurry of punches. He storms toward me, so absorbed in his assault he doesn't notice the Aturnian soldiers flinging through the air, landing far afield. But I see them, through De'ral's eyes, because I'm the one throwing them, still sharing his perspective with my own.

My phantom is free!

Through rage-red vision, I see the Aturnian captors slapped hard to the ground. They worm to get away before being crushed underfoot by my phantom's boots. The *ousters* back away, whipping their hands about, but not fast enough. Enemy soldiers sail through the sky, heading toward the ocean in high, blood-streaming arcs, their cries cutting short on impact. The giant *warrior* rips apart enemy phantoms with his teeth.

The guards release me and back away to the stable wall but Destan still hasn't seen. He grabs me by the hair. "Call it to ground, Baiseen, or I'll kill you, no matter what my orders."

Through swollen lips, I shout, "To me!" Blood spurts from my mouth. "To me, now!" It's not a call to ground, and De'ral and I both know it.

Destan's breath comes in deep gasps, blowing air across my face, cool against broken, wet skin. The ground shudders from De'ral's pounding stride. He runs low, nearly on all fours, spears sticking out of his hide, pieces of savants and soldiers spilling from his mouth. I see him, I *am* him, mimicking chewing motions with my own teeth.

Destan drops to one knee, clearly intending to bring his phantom in and raise it again right in front of me, but I lunge and catch him from behind, a death grip. My teeth sink deep into Destan's shoulder while choking him down.

Destan's war cry turns into a deafening shriek when De'ral smashes his fists into the earth, crushing the rising demon, sending it back to ground. Dirt rains and the giant *warrior*'s mouth closes around Destan's kicking legs. I let go my grip and De'ral snatches him up. Leg bones crush under phantom teeth. Destan's face, hanging upside down like a savaged bat, twists horribly as he swings, blood flowing over his body, dripping down his arms, fingertips, and from the top of his head.

I stare into De'ral's face, seeing my own eyes, wild and black and furious. It revives me, though blood runs from my hands and down my wrists as well when I raise them high, the victory now mine. We stand to full height, phantom and savant. The rage buried for so long is free. Destan's eyes bulge, his spine breaks, and the last sound he utters drifts over the wind, a shrill cry for help.

The advancing troops have weapons drawn, but they cower at the darkness in me, in De'ral. All save one. He rushes forward, spear raised as he drops to the ground. His phantom erupts—a white-furred ape with long yellow teeth and fisted hands. Its arms spiral in classic *ouster* movements, and chunks of wood and tiles fly toward us, the stable rooftop breaking free. With phantom arms I block before impact and punch the roof midair, sending it down the road. Enemy soldiers are strewn aside like windblown leaves, the rooftop skidding along until it flips, breaking into pieces. The smaller bits skip farther down the road, hitting troops as they dash out of the way. Some evade. Others are smacked to the ground.

In the midst of battle, I pull more of my awareness back into my body.

In savant form, I rush the ape and bowl it to the ground. Straddling the *ouster*, my elbows rain into its face in place of curled and bleeding fists. The phantom's bones cave, and it melts into the ground.

Power engulfs me, my vision tunneling into a tube ringed in dark blood.

"More!" I shout and leap to my feet. De'ral and I challenge the enemy coming up the road. They flee, De'ral pounding after them in pursuit. Those too stunned to react, or too slow, are stomped flat. My phantom's grinding jaws finally open and Destan, what is left of him, a scrap of torso, a bit of his worn green robe, falls out.

When I catch up, De'ral and I stand over the remains. "You lost," I tell him. Ignoring the searing pain in my hands, I yank a spear out of De'ral's flesh and plunge it through Destan's rib cage, aiming for the meat of his heart.

"Marcus, stop. He's dead." Samsen runs up from the ravine behind the stables, his face pale, blade wet. "Enough. Bring him in."

De'ral snarls and charges after more retreating soldiers.

"To ground," Piper shouts, panting behind Samsen. She stands with a short knife in each hand, snake around her neck, her chest heaving. "Before it's too late."

I can barely understand her words. Too late for what?

Samsen shakes me. "Bring him in! You're going to bleed to death if you don't."

My eyes flutter, knees going weak.

"No!" Samsen slaps my face. "Stay awake and bring him in!"

The part of me that is trapped in phantom perspective seeks the door, the barrier De'ral tries to keep me from crossing. I reach for it in my mind and wedge it open with my thoughts. It burns, acid on skin, but I struggle, push, and squeeze my way through. "To me," I say, returning completely to my own mutilated body.

With no more hold over me, De'ral melts into the ground, leaving broken spears, swords, and knives behind on the road.

I glance briefly at my friends before falling forward, the phantom energy sustaining me dissipating like the mist.

"Marcus!" Piper's snake scents near my face as she lifts my head out of the dirt.

"Off the road!" Samsen tries to hoist me, but I resist.

"I won't desert Aku." My voice is low and rasping.

"And I won't let you throw your life away." Samsen shakes me again when I close my eyes. "You're the Heir of Baiseen, and Aku has fallen. Come. We must find Ash and escape the Isle."

At the sound of her name, my heart turns black and squeezes shut, along with my eyes. "She was in the library..." Salt tears burn down my face, cutting pathways through blood and dirt.

Samsen curses. "Stand up, man. Ash lives. My phantom tracks her now."

I open my eyes, push up to my knees. "Where?"

"With Kaylin. Coming this way."

I throw every ounce of remaining strength into gaining my feet. "Ash lives?"

"Hurry!" Piper says, guiding me.

I stumble off the road, leaning hard on her and Samsen both. Ash lives, and the thought brings me a few inches back from the brink.

57

ASH

"I'm holding you back, aren't I?" After making it down the three-story-high building, I haven't let go of Kaylin, forcing him to swing his blade one-handed. I'm wielding a short sword with my free hand as well, but even so...

He drops his eyes to where I cling to his sleeve. "You could never hold me back, lass."

"Liar." A dozen times already I've nearly been killed by the swinging blades of enemy phantoms and savants. *Ousters* slam us into walls and *callers* snatch our weapons away as quickly as we pick up new ones. Many of the *warrior* phantoms are short and strong-limbed, like Destan's, and fast as snakes, armed with spears and blades, spiked balls and war hammers. The main boulevard is slick with blood. Puddles and streaks of it. The catapults knocked the strength out of us before we knew what was coming.

Kaylin motions to the south. "The other side of the field. By that line of trees near the stables. They're moving off the road."

The field is filled with phantoms and savants who fight each other around mounds of debris, twisted doors, upturned carts, and strewn bricks. "I don't have your eagle eyes."

"Trust me." Kaylin takes my hand and we're off.

We cut our way through, but by the time we reach the center of the field, the enemy closes in again. Kaylin loses his sword to an *ouster* and sends his other toward it, end over end, skewering the phantom through the middle. I cringe as it starts to gush ichor and more *ousters* step up, twitching their fingers, gathering air. My arm falls, aching as I use both hands to hold the thin blade in front of me. It's not much of a shield. The *ousters* have a straight shot to us, and I can't see a way out until spotting a flatbed wagon with big iron wheels. "There." I point, meaning we can hide under it, but Kaylin has another idea.

He pulls the wagon around, tipping it on its side with some kind of leverage. I can't see how he does it, but we jump behind as the first blast strikes. It blows off the wheels and flings them through the air like saucers. The next strike hits harder, pushing us back, wagon and all, as we brace behind the floorboards. Another hit and the metal straps rip from the wood and the whole thing breaks apart, leaving us exposed again.

"I'll be right back." Kaylin takes my sword and springs into the air, disappearing as I crouch low, covering my head with my hands.

The next blast never comes.

When I peek around the rubble, Kaylin is bounding back to me, a blade in each hand, face splattered with blood, smile bold as dawn.

"You got them?" I ask, taking one of the swords.

"And their savants." He offers his hand again. "This way."

"He's quite talented with a sword."

I fight for my life and this is what my inner voice wants to comment on? *Where have you been?*

"You seemed busy. I didn't want to interrupt."

I shake my head, too distracted to answer.

By the time we reach the other side of the field, we run without challenge, the battleground littered with bodies. The gates have fallen, and the stable is demolished, the roof gone. Rock, rubble, and blood cover the road. Broken bodies and crushed bones are everywhere. My eyes well and the tears fall unchecked. "Marcus?" I can't see him anywhere.

"Over here." Kaylin leads me around the corpses, but my boots don't always come to rest on hard ground.

"Ash! Kaylin!" Samsen calls.

I see them! Off to the side of the road.

When we're a few steps away, my hand goes to my mouth as my stomach heaves.

Marcus looks like raw meat. His phantom's gone to ground, the ruin around us overwhelming. Belair lies unconscious with a terrible bleeding wound on his chest and face. Piper's phantom has its double-headed fangs into both of them. I drop to my knees beside Marcus, not knowing where to touch or how to help. Tears well again as I hold his beautiful tapered fingers in my hand. His palms are full of holes and packed with blood and dirt. He is so badly harmed, I can't make out where one wound ends and another begins. "Marcus," I whisper and press my forehead lightly to his. He doesn't seem to know I'm here. "Marcus, you're going to be fine."

I feel Kaylin's hand on my shoulder and turn to look up at him.

"We have to get off the island," he says softly, his eyes on Marcus.

"Retreat to the ravine," Piper says. Her snake releases Marcus and Belair before entwining her neck. "We'll make a plan there, out of sight."

Marcus stirs and turns toward me, and I'm forced to swallow back tears. "Where's my sword?" His voice is gravelly, his eyes swollen to little more than slits. I am certain he can't see a thing through them.

"You'll not be needing it just now," Samsen says. He and Piper pull Marcus up and walk him toward the deep ravine to the right of the road. I grab his sword while Kaylin hoists Belair over his shoulder as if he were a sack of feathers. At the bottom of the narrow ravine, we stop to assess.

"I suggest you take the Heir back to his realm as fast as you can," Kaylin says. "Aku has lost this fight."

"Agreed, but how?" Samsen asks. "We've seen the docks and the southwest shore. They're ringed with warships."

"We could work our way north and hide, but without supplies, stretchers to carry them…" Piper doesn't have to finish her thought.

"Aye, Aku's besieged," Kaylin says. "But I know a way off the island, if we go now."

We all stare at him.

"The leeward cove, one bay over from the main docks. There's a small sloop there, not heavily guarded." He tilts his head skyward. "Send your hawk to confirm, but I guarantee it's the only way out."

Piper looks from Kaylin to Samsen. "The road's swarming with enemy phantoms, and the beaches are full of savants."

"Trust me," Kaylin says. "I can secure the ship."

"With Belair over your shoulder?" I ask.

"I might have to put him down for a moment."

Samsen and Piper seem skeptical but relent. "What choice do we have?" Samsen asks.

"Follow along with Marcus as you can." Kaylin adjusts the unconscious Belair. "I'll have the ship ready."

"I'm coming with you," I say.

Kaylin nods and we take off toward the leeward cove.

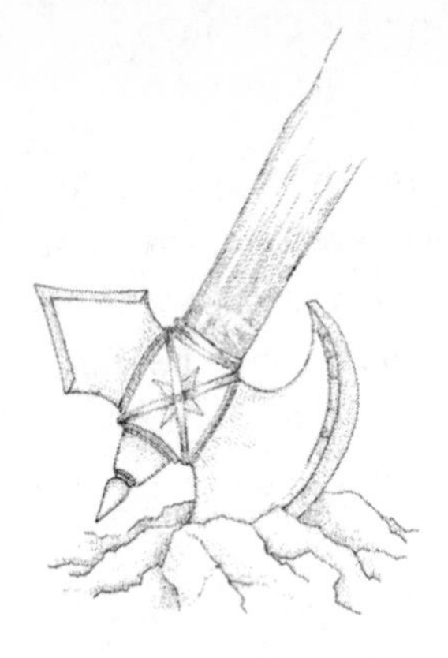

58

MARCUS

I wake to throbbing pain consuming every inch of my body, and Piper and Samsen conversing over my head.

"...already two transfusions. He'll survive, but..." Piper's voice trails off and I can't yet open my eyes to see her expression.

"He mustn't raise his phantom again," Samsen says. "Not until we find a red-robe warrior who understands this sort of problem. What I saw—"

"Samsen, he's coming to."

"I need a red-robe-level healer?" I feebly pat at my body, trying to make sure I still have all four limbs.

"Your body isn't the problem, Marcus."

I blink at Samsen as he speaks, his face grim.

Piper brings her phantom in as she and Samsen lift me to my feet. The world spins and nausea sweeps through me in waves. I nearly throw up.

"Easy, Marcus. We're going to get you on a ship."

"Yuki," I say, but they take it for a grunt and carry on.

They hurry me down the ravine until a sweet call fills the air. The next moment, Samsen's blade is gone, ripped out of his hand. It arcs toward the stables at high speed along with abandoned weapons on the road. There are multiple *thwacks*, followed by screams. Piper's long knife flies out of her free hand as well.

"What's happening?" I choke out the words, trying to stand on my own.

Samsen points to his phantom circling above. "It's Tyche."

"She disarmed us?" Piper asks.

"Aturnians have her cornered on the other side of the stables. She's calling weapons to impale them."

"Help her." I manage to speak more clearly. "Leave me. Go help her."

Samsen calls in his raptor to hover over me and runs back up the hill. Piper drops to raise her phantom and then follows on his heels. I stagger behind them. *"Where's my sword?"* I ask my phantom.

With Ash, De'ral says from the depths.

It's impossible. I haven't seen Ash since walking her to the library this morning. How could she have my sword? I remember Samsen telling me that she survived the attack, but…where is she?

With the sailor.

It disturbs me that my phantom has more awareness of what's going on than I do right now.

When I reach the stables, I stop short and blink, forcing my eyes to open wider. At least two Aturnian guards are on the ground riddled with weapons. Samsen pulls his blade from one's back. Piper retrieves her long knife from the other's chest. Tyche stands in the corner of a roofless stall, her hands in irons, her little impala phantom trembling.

"It's all right," Piper says. "You're safe."

I want to point out that safe is the last thing any of us are, but I don't have the strength.

The girl stares at the bodies. "I killed them."

"You defended yourself," Piper says calmly. "Well done. Are you injured?"

Tyche shakes her head.

"Do you know where Yuki is?" Samsen asks.

"Dead," Tyche says in a small voice, her eyes dry and hollow.

"Peace be her path," Samsen says gently. "How did it happen? Boulders?"

"A red-robe." Her eyes look away.

"Which red-robe?" Samsen asks

"Tann, High Savant from Sierrak," I answer for her.

Piper gasps and she and Samsen swing around. "What are you doing? Marcus, you're in no condition—"

"Destan told me," I say. "Tann leads the attack on Aku."

"Tann," Tyche says in a hollow voice. "He marched me into Yuki's hall, his *ouster* clearing a path for the brown-robes—"

Samsen swings back around. "Wait. He brought initiates here?"

She shakes her head. "Cowled savants, not children. Couldn't see their faces, but the *ousters* and *warriors* guarding them were fierce. They carried a chest." Her brown eyes are vacant, even as tears spill down her cheeks. "Tann said if I called the first whistle bone, he'd let Yuki live." She bows her head. "I did what he asked, but once he had the Crown of Er…"

"Aku's first whistle bone?" Piper asks.

She nods, sobbing. "He cut her throat, filled the chest with her blood, and locked the bone inside."

I can hardly believe what I'm hearing.

Piper lifts her to her feet. "Tyche, listen to me. It's not your fault."

"Now he's after me. After all the *callers* on Aku!"

Tann is after *callers*? My head spins, on the edge of understanding, but I can't quite grasp why.

"We're going to keep you safe," Samsen assures her.

"Call the key to these irons, and a warm coat." Piper looks down. "Boots, too. We have to hurry."

She doesn't respond, but the phantom sings, and moments later an embroidered, mid-length coat flies to her, along with brown leather lace-up boots. From the coat pocket spills a little bean-stuffed toy, a replica of her impala small enough to fit in her hand.

"Imp," the girl whispers and picks it up, red eyes turning to Piper. "Yuki made this for me when I was born. She knew what my phantom was before anyone saw it."

Piper's expression breaks, but she's quick to pull herself back together. "Come now. Up you get." She lifts the girl by the armpits, drapes the coat over her shoulders, and does up the top button like a cape. She pushes the toy deep into the pocket, knots the bootlaces together, and slings them over her head. "The key?"

Tyche shakes her head. "I don't know what it looks like."

"Shh!" Samsen hushes us at the sound of advancing boots. He motions toward the ravine. "Keep to the cover," he whispers and picks up the child.

"Her manacles?" Piper says.

"No time."

Piper glares at me and turns me around. "You were supposed to wait." She wedges herself under my arm and limps me to the edge of the ravine.

I lean heavily on her. "How are we getting off the island?"

"Kaylin has a plan."

I groan but keep moving. "I hope it's a good one."

59

KAYLIN

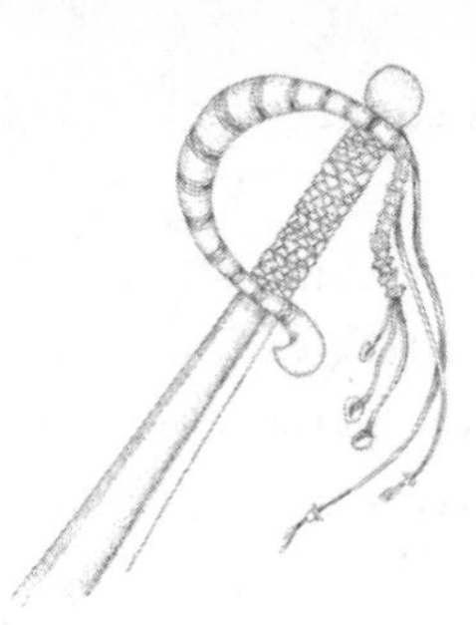

"I see guards," Ash whispers to me as we crouch behind tree cover. I love how she leans in to share her observations. The westering sun is behind her, magnifying the red in her hair. She catches me looking and tugs the knit cap down, smiling shyly. "The guards?" she asks.

"Aturnian soldiers left behind to mind the sloop."

"We aren't worried?"

I shake my head and hold a finger to my lips.

She nods, pressing her lips together. Her cool, turquoise eyes are calm, and she's recovered from her shock of battle. I have to get her off this Isle, away from the enemies of both land and sea. I wish there was a better plan, but the sloop is all we have.

The little ship rides high in the water, moored at the end of the pier. It's large enough to sail us over the channel yet not so big I can't handle it on my own. Remembering them all on board the *Sea Eagle* doesn't give me much hope of seaworthy assistance. I shift Belair's dead weight and gaze at the docks.

"How do we get past them?" Ash follows my eyes to the hundred or more warships across the channel.

"First things first," I whisper.

"The sloop?"

"Exactly."

"Again, how?" she asks.

I'm about to explain, then shake my head. "It'll be easier for me to show you." As we creep forward, I hum my favorite battle tune to myself.

She gives a nervous laugh. "The world's in ruin and you're enjoying yourself, aren't you?"

Heat needles my skin. Did my lass hear me or is she just that sensitive to my expressions? "This is not the world in ruins, lass. Nothing close."

Her smile falls, and I regret my words, wondering how I can undo them.

"You see the flag?" She lifts her chin to the banner tied to the mast. Like the ones from the camp, it has a white background with two stylized spheres—the large one bright orange and smaller dark red. "The twin suns. Is that the new Aturnian emblem?"

"Tann's, I'd say, given he leads this fleet." I give her a wink to lift the mood. "I won't be long."

The guards are not terribly alert. Dressed in Aturnian coats and sheepskin boots, they aren't geared for the sea, either. But some are savant. I lift my face to the phantom birds circling overhead, mixing with the gulls, terns, and cormorants.

"Oh," she whispers, looking up as well.

There are also three hounds at the base of the pier—tall, liver-colored dogs with tan legs and pointed ears. Their hackles are up and their long faces snarling. They smell us already. One of them breaks into a series of deep, throaty barks.

"We have to wait for the others." Ash checks back up the hill for them.

I study the bay, spotting a rowboat full of savants pulling their way through the water, heading for the dock. They could reach it before I do. "I don't think we can."

She sighs. "I was afraid you'd say that."

I shift Belair higher on my shoulder and we hurry down the hill, crouching low to stay out of sight.

"Kaylin!" A lilting voice sounds in my head.

"Salila?" For once, I am not opposed to the Mar woman's presence… that is, if I can persuade her to help.

60

SALILA

The surface breaks as I leap out of the water, air flowing over my skin, tickling my toes, making every pore gasp at the shock. It's a sensation I don't mind, but now's not the most conducive time to linger in it. *"There you are…"* I dive straight back in then dart to the surface to watch.

He runs half crouched toward the pier, carrying a body—dead or alive, I can't tell. *"What are you doing? The Isle's in flames, or haven't you noticed?"*

He's not answering me, but then, he probably can't hear much with his feet on dry land. I swim in circles under the surface, waiting. Once he's in the water, I'll grab him. We can shoot under the hulls and across the channel, none the wiser. I stop suddenly, my hair floating away from my face. Was that the girl running with him? Still alive? *"Can't you get a single thing done right anymore?"*

I roll on my side and break the surface just enough to have a better look. *"Kaylin!"* If I were prone to cursing, this is where I'd release a string of them. It *is* her, alive as the day she was born. Does he know the tidal wave of trouble he's bringing down on himself? No one crosses Teern.

I frown at that. There have been one or two instances in the past, resulting in mixed levels of success, but *almost* no one crosses Teern, certainly not the favorite son who bears the Sea King's trident.

I stream toward the pier, rehearsing how I will talk sense into him, but find I'm not alone. A rowboat, oars dipping and pulling through the chop, parallels me, riding low in the water. It's overfull of savants. *"Ha!"* I run my tongue over my teeth. Nothing like a good complication to push the point along, or points, in this case.

Kaylin wants the sloop, that's obvious. But he'll need help with this mob on their way. I smile at the little boat's hull, wondering if these landers ever learned to swim. In my experience, not many have. *"Kaylin, if you're listening, you owe me for this."* I divert my course, straight toward the little boat. The current ripples over my body, and bubbles escape my lips as I laugh under the waves. This will be fun.

The oars continue their rhythmic dips in and out of the water, two on each side working in perfect harmony. The boat makes good speed. They're already shouting to the soldiers on the dock, alerting them of their approach. Good idea if they don't want to be mistaken for Aku savants and end up full of arrows.

I come up under the hull and cling there like a long, lean remora. The planks are mostly strong as I tap—solid, solid, not so solid, weak… I punch my fist right through the planks, and the wood splinters to bits, water sucking into the hole. The inevitable cries and chaos ensue. I love this part.

"Shark! Shark!" they cry.

"Not yet, but soon, little baitfish." I grab the lead ore, snap the paddle off, and flip the rower out of the boat before he can let go of his end. Such a lovely splash he makes. I circle the boat, breaking the other oars and tossing them, some with clinging landers attached, some without, into deep water.

They all climb on top of each other to reach the bow—the only part of the vessel still above water. It sinks quickly with the added weight, and they thrash about until their heads disappear under the surface. Such a noisy lot, and nary a swimmer among them. I can't help but smile and bare my teeth. Fifteen, I count. *"Shall we put you out of your misery?"* I take the horrified expressions as a yes and bite them all, through skin and into belly or throat, until the crystal water is tinted red with their blood and guts.

"Now you can cry shark, my silly landers."

They'll be here any minute.

61

ASH

"Blazes' dak, what's happening out there?" We're hiding behind a head-high mound of coiled rope, thick as an arm, stacked neatly at the edge of the dock. "Can you tell?"

Kaylin gently lays Belair down, checks his pulse, and then peers around the coils. "Mother of Ma'ata…" he mutters under his breath.

"Ma'ata?" The word is faintly familiar, but from where? I make a note to ask Kaylin later, if we survive. "What's wrong?"

He sighs. "There was a rowboat full of savants heading for the pier."

"Was?"

"It appears to have sunk."

"How?" When I look back, a bit of hull sticks out of a widening circle of dark water. "What are the odds?"

"In our favor, lass." He doesn't look so thrilled about it. "This is our chance."

The Aturnians guarding the ship are alarmed by their drowning comrades. Six of them bring their phantoms to ground and man a lifeboat to row out and save them.

I peer around the coils next to him, even though he can see it clearly himself. Out at the far end of the bay, the only sign of the rowboat is a few bits of floating wood.

"I'll be back." Kaylin draws his sword and strides away.

He's halfway to the ship before the remaining guards notice him. They draw their swords and call their phantoms. Two gulls zing in. Kaylin ignores the birds and swings twice, slicing one guard from shoulder to hip. The other he impales in the chest. Their phantoms vanish like smoke on the wind. My stomach tightens as I'm again reminded of how fast and deadly Kaylin is with the blade. He searches the dock for more guards but finds none.

I scan the hill for the others but there's no sign. What's taking so long?

"They're coming," my inner voice reassures me.

When my eyes return to the cove, the second rowboat lurches and capsizes, spilling out the guards, the rescuers joining the victims. My brow pinches tight. What in F'ndnag is going on?

"Ash! Here you are!"

I stifle a yelp as Samsen comes crouching in behind the cover of the ropes.

"Where's Kaylin?" he asks.

"Over there, killing people." I check again and wrinkle my nose. "And taking off their coats."

Samsen doesn't seem bothered by it. "Is it safe to bring Marcus down?"

"I think so. How is he?"

"Unconscious again." Samsen's face is grim. "Belair?"

The Tangeen hasn't stirred, but the rise and fall of his chest under my sheepskin coat is comforting. "He's alive."

Samsen nods and is gone.

The cove is empty when I check again, save for a few broken oars floating toward the docks. Beyond it, a huge fleet anchors on the far side of the surrounding reef. How we will sail past them without being stopped is beyond me, but on the pier, Kaylin heads back our way. *"I hope you have a plan."* I think the thought in his direction.

"I do, and we can start by boarding the sloop." I startle as he hands me a dead guard's wool coat and puts one on himself. "This will fool them, from a distance."

I start to push my arms into the sleeves. There is a slice from the shoulder to the waist, wet with copper-smelling blood. "Kaylin, this is—"

"Necessary." His voice is light, carefree.

Naturally, it would be. He's been chopping and slashing the enemy to bits. "They're bringing Marcus down the hill."

"Good." He lifts Belair over his shoulder again. "This way."

I trot after him down the pier. The coat is still warm and has a man's strong scent on it. I try to focus on something else—the sound of my boots on the wooden dock, the smell of salt water and bird droppings, fish and tar, how Kaylin, once again, appears to have heard my thoughts. Anything other than the dead man whose body I'm about to step over. I avert my eyes and hurry on. *How wrong can an entire initiation journey go?*

"Maybe don't ask that question until it's over." My inner voice's wry

tone is a warning all its own.

Kaylin takes my hand and helps me up the gangplank. "To the helm."

I walk along the spotless deck.

"Other way," he calls out. "Hold the wheel. Be ready to turn her hard to port."

Back of the ship. Be ready to turn hard…I squint. *"Left, isn't it?"*

"Aye, lass."

There is no question that he heard that one. I file the information away for later, when we're not in immediate danger of being killed by an enormous enemy fleet.

The sloop is a small ship, and it doesn't take me long to reach the wheel behind the cabin as Kaylin takes Belair below. I stand tall and grip the smooth wooden helm that comes up to my shoulders. I've both hands holding on, knuckles white, eyes fixed straight ahead, even though we are moored to the berth. The others climb up the gangplank. "Piper's keeping her phantom up?" I ask.

Samsen dips his head to the hold where he takes Marcus. "They'll need it."

"True." I glance back to the plank. We've acquired another passenger, or is she a prisoner? The girl's in irons, unrecognizable with her head down and long hair tangled, robes torn, a dark embroidered coat over her shoulders. Orange-robe? Samsen pauses to help her onboard.

My mouth falls open. "Tyche!" Where did they find her? Before she can respond, Kaylin ushers them all below.

"Be ready, lass," he says to me. "This could get dangerous."

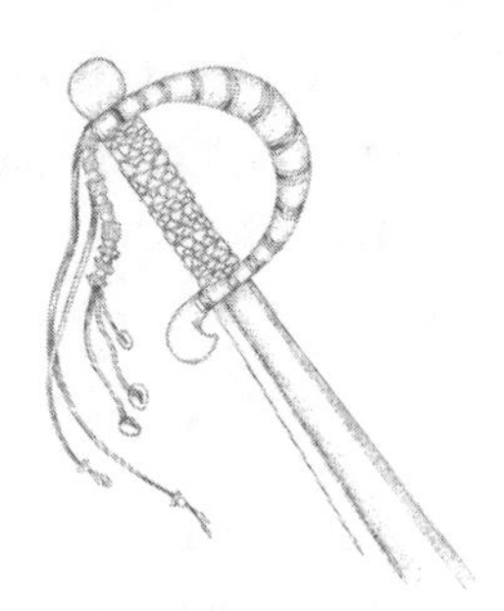

62

KAYLIN

I've stowed Belair in a hammock while Samsen and Piper do the same with Marcus. "There'll be bolt cutters in the bulkheads. You can free the girl."

I study Tyche for a moment. It's a new development, having Yuki's granddaughter in my care, the only survivor of the High Savant's house, I'm guessing. One complication after another…

Piper's snake flicks two blue tongues toward me.

"Do you want to bring it in, before we set sail?" I nod to her phantom.

"They need healing still." She tilts her head to the hammocks. "I've more hours in me."

She means more hours to keep her phantom raised. There's no bringing it in, once over water. "Good. Stay below, for now."

Samsen stops me. "You can't just take over. I've—"

"The sea's *my* realm, savant. Do as I say and we might make it across the channel alive." I don't wait for his answer. "Save them." I indicate Belair and Marcus. "And arm yourselves. The girl, too." I climb out of the hold and close the hatch. A moment later, I scramble up the rigging to the crow's nest. Below, Ash has her hands on the wheel as if she's already sailing the high seas. That's my lass. She's beautiful, strong, and something else…

I turn to the sea and catch a splash headed our way. *"There you are, sister."* I release the jib. There's no telling what Salila's game is today, if she's here to help or harm. As the sky clears, all I can think of is fog. Where is it now that we need it? "Hard to port, lass," I call and ride the rope down to the deck.

"Like this?" She turns the wheel with all her might. It spins freely, and her face lights up with a smile.

"Aye, that's the way." I tie the jib, keeping it slack, then run down the plank, untie the mainlines, fly back up the plank, and haul it in. Wind fills the sail as I tighten the jib just in time to lean over the rail and catch Salila surfacing. "What are you doing?" I ask as the sloop glides out of the berth.

"Helping," she says, her face out of the water.

"Thanks for the rowboats." My jaw tightens. "I've got it from here."

"You can't sail this tub across the channel by yourself."

"I'm not alone."

"Her?" Salila submerges and comes up sputtering. "You think she can steer you out of the bay? If so, there are a hundred warships waiting on the other side, don't forget. I can't sink them all, if that's what you're going to ask." She spits water at me and smiles. "Come, Kaylin. Come into the sea. This is where you belong."

It's tempting, always. "Soon enough, Salila."

"Did you say something?" Ash calls out.

"Ease to starboard, lass. That's it." We're nearly clear of the breakwater.

Ash spins the wheel, but she gazes over her shoulder, down into the water. Her eyes go round. "Kaylin? There're sharks everywhere. I think they're feeding on…" She turns away and keeps her eyes straight ahead. "Drowned savants."

"Steady as she goes," I say, ignoring her distress and leaning back over the railing. "Get out of it, Salila. Did you hear her?"

"I can out-swim a shark."

I exhale through my teeth. "Still, I'd rather she not see you do so."

"Why? Would it ruin your plans?" she asks.

I shrug one shoulder. "I don't know what you mean."

"Your obvious plan. To ignore Teern's orders to put these landers in the ground. Have you told Father what they've discovered, this motley crew you lead? Have you explained why they aren't dead?"

"We don't know anything for sure." There is so much more to say, but there's no time to explain this to Salila now.

"Don't know for sure?" She laughs. "Mossman's Shoals, Kaylin. I know they call it the Ferus River Falls now, but it's one and the same. They came by way of Mossman's Shoals, as foretold. Straight over the Falls. Don't play naive. You led them to it."

"I meant to go around—"

"Face it, Kaylin. The throw of the bones takes its course. Because of you." She pouts but I know by the light in her eyes the whole thing excites her.

"Maybe." I want to argue, but I *was* the one to set the five on the river and cut the raft free.

"Yuki thought so, or she wouldn't have sent five ships."

"And Teern sank them?"

"He let me do it." She gives a smug smile that quickly turns sour. "But that Sierrak, Tann, claims it was him."

"Was he there at the time, lobbing his catapults?"

"I guess, but the point is, Teern knows what was in those messages Yuki wrote so fervently, and if he wanted the Heir dead before, he'll want it all the more now. Are you willing to risk so much?" Salila rears up and bares her teeth. "Behind you!"

Ash screams at the same time.

I swing around to see the hatch fling open. Tyche is forced out at knifepoint, an Aturnian guard behind her. Piper and Samsen follow, their hands bound behind their backs. The phantom serpent hisses, and its long coils writhe around Piper's neck and chest. They drag Marcus out, even though he's barely able to stand. "Damn the bones," I say under my breath. It seems not all the guards had been dispatched after all. Two stowed away in the hold.

The one guarding Tyche is a broad-shouldered man with dark red hair and a reddish-black beard. He grips the girl tight, one arm around her chest. His other hand holds a knife under her chin. "Do as I say, or I end her life."

"Aye, and what is it that you say?" I ask, as if it matters little either way.

"Turn this ship around."

So, they can't sail. Judging by their accents, they're Sierrak, not Aturnian. Useless at sea.

"Happy to," I answer. "One master is as good as another, though I do have a price."

The others turn my way as if slapped. Even Marcus shoots me a grimace through his battered face. I hope he can keep his mouth shut, though. These enemy soldiers don't realize who they've captured. Marcus must go unnoticed—just a badly wounded savant, a green-robe trying to escape. No one of import or value. Will he be aware enough to appreciate the situation?

"Ease to port," I call to Ash without looking at her.

"What are you doing?"

"Trust me, lass." I'm not going to announce to the captors that there's no point running the ship aground while I work out how to kill them, so

I carry on, and Ash does as I ask. Bless the bones for that.

We're leaving the inlet behind and coming out into the larger bay. For a moment, the guards lose focus as they see the wreckage from the rowboats float by—broken oars, planks, limbs, shark fins. Bright blood spreads through the water.

Then the redheaded guard steps up to me, pushing Tyche in front of him. He keeps the knife tight on her throat. "You do that? You kill my men?"

I study the water as if considering. "Not me."

The guards eye my coat and the bloodstained collar. "I should skewer the lot of you right now and feed you to the Drop."

"But then how will you reach the shore? Can you maneuver the razorback reefs? They are called that for a reason, mate."

The man glances at his companion, who shrugs.

"Worth a price if I return you to the dock, don't you think?"

"What kind of price?"

"That gold inlaid chest I saw in the hold for a start, and my crew. You'll have to spare their lives."

He laughs. "I think it goes more like this. You do as I say, or I kill your crew, starting with this girl." He shakes Tyche. "Turn the ship around."

I raise my brow, as if impressed. "Aye, aye. Just let me set the mainsail."

"Hold! I'm no fool," the Sierrak guard says. "You got her out with the small one. You can sail back with it, too."

I chuckle at that. "A sailor you are not. We will have to tack back. That means sailing into the wind, if you don't know. It'll be slow going without the mainsail up."

The Sierrak again looks at the other guard, who nods. "Be quick about it then."

I make eye contact with Ash for the first time as I climb the mast. Her jaw is set and her eyes say *no* as she stares back at the pier. I continue my climb and see why. The little pier is swarming with troops. That way is not an option. I can snap both their necks, but Tyche would die. Unavoidable, unless… I grab the mainline and scurry back down the rigging. When I jump the last several lengths, I land right next to Tyche. "Little lass, I'll need you to hold the jib."

The Sierrak doesn't comprehend.

"Wind's up. Can't you see?" The mainsail dumps air, but the jib fills and strains. The sloop races through the water just an arm's length from the shallow reefs. "If we rake the hull at this speed, it'll gouge out the bottom. We'll join your men in the depths." I reconsider. "Unless you want to give me your sword and you can hold the line."

The guard nods to Tyche. I see what he thinks—she's a strong girl, but harmless in her iron cuffs. An orange-robe, yes, but unable to raise her phantom over water, no matter what it is. "She can do it."

I'm careful not to smile as I tie off the mainsail, keeping it slack, and hand Tyche the jib line.

She takes it with her bound hands.

"Lean back," I instruct her. "Use all your weight. It's going to be a sharp turn."

The guard draws his sword and keeps it pointed at her chest as she throws her full weight back toward the starboard railing. "I'm watching your every move, sailor."

"But are you watching mine?" a woman's voice calls from above.

63

ASH

My heart's hammering as it is, but when the woman jumps out of the sea to stand on the railing, my mouth falls open. I fix my eyes on her as a single thought reverberates through my mind. *Mar… Mar… Mar…* There is nothing else that explains her, this living, breathing vision from legends and myths. She balances effortlessly on the narrow rail, her long toes gripping tight, water sluicing off her body. All that creamy white skin and wavy, coppery gold hair falling down to her thighs.

"Mar," I whisper, both hands glued to the wheel, heart banging double-time in my chest. I can't pull my eyes away. She's very tall, incredibly beautiful, and terrifying all at once. Water beads on her skin and drips from the ends of her hair and fingertips down to her feet. Strands of the honey hair cling to her body. And, most disturbing, her eyeteeth are showing as she snarls at the guards. Before anyone moves, she leaps onto the nearest one, breaks his neck with her bare hands, and rips out his throat.

My blood and bones freeze.

Kaylin, already moving, draws his knife and slices the jib line in two. Tyche falls backward over the railing and into the sea before the guard can skewer her. He tries to turn his sword on Kaylin, but our sailor's already plunged a knife in his neck. The guard staggers, clutching at the short hilt, blood spurting in a high arc. Effortlessly, Kaylin hoists him overhead and throws him into the sea, but not before pulling his knife out of the man's throat. Ever practical, my Kaylin.

"Salila," he says, his voice more commanding than I've ever heard it. "You will harm none!" Then he turns to me. "Keep to the center of the bay, lass, whatever you do. I'll be right back." In a graceful motion, he dives over the railing and into the water.

"Kaylin!" I stare after him as the sea closes over his head. How can he hope to find the child? He's a powerful swimmer, but Tyche is weighted with chains, and the ship's moving fast. She's at the bottom of the channel,

and no doubt the sharks are in a frenzy, looking for more. "Bones be chac." I press my lips together, holding to Kaylin's last command—keep to the center of the bay.

Fortunately, the sloop is slowing down. Or, unfortunately… In a moment, I have to reassess. "It appears I might have overturned the wheel." No one listens to me. Would they have advice if they heard? The sails flap like sheets on a line, spilling wind.

"Keep us safe, to the center of the bay."

I hear the command, his voice in my head. And not a moment too soon. The ship turns decidedly sideways and drifts back toward the Isle and its razorback reefs. To make matters worse, several vessels come into view, heading straight for us. From a distance, they might think we're sailing to meet them, the siege complete. Up close, with me at the helm, stunned savants on deck, and a Mar licking her blood-soaked lips, it might be a different story. A Mar! I stare at the woman again, in awe. Kaylin called her by name, Sah-*lee*-la. Currently, she's ripping the Sierrak guard open with her bare hands and teeth—a messy and disturbing process. As she continues to eviscerate him, it appears she's lapping up his blood. I turn away, bile rising in my throat, but my gaze draws back to her of its own accord.

Salila stands over her victim, eyes all pupil, as far as I can tell. Finished with the Aturnian, her focus shifts to Marcus. He's hunched between Samsen and Piper, who look on as shocked as I do. "Stop!" I gasp but then see by her posture she isn't going to hurt him, at least not right away. There's something quite different on her mind. She licks her lips clean and sucks blood from each finger until she's alabaster again.

Marcus is too injured, and too dazed, to do more than hold up his bound wrists.

"Would you like me to help you with that?" Salila asks, her voice soft as kittens. She leaves blood and water footprints as she walks across the deck to him. Her hips sway and the ends of her hair lift in the breeze. "They can't feel good." She traces her finger over his knotted bindings. "Poor hands."

I'm surprised that Marcus finds his voice. "It is a bit tight for my liking."

"Let's fix that." Salila grasps his bindings and draws him close. Will she gnaw the ropes off, or his fingers?

And ropes it is, as the frayed ends fall from the Mar's teeth. Salila holds Marcus's bloody hands in hers and gazes into his eyes. "You've fought hard against the traitor."

My heart skips a beat. Traitor? What does she know?

Marcus startles as if coming out of a deep sleep. "Mar?" he whispers.

"That's right," she says. "You can release the others." Salila pulls a short knife from the dead guard's midriff belt, which is nowhere near his legs at this point, and hands it to Marcus. "Then have a spell with your healer, while I introduce myself to this girl." Salila turns and heads for me.

"Tyche will drown." Piper points to the railing where the young savant went overboard a quarter mile back. The healer's serpent is moving, scenting as it rearranges itself around her body. "You can save her."

"Let's let the little brother be a hero this time, shall we?" Salila turns my way, hands on hips, gaze combing over every inch of me, up and down. "Now, what does he see in you?"

I'm tense as a bow. *The little brother?* They're related? I keep my mouth shut, struggling with the wheel, trying to hold to course.

The ship continues to drift toward the Isle, and I have no idea what to do about it. I'm about to ask her if she can offer a suggestion when Marcus comes staggering up to stand between me and the Mar. Piper's snake is latched onto his neck, and he is recovering somewhat, but I find him almost scarier than Salila in his bloody, battered state. *"Just don't say your name, whatever you do."* I send the thought to him, like I do with his phantom. Maybe one of them will hear me.

"I'm Marcus Adicio, the Heir to the throne of Baiseen," he says as his eyes swim in red sockets. "Anything you have to discuss with her will be said directly to me."

"Dead bones and rit'n stuggs, Marcus! Can you not remember the importance of anonymity, just once?"

Salila shrugs elegantly. "Thank you, Heir. I know who you are, and I'm not interested in you or your realm at the moment." The Mar pats his chest as her eyes go to me. "I'm interested in her."

Marcus staggers in my direction like he means to intercede.

"It's all right," I say. "Salila and I can chat, but I think we have more urgent concerns."

Marcus follows my gaze to the horizon where the approaching ships tack into the wind, getting closer every time they make a turn.

"Them?" Salila laughs; her voice is a melodic stream. "I'd be more worried about the reef. It's just under the hull, don't you know?"

My whole body goes cold. "Can you help, then?"

She cocks her head. "Let me think. What do you reckon will remedy our situation? Hard to port? Starboard? Fifty-fifty chance either way."

And that is all I can take.

"Samsen, hold the wheel." He comes up beside me and I plant his hand on the polished wood and walk away. "Keep the nose pointed toward the center of the bay. This won't take long."

The Mar woman laughs. "What won't take long, little starfish?"

I step up, grab her wrists, spin, and drive my knees in behind her legs. In a breath, I flip her onto the deck and press my knife against her chest. "This. You can talk to me all you like, Salila, but I've got some things to say first."

The Mar smiles up at me. "By all means, please do."

"Either you help me turn this ship around and find Kaylin and Tyche, or you die here at my hand."

Salila glances at Marcus. "I think she means it."

"I assure you, she does," he says through swollen lips.

"A lot of pluck for a lander girl, I'll admit, especially a non-savant." Salila erupts from the deck, flips me midair, and slams me down hard. The wind rushes out of my lungs in one giant exhale, and I can't breathe or speak. Samsen lets go of the wheel and jumps the Mar, but she ducks and rolls him off her back. Piper comes at her next. Marcus follows, though he can barely hold his stance. Salila springs through the air, jerks the blade from my hand, and lands behind us all. She has Samsen around the chest in a viselike grip and holds the blade under his throat. "Does this one mean anything to you? If so, I suggest you back off!"

I'm trying to breathe as I struggle to my feet in time to stop Marcus from lunging forward. "Don't." I recognize the rage in his eyes. He'll get himself killed. In the background, the Aturnian ship continues tacking toward us. The man in the crow's nest waves a warning. Just then our sloop makes an awful groan as the wheel spins freely. The hull grates over the reef and catches for a moment before rolling forward again. I lose my footing, and Marcus falls on top of me.

"Grab the wheel and turn hard to port!"

"Kaylin?" I whisper, my face pressed flat on the deck.

"Let's avoid the razorback reef, shall we, lass?"

I push Marcus off. In two strides, I'm at the wheel, wrenching it to port. When my eyes find Kaylin, he's on the railing, dripping wet, his fisherman's pants hanging low on his hips, hair plastered to his face and shoulders. Draped over his back, he carries a drowned girl.

64

KAYLIN

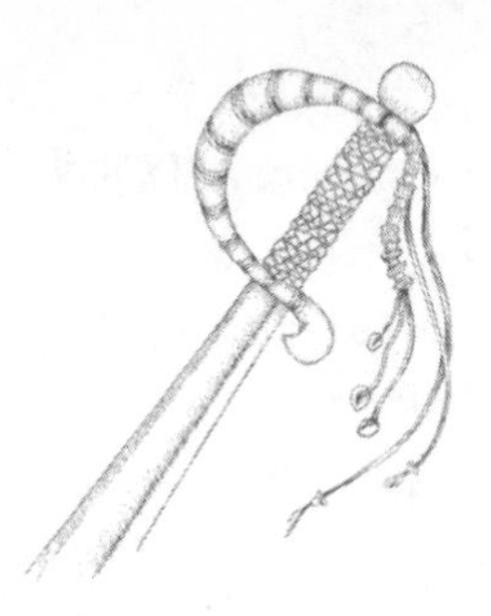

I swing wet hair out of my face and shift the girl's weight. Her manacled hands are looped around my neck, limp body hanging down my back. It probably doesn't look good. "Samsen, you and Piper toss the guard." I check the distance of the approaching vessels. "Salila!" I growl her name.

"You didn't drown," Ash says, her voice small.

"Not enough water in the sea for that."

Salila chuckles. *"At least you've kept her in the dark. It might help your case with Teern."*

"Shut up, sister."

I let Tyche down on the deck, where she lies like a broken doll, her head lolling to the side, lips and skin blue. Piper tries to resuscitate her, the serpent latching onto her wrist, but there's no response.

I tap Piper on the shoulder and tip my head toward Marcus. "Take him below before he topples overboard."

Piper looks up at Marcus with tears in her eyes.

"Samsen, check the water level in the hold."

Piper ignores me and keeps searching for Tyche's pulse. I can tell from here there is none. Samsen helps her up as her serpent retracts its fangs. "It's too late."

Ash holds the wheel, her tear-filled eyes resting on me. "I know you tried."

"Lass, wait for my signal." She's about to protest, but I cut her short. "Salila, revive the child."

"Revive?" Ash's eyes go round. "She can do that?"

Piper looks over her shoulder and shakes her head. "We're too late."

I don't try to explain but climb the rigging to retrieve the jib line that's lashing against the mast. Salila needs watching. She's unpredictable at the best of times, and the blood has to be driving her crazy. I know it is me. *"Quickly, Salila."* I wave toward the lead Aturnian ship. *"On Teern's wrath, you've made a mess of it."*

"I've *made a mess of it? Oh, that's rich."* She lets out a snort but goes to Tyche.

"Samsen," I call down the hold from my perch on the mast. "Water level?"

"Ankle deep."

"Excellent!" I feel Ash's teary eyes on me and give her a wink. "There's a distance viewer in the galley, Samsen. Get it and go aft. Keep watch on the pier." I check the horizon. "Ash, hold the wheel tight. She's going to want to spin to starboard." I jump and catch the jib line, riding it down to the deck. Once my feet touch, I haul it taut. "Now, Ash. Hard to port. More. More. Enough! Hold it for all you're worth!"

The sail flutters for a moment then billows full. The sloop comes around fast, the prow heading toward open water. With the wind in the sail, it arrows straight past the approaching vessel, leaving the bewildered Aturnians behind, but not before they take in the deck with its spilled intestines, drowned child, and a tall, naked woman.

I'll have to deal with them later. Right now, there's too much else at stake. "Salila!"

65

SALILA

Kaylin's throwing orders around like the King of the Sea. Sure, I'll play along, just to see where he takes this, but really, it's getting up my nose. I kneel down to the child, putting all my focus there. "You have a pretty face, don't you, polyp?" I touch her freckled cheek. Her skin is leached to gray, cold to the touch. I put my hand on her chest. No heartbeat. "Tell me she's savant." I glance at Ash.

"She was, peace be her path." The girl challenges me through red-rimmed eyes. Landers are such an emotive race.

"Good thing I'm reviving her, then." I say it under my breath, but she hears me. Her eyes widen and her mouth gapes like a fish. "How big's her phantom?" I ask.

"Impala."

"Describe?"

"A half-size deer. Long neck. Like a goat only more—"

I brighten. "That'll do." I ball my fist and slam it into the girl's chest. It seems to go straight through her to the deck while the girl arches her back and opens her eyes. From her chest explodes the impala. What a creature! It flies into the air, brown eyes wide, ears flapping, and tiny hooves flailing. In a flash, I catch it around the neck and shove it back into the girl's body. The little savant sits upright, sucks in a huge breath, and coughs violently before rolling over on her side to throw up half the bay.

I grin at Ash while patting the child's back. "Not so dead after all, is she?"

Ash's lips form a perfect *O*.

"Free her!" Kaylin commands.

He's so cocky in his captain's hat. "Not a prisoner, then?"

"Hurry up, Salila. You have a fog to raise."

I toss him a dirty look. "Aye, aye." I examine the girl further. "What's your name?"

"Tyche." She coughs. "Who are you?"

"Call me Salila."

"Are you Mar?"

"Obvious, isn't it?" I laugh. "Come, little nudibranch. I saw your phantom. All's well in your world, so show me your bindings."

Tyche sits up and holds out her hands. Her wrists are chafed and bruised.

"Hold them as far apart as you can. Like so." I place one manacle over an iron ring in the deck and bring down the edge of my hand like an axe. Sparks fly and the iron cracks. With another lightning strike, I split the second cuff apart. Tyche clutches her wrists and tries to catch her breath, her wet hair dripping down her face. "The words you're looking for are *thank* and *you*." I glance at Kaylin meaningfully then sweep up the irons, flinging them far out to sea. "Only monsters put children in chains."

Kaylin continues to fire orders at us all. "We have to sail across the channel as fast as possible. I'll want—"

"One moment, oh Cap-i-tán." I take the jib line from his hand and pass it to Samsen. "Do you mind?"

I push Kaylin in the chest, and he steps back. I push again, and he's nearly to the railing. "We need to check the hull, little brother." Before he answers, I shove him a third time, and he sails backward over the edge of the rail. "We won't be long." Their faces are stunned as I dive headfirst into the sea.

66

KAYLIN

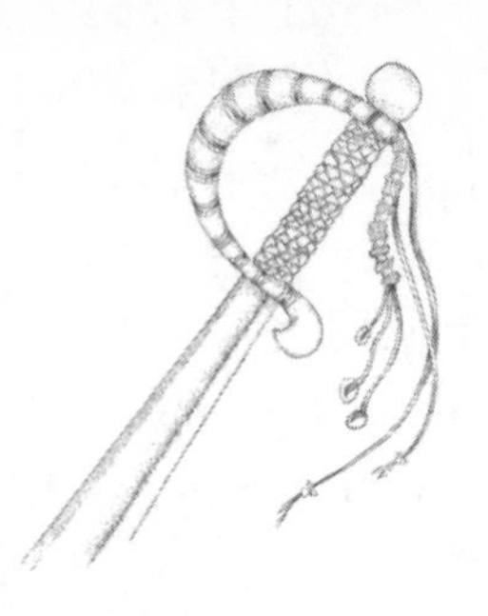

"*Was that completely necessary?*" I snap at Salila as I run my hand along the hull, feeling for damage.

"*How else to get you alone? You're up there, shouting orders, playing swashbuckler, and the deep Drop knows what else with the girl.*" She glides beside me but pays no attention to the hull.

"*It's not a game. The landers' lives are in our hands.*"

She gives me an incredulous look. "*Since when do you care about landers?*"

"*Since I've gotten to know them.*"

"*Pfft.*" Salila crosses her arms as we kick along, keeping up with the sloop. She finally turns back to me. "*You look ridiculous in clothes.*"

"*I look like a lander.*"

"*Exactly.*"

I press my lips tight. "*Salila, have you forgotten why I'm here?*"

"*To assassinate the Heir and his company, which you have failed to do, though abundant opportunities presented themselves.*"

"*That's what I'm trying to tell you. Teern has it wrong. Once he listens to me...*" I pause to feel a crack in the hull. The ship will stay afloat if we avoid any added strain, or another rake over the reef, but a good jar might split her open.

"*Have you lost your mind?*" Salila pulls on my shoulder. "*Teern's not going to listen to you.*"

I shake her loose. "*If anyone's lost their mind, it's you. Showing yourself to landers? How long will Father punish you for that?*"

"*They won't live to tell, I promise. When will you get it through your thick narwhal skull he wants them dead?*"

I thrust out my chin. "*Not going to happen.*"

"*Why not?*"

I hesitate, studying the surface streaming by. "*You don't know the whole story."*

She throws her hands up. *"Because you haven't shared it with me!"*

"There's no time now," I say, pressing the crack again, testing its integrity. *"We have to evade the fleet."*

She picks at the barnacles on the hull. *"How do you suppose we'll do that?"*

"You're going to call up a fog, remember?"

"I don't want to." Her mouth turns down. *"It taxes me."*

"You will call a fog, Salila," Teern's voice booms.

We both startle. The sloop sweeps over us as we hang in the water, the ship sailing on.

"Father," Salila recovers first. *"We were just thinking about you and I—"*

"Salila." Teern cuts her off. *"You will guide them now that you've interfered. I will help with the fog myself. And then..."*

"Yes, Father?"

"You'll come with me." He thunders the command. *"Kaylin, get back on that ship. Once you're past Capper Point, run this sloop aground. When you do, find which ship carries Tann and get me Aku's whistle bone. Understood?"*

"Tann snatched Aku's whistle bone?" Salila glares at me. *"I could have heard this sooner."*

"He'll have the whole damned crown if we don't stop him," Teern says. *"Why are the landers still alive?"*

Salila smiles. *"Ha!"*

I talk fast. *"It's not Marcus you're after, or any of the others. I'm sure of it. He barely has rapport with his phantom, the girl is non-savant, and—"*

"Sink the ship." Teern's voice sounds in my head. *"Drown them all and get Tann's whistle bone chest. Meanwhile, I'll ponder your disobedience."*

I tread water, stunned that he wouldn't even hear me out.

"Ta-ta, brother. I'll see you in the fog." Salila jets away. *"I did try to warn you."* Her voice wafts back to me in a whisper.

I drift in the current, gathering my thoughts before arrowing toward the sloop. In a few strokes, I'm at the rope ladder but make a show of gasping for breath while I climb over the railing. Business first. "The planks are cracked where the reef gouged them. We need to tar them on the inside."

"We thought you drowned." Piper looks angry.

"Again." Ash glares at me. I don't think they can take too many more of my near deaths.

"Are we going to sink?" Samsen's still holding the jib line. Good man.

"Not right away." I take the rope and secure it. "The ship is sound enough to sail us across the channel and well down the coast."

Their strained expressions don't change. I follow their gaze to see another sloop looming behind us. The Aturnians have come about quick and are gaining.

"We're going to disappear and glide right past these ships." I try to smile. Teern's orders sink in my head, and my plan sinks along with it like a rusty anchor.

"Disappear?" Marcus struggles back onto the deck.

"What part of *stay below* can't you hear?"

"I have questions." He holds his hands as if they'd been trodden on by horses.

"No time."

"Then just one. How exactly do you know the Mar woman?"

They all wait for my answer. Ash's eyes burn into me until I'm sure smoke rises from my skin. I take a deep breath. "Salila is Mar, true enough." I let my eyes rest on Marcus. "What you may not know is that some sailors have a connection with the sea people."

"She called you little brother," Ash says, her tone accusatory.

"True. Brother or sister are terms the Mar use for those connected to them."

"Connected?"

"Salila saved my life once, when I was very young, and has kept track of me ever since." All true.

Their faces are a mix of surprise and disbelief.

"And be glad of it." I take back control. "We'd be dead if not for her." I tighten the mainsail. Well, they'd be dead, but I'm not going to put it that way. My eyes go to Ash. I can't think straight, knowing her life is in danger.

"And the hull?" Samsen asks.

"Needs patching. There's a barrel of tar in the hold. Paint it on thick." I check the wind and shout out. "Hard to starboard, Ash." I can smell the fog rising. Soon all the harbors of Aku will be socked in, with the Sea King's help. "Samsen, grab that rope and haul for all you're worth."

He jumps to it while Piper heads down to the hold.

"Ash, keep your eyes on me. I'll signal you from the prow as I watch."

"Watch what?" Her words are clipped in my mind.

"Salila. She's guiding us across the channel, out of sight and harm's way of the other vessels."

"How in the depths of S'rak al Mor are we going to be 'out of sight'?" Ash swears aloud, her curse nearly bowling me over. Does the lass know what she's saying?

"Of course, I do. Now tell me how!"

"Salila's raising a Mar fog, don't you know?" As I say it, the air turns thick like a winter blanket, and soon all forms beyond a handspan wink out.

Ash whistles through her teeth. "Another myth comes to life?"

Seems she's heard of a Mar fog. Of course she has, with all that research for Brogal. Must tell Father about that, if he doesn't already know. What I'll *not* be sharing with the Sea King is Ash's unique ability to converse with me. No. I labeled her non-savant and her life may well depend on others believing her completely so. "Steady as she goes, lass. Don't let the wheel spin." I secure the mainsail line for Samsen and direct him to the crow's nest with the distance viewer. "Keep your eyes fore and aft." I watch the crow's nest vanish in the fog. "Not afraid of heights, I hope."

"My phantom's avian, remember?" Samsen starts to climb, moving faster than I expect.

The sloop leans into the winds and picks up speed, cutting through the rising mist. If I know Salila, she'll cause more than a few ships to ram into one another today as she leads us across the channel. As long as it isn't this one, I don't mind. As for Teern's orders, I begin to form a new plan, and it's not a good one. Not yet. How can it be when I'm sailing Ash and the rest of the company toward certain death?

67

ASH

G*ut'ns tish, I have conversed with a Mar.* The thought stops my breath and makes my legs go weak. *The sea people really do exist.*

Like the headlands of Clearwater Road, the fog saturates everything, and cold doesn't begin to define it. It dampens any distant sounds and acts like a megaphone to those nearby, the rhythmic spray of water hitting the prow, the creak of ropes and whoosh of wind through the rigging. The mainsail is down, and we run with the jib only for maneuverability. But the sloop makes good speed, which is lucky, because we need it.

Lucky also, I'm told, is that Salila, the Mar, leads us to safety. My mind spins with other possibilities. Maybe she leads us to the mouth of death, to the freezing waters of the Drop. I can't see Kaylin but can hear him over the sounds of the ship and the sea. From time to time, Salila's voice rings out as well. Her attitude ranges from cutting sarcasm to outright flirtation. It makes me question if Kaylin is the same man I knew this morning. The sailor who took me swimming, brought meals to our room, and explored the secrets of the ancient texts in the library of Aku. Who shared a kiss, or three… My companion who led me out of the library right before it fell? *That* Kaylin saved my life, and I want this version to be the same person, but it's not clear to me if he is.

Kaylin's all over the ship, a single man crew, calling out course corrections, trimming the sails, running up the rigging and adjusting whatever there is to tighten or loosen. He never tires, but then, he never did. That's the same. He hurries by me now, and there it is again, a smile that isn't quite right. And, if Kaylin is worried, there must be something catastrophic going on. A pressure in my head makes it hard to think straight, let alone talk. When Kaylin pauses next to me at the wheel, I force the words out. "She…the Mar…"

"Salila?" He modifies the heading slightly for me, though how he can see past his elbow in the fog, I don't know. "Ask me anything you like."

That's willingness, but I hardly know where to begin. "She saved your life?"

"Aye."

"When?"

His eyes grow distant. "Two turns to starboard," he says then studies my profile. "A long time ago, Ash. I was a child."

"Can't have been that long ago," I mutter. "And so, now you two are what, exactly?" I sum it up in a word that I hope is ludicrous but must be tested. "Betrothed?" The blood drains from my limbs as I wait on his answer.

A genuine laugh escapes his lips. "No, lass. Nothing like that."

I relax, then tense again. "But she's so provocative."

"She's Mar." He shrugs as if that explains everything.

"Yet she calls you brother?"

"As I said, a Mar's term for those they know. A familiar one."

I chew on that and decide not to ask exactly what "know" means in this specific instance. "But you're somehow entwined."

"Betrothal, in *any* sense, is not the way of Mar."

He's not really answering the question. I hesitate, then whisper, "It's not the way of Mar. I get that now, but is it your way, Kaylin?"

"It never used to be."

He looks at me with such openness my lips part.

"Port. Half a turn. That's it. Steady." He's back to being the captain.

At the risk of sounding childish, I ask one more thing. "Why didn't you tell me about her?" I turn and face him. "You lied."

"I withheld about Salila, but I've never lied." His brow wrinkles, as if considering how to proceed. "Mar hide their bonds with landers, never wanting them to be known. It was not my secret to tell."

"Bonds?"

He pauses and looks at me.

"Do you think you're pushing him away yet?" my inner voice asks with a cheerful lilt.

You disappeared again!

"Other way around. It's you who stopped hearing me."

Right. The messy business of being under attack, the escape from Aku, the guards, the Mar…

"Maybe pay attention to the outer conversation for now?"

I realize Kaylin is talking.

"...the bond is a greater agreement, Ash," he says. "Please forgive me if I offended you."

Offended is not the word I'm searching for. My heart sinks under his formality, and heat stings my face. I change paths. "There are more lander-Mar bonds that you know of?"

"It's rare." His eyes melt into mine. "But I believe so, yes," he whispers. "I hope so."

I fall into the softness of his voice, for a moment, before breaking the spell. "You speak in riddles, Kaylin of Tutapa," I turn back to the fog, which is all there is to look at, and stare straight ahead.

He places his hand over mine as I grip the wheel. "I was asked to keep a confidence, an extraordinary one, and I did."

"Fair enough. But it's out now, this relationship you have with her. It's out that Mar exist beyond myth and fancy, and that changes everything. You know Jacas Adicio has called a halt to the sacrifices, saying the Mar never existed, nor did the old gods. Now people will be tossing marred children into the Drop again, to placate the likes of your disemboweling Salila."

"Is this Teern's plan all along?" Salila's voice echoes.

"Maybe." Kaylin allows. *"You know the ban has left empty tombs."*

Salila laughs. "*We could have been played, but then why have them all killed? There'd be no one left to report it.*"

"What are you two talking about?" I press my hand to my forehead. "Who's Teern? Who's to be killed?"

Kaylin startles. "Teern?"

"I heard her say the name." I look for Salila on deck. "Where is she?"

Kaylin is speechless for a moment. "Guard your thoughts, lass." His composure returns. "When we're safely away, I'll explain everything. I promise."

"Oh, Cap-i-tán?" Salila interrupts.

"There she is again." I shake my head. Is this imagination?

"It's not." He presses his finger to his lips. "Keep her out of your head."

I stagger, bracing my legs in a wider stance to stay upright. She's in my head, too? And I'm supposed to keep her out, how?

"Can you come aft for a moment, brother, if you aren't too busy toying with your—"

"Steady on," Kaylin says to me. "Salila's—"

"I know. She's calling you. I'm not deaf! And what does she mean, toying? Is she talking about me?" I'd cross my arms and puff out my chest if they weren't clamped onto the wheel.

"Toy…it's a Mar word for *bantering*," Kaylin says quickly before disappearing into the fog.

Somehow, I don't think that's precisely true, and neither do I trust that Mar is leading us to safety after all.

68

KAYLIN

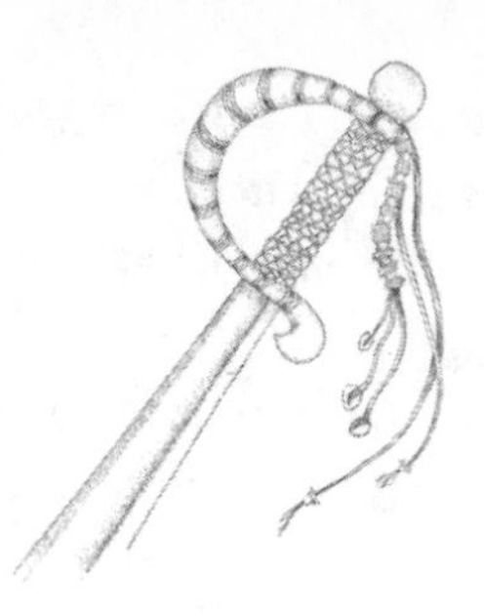

"*Kay…lin.*" Salila calls my name like a song. "*I'm wai…ting.*"

I scale down the net ladder and lean over the water, letting my free hand stream in the wake of the bow. The sea wraps around my fingers like a second skin as Salila's voice fills my mind.

"*We're coming out of the channel.*" She sounds very pleased with herself.

"*Excellent. You can go now.*"

"*I'd rather help with—*"

I narrow my eyes. "*I know what you'd rather help with, but Teern has it wrong. No one needs killing here.*"

She cocks her head just under the surface and smiles. "*What Teern has is a plan.*"

"*And you think part of it is seeing you revealed to the landers?*"

"*If it's true.*" She leaps out of the water and splashes my face. "*Then he has an even bigger plan than we can imagine.*"

It can't be true, can it? I resist the urge to jump in and strangle her. "*Just go. I've a plan of my own.*"

"*With the entire Aturnian fleet after you?*"

I give her a bland look. "*A fleet of landers, Salila. Barely a challenge.*"

"*Fine.*" She leaps again and nips at my hand. "*But don't forget, Teern is watching, and you have the Heir's company to drown, the girl included.*"

I catch her wrist, pulling her toward me. "*You will stay out of it and say nothing to Teern.*" I slowly let go and she darts away.

"*Crush the bones, Kaylin. What's eating your guts?*"

"*I told you, I have a plan. Don't interfere.*"

She sends me a mental huff. "*I won't tell him, but when Teern finds out, you'll be back in the Ma'ata until the next Great Dying.*"

"*The risk is mine to take.*"

69

ASH

I wake to the rise and fall of the ship, a ton of weight crushing my body, limbs aching, blisters from gripping the wheel overlong, weeping. I don't think I can lift my hands to examine them let alone climb out of the hammock. My muscles groan when I try to stretch, utter anguish from yesterday's sword swinging, wall climbing, and helm turning.

We filled in the missing pieces for one another last night around the galley table. Tyche spoke only when forced to, her voice flat, words fragmented. As for the procuring of the sloop, the appearance of Salila and the Mar fog…we were all present for that, though it's hard to believe.

Poor Tyche… This is worst for her. I swing out of the hammock, grunting when my feet hit the floor, and am off to find the girl. Piper tucked her into an aft bunk hours ago, and I don't want her to wake alone. But it's too late. In the galley, Tyche sits under the single lamplight, all by herself at the large table.

"You're up." I'm all smiles. "Are you hungry?" When Tyche doesn't answer, I keep talking, filling in the space with chatter. "There's some bread and dried fruit. Water, too. You must be parched."

Tyche's face remains vacant as she stares at her hands.

I fumble the cup when I pour her drink. "Lemon?" I reach for one from the hanging basket and slice it in half, nicking my finger as I do. "Brik on a bone fire, that stings." I shake my hand and blow on it as lemon juice seeps into my raw blisters. Tyche doesn't bat an eyelash at my antics. Finally, I manage her lemon and honey drink. "Try this, Tyche. You'll feel better for it."

She moves as if in a trance.

"Tyche?" I sit next to her and pull her close, whispering softly while the sea rocks us up and down. The nurturing soothes me, but the child won't speak. Her eyes fixate on an unseen object until I wish for her to close them. "Things could be worse," I say, getting up to rinse my hands.

"Last time I was on a sea voyage, I spent the first three days spewing my guts into a mop bucket." I detect the tiniest flicker of a smile on her lips. Progress. I go on to tell the tale. "Then Kaylin—such a fine sailor—he showed me this." I press the points on Tyche's wrists, wondering if it quells despair as quickly as nausea.

"Kaylin's not a sailor." Tyche speaks to the wall.

I put a piece of bread in the girl's hand. "Sure he is. What else would he be?" I try not to think the word *assassin.*

"Salila knows."

"Salila knows what?" Marcus asks as he enters the galley. He's cleaned up a bit, but he's still covered with raw flesh and gouges. Large purple bruises spread across his face and no doubt everywhere else on his body.

I stop myself from gasping and paint on another bright smile. "You're up, too."

Tyche doesn't seem to notice Marcus is injured, which is probably a good thing. He walks toward us with a limp. My eyes dart from him to Tyche, my brows raised. Maybe he can offer her some solace.

Marcus sits beside Tyche and lowers his face level with the girl's. "How are you feeling?"

She slowly digs into her coat pocket and pulls out a little stuffed impala, a miniature of her phantom. "Imp was nearly drowned."

Marcus examines the stuffed animal. "Seems to have survived, but we'll get the healer to have a look, shall we? Piper's very good with small creatures."

Tyche wraps her arms around Marcus's neck. He stiffens at first, and I send encouraging nods as he shifts her into his lap and strokes her hair. She holds tight to him and sobs.

"Good." I reach toward Marcus and grip his shoulder. "Are you…?"

"I'll live." His eyes are black circles in his skull.

I hold back the tears and try to stay clear. I know he'll recover from the physical wounds. That wasn't what I was asking. Samsen said he killed more yesterday than some warriors do in two lifetimes. At what cost to his heart?

"Where are we?" He gazes out the small porthole.

"Open sea, south of Capper Point by now. If the wind is behind us, we'll make Baiseen in five days, but we have very little food or water." I blow stray hair off my forehead. "And there's the issue of the crack in the hull."

Marcus frowns. "That bad?"

"I'll talk to Kaylin. We'll have to put to shore at some point for Piper to bring her phantom to ground anyway. Maybe it can be fixed then?" I dip my head to Tyche. "She needs…"

Marcus nods and holds her mug. "Try some, Tyche." I've never seen him in such a tender mood. From one extreme to another…

I offer him a ration of bread and a lemon drink. "I'll take water topside." I lean down to kiss Tyche's cheek, and then Marcus's. "Get more rest, both of you."

On deck, the north wind stings my face. It fills the mainsail and spinnaker, the big sail over the bow. The Mar fog is gone, left behind along with Salila, I guess. That revelation is still looking for a place to land in my mind. I head toward the mast and offer Piper a drink from the wooden bucket and ladle.

"Let me see those hands." She winces at the sight of them. "You need bandaging before you touch that wheel again." She pulls out rolls of cloth from her deep pockets and does it on the spot. "How are the others?"

"Marcus and Tyche are up." I'm not sure what expression I offer, but she turns toward the hatch. "I'll go check."

I tip my gaze to the crow's nest where Samsen has his eyes fixed on the horizon. "How far behind can he see?" I ask Kaylin when I reach the helm.

"In this haze, maybe three leagues."

I offer him water, but he declines. "The fleet could be right on our tail and we wouldn't know it?"

"Lass, in all probability, the fleet *is* on our tail." He turns the wheel a fraction. The swell crashes against the prow and white water sprays the air as we rise up and slap down.

I grab at the quarterdeck railing and brace my legs. "Will they catch up?"

"Aye."

My stomach knots. "Can't we go faster?"

"We could cut loose the lifeboat."

I don't like the sound of that. "Should we?"

"No." Kaylin stares at the rigging. "If I put up the topsails, we might outrun them for a while."

"Why don't we do that?"

He grimaces. "Because her hull won't take the stress for long."

I'm about to respond when Samsen yells from the crow's nest. "Ships behind us! Gaining fast."

"More sail it is." Kaylin finds his smile. "Ash, I wanted to say..." He shakes his head. "More than we have time for. Can you take the wheel?"

I step up, cringing as blood seeps through my bandages.

"Steady ahead. Sing out if you can't hold her."

I have to brace against the pull of the vessel already, but I won't let go.

Kaylin calls down the hatch to Piper before running up the rigging. "All hands!" He's above the crow's nest in seconds, releasing the topsails when she appears. "Catch the lines," he says as he drops them. "And heave ho!"

The ship lurches ahead and I hear a loud crack. *Oh no.*

"Ready to bring her to starboard, Ash," Kaylin calls down to me.

"Toward the coast?" I'm sure we are meant to stay in the southern current, out of sight of the great coast road and clear of any reefs.

"Trust me, lass. I have a plan." Kaylin drops to the deck and gives the command, "Come about!"

I spin the wheel hard to starboard, and the others duck under the boom.

Kaylin seems relieved as we cut across the current and head straight for the Aturnian shore. "Well done."

"What's the plan?" I ask as the little ship strains against the sails.

"We can't outrun them for long in the open sea," Kaylin says as he ties off the topsail lines. "But we can lose them in the shallows along the coast. Near Gleemarie, there are hundreds of shoals, river mouths, and islets."

I frown. "Aren't we worried about those islets and shoals and such?"

"Not as much as we're worried about being caught by Aturnian warships."

I look over my shoulder. "But they'll follow us."

He smiles. "To their demise, lass. They draw too deep for what lies in wait."

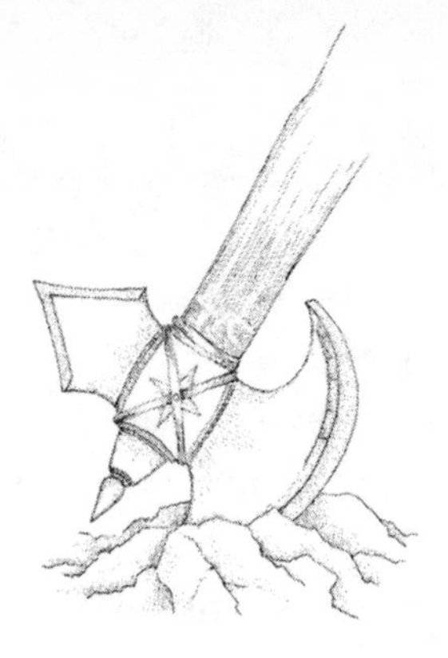

70

MARCUS

There's a chasm of darkness at the edge of my mind, briefly held at bay while I focus on Tyche. It roils back up once she falls asleep in her bunk. I pull the blanket up to her chin and turn away. If there is any chance this darkness is contagious, I don't want to infect her dreams.

As I walk away, the ship lurches and I stumble.

"What's the sailor doing now?" It feels like we're heading in a different direction.

I pull on my coat and climb the ladder. As my foot rests on the bottom rung, I hear a snap and the hiss of water spraying. I hurry down to the darkness of the hold to check the patched hull. My stomach drops. It might as well be Aku's fountain, water spurting everywhere! I go topside as quickly as my aching body will move. "The hull's breached!"

"Man the bilge!" Kaylin shouts.

I turn to go back down then stop and come back. "Man the *what*?"

"Landlubbers," Kaylin curses. "Below, in the aft bulkhead. A pump. Use it." Kaylin signals Piper. "Help him."

I hurry down the hatch and knock Belair over at the bottom of the ladder. The Tangeen is up but glassy-eyed and hunched, cut and bruised, a chunk of his earlobe missing. A phantom cure won't regrow that. But he pushes up his sleeves, ready to work. "There's a leak in the ship, I hear." How does he stay so calm?

Piper follows us below, her serpent rearing up over her head and swaying back and forth. "It's flooded already."

We slosh through the galley, knee-deep in ice-cold water, and past the high bunks where Tyche sleeps. I make a mental note of the quickest way to get her up on deck if the time comes.

"Here!" Piper says. She releases the pump locks and works the handles up and down. I go to the other side of the two-man pump and Belair braces it with his boot.

"Is it helping?" Piper asks. Water sprays her face from the growing crack.

I keep a close eye on my legs, watching for the water to recede. It doesn't, but then it isn't rising anymore, either. "Keep at it."

After an hour, I'm completely exhausted. My hand wounds have reopened, though Piper stops long enough to kneel beside me in the water. Her serpent is hard-pressed to find a vein that has not been punctured, but it manages to latch on to my right wrist and inject a restorative serum. When it releases me, my hands drip blood.

"Wait!" Piper says and pushes back from the pump. Belair takes a short turn on his own while she bandages my palms. "You have to rest. Let the healing take hold." The sloop rocks with the swell. "You too, Belair. Rest. I've got this." As she speaks, her phantom sinks its teeth into her own neck and her eyes widen, pupils dilate.

"Kaylin needs one of you on the deck," Samsen yells down the hatch.

"Dead bones, he does," Piper mumbles. She tries to hold me back. "Is he sailing us straight to our death?"

"I can do it." I pull out of her grip. It's a long climb out of the hold, but the fresh air slaps me awake. That, and the serpent's elixir. "What do you need?" I ask as I find Kaylin waiting at the prow. The sun is lowering in front of us and the water turns to gold.

"Watch for land."

Did I hear right? "Land?"

"Reefs, too, but you'll likely not spot any until we're right on them." Kaylin starts to walk away.

I catch him by the arm. "Why are we heading for land?"

"Ship's taking too much water. You best hope we find land quick. The enemy will surely catch us in a rowboat."

"And what then, when we reach land?"

"That would be your domain, Heir." He turns to go, but I stop him again.

"I don't know who you serve, and right now I don't care, but the safety of all on this ship does concern me." I push my voice low and threatening. "And I'll not see you hurt Ash, in any way."

Kaylin looks down at his arm where I grip him.

I let go but don't step back.

His expression changes suddenly, as if he'd heard something. "Keep watch." He leaves me to my new task and the sloop carries on, sails full and lines tight. I glare after the sailor, then face the horizon, doing as I'm told, scanning for land. What choice do I have?

Before long I hear the familiar cry of gulls, squint, and see the reef. "Stop the ship!" I wave toward the helm. "There's a reef. Coming up fast! Turn away!"

Kaylin is at my side. "Perfect. Well done."

"Perfect? Look at the depth. It's a child's bath." I don't even try to keep the alarm out of my voice. "It'll tear her bottom right out."

Kaylin laughs aloud. "That's what I like to hear, talking of this vessel as if she has a heart. You'll make a sailor yet."

"Bones be damned about making me a sailor, Kaylin. The reef!"

"I think we'll just skim over it, but I know they won't." He sticks his thumb out behind him.

I turn around. Not a quarter of a league away is a tall, double-mast warship bearing down on us.

"They're running with full sails," Kaylin says as if that explains it all.

It doesn't. "So?"

"There's not a crew in all the realms that can drop enough cloth in time to stop. She's going to rip over the reef if they can't turn her about. Either way, we slip through and lose ourselves in the shoals, abandon ship, and row to shore."

There is no part of this plan that I like, save for the Aturnian ship going down. A moment later, our hull scrapes the reef and Kaylin's smile fades.

"What's happening?" Ash shouts from the helm.

"The extra water in the hull's made us draw a touch deeper than I'd hoped." He heads for the hatch. "Bilge!" he hollers. "Keep pumping!" Then to me he says, "Marcus, find us land!"

All I can do is watch the horizon as we skate over the shallow reef, gulls crying above. Shading my eyes, I finally see it. "Land ahoy!" Relief washes over me. Safety's ahead, but really, I should say *distant land ahoy*. The hazy cliffs and long white beaches are much too far away.

If I believed in the old gods, I'd be on my knees praying.

Pity they are no longer among us.

71

KAYLIN

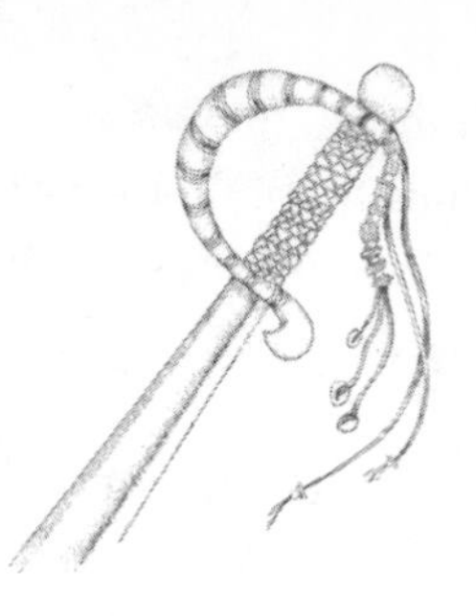

As I race past the helm, it's all I can do to keep myself from slowing down, taking Ash in my arms, and explaining everything. Promising that even in these dire circumstances, everything will be all right. I keep running instead. I deceived her from the start. There's no time to beg forgiveness now.

When I reach the stern, out of sight, I pull my knife and squat to the deck. The rowboat's mooring line is tied fast to the cleat. I haul up the slack until wet rope is in my hand. I make a loop and slip the knife against it, ready to saw back and forth. It would look like the reef frayed it. These things happen…

But my knife doesn't move, the landers' lifeline intact while voices battle in my head.

Sink the ship, the Sea King ordered. *Kill them all and get me Aku's first whistle bone.* It's Father's will, and he expects me to obey.

If you betray Teern, you'll not see the surface again. Salila's warning rings true.

But Ash's soft words are there, too. She speaks from the battlefield of Aku when I urged her to flee the island. *They are our people,* she tells me. *We don't leave our people behind.* And her face when we found the Heir? The love and care in her eyes blinded me. I imagine her turning those sparkling eyes my way, meeting me without reservation.

But if I cut the rope, saving only Ash, and manage to hide her from Teern, what of the others? Can I let those who matter to her most drown?

Do not fail, Teern's voice echoes. *None must survive.*

"None must survive what, Kaylin?" Ash's question sounds directly in my head.

She's at the helm, her back straight, bandaged hands on the wheel.

My heart tightens in my throat as I boil it down to one of two things—save only Ash or save them all. Either way, I cross the Sea King and forfeit my life… The truth is, there is no choice at all.

I drop the rope, uncut, and sheath my knife, making my way back to the wheelhouse. "Be ready, lass." I rest my hand briefly on her shoulder. "We're in for a rough ride."

72

ASH

"I can't hold it!" I cry out as the wheel burns through my bandaged hands. Kaylin said to be ready for a rough ride, and this is it.

"All hands on deck!" Kaylin commands.

In moments, Piper comes out of the hatch with Tyche in tow. Belair stumbles topside behind her, his fair skin paled to an unnatural white. They carry a few bags and the water barrel. I want to race below and get my pack, but I'm wrestling the wheel. I shout to Piper over the wind. "My satchels are hanging in the galley. We have to preserve those books, my records."

"Too much water," Piper calls. "Can't get back down."

The wheel spins and I clamp harder, using my whole body to brace against the drag. Then it suddenly breaks free and I hit the deck.

"Lass!" Kaylin picks me up.

"What happened?"

"Rudder's broken." He tests the helm. "To the lifeboat. Abandon ship!"

"Abandon ship?" Marcus cries out.

I dart back to the hatch. "I can't leave the records behind. It's the proof…"

Kaylin catches me. "I'll find them. You help Tyche to the boat."

I take Tyche's hand and guide her to the lifeboat as the ship slows, listing hard to starboard. I don't even know if the girl can swim, but her face is so void of life, I don't bother to ask. Samsen and Marcus lower the rope ladder. It slaps against the side of the hull but doesn't reach all the way. The onshore wind stings as my hair, long escaped from the ponytail, whips about my face. I look beyond the stern as two Aturnian vessels carve through the sea straight for us. The nearest makes a sudden shift in its sails, many of them spilling wind. Cries rise up from the crew, and then orders are shouted in Aturnian.

"Hard to port! Come about!" But the warship has too much speed. It doesn't respond, and they go aground on the reef, wrenching and splitting the hull.

Marcus jumps the distance to the lifeboat as it rocks wildly next to our sinking ship. He turns around and reaches for Tyche.

"Let go. I've got you."

Tyche drops from the ladder and Marcus catches her in his arms. He carries her to the stern and sits her down.

I keep an eye on the warships. The one in the lead hit the outer reef side-on, mid tack, its deep-drawn hull slicing into the barrier much sooner than we had. The deck hands scatter in every direction, their lifeboats lowering. Before they reach the surface, the ship booms, a geyser spraying up from the prow. It sinks like an anvil, right before my eyes, sucking the crew and the lifeboats down with it.

"Ash, you're next." Kaylin's soaking wet but over his shoulder is my satchel and, in his arms, the last water keg.

"Thank you." I grip him for support and climb over the rail, turn around, and cling to the thick, wet ropes. My blisters scream at the touch of salt water, but I make it down and jump to the lifeboat, finding a bench seat on the other side of Tyche. Samsen follows with Belair and Piper. Her serpent's heads are up and scenting in every direction, reflecting the panic on her face. Marcus, Belair, and Piper man the oars to port, Samsen and I to starboard. Kaylin unties the mooring line and throws it down. He lowers the barrel in a net and follows. "Row!" he hollers, taking his place at the last oar.

The sloop lays over the surface, the hull cracking wide, sucking in water. It tries to draw us down with it, but we pull hard and eventually break free. Once gliding over the reef, I keep my head down, putting all my mind and strength to the rowing. Whether the second warship came about or not, I don't know. When I look, none are on the horizon. I check over my shoulder toward the shore, the setting sun burning my eyes. I can't see anything that way, either.

I row until my mind is numb. My back aches, palms bleed. I tear the cuffs off my sleeves to wrap them thicker, but the makeshift bandages stick to the weeping blisters and chafe worse. Kaylin assures us the shore is coming up soon.

Land. It is my only goal.

How Kaylin guides us after the sun sets, I don't know. Maybe he doesn't. Maybe we're going in circles, or worse, back out to sea.

"Trust him," my dry inner voice tells me. *"He guides us true."*

Kaylin turns to face us many times as the sky darkens, and finally, he calls out, "Land ahoy!" His eyes narrow. "Hold. There's a bit of a swell." He stands on the bench, rocking with the boat, surveying the coastline. All heads follow his gaze as we lift the oars out of the water. I barely discern the outline of tall cliffs and the churn of white shore break. The strongest feature is the jutting breakwater, a natural string of islets protruding from the beach. The waves rolling under us are huge, lifting the little boat high and rushing us toward shore.

"Hard port!" Kaylin calls as he turns back to the sea.

As one, we pull the left-hand oars and the boat starts to come around, but not soon enough. I watch as a wall of black water rises behind us, gaining size and momentum by the second.

Kaylin's last command as the swell picks up the boat, tips it on its side, and flings us overboard is, "Swim!"

"There are at least three who can't!" I shout back in my mind as I free-fall through the air.

"Maybe focus on holding your breath for the moment," my inner voice suggests.

I have the vague feeling that the rowboat is falling, too, just above my head. I grip the oar, but it sticks into the dark wave and is ripped out of my hand. So much for flotation. The next thing I know, I slap the trough of the wave and plunge into the ice-cold sea. It tumbles me like a rag in a washtub. My breath escapes as something clubs my head. A stray oar? Marcus's boot? I have no idea.

"Swim!" Kaylin's voice booms in my head.

I can't do anything but be tossed about until the wave finally lets me go. I shrug out of my waterlogged coat and a few seconds later I break the surface and gasp in a breath. I get half a lungful, mixed with seawater, before the next wave lifts me like a cork and dumps me into the deep trough.

"Dive under it, Ash!" Kaylin shouts when I surface a third time.

Too late. The wave smacks my face before I take a breath. But this time it drags me down to a sand bottom and, as the white water pushes me toward shore, I find my feet, shoot to the surface, and take a glorious deep breath of air. Behind me comes another tumbling wave, but it has already spent most of its fury before striking and merely knocks me to my knees. I swim, ahead of the next wall of white water, kicking hard, and catch the momentum, riding it to shore. It drives me along, and I bump and skip like a stone until my belly scrapes over the coarse sand.

On hands and knees, coughing and retching, I crawl the rest of the way out of the water. Once up to the dry sand, I turn over onto my back, brace my elbows, and search the darkness. The next wave rushes in, not reaching my toes.

When it sucks back out, I find I'm the only one left on the beach.

73

KAYLIN

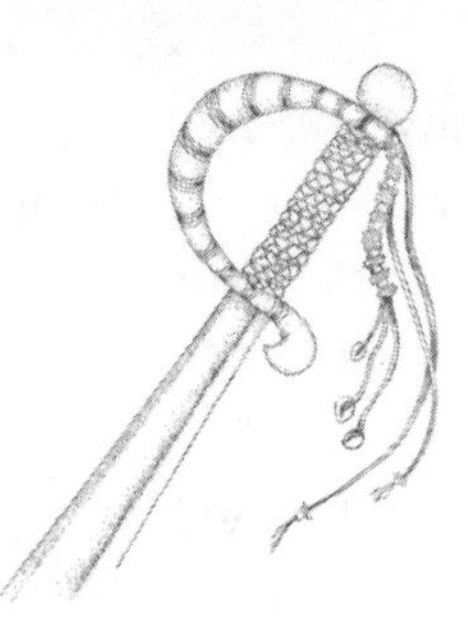

I reached for Tyche when the boat capsized, dragging her down into the depths. If nothing else, it gives me time to think. I can't get them to shore on my own, not fast enough to keep Teern from catching wind of us. I send a silent plea to Salila, which she will *love* as it puts me even further in her debt. Soon, I'll owe her all of Amassia. But what to do with the little savant? Instinct tells me to draw the line here. She's seen what I am, and no doubt when she finds her right mind again, she'll accuse me of it.

Tyche fights against me, not the sea, which isn't what I expect. The little thing swims like a fish. As I hold her to my chest and deliberate, the girl's small fists swing harmlessly at my face. For a moment, I see not Tyche struggling, but Ash, and Ash's expression as if she knew what I'm contemplating. In an instant, I turn Tyche around, keeping her back tight against me. After the next wave passes over, I shoot to the surface. "Stop your beating, little lassie. I'm trying to save you."

Tyche struggles to pull away. "I can swim!"

"Not in this swell, in the night."

She elbows my nose hard and tries to bolt. The next wave comes, and again I dive, taking her down with me. Has she caught a breath? I hope so. She still fights, so I push her down to the reef. It's impressive that she instinctively grabs it and holds on until the churning water passes overhead. We swim to the surface together and I catch her again. This time I flip her on her back and speed toward the shore before the next wave breaks.

"Take a breath," I say before we go under again. I swim ahead of the swell, one arm around the girl and the other blocking her strikes. We come up in waist-deep water and I let her go. She stumbles away from me without a glance back. I dive over the next wave and out to search for the others. *"Salila, where are you?"*

"Lose your little lambs, did you?"

"Help me."

"Why should I?"

"Because there's a chest of Sierrak gold in it if you do."

"Then don't fret. I've got the Heir in my arms already. It's a feeling I could get used to..."

I shoot to her like a comet. *"Take him to shore unharmed!"*

She snarls but sweeps Marcus toward the beach. *"I wasn't going to hurt him."*

Another Mar appears beside me. *"Shashida, you came, too?"*

"Did you say gold?" She smiles at me. *"And these are your prey?"* Shashida glides around me as another set rolls through.

"Not prey. Will you help me save them?" I reach out, fast as a snake, and hold her arm, forcing her to stare into my eyes. *"Do them no harm?"*

"Salila said you were testy. But for gold, I will do as you wish." She swims over me. *"Can I have first pick of the males?"*

"You will have no such thing." My grip clamps around her arm and I squeeze until she winces. *"There are three more, Shashida, so be quick."* I speed after Salila. *"For the Drop's sake, sister. Keep his face out of the water! Landers breathe air, remember?"*

"But I want to resuscitate him. See what his phantom's like."

"I promise, you don't."

She pouts. *"But he will be quite grateful, don't you think? If I save his life?"*

I come up a handspan from her face and clutch her shoulder, fingers cutting into her neck though she doesn't bleed. *"You rescue, revive, and you disappear, without a word to Teern. Do otherwise and I'll hunt you to your death."*

74

ASH

I don't believe my eyes when Salila comes out of the surf with Marcus in her arms. He's alive! Still, my hand goes to my sword, which isn't there. Useless.

"Stay back." I motion to Tyche.

Salila has her mouth on Marcus's, breathing for him until he splutters and coughs, drawing his own breath. He gains his feet as she puts him down, and Salila returns to the sea without a word.

"You're alive." I lead him to the shallows, but Marcus looks confused. He shivers in the darkness, his hands curling into his chest. The bandages are loose, hanging in strips, the ends floating on the water as his teeth chatter.

I know what salt feels like on my blisters. What he must be experiencing with all his gaping wounds I can't imagine. I stagger with him toward the cliffs. Tyche slips over wet kelp as she comes down to greet us. "More." She points back toward the sea.

Kaylin walks out of the surf with his arm supporting Piper. Behind him is Belair, falling to his knees, crawling, but managing on his own.

"Stay here, both of you." I let go of Marcus and he crumples to the sand.

I run to Kaylin as Piper drops to all fours. Her serpent immediately goes to ground. "Samsen." She gasps and coughs up water. "Find him."

"Already done," Kaylin answers as a tall, dark-skinned Mar emerges from the sea. She's like Salila, female, yes, but longer of limb. She carries Samsen over her shoulder. I run to her. "Is he alive?"

The Mar hisses at me, but I don't back away. Before I speak again, Kaylin stands between us.

"Shashida," he says, formally. "For your help, we are grateful."

"You know her by name as well?"

Kaylin takes Samsen out of her arms.

The Mar woman leans very close to Kaylin. "You play a dangerous game with Teern, brother." Her voice is husky and moist, more phantom than human.

"I hold you to your vow, on your life." Kaylin turns away, and Shashida disappears into the sea.

My breath catches. "Did you just threaten her?"

"I promise, when we are safe, I'll explain everything." Kaylin carries Samsen to shore.

We huddle under the towering sea cliff while wind whistles through headland pines. It's not much shelter, and it certainly isn't warm. I'm shaking uncontrollably. We all are. I go to Tyche, hoping to comfort her.

The girl nurses her soggy wet toy to her chest, the little replica of her phantom. Her hair sticks to her soaked clothes, and she's cold beyond shivers.

"We have to make a fire." I repeat it a few times before anyone responds.

"I think we must," Marcus agrees. "Though it's a beacon to our whereabouts."

"If anyone is looking." Kaylin turns to Samsen, who sits hunched next to Piper. "Can you call dry wood?"

"Give me a minute."

"I can do it." Tyche sounds small in the dark.

"Do you have the strength?" I can't see how.

She tucks the stuffed toy deep into her pocket and rises to her feet.

"Let her," Kaylin says quietly in my ear. "She'll gain comfort from raising her phantom."

For a sailor, he knows an awful lot about savants and their phantoms. Tyche avoids eye contact as she walks away from our circle.

"I'll come with you." She doesn't indicate she's heard me, but I follow anyway.

Farther down the cliffs, the young orange-robe drops to her knees and up comes her phantom, sand flinging everywhere. It shakes kelp and bits of shell from its hide and turns to lick Tyche's wet, salty hair. The intimacy warms me and makes Tyche sigh. Kaylin is right. It's the first relief I've seen in the girl's face since Aku fell.

There's no sign of shock or confusion in her phantom's expression. That makes sense. Going by what Marcus once shared with me about De'ral, the little impala has been watching from the depths through Tyche's eyes, feeling through her hands, hearing through her ears.

Tyche lifts her chin. "Dry wood, please."

The phantom blinks its big brown eyes and sings. The melodic tune lifts above the pounding surf, enchanting me, and all the nearby driftwood on the beach. When that's piled high, dry branches rise from the wooded glen beyond the headland. Piece by piece they float toward Tyche, stacking neatly at her feet. I grin through chattering teeth. The tone of the phantom song is so soothing; it calls up feelings of peace and warmth inside me, and I think everyone and everything on this beach must be touched by it. I sweep up an armful of wood to take back to the others. "Well done."

Together, Tyche and I lay the fire. The tinderbox from the gear is long gone, but being the resourceful sailor that he is, with only a dry stick and a flat piece of driftwood, Kaylin sparks a flame.

"Is there anything you don't know how to do?" I ask him.

"Aye, lass. Plenty." Not boasting makes him seem even more capable.

Cheered on by the breeze, we have a roaring flame in no time. My arms and legs tingle as blood returns to my limbs. Everyone else relaxes as well, clothes steaming in the warmth, blue lips turning to more natural tones. For Tyche, the heat is a sedative. She rests her head on her hands and falls fast asleep. The rest of us talk quietly while we busy ourselves drying our clothes in front of the fire.

"Do you know where we are?" Marcus asks Kaylin.

"I have us north of Gleemarie."

I sit next to him and pull up a mental map of the area. "How far would that be? One hundred and fifty leagues from Baiseen?"

"As the crow flies. On horseback, farther."

"Horses," Marcus says. "We'll need fast ones."

"To reach Baiseen in time to warn of Tann's madness, and for the southern realms to hide their first whistle bones?" Kaylin asks.

"Is there any other goal?" Marcus's voice is challenging.

"Survival in enemy lands comes to mind," Kaylin says to us all, but his eyes rest on me.

"If we replace the horses every night and morning and stick to good roads, we can reach Baiseen in five days or less," Marcus says.

"Ahead of the warships?" I ask.

Kaylin shrugs. "Depends on winds and currents." He looks at the faces around the fire.

"We need rest," I say, letting my eyes fall on Belair, who hunches like an old man.

"Don't look at me like that. I can ride," he answers, straightening. "But how do you propose we find fresh horses, morning and night, and disguises to keep us out of shackles, seeing as we must stick to well-trodden roads if we are to reach Baiseen ahead of the fleet? *Enemy* roads, I might emphasize."

"Gleemarie has plenty of farms." I frown. "There's no coin, though, is there?" I look hopefully at Kaylin. "That chest of gold?"

"Gone," he says. "But that shouldn't slow down a band of savants."

I pinch my brow, guessing what will come next.

"Will there be food?" Tyche's eyes open again, large and luminous.

"Hungry?" Kaylin asks.

She frowns at him, and then, as if making a decision, she says, "Yes, please."

"That I can see to." Kaylin chooses a straight branch from the wood pile, pulls out his knife, and in two strokes, gives it a sharp point. "Fancy fresh rock cod?"

Tyche nods again.

He pulls off his shirt and starts to walk away.

I run to catch up. "You're going to spear fish? In the dark? After what we've just survived?"

"The little lassie is hungry." His eyes crinkle as he smiles.

A bubble of laughter escapes my lips. In spite of everything, he has our well-being on his mind. Still, I force a mock frown. "And I suppose I know what you mean when you say lack of gold won't slow down a band of savants?"

He leans in close, his arm going around my shoulders, seemingly unconcerned that all eyes are on us. "Aye, lass," he whispers. "I'll make fine thieves of you yet."

75

MARCUS

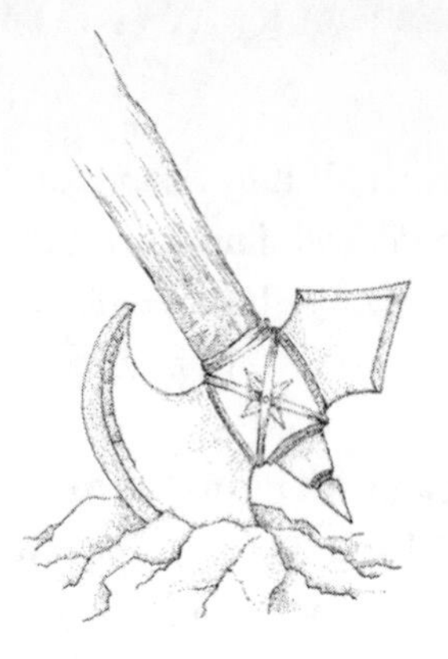

I scan the road as it curves close to the tree line north of Gleemarie. It's a perfect ambush point, according to Kaylin. He waves me back, and I duck out of sight. I can hardly fathom what we're about to attempt.

Kaylin, Samsen, and Belair hide with me in the pinewood, silent save for a few stomach growls. Kaylin's rock cod satisfied us for the night, but with the urgency to reach Baiseen ahead of Tann's fleet, we spared no time to fish and cook in the morning.

The plan is to steal military mounts, the logic being if we're seen galloping south on the coast road in Aturnian military uniforms, it's less likely we'll be haltedor reported. The war-trained horses should be the fittest, too. The problem is, as Ash predicted, so far, no troops have come by.

Until now.

"Steady," I say and make a fist, keeping the pain to myself. Deeper in the woods I spot De'ral and the sun leopard awaiting orders. So far, my phantom hasn't eaten a whole village or churned the woods to pulp, which is good, considering I promised Piper he wouldn't. We had a fierce argument, but in the end, I am the Heir, even without my official seal, which is at the bottom of the sea, or my yellow robes, which must have burned along with all the other neatly folded robes in the main hall of Aku. Still, I remind De'ral. "*No killing the horses. No squashing the riders. We steal the mounts only. Do you understand? Catch, not obliterate.*" Part of me is so confident I want to laugh. Another part of me, like Piper, is riddled with doubt.

And she has reason for concern, good reasons for wanting to find me a red-robe warrior to teach me greater control. Because she saw the results firsthand. I'd been self-assured in my final days of training, convinced Zarah's instructions were paying off and De'ral and I had finally found our rhythm. But that was before the attack that changed everything. And in those moments when De'ral and I were fully joined, when nothing mattered save annihilating every threat to Aku and her people, both real and perceived, I knew not who was in control. Or if there even was control. I recall only rage and blood and a savagery that seemed to be such a part of me I fear perhaps I've always been more monster than man. *The savant and the phantom are one*, I think as Kaylin's words come back to me. I must stay in control this time. No second chances.

Samsen slips deeper into the woods and calls over his shoulder to Kaylin. "Try not to get blood on our coats this time, will you?"

The sailor chuckles. I grimace.

Much deeper in the woods, Ash and Tyche wait, ready to call and calm the horses while we disable the riders.

Samsen's phantom circles overhead in the form of a large tern. It sings its clipped tune and suddenly the riders heading down the road find themselves on runaway steeds. The horses race into the woods as Piper and I close in behind them. The moment the phantom stops singing, De'ral and the sun leopard jump from hiding, turning fear to terror. The horses drop their haunches and skid to a halt, rolling back, trying to escape the ambush. Five of the riders fling from their saddles. Before they pick themselves up from the ground and draw swords, we are on them.

De'ral punches the remaining riders out of their saddles, using wild swings left and right. They hit the ground and don't move. I have to work harder than my phantom, but I flip, head-butt, and knock out two while Samsen, Piper, and Kaylin take care of the rest. Belair stays by the road, keeping watch in case anyone sees our highway robbery and tries to intervene. I hear Tyche in the distance, chanting, gathering the mounts.

"That's enough!" I command De'ral when he picks up a body and opens his mouth. *"Leave them be."* I shake with the effort to stay in command. *"To ground,"* I order, and De'ral melts into the earth, rushing back to me. I turn to see if anyone noticed my inner struggle, but they're all busy with their own concerns.

"Hold!" Samsen yells to Kaylin. The sailor's arms are raised, gripping a sword doublehanded, ready to swing wide. "No blood, remember?"

Kaylin reverses the blade, thwacking the hilt into the back of the rider's head and knocking him out. "This one looks about your size," Kaylin comments as he measures up the Aturnian slumped on the ground.

We're into the Aturnian uniforms in moments, keeping the smallest for Ash, Piper, and Tyche. Even then, they have to roll up sleeves and cuffs. I notice they all strap on swords, including Ash.

"I think I'll never be without a weapon from now on," she says.

After what we've been through, I fully understand.

The entire exercise takes less than fifteen minutes, not counting the roadside wait. We pass around the soldiers' waterskins and rummage in the saddlebags. They are well stocked with thick brown bread, dried meat, fruit, grains for cooking, and rounds of cheese. We stand in a circle together, sharing food and deciding the best match of horse to rider. I wipe crumbs off my chin stubble and give the command to mount up.

By the time the sun reaches midmorning in the east, we are south of Gleemarie, galloping full tilt toward Baiseen. I'm not sure of the others, but my horse, a tall, stocky brown mare, is smooth and easy. I have to admit, she's even more responsive a mount than Echo, long be her path. The Aturnians have fine bloodstock, certainly. If we could only reach mutually beneficial trade agreements instead of trying to cut one another's throats. Then again, after the attack on Aku, what chance for peace could there possibly be? It hits me in that moment, the irony. For so long, I've thought only of my seat on the Council, the many ways I'd bring about better diplomacy and peace. Perhaps I'd been blind to it, or naive as Father often said. Well, if Tann wanted a war…

"We can do this," I encourage our company. "We can reach Baiseen before the fleet, secure our whistle bone, and send word to Tangeen and Nonnova. We can be ready for the attack."

"I could call a headwind to slow the fleet," Tyche says over the thundering hooves. She rides well considering the saddle's two times too big and the stirrups, shortened as far as they go, are barely within reach of her toes.

"Tomorrow," I say. "We'll be stronger then." I look over my shoulder at them all. "Ride on!"

76

ASH

If I hear Marcus say, "Ride on," one more time, I'll purposely spill from the saddle, hit my head on the ground, and never rise again. In years to come, they'll find my skull and spine curled like a child, with scraps of fabric scattered about, pale and rotting from seasons of decay. They'll think I was a soldier in the Aturnian Army, maybe even savant. The black-robes might carve whistles from what's left of my arms and legs. Wouldn't that be something?

"A tad dramatic, no?"

"Ride on!" Marcus yells.

"Dakin deep," I curse but stay in the saddle. One more time, though, and that's it.

I've lost track of the days and nights and the number of horses I've sat. This one is a dark bay with straight shoulders and a relentless, choppy stride. Each hoof fall hammers my backbone like corn popping in a pan. I won't be surprised if all my bones are knocked ajar and I'll need months of healing to recover. Pins and needles prickle my limbs, and what used to serve as sit bones are now raw stumps. Our horrific journey to Aku, with its mercenaries, scouts, and near drowning in the Ferus River doesn't compare to this nightmare that won't end. I would like to say something to the others, if just to commiserate, but the cold and exhaustion silence me—and the hunger. I'm almost thankful for the tailbone pains; they at least distract me from the gnawing in my empty stomach.

After a series of hills and valleys, we slow to a walk on the nearly spent horses.

Marcus raises his arm and halts at the bottom of a valley. "A short rest, then we keep moving." He looks hollow, a ghost of himself. I guess we all do, even Kaylin who gazes yearningly toward the eastern seaboard. We're drawn and haggard, dark circles under our eyes.

"Nearly there?" I feel certain we crossed into the realm of Palrio a few hours back.

Marcus nods, and Samsen confirms it. "Home realm."

I want to cry.

Kaylin finds a clear spring and returns with full waterskins. He must have immersed, as his hair is wet, eyes clear and revived. We water the horses and build a fire at Piper's insistence.

"There must be a hot meal," she says, shaking out the last bag of oats and cracked wheat into a pot. "Little point arriving at Baiseen's gates in time only to drop dead before delivering our warning."

There's no salt or cream or honey, though the gruel is warming and fills a gap. After the bland meal, I stare at the coals and hold my hands up to them. The others are silent. Tyche curls up and dozes next to me.

"We might beat Tann yet," Marcus says, scraping his bowl. "If we keep going tonight."

"There's a chance my phantom could make the flight from here," Samsen says, "though I'd have to stay in its perspective…"

Meaning we'd have to leave him behind, unless we tied him to his horse or—

"Out of the question," Marcus says. "I'm not leaving you for the Aturnians to find."

I have no strength to argue. None of us do. At least we're getting better at the theft. Between Tyche and Samsen's *callers* and Belair and Marcus's *warriors*, it has become a smooth business to lure riders off the road and knock them out. Piper suggested a few days ago that we call mounts in from isolated paddocks. It sounded like a good idea at first, but we tried it only once, finding out the hard way that not every full-grown horse in Aturnia is broken to ride. What a fiasco. We'd lost two hours of daylight that morning, and Piper was nearly trodden into the ground.

The whole business is worse for Tyche. She remains mute, for the most part, a contrast to the young girl she'd been before the attack on Aku. I have no time to talk with her about Yuki's death, not to mention the Mar who saved her life or the possibility of the next Great Dying. It feels like a huge store of knowledge long hidden was coming to light and now it might all be lost again. Certainly, the references from Aku are gone.

"One problem at a time," my inner voice counsels.

You're right.

Finally, Kaylin speaks up. "We have to make a choice."

"We do." Piper levels her eyes on Marcus and summarizes the situation. "We are approximately thirty leagues northwest of Baiseen. We can either carry on, hugging the west coast, or cut east and follow the larger, more trafficked East Road to Cabazon and across to Baiseen."

Everyone speaks up. Some are for and some against, and I'm uncertain where I stand.

"The west coast is severe terrain," Kaylin says. "Also, the settlements are few and far between. If we lose a horse or two and can't replace them, it will slow us down, and these are already spent. They have to rest."

"Five days and you're an expert on horses?" Marcus says.

Kaylin rubs his shoulder. "A city dweller could tell these animals are done."

"What about the marauders?" Tyche asks as she sits up. Her eyes are round and black in the firelight, her face filthy.

Everyone stares for a moment, surprised to hear her speak.

"Who told you there were marauders?" Marcus asks.

"Savants from Nonnova. The west of Palrio crawls with Gollnarian thieves, they claim."

"My realm isn't crawling with any such thing," Marcus says. "It's our best option. Going east will take too long."

"True," I say, seeing his logic. "It would be hard to slip past unnoticed that way, and we have no travel documents, not to mention the little problem of our uniforms. We'll be shot on sight as Northern Aturnian soldiers."

"Why not follow the Waindown River—" Kaylin begins but everyone protests. He holds up his hand. "Hear me out. We could skirt the foothills of the Hugon Mountain Range and come out north of Cabazon."

"Too risky." Marcus breaks a branch and tosses it on the fire. "Without an update on the temper of the realms, we can't go shouting out about a pending Aturnian attack to just anyone. The roads could be full of sympathizers, or non-savants."

My ears burn. "Meaning what?"

"Non-savants?" He rolls his neck. "They're mostly uneducated. Given to panic."

"Subtle," Kaylin says, staring at the fire.

"Is that what you think of *us*?" I stab the ground with a stick.

Belair jumps in to help Marcus. "No matter who we encounter, word of an Aturnian attack will be received in a mixed way, especially if it reached the east coast cities before we're in Baiseen. We have to know the status quo first."

"Exactly," Marcus says.

Their babble does nothing to appease me. "I wouldn't worry so much about us *non-savants*," I say. "We'd hardly have the presence of mind to organize an uprising, being uneducated, and…what was the other thing? Given to panic?"

"I didn't mean you." Marcus looks confused. "You're the smartest person I know."

I open my mouth to speak, not sure where to start.

Kaylin raises his hand, signaling for silence. Without explanation, he disappears into the night.

Marcus motions to Piper and Samsen, and they silently melt into the surrounding bushes as well.

Kaylin returns soon after with Piper and Samsen behind him. "Trackers."

"Be ready to ride," Marcus says. "We leave now."

My eyes widen. "Who comes?" I ask, buckling my sword back on.

"Northern Aturnian troops."

Belair helps me pack up the cooking gear without cleaning it. "They must want their horses back."

"The fire." Marcus goes to kick dirt onto the flames.

"I can do it," Tyche says. "No smoke."

She raises her phantom silently, and it leans in to her, rubbing its nose on her cheek. They chant softly, and the fire vanishes without a trace, plunging our camp into darkness. I have to wait a moment for my eyes to adjust, then I lead Tyche to the picket line where seven horses stand, hind legs cocked, eyes closed, steam rising from their backs. I tighten the girth on my tall military mount and on Tyche's horse, too. She scrambles up into the saddle without complaint, but I can't stifle the groan as I do the same. The horses sigh, resigned. In moments we are riding out of the valley, single file under a third-quarter moon.

When we reach the crossroads, Marcus points west, the trackers making the choice for us. "We cut across to the coast. Samsen, keep watch from above, and lead them falsely if you can." His jaw is set. "They have broken the treaty by their presence here. It's an act of war."

I roll my eyes. "I think we might have beat them to it when we stormed through Aturnia, North and South, stealing horses and knocking troops down like chaffs of wheat." I know he doesn't want to hear that right now, but I say it anyway.

Marcus isn't listening. His eyes take on a faraway look, and then he says those bones-chac'n words I hate, "Ride on!"

77

ASH

My eyes widen as the exhausted horse stumbles to his knees. The only thought I have while pitching out of the saddle is the certainty that I will hit the ground, which happens a breath later. I land hard on my shoulder, and as much as I would like to lie there, close my eyes, and sleep, I struggle to my feet and catch the dangling reins. Poor beast doesn't even have the strength to run away.

I guess things could have been worse. We're on a narrow goat track, at the cold crack of dawn, skirting a ravine, and I didn't roll to the bottom with the horse landing on top of me. But then I see his front legs, and I change my mind. "Oh no..." The fall did me little harm, but my mount's dead lame, his left knee already swelling badly. He'll go no farther tonight.

Marcus quickly assesses. "Double up, Ash, and be quick." I frown at his lack of concern. But I suppose, since he can see I'm in one piece, I guess there's no need to ask if I'm all right or need help.

I go to untack the horse and turn him loose.

"No time!" Marcus calls as he moves on.

"Ridiculous," I say under my breath and unbuckle the girth anyway. The saddle hits the ground, then the bridle. "Safe be your path," I whisper in the loyal horse's ear. When I look up, Kaylin extends his hand.

"Ride with me?"

"Yes, but a little warning. I—"

"She stinks," Tyche interrupts, wrinkling her nose.

Heat spreads across my face. "Not what I was going to say," I grumble, "but probably true."

"I don't care." Kaylin takes my hand.

I mount up behind him, circling my arms around his waist. It seems like decades since our roles were reversed and Kaylin rode double with me on Rita. "This is different."

"Aye."

From him, I detect the faint scent of river water and campfire smoke. "You've been washing in the ice-cold streams."

"And you haven't."

I smile, though he can't see it. "This coat was ripe when I got it." We follow the others, my lame horse dogging along behind us until it can't keep up. I hate this marathon we run. But we have no choice. The very thought that Baiseen might share Aku's fate…

By late afternoon we've reached a wide, shallow river where the horses drink their fill.

"How close are the Aturnians?" Marcus asks Samsen.

"An hour back. They're having trouble tracking us. I've called their dogs off course more than once. But we've more immediate trouble."

"More?"

"A large bat and a condor are circling to the south," Samsen says. "Together."

I frown as I wash in the stream. The water is freezing, but it wakes me, and more importantly, it cleanses the dirt and sweat away. "Must be phantoms."

"Gollnar *alters* often take the form of large bats. But if it is from that realm, what is it doing in Palrio?" Marcus asks.

"Your city might be under attack from more than one quarter." Kaylin's knee-deep in the water, holding our horse. For a moment, he closes his eyes. "This is the Suni River, if I have my bearings right."

I shake my head and tighten my sword belt. "Your bearings astound me." We smile at each other openly for the first time in days. The questions I have for him go unasked and unanswered, but holding onto him since dawn has had a healing effect. Our closeness comforts me, renews my spirit, and the explanations can wait.

"I know my waterways," he replies.

"If this is the northern branch of the Suni, it puts us seven hours hard riding to Baiseen." Marcus gets that faraway look again. "We must—"

"Ride on?" I supply the words as I study the horses. They don't look like they have seven hours at a dog walk left in them. "And if those things overhead are phantoms?"

"We'll keep to the trees and not be spotted." Marcus rubs the back of his neck. "We'll stick to a trot, conserve strength, and reach Baiseen by midnight."

"He's an optimistic lad," Kaylin says as we move under the pines that fringe the western trail. "One moment he's beaten down, bereft of hope, the next he's a shark headed to the frenzy."

"That's Marcus," I murmur. "But you're one to call him lad. He must be your age, or even your senior." I pinch his waist. "How old are you?"

He pats my thigh. "Old enough."

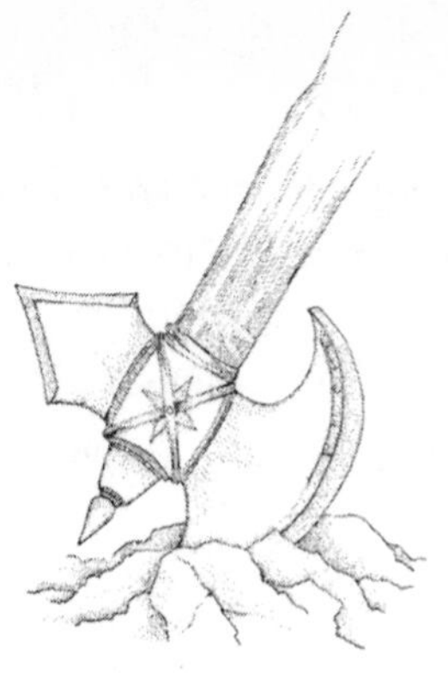

78

MARCUS

On the verge of a steep climb, I signal a halt. I'm slumped so far forward all I see is my horse's cresting mane and the ground below. Behind me, I hear the others exhale as one. I turn to face them. "Dismount. We'll have to lead them up."

Ash slides off first. "You mean we'll have to carry them up on our backs, don't you?"

Samsen waves down our chatter and points skyward. Against the stars, I barely make out his phantom circling the next valley over. He presses his finger to his lips. Smoke rises in thin plumes, undisturbed by wind.

"This is good news," I say in a hushed voice. "It must be Hayvale, the township north of the Suni's outlet. We can procure horses and—"

"It's not Hayvale." Samsen hands off his horse to Piper.

"What then?"

"Let's take a closer look."

I dismount and pass my reins to Belair, not that the poor beast has the strength or inclination to wander. Samsen and I hike to the top of the ridge, and as the valley comes into view, we drop to our bellies. Soldiers, phantoms, savants… It's a moment before I can manage a whisper. "How many do you reckon?"

"Over five hundred if there's one."

"All soldiers, and notice the phantoms by the watch fires. More near their horses."

"There must be fifty savants at least."

We hurry down the track. "We've found an encampment," I tell the others.

"Large?" Belair asks.

"Very." My voice snaps like a dry branch.

"And they're well-guarded," Samsen says. "Phantoms up, Gollnarian, by the look of them. Likely *alters* or *warriors*. Or both."

"We'll have to give them a wide berth, which will slow us down."

I study their faces in the rising moonlight. Kaylin doesn't seem surprised by the news. I store that thought for later, though my "later" list is long, *very* long, including most everything that has happened since the last morning I woke up on Aku.

Kaylin shrugs. "It could be an opportunity."

"How so?"

He pats his mount's neck. "We need fresh horses for the final gallop. Without them, we cannot gain Baiseen before dawn."

I rub my jaw, knowing the sailor's right. "Their horses are hobbled to keep them close by. Front legs only, so they can still move around to graze."

"Not ideal for us, but better than being tied to pickets." Ash slides to the ground and the horse sighs. "Where are they, exactly?"

"West end of the valley."

"Watched by phantom guards," Samsen reminds us.

"Perfect."

Ash throws her hands up in exasperation. "How in the F'qadin Bone Thrower's behind is it perfect? Do you know how fast the Gollnarians can amass an attack? We'd lead them straight to Baiseen if by some miracle we *did* get the steeds and galloped off."

"We'll just have to be faster," Kaylin says with a wink. "And smarter, but your fair city is their destination by any course, wouldn't you say?" He looks directly at me.

Unfortunately, I would. "Let's hear your plan."

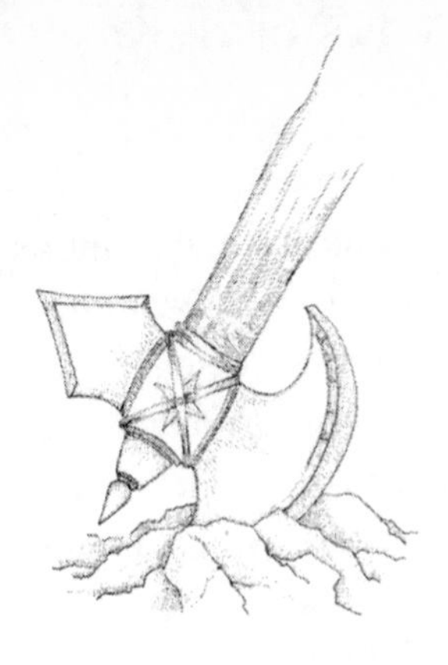

79

MARCUS

I crawl on my belly to peer over the ridge, staying low and out of sight. The wind whistles through the pines, bringing with it the smell of wood smoke from the camp below. "How far behind are the Aturnians?" I ask Samsen, who still has his phantom up.

"Two hills back."

"Not long to wait." Kaylin rubs his hands together like we are about to bet on a sure-to-win horse.

The plan, simple if not foolproof, is to nab the mounts just before the Aturnian troops stumble over this ridge. Just in time to take the blame for our theft. "I hope this works."

"It's Gollnar down there." Kaylin chuckles. "They fight first, ask questions later."

He might be right. "Two birds…"

"One stone," Piper agrees. "Gollnar's love for Northern Aturnia is fickle. They may be aligned, but at least they'll argue, giving us a head start."

"And please," Ash says. "Speak Aturnian if chased. It will add to the ruse."

I motion Tyche forward. "You're in first. We'll be right behind you."

She stares blankly, taking halting steps.

"Tyche? You can do this?"

She presses her lips together and nods.

I turn to Samsen and Piper. "Ready?"

They raise their fists and silently melt away.

I point back toward the tree line as Ash and Kaylin lead the horses away. We're set.

Belair and I climb over the ridge then crawl on our bellies, concealed in the tall grass. When we reach Tyche, we raise our phantoms, insisting they be silent as we creep closer to the camp that shines like a small city beneath us.

I raise my fist and pump it once.

On my signal, Tyche calls air from all the fires and the light in the valley winks out. While the camp stirs, shouts going up, Samsen calls seven fresh mounts. They look like rocking horses, the way they move with their hobbled front legs, rearing up in short leaps until Piper and Tyche can unbuckle the restraints. Samsen's phantom hoots, keeping them quiet and under control. In moments they are away, the steeds following Piper and Samsen into the woods. Tyche runs after them. Hard part done.

But the fires are quickly relit. Suddenly, two enemy phantoms, a razorback hog and a short, twisting *alter* that rolls end over end, spot the thievery and charge after Tyche, bringing up the alarm.

"Grab Tyche and run!" I shout to Belair in my best Aturnian.

He sweeps her up onto his back and sprints for the woods. The sun leopard, almost black under the stars, lags behind, ready to deal with the guards. The razorback gives chase, but it's no match for the cat. Belair's phantom turns on it, shows fangs, and lunges, saber claws extended. The razorback bucks and squeals but can't throw the cat. The red leopard rips into the hog's throat and it goes to ground, but by now, our location is no longer secret.

The other phantom, the rolling and twisting *alter*, heads straight for De'ral. When it reaches his feet, it turns into a thousand stinging tendrils, roots digging into the earth to trap him. Each vine climbs up the *warrior*'s thick legs. I'm half in, half out of phantom perspective and seeing everything from above as well as the sidelines. De'ral tries to kick free of the vines but they cling tight.

"Rip it out by the roots!" I boom, the pain bringing tears to my eyes.

De'ral reaches for the base and tears it out of the ground. Using my phantom's hands, I crush it to powder that floats away on the breeze. By now the camp is armed and heading straight for us. The guards spread out, searching the valley. Calls go up, all Gollnarian. I stand beside my phantom, ready to fight. Samsen knows what to do if I don't make it back. Warn Baiseen. That's all that matters. I grit my teeth and take a deep breath.

But nothing happens.

The night breeze ripples through my hair, strands sticking to the stubble on my jaw. Where are they? The guards and their phantoms don't come up the rise to give chase. They run the other way. I hear shouts and challenges, but the object of attention is not me. Are they blind? Can they not see the threat before them? I stop questioning it and, De'ral at my side, run flat out toward our rendezvous point.

Deeper in the woods, I spot Tyche, her phantom up and calling.

"You sent the entire camp in the wrong direction?"

"Seemed best."

"So it is. Well done." I help her up. "How would you like a ride on my *warrior*?"

She swallows, and her impala squeaks.

"He won't drop you, I promise, and we must be very fast."

Tyche kneels for a moment, and her phantom disappears. De'ral picks her up and holds her close to his chest with both hands.

"Run!" I lead the way, charging through the woods until the clearing is in sight. Ash and Kaylin have tacked the new mounts and released the old ones that linger around the fringe.

"Marcus!" Ash waves, holding a spare horse. She rides bareback, her saddle left behind when she fell. "This one's for Tyche."

De'ral tries to put Tyche straight into the saddle, but the horse shies away. He sets her down on the ground and I call him in, the horse calming immediately. The girl climbs into the saddle, the stirrups already shortened all the way, and I mount the horse Samsen holds for me.

"Ride on!" I cry and set the pace, a dead run to Baiseen.

80

MARCUS

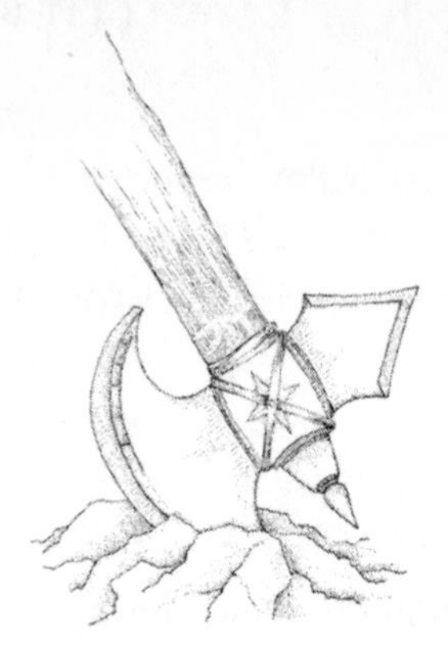

"Open the gates!" Samsen shouts as we ride breakneck toward the west entrance to the city. "Open for the Heir of Baiseen!"

My horse is lathered, her flanks heaving like bellows. I'm gasping for breaths as hard as she is, but on we go, churning down the headland road to the gates. But we've made it! From this height, all appears peaceful below. No scent of fire, metal, or blood. No sound of battle. The palace torches are alight. The Sanctuary's, too. The masts in the distant harbor rock back and forth. Flags, from what I can see at a squint, are all the ancient shearwater. Ours.

"No warships," Ash says holding fistfuls of mane as she gallops bareback beside me.

True, but they must be nearly upon us.

We skid to a halt, the gates not budging.

"Open for the Heir!" I shout.

There's a stir in the tower. "Who goes there?" a voice challenges us.

The horses shake and huff as Samsen stands up in his stirrups. "Are you listening? The Heir of Baiseen, Marcus Adicio. We bring news of imminent attack."

The guards above us converse in hushed voices. "Come into the light, you who claim to be the Heir."

"Claim?" I will give them five more seconds before I raise De'ral and point him at the gate, though with the Gollnar troops on our heels, I'd rather not. It would be good to be able to close this door behind us.

"It's a reasonable request," the guard says. "You ride Gollnar horses and wear Northern Aturnian uniforms, yet call yourself the Heir? Marcus Adicio never had a beard, even when he was in this world."

"I most certainly am in this world, beard or no!"

"Not by the Magistrate's account." The Baiseen guards march out single file from the tower but do not open the gate. In moments, they have us surrounded.

"Fools!" Samsen steps directly under the torch light. "The Heir is right before you, very much alive, though the Bone Throwers know we have nearly been swept from the path." He pushes back his hood and his pale-yellow hair dances around his face.

"Samsen?" the main guard says. "What trick are you playing?"

I rein my horse next to Samsen, recognizing the man. "Open the damn gates, Adrick, and let us through. It won't go well if you don't."

His eyes meet mine and he audibly gulps. "Make way for Marcus Adicio!" He salutes with his sword and drops to one knee. "Forgive me, please. We were told of your passing—"

"You were told wrong," I growl, more De'ral's response than my own. "To the Sanctuary," I command as the gates open. "Wake Master Brogal at once."

But still, the gate is closed. "I'm sorry, sir." Adrick catches my reins. "All petitions to the Sanctuary must report to the Magistrate first. No exceptions."

"Since when?"

"A recent decree by the Magistrate."

"My father will understand in this case. We must speak to Brogal immediately. Wake Father, too, of course, but it's Brogal and the war council—"

Adrick wavers and coughs. "We will accompany you."

"Fine, if you must, but let us in, and lock the gate behind. Gollnar troops camp a few hours to the north, waiting for a signal to attack. I'd rather you didn't let them in."

Adrick signals the gates to open but doesn't let go of the reins. At a quick march, we are escorted into Baiseen. Finally.

Ash keeps her horse at my side. "It's all right, Marcus. They'll wake Brogal."

"By my word, I will if they don't." I stand up in my stirrups and command. "At the trot! We have no time to lose."

81

ASH

I squeeze the hilt of my sword as the minutes tick by. If I had an ounce more strength, I'm sure it would snap. How can they treat the Heir of Baiseen this way? We're still waiting in the empty throne room, huddled around a few embers in the giant stone fireplace. No savants arrive, not Master Brogal or his ever-present assistant, Nun. No Bone Throwers. Not even a palace servant to add wood to the fire. I'd do it myself, but the hearth box is empty. To run so far and so fast to *this*? I turn to Kaylin and unclench my jaw. "We're usually more welcoming of our own in Baiseen."

"I have no doubt." He gives my free hand a reassuring touch, and I try to smile.

Marcus grumbles something inaudible, his arms crossed, fingers tapping against his biceps.

I'm furious, but it won't help our cause to lose control. It definitely won't help if Marcus does. I swallow the sour taste in my mouth. "It's terrible, this treatment, but Marcus, we made it. *You* got us home in time to deliver our warning."

"And you saved us from certain death on Aku." Piper puts a calming hand on his shoulder.

Marcus nods, and I see a gleam in his eye as he lets it in.

Moments later, the High Savant strides into the hall. My heart quickens at the sight of him, and I go back to gripping the hilt of my sword. Following behind is Nun and four savants, orange- and yellow-robes with council member medallions visible around their necks.

Brogal whisks up to us in his flowing red robes, his straight white hair tied at the nape of his neck, dark eyes searching, but not for me. They shoot to Marcus, and the High Savant's face contorts. It's shock, I think. Did they really not expect to see us again? Was the message from Clearwater not received?

I know how we must look, filthy in our stolen uniforms hanging loose over dirty, frayed robes. We're hollow-eyed and gaunt, not to mention the cuts and bruises. None of us have fully recovered, in spite of Piper's healings. All except Kaylin, but he hangs back.

I swallow the grime in my throat and straighten, knowing my role as recorder to speak first. "Master Brogal—"

"So it's true!" The High Savant interrupts me and extends his hand to Marcus. "Bless the old gods, you survived." His face is grave. "Sadly, it's too late."

The council members form a semicircle behind Brogal. They nod, miming the disappointment, or concern, or whatever distress I'm reading on their faces. That's when it sinks in. Marcus's claim to the throne. His place on the council. Proof of his ascension to yellow-robe. Is it all lost?

Kaylin stays behind me but touches the hem of my sleeve. *"It'll be all right, lass."*

I can't see how.

"We bring news," Marcus says, shaking Brogal's hand. "A dire warning."

"*Dire* is dramatic, especially at this hour." Brogal attempts a smile as he greets the others, clasping his savants' hands, nodding to Belair, Tyche, and Kaylin.

I wait for his eyes to find me, but when they do, there's no warmth, only a slight lift of his brow, so brief it's over before it begins.

Ice forms around my heart. Why do I ever expect more from him?

"Because you deserve more," my inner voice says.

I fight back the tears.

Marcus puts his hand on the hilt of his sword, the leather scabbard creaking. "Dire is no exaggeration, High Savant."

Brogal's attention is back on Marcus. "By the look of you, I think it might be true. Tell me."

"Tut-tut, Master Brogal."

All heads turn to the dais, and my jaw drops.

"Is that my brother among you?" Petén makes a show of pressing a hand to his heart. "Bless the bones, I thought you were dead." He's dressed in a thick, fur-lined coat and leads a woman onto the dais with him. My knees nearly give out when I recognize Rhiannon. She's wearing a quilted, knee-length robe and sheepskin boots, her strawberry hair in a single braid as for sleep. Petén and Rhiannon together? Receiving us? I can't make sense of it.

And then, my breath catches as Petén walks to the throne. "He will sit there?" I whisper.

"It appears so." My inner voice is enduringly calm.

But only the Magistrate of the Realm can take the throne.

"True."

The reigning seat of Baiseen is as majestic as ever with the carved phantoms of Marcus's ancestors springing from it at all angles. They seem to animate as I watch, but it's just the exhaustion behind my eyes.

"Is it?"

My hand clamps over my mouth as Petén takes his place on the throne. I've never seen anyone look more out of place. While he smooths his coat, Rhiannon sits in the smaller throne beside him, previously empty since Marcus's mother died.

For a moment, no one but Petén moves as he situates himself on the oversized seat.

"Your Magistrate." Brogal goes down on one knee and dips his head.

"Your *Magistrate*?" Marcus says, but the rest of us follow Brogal's example, as is customary. What else can we do?

Suddenly it's quite clear what has happened, and it numbs me to the core.

Marcus remains standing, his hands on his hips. "What are you playing at, Petén? Where's Father?"

"Rise." Petén sweeps his hand over our heads before answering. "Father's gravely ill, not long on this path. When you were presumed dead, he named *me* Heir. Practicalities, you understand. Couldn't have the throne contested by an outsider." He smiles. "Just days ago, the Magistrate ceded rulership to me, all legal and correct, documents witnessed and signed." Before Marcus can respond, Petén claps his hands. "More firewood and bring food and hot drinks." He studies Marcus. "What a mess you are, brother. Did you travel the length of Amassia on foot after running into a wall?"

Rhiannon stifles a laugh, and a furious pressure begins to build at the back of my head. To speak publicly of the Heir in such a manner…

"Lass, I don't know that he is still the Heir," Kaylin says softly in my mind.

Marcus's face is stony as he looks to Master Brogal and the council members for support.

They avert their eyes.

"The 'mess' will be much greater if you don't pay attention, *brother*." He exaggerates the endearment. "We've ridden day and night from Northern Aturnia to warn of an attack."

"Well then, best give us the details." Petén reaches across to take Rhiannon's hand. He kisses it as if they were the only two in the hall. "But first, I'm dying to hear. Did you actually reach Aku?"

"I did, in time for training and trials." Marcus's voice is steady and measured. "But that's not important now—"

Rhiannon whispers in Petén's ear.

"Not important? Don't be so modest, brother," Petén cuts in. "Let's see the records of your feats and successes. Admire your new yellow robes." Petén raises his brows. "You won them, didn't you? And the Tangeen?" He claps his hands again. "Let's hear it from your little recorder. The non-savant you insisted on taking. I see she's still with you."

I step up, hands clenched behind my back to keep from shaking them at our Magistrate. "The records were lost when our ship went aground on the reefs, and Aku was attacked before the award ceremony. We have ridden this far to warn—"

"Went aground! Aku attacked?" Petén cuts me off. "Dead bones and fat, you have had *adventures*!"

"The warning, your Magistrate—" I try again.

"You're saying the yellow robes were not won?"

I shake my head. "Marcus and Belair did earn them, indeed, but there was no chance once—"

"No chance? What a pity." Petén sounds elated. "And no proof of advancement, either?" He lifts his gaze to the council members. "Looks like I'll be the only Adicio in your ranks, come the next Council meeting."

Marcus hisses, exhaling through his teeth. "The color of our robes is inconsequential, brother. Ability stands on its own. One of the many things I've learned on Aku."

Goose bumps rise on my skin as Marcus's words boom to the ceiling, De'ral's voice bleeding into them. With several curt sentences, he tells of Tann's attack on Aku, Yuki's death, our escape, and pursuit of the Aturnian fleet. I've never seen him more powerful in my life, and if I could stop the waves of anger coursing through me, I'd beam with pride.

"Yuki's dead?" Brogal can't hold back. "I will not believe it."

"There is more, Master." I step up, ignoring an indignation so deep I think it will split me apart. "The High Savant Tann led a group of cowled brown-robes and forced Yuki's granddaughter to *call* Aku's first whistle bone." I hate being cold with the facts in front of Tyche, but something has to be done to convince him. I tell him of the bone being placed in a chest with Yuki's blood, the bits and pieces Tyche revealed. "Tann took caller savants prisoner, murdering every other class. It was a slaughter yard, sir. Worse—"

"Did you witness this yourself?" Brogal asks, his face paling.

"Not Yuki's death, sir, but the taking of callers, yes." I turn to Kaylin. "We both did."

Rhiannon is in Petén's ear again. My body goes cold as I start to see who is in charge of Baiseen.

"I find this all very hard to believe," Petén says. "Did any of you actually see Yuki die? Meet this red-robe face-to-face?"

"I did," Tyche says, finding her voice, though it sounds hollow in my ears.

Petén frowns. "Who are you?"

Marcus puts his arm around the young girl's shoulders. "This is Tyche, orange-robe savant of Aku."

"Orange, is it?" Petén makes a face. "She's just a child."

"A child of Yuki's," Marcus says, barely holding back his rage.

"The High Savant of Aku was my grandmother, peace be her path," Tyche says, her eyes focusing into the distance. "I watched her die by Tann's sword. His cowled brothers captured me, though I escaped. Believe it or not." She turns defiant. "Tann wants the Crown of Bones, Master Brogal. He stormed Aku for our first whistle bone, and Baiseen's is next."

Brogal stumbles, and Nun has to support him. "It's not possible."

Even Petén is silenced.

"Hence, our race here to warn you," Marcus says. "From the pursuit, it's clear, as Tyche says, Baiseen is next."

Master Brogal presses his hand against his chest and tries to steady his breathing. I've never seen him so unnerved. He gives instructions to Nun, who nods quickly and slips away. Brogal turns back to us, his face gray, eyes unblinking.

Petén recovers quickly and brushes lint from his sleeve. "This is all very interesting. But where are the refreshments?"

Two attendants scurry away. Others bring a box of wood for the fire and set up tables and chairs in the center of the room.

Marcus refuses the seat offered him. "Are you not listening?" He looks from his brother to Master Brogal. "The Gollnar army and Aturnian fleet are nigh."

"Gollnar, too?" Petén shakes his head. "Stop worrying, Marcus. We have gatekeepers if our neighbors come to call, and the watchtower guards will see ships off the cape before they near."

"In the night? Running dark?"

"Dawn is breaking. They'll see them." He smiles, showing too many teeth. "Sit! All of you sit! We'll discuss appropriate actions in due course."

I persuade Marcus to take a seat, though I can barely do it myself. At that moment, U'karn walks in, followed by more members of the war council, three Bone Throwers, and Nun who must have gone to fetch them. Something Petén should have ordered from the start.

"I understand I'm needed, your grace?" U'karn bows to Petén while his eyes fall on Marcus. "I see. Marcus lives?" His expression warms.

"I don't think any of you see!" Marcus shouts. "If the Isle of Aku is anything to go by, we must prepare for a full-scale attack."

U'karn waves him off. "The watchtowers have no such reports off Port Cabazon or rounding the cape. We have ships patrolling the channel."

"Are you so quick to dismiss the warning?" Kaylin asks, speaking for the first time.

Brogal's assistant, Nun, startles as Kaylin pulls off his knit cap. His dark curls fall about his face and he brushes them back. Nun recognizes him? How?

"And you are…?" Petén asks.

"A sailor, for one, who knows the sea," Kaylin says before I can introduce him.

"Kaylin, from Tutapa," I rise to say.

"You should know," Kaylin goes on, "the Great Eastern Current widens south of Toretta to five times its normal span."

"Our sea captains have spoken of this," U'karn confirms.

"Then consider how a fleet, one hundred strong, can sail for Baiseen, rounding the cape far beyond the watchtower's or patrol's vision, even with distance viewers." He rests his eyes on Nun. "I promise you, that's exactly what is happening as we speak."

Petén dismisses it, but U'karn eyes Marcus as if asking if the sailor is trustworthy.

Marcus gives an approving nod.

"Can you show us where such a fleet would cut back to the coast?"

U'karn asks Kaylin directly.

"Aye, that I can do."

U'karn tasks two men under his command and they follow Kaylin out of the palace at a fast clip.

"I won't be long, lass."

In all the exasperation and fury of this moment, his words are joy, sparking hope, and something much warmer within me. *"Good luck."* Maybe Kaylin can convince them.

"Ahh, finally," Petén says as the food and drinks arrive, not seeming to be listening to us at all now.

"Enough." Marcus stands, his hands splayed on the table. His face is red, muscles straining under his skin. Slowly, he lifts dark eyes to the throne. "*Enough*," he growls again, all patience gone. "There can be no more debate!"

As his words hammer into my mind, an excruciating pressure builds at the back of my head. "Marcus—"

He pounds his fists on the table, making everyone jump. "I'm telling you, Petén, Tann is nigh, leading a fleet of warships while Gollnar gathers to storm our gates. You *must* sound the bells. Prepare Baiseen for attack!" He strikes the table again, and the wood cracks.

A wary servant approaches carrying a tray of steaming mugs.

"In due time, brother." Petén draws a deep breath. "I'm finding your demands—"

"*Demands*." Marcus swings his arm, smashing the offered drink out of the servant's hand. It flies through the air and shatters against the wall behind the throne, missing Petén's head by inches. "Heed my warning, Petén Adicio," he snarls. "Or step aside so someone more capable can!"

Petén's face turns crimson, his voice shrill, as he swipes at his wet robe. "Guards, escort them out!"

The palace guards move toward us, pikes raised.

My body goes rigid and I don't breathe. It's like I've forgotten how. The pressure in my head hits a wall and shoots back down my spine only to bolt up again. My limbs shake and my eyes bulge like they're being pushed from the inside out. I want to scream, but I have no air to release, no way to draw more in.

"He belongs not on the Phantom Throne!"

My inner voice is an explosion inside my head that shakes the center of my being. I grasp Marcus's arm for support, fingers tight, but as soon as I touch him, everything shifts.

A single moment stretches into a hundred, the collective stillness like a glimpse of eternity. I'm aware of every detail around me, my hold on Marcus, the guards rushing toward us, the sound of their boots over the white marble floor, Rhiannon shouting…

The marble cracks under my feet. Bolts of lightning split the floor in jagged lines toward the throne. Fractures go up the walls and across the ceiling, chips of rock tumbling down. The weighted pause gathers like a storm, funneling all the energy in the room as if I could catch it in the palm of my hand. I feel it, the spirit of this storm about to fly out of my fingertips. The pressure builds higher until everything snaps back to full speed.

The room itself rocks with a thunderous boom.

A fissure breaks open inside my skull while the floor reels and tilts. There's a wild energy in me, rushing, pushing, seeking a way out. I scan the room until I find Master Brogal watching me. His face turns from disbelief to shock, and then finally twists in horror.

The energy inside me rolls under my skin, coursing down my arm, forcing my grip on Marcus to cinch tighter. As my nails dig in, the energy surges from me into him, *calling* De'ral.

And he answers.

The lightning bolts open wider, and white rock sprays to the ceiling. It pummels the guards' shields and showers down like spears of ice. Everyone scatters, hands over their heads, as De'ral erupts to his full height in the middle of the royal hall. He bellows a war cry and Petén topples out of the throne.

I back away fast, along with Piper, Samsen, Belair, and Tyche as guards converge. Before De'ral can sweep them aside, a pealing cry calls for silence.

"Marcus Adicio!" The High Savant's voice is phantom strong and piercing. "Stay your *warrior*!"

The entire throne room freezes, and in that moment of silence, I hear the coastal tower bells ring the alarm.

U'karn draws his sword and calls for the palace guards to hold. Brogal orders all savants to him. A messenger, faltering for an instant as he takes in De'ral and the wreckage in the throne room, runs straight to U'karn and Brogal. He delivers his message, between gasps of air. He talks quickly, although I'm too far away to hear until U'karn shouts, "Marcus speaks true!"

"Meet at the lookout and sound the Sanctuary bells," Brogal commands. "Baiseen must prepare for attack!"

With one last glance in my direction, Marcus springs after De'ral already running to the door. "Follow me!" he orders. "We must raise the defenses!"

Shouts and cries well up as everyone sprints after them, troops, savants, and non-savants alike. I grip my sword hilt and try to keep up, dodging slabs of marble scattered like giant teeth over the floor. Ahead, De'ral punches out the door. The hinges twist and splinters fly in every direction. The archway fractures and the support beams groan.

At the grand steps, Kaylin appears at my side. "Lass? What happened? I felt…I don't know what I felt."

"Marcus raised his phantom, in the middle of the palace hall."

"I can't believe I missed it!" A fresh smile edges onto his face and he leans in close to whisper, "Tell me, lass, did your Bone Throwers see *that* coming?"

I smile to myself, feeling strength and power bloom inside me. "No, but sometimes they get it wrong."

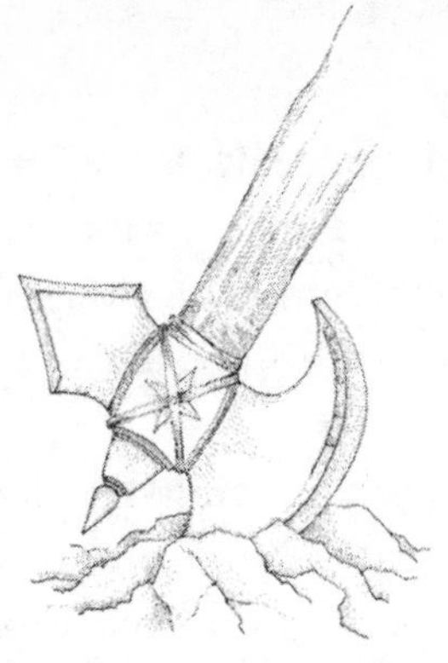

82

MARCUS

"Savants of Baiseen," Brogal cries from the lookout above me. "Raise. Your. Phantoms!"

With his red robes pinned tight under crossed arms, white hair streaming free of its customary tie, the High Savant jumps off the ledge to land in our midst, one knee smacking into the cropped grass. Dirt sprays as his bird of paradise rises. It heads for the clouds, dirt rolling off the blue and vermillion feathers. "*Callers* ready! We must keep the ships to sea!"

He throws an imaginary spear into the sky. His phantom darts after it, a euphonious trill echoing back to us as the *callers* of Baiseen erupt from the ground. Samsen sends his eagle toward the forming clouds and adds his own rich voice. Larseen and his jackal step up beside him, the phantom's head back, baying. Cybil directs her chanting cormorant up to meet the others as it counterpoints the High Savant with perfect tone.

I startle to see Rhiannon rushing down from the lookout, royal sleep garments replaced with yellow robes. The sight of her, and the meerkat, makes my guts twist, but this is not the time. She is trained. She is capable, and every *caller* in Baiseen must contribute. Every phantom and savant.

Rows of them have gathered, green, yellow, and orange robes fluttering in the rising breeze. They fill the lookouts and line the streets, uniting their voices with their phantoms that race to the sky.

My ears ring. My heart pounds at the splendor of it.

Deep within, I feel De'ral's pride, too, but something still makes my forehead sweat. In the throne room, his rising… It was unnatural…

But this is no time to puzzle it out. Not with Tann's ships on the horizon.

The clouds gather, the winds blowing overhead so fiercely they circle like a cyclone in the sky. And still the gale grows.

Over the bay, warm air rises from the sea, a mist sucked into the heavens as the wind builds. The sky above is thick with phantoms, dark shadows in the gray light until suddenly they ignite in color when the sun cracks over the hills behind us. Phantoms turn bright pink and orange and red as they circle the heavens over a rising purple swell.

In a crescendo of sound and wind, the storm courses off the cliffs and slams into the ocean.

Waves as high as the city gates riot into the air and push back the sea. A veritable wall of water moves with the force of a hurricane. The boats not tethered in the harbor bob like corks and are swept away.

On the highest crenels of the palace, black flags with the red shearwater insignia strain in the furious offshore winds that continue to blow. The watchtower bells started it, and, now—thankfully—the full measure of my city prepares for war. Even as the bells continue to toll in the distance, my thoughts turn to my father. Does he hear them? Is this his favored dream or worst nightmare come to life? All I know is that perhaps for the first time, I'm grateful for his preparedness, for every grueling hour he drilled me with the defenses, the steps, the protocols. *"As Heir to the Phantom Throne, Marcus, you must know this by rote. The people of the realm are depending on it."* I'd dismissed his militaristic ways for most of my life. But, because of them, Baiseen readies for attack in perfect harmony.

Healers guide the non-savants along the streets. Blue-robes usher the livestock and horses from the stables. I'm saddened by the need for it even as I long for my father to be able to see this and see me do what must be done.

"Oba," Brogal draws his perspective out of his phantom to address the highest Bone Thrower. "Send your strongest black-robes to the Sanctuary gates."

Oba nods and her crimson phantom, blinding in the morning light, flares. Other savants step aside, making way for them, their black robes wafting…the eerie result of their phantoms, formless but somehow woven into their shadows.

"Master Brogal!" I call his attention to me. "I am ready."

The High Savant turns his weathered face between me and De'ral, Belair and his sun leopard.

My mouth tightens. "We are, and throne or not, running the city defenses is my inheritance. I know what to do as well as my heart knows to beat."

He hesitates still.

"And we *did* pass, Master Brogal. On Aku, Belair and I trained and fought beyond reproach."

De'ral growls and I send a silent plea for him to hold steady.

"Mistress Zarah…" I begin, knowing he cannot possibly deny what I'm about to say. "Upon the last day, she named us both yellow-robes, and stopped calling us Baiseen and Tangeen."

Master Brogal's brow twitches as he looks back toward the palace. "Do it, Marcus. I leave you to oversee the defenses in your father's stead."

I motion for my company to follow but Brogal stops me mid-step. "Ash will come with me."

Kaylin raises a brow and I tilt my head, about to ask why.

"We won't be long." The High Savant drops to one knee, bringing his phantom in.

Ash waves goodbye and hurries toward the Sanctuary with the High Savant, a smile on her face.

But Kaylin's eyes still follow them.

"Don't worry. He's her guardian, and the most powerful savant in the realm. She couldn't be in safer hands."

I lead the way to the west gate, three dozen *callers* behind me. Our march is silent, save for Samsen's quiet instruction to Tyche so she can visualize what to *call*. But still the streets are crowded and noisy. People spill out of their homes, many with children and elderly in tow, jostling all the belongings they can carry as they race to the Sanctuary.

When we reach the gate, I take a deep breath. "Caller savants, take your places!" I raise my voice above the raging winds.

The savants divide into three groups. When in position, I command them. "Raise the columns!"

The chant starts out thin and high, escalating until I am sure it will break glass. Then it falls to a bone-jarring register, then up again, like a serpentine of sound. In response, the earth quivers and groans, dirt launching skyward as the first of the tessellated columns erupts. Then up rises another, and another in fast succession.

Everyone shields their eyes as the dust and bones of the earth blow off the black surfaces, sweeping the monoliths clean as they surge to near five stories tall. Carved from obsidian found in the high ranges of Palrio, no one knows how they got here, let alone were buried so deep. Ancient legends say they were set by Mar, back when this part of the land was under the sea.

Whoever fashioned them, they rise now for Baiseen—impenetrable shields to block *ouster* winds, checkpoints to stop the enemy's advance to the heart of the city.

I hood my eyes, watching the distant columns continue to shoot up, one after the other, all the way to the southeast tower.

"Well done!" I pump my fist and the savants crowd in, responding with boisterous cheers.

De'ral tips back his head and adds his victory cry.

"Gollnar won't trouble us this way," Kaylin says as my company draws their swords and rallies around me.

"We defend Baiseen!" I shout, rejuvenated by the glory of it all.

But then a small shadow crosses my mind.

Where is Ash?

83

MASTER BROGAL

Impossible! What I saw in the throne room… It can't be. Not after all these years. Yet there is no denying it. Ash's bound phantom could break free any moment.

I must act fast. But how?

For a brief instant I'm tempted, like a moth to flame, to let it rise, to watch it burn the enemy to dust. But I know the destruction this anathema is capable of. It is why I bound it in the first place. Some phantoms are too raw, too insatiable in their need for bloodshed. I cannot risk Ash destroying as many innocents as enemies.

"Fetch rune bands from Oba," I whisper to Nun, who runs up as we approach the Sanctuary. I don't know how much time there is, but thanks to Marcus, we are not taken unawares. For that, I am grateful. But regardless, I must bind this phantom back down. Before it's too late. I look across at Ash as she runs with me. Poor girl. She has no idea what is happening. At least I did that part right. But I saw. Marcus's phantom rose at her behest, not his. He has no idea, either…

My chest tightens. I wonder what other impulsive actions she provoked while they were on Aku.

How did this happen? Her phantom should have grown weaker over the years, not stronger. It should be charred powder by now, but to the contrary, power moved through her like a red-robe's might.

We turn the corner at full speed. One breath later we are hit with a searing blast.

Ash cries out. Her skin splits open like it's whipped, and beads of blood well.

"*Ouster* wind! Close your eyes!"

As I speak, she's torn from my grip, slammed across the breezeway and into the library wall. Her shoulders droop, and blood seeps through her coat.

Before I can move, another wave hits, throwing me through the air. My head smacks the pavement and I lie on my side, unable to draw breath. The morning light is thin, but in the distance, I make out five orange-robe savants. They push before them five reptilian *ousters.*

The enemy, I realize. It is already in our midst.

I struggle to my knees just as the ground heaves and cracks, like a forest of trees ripped out by the roots. The tremors topple me over and I fall hard again.

On my side, cheek pressed into the grass, I see Ash, still pinned against the wall, her face in agony, blood staining her clothes, so much blood. But high above her, to the side—I can't quite tell as my vision pulses in and out of focus—towers a huge phantom's profile, a crested neck, claws with nails as long as scimitars. Its skin is scaled and blackened, raw in places as if burned, but its action is supple, undulating. The prehensile fingers weave and twist and suddenly the wind tearing at Ash's body is blocked and sent back as a focused beam of searing light. It cracks like a whip toward the approaching orange-robes, splitting a phantom in two and impaling its savant. The man's face goes slack and then his entire body bursts into flames.

I swallow hard.

Old gods have mercy, what does she raise?

I blink my eyes and the claw alters into a disk and shoots out toward the next approaching orange-robe. She's decapitated before she sees it coming, her phantom dissolving into the ground.

Two savants approach at once, increasing the razors of wind their phantoms wield. I struggle to rise, my head spinning as a single golden tendril, the likes that float around the mythic sea dragons of old, coils and springs, hitting the ousters, one then the other, piercing their chests. On contact, the savants cave in on themselves as if every drop of moisture is sucked from each cell, the bodies turning into husks amid horrendous screams. The gold tendril recoils to encircle Ash as she slumps down the wall, the *ouster* wind gone. A light pulses from the tendril and her crumpled, bloody body sits up, eyes shining, hand reaching to her phantom.

"Dead bones and throwers," I whisper, but there's no time to think. I gain my knees and raise my phantom just as the remaining orange-robe draws her sword.

Before C'sen can fully rise in a gust of blue and red feathers, Ash's phantom *calls* the weapon, turns the blade, and shoots it straight back into the savant's heart.

My head slumps. But I must sound the warning. *"Spies in our midst!"* I tell C'sen. *"Scout the Sanctuary!* Call *the warning bells."*

As my phantom shoots off, I fall back to my side, paralyzed by fear as the huge, luminous eyes search for more threats, and find me. The one who bound it. Regardless of my intentions, I have wronged this girl in many ways. My first thought is to throw all my awareness into C'sen and flee, but what will that achieve? If this is my last breath on the path, so be it. My body shakes as the inner Sanctuary alarm bells toll, but I take another breath.

And another.

Her phantom turns away, uninterested, and I exhale into the grass.

Slowly, I find my feet and stagger toward Ash. When I reach her, I pause at the carnage.

Five *ousters.*

Five savants.

All gone, destroyed in a blink by a phantom bound and crippled for nearly a decade.

I catch a movement, and I tense all over again. It's still there, in the shadows, tall as a tree, leaning over Ash. All I see this close is the burned skin, the harm and abuse I caused. Then, a steaming orange and black mane, serpentine body, a wraith of a creature, contorted from the binding. Patches of singed scales fall like tiles from a roof, leaving raw flesh as it ripples in and out of view...a tortured thing seeking comfort from its savant.

Ash reaches up and kisses its massive muzzle, multiple gold tendrils dancing as she presses her forehead into the shimmering scales.

"Ash?" My voice catches and I clear it. "Ash, bring it in, to heal."

I hold my breath as slowly, like drowning without struggle, the phantom sinks back into the earth.

When it disappears, strange vines begin to grow, climbing up and over the lip of the crater it rose from to twine around the cracked pillars of the walkway, reaching coils toward the growing light. I watch, open-mouthed, as one by one they bloom with hundreds of tiny red blossoms.

A single name forms in my mind—*Natsari*—and I banish it like a demon as C'sen wings back to me. *Nun has everything in place.*

"Thank you. Wait for me there."

I look back at Ash, her face enraptured.

We are running out of time…

"Master Brogal? Did you see? This wasn't a dream, was it?" Ash glows in the warmth of the memory.

I steady my mind. I can't risk lying or revealing my intentions while the phantom can hear me. "No, Ash, not a dream. You did it. Against a millennium of likelihoods, you have raised your phantom and saved our lives. Saved the Sanctuary." I reach out my hand and pull her to her feet. "But you've so much to learn. It is untrained. *You* are untrained."

She nods, taking in the bodies of those she's killed.

"This is your first day as a blue-robe savant." I allow a small smile as she beams. "Such an amazing feat. It makes me so proud." I press my hands together in prayer and bow my head to her.

Her eyes shine up at me, tears running down her cheeks, and it's all I can do not to flinch.

It will not harm you now, C'sen bespeaks me.

I waver.

Her phantom will take time to recover. We are safe, but not for long.

"No, not for long."

"Come, Ash." I take her hand again. "Let's get you started on your new path."

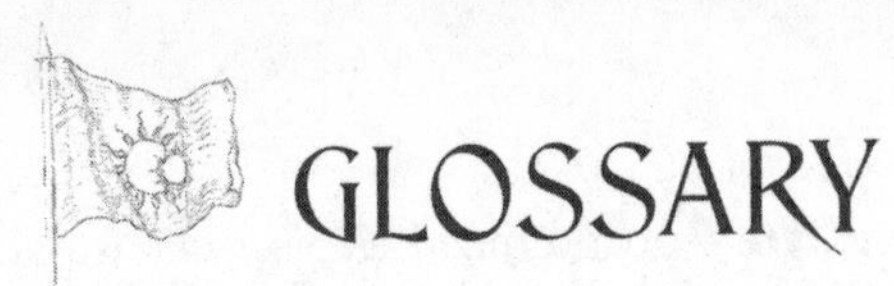

GLOSSARY

Aaron Adicio—first born son of the Magistrate of Palrio, deemed marred by the Bone Throwers and sacrificed to the sea, an act which has fueled the Magistrate's hatred of the black-robes.

Agahpa—a tree-like *warrior* phantom with incredible endurance and strength.

Aku—also referred to as the Sacred Isle of Aku, a politically neutral island realm where all initiate savants go to train for advancement to yellow robes.

Alters—phantoms who can change shape from one solid form to another. They are most common in Aturnia and Gollnar but can be found in any realm.

Amassia—the third planet from the sun whose seven continents have, over millenniums, formed a single landmass surrounded by sea. Alternate spelling is Amasia.

An'awntia—pronounced an-ON-tee-ah—the highest state of mind-body-spirit unity an Amassian can embody, where they have mastered every lot and reached the end of their path.

Ancient Sea Scrolls—historical fossil records, preserved in petrified tablets, that record the histories of the realms previous Great Dyings. Only fragments have been found to date…

Ash—orphaned at age eight, Ash, best friend of Marcus Adicio, is a seventeen-year-old non-savant wordsmith whose dream is to set foot in every realm of Amassia. Though she doesn't raise a phantom of her own, other phantoms are oddly curious about her.

Asyleen—the Sierrak Sanctuary in the far north of the continent lead by the red-robe Zanovine and the Magistrate, Rantorjin.

Atikis—the red-robe of the Sanctuary of Goll who raises a monstrous *alter* phantom.

Aturnia—the realms of both Northern Aturnia and Southern Aturnia are to the north of Palrio and hostile. Tann of Lepsea has taken over from their deceased red-robe, peace be his path. Due to political misconduct, Northern Aturnian savants are banned from training on Aku.

Avon Eyre—pronounced *ah-von-are.* Stories describe it as a small island at the top of the world reached only by an ice bridge in winter. It hosts a Sanctuary where the fabled Brotherhood of Anon dwell.

Baiseen—the seat of the throne in the realm of Palrio. Home city to Marcus and Ash.

Belair Duquan—a green-robe warrior savant from Tangeen who joins Marcus on the initiation journey to the Isle of Aku.

Black-Sailed Ships—outlawed in Palrio, these vessels hoist black sails when they carry a marred child to the Drop to be sacrificed to the sea.

Bone Throwers—those who carve and throw the whistle bones, belonging to a sect of savants whose phantoms never take solid form but remain as wisps of energy and colored light. They wear black robes, no matter their rank, and are oracles, throwing the bones to determine when to sow, harvest, go to war, and most importantly, which child has the potential to be savant, non-savant or marred.

Brogal—the High Savant of Baiseen and Ash's guardian. He raises a bird of paradise *caller*.

Brotherhood of Anon—an ancient sect of savants from the far northern Sanctuary of Avon Eyre who worship the Second Sun.

Bucheen—the orange-robe master healer on Aku. Raises a chameleon *healer* phantom.

Callers—phantoms who use vocalizations to *call* things to them, such as: fish to nets, weapons from a warrior, weeds from a garden bed, or in rare cases, blood from bone or memories from the mind.

Council members—high-ranking officials of the Sanctuary and Magistrate court allowed to attend policy meetings and vote on the Summits.

Crown of Bones—the group of twelve original whistle bones, when collected and played together at once.

De'ral—Marcus's w*arrior*, a phantom of massive size and will.

Destan—an Aturnian green-robe with a *warrio*r phantom, training on Aku.

Dina—an orange-robe healer savant at the Sanctuary of Baiseen who specializes in herbal medicine.

Drop—a deep-sea trench along the continental shelf where the black-sailed ships take the marred children for sacrifice.

Er—King of Se Er Rak (now known simply as Sierrak) the northern realm of Amassia. King Er was thought to be the first known savant, and from his skeleton the original whistle bones were carved.

Ferus River Falls—originally named Mossman's Shoals, the falls above Capper Point.

First Whistle Bones—also called the original whistle bones—the first twelve whistle bones, purportedly carved from the skeleton of King Er, which actually stem from much earlier times. Each represents one of the lots or *ways* on the path to An'awntia. Once made into a Crown of Bones, eventually they were dismantled and sent to the sanctuaries for protection. Each is kept in a place of honor, symbolic of the responsibility and privileges of being savant. In order, they are:

Crown of Er (jaw) —First Lot—Awareness of Self

Tree of Eternity (vertebra)—Second Lot—Awareness of Body

Ancient Shearwater (scapula)—Third Lot—Awareness of Mind

Ma'ata (Femur)—Fourth Lot—Awareness of Feelings

Water Serpent (coccyx)—Fifth Lot—Awareness of Creativity

Mummy Wheat (radius)—Sixth Lot—Awareness of Service

Mask of Anon (cranium)—Seventh Lot—Awareness of Relationship

Scroll of Hetta (rib)—Eighth Lot- Awareness of Renewal

Arrow of Nii (femur)—Ninth Lot—Awareness of Expansion

Jenin Stones (Tibia)—Tenth Lot—Awareness of Leadership

Eye of Sierrak (fibula)—Eleventh Lot—Nonjudgment

Prince of the Sea (scapula)—Twelfth Lot—Self-acceptance.

Gaveren the Great—a celebrated Sierrak warrior out of history whose phantom was thought to be the largest and most powerful ever raised.

Ghost Phantoms—a rare occurrence where, upon the death of its savant, the phantom becomes untethered from the depths of its being. A ghost phantom roams for an unknown time, always in search of a new savant to serve as host.

Goll—the main Sanctuary in the northern regions of Gollnar, led by the red-robe Atikis and his terrifying, multiformed *alter* phantom.

Gollnar—the realm to the northwest of Baiseen, home of the red-robes Atikis of Goll and Zekia of Kutoon.

Great Dying—the once every twenty-five-million year extinction that wipes out most of the life forms on Amassia, leaving what survives to evolve along a new path.

Healers—phantoms devoted to the care and well-being of all life no matter the realm, rank, or species. *Healer* phantoms are found in all the realms.

High Savant—a red-robe savant who has obtained the highest level of aptitude and rank. They usually oversee one of the Sanctuaries.

Huewin—the orange-robe library master on the Isle of Aku.

Initiate—a green-robe savant who has advanced in training far enough to attempt the journey to Aku to earn their yellow robes.

Jacas Adicio—Marcus's father and Magistrate of Palrio, savant to a *caller* phantom and lord of the throne of Baiseen.

Kaylin—a bosun's mate who guides Marcus and his company when they are stranded on their way to Aku.

Klaavic—Palrion fish stew with prawns, crab, fish, mussels, and clams in a tomato, garlic, and basil broth.

Kutoon—the main Sanctuary in the south of Gollnar, led by the High Savant Zakia and her *alter* phantom.

Landers—a term for those who cannot swim, or when used by Mar, for those who do not live beneath the waves.

Larseen—a yellow-robe friend of Marcus who raises a jackal *caller* phantom.

Lepsea—High Savant Tann's Sanctuary on the far northeast of Sierrak.

Lots or "Ways" to An'awntia—twelve in number, they are: receptivity, awareness of body, awareness of mind, awareness of feelings, play, work, partnership, renewal, travel, leadership, nonjudgment, and self-acceptance. The journey begins on the eastern point of the great circle and travels like the visible sun around the Earth. Once the first twelve ways are taken, the journey begins again, each lot building on a theme that, over lifetimes along the path, develops to its highest form of expression.

Ma'ata Corals—the ancient polyps that grow from the bones of the old gods and surround the tombs of the Mar. Sometimes written ma'atta.

Ma'ata Keeper—a Mar who tends the underwater tombs and oversees the turnings of sacrificed children into Mar.

Mar—long thought to be a mythic race who live beneath the sea but can pass on land as non-savant, or even savant, under certain circumstances. Some say they feed on the child sacrifices; others say they turn the drowned children into Mar.

Marcus Adicio—the green-robe Heir to the throne of Baiseen, Marcus is the third son of Jacas Adicio and raises a *warrior* phantom. He's also Ash's best friend.

Morning Ritual—An early morning practice on the Isle of Aku where all gather for a short meditation followed by rigorous, dynamic exercise.

Natsari—a phantom told of in the ancient sea scrolls who rises to bring balance to the world.

Nonnova—the island chain to the south west of Baiseen, allies of Palrio, led by the High Savant Servine and her *healer-caller* phantom.

Ochee—a Tangeen spiced tea made from an aromatic mix of ginger, cinnamon, cloves, cardamom, black tea leaf, and dried orange peel.

Old gods—a pantheon of deities said to have been trapped under the earth eons ago, before the last Great Dying. From them the Ma'ata rose.

Ousters—these phantoms dispel or vanquish objects, weather, animals, or people. The more advanced ones are very specific. They can push away certain types of objects but pass through others. The Aturnians originally used these phantoms to control weather and rain cycles but in the last five hundred years they have been trained for war/battle. Opposite of a *caller* but can create similar results.

Palrio—the realm south of Aturnia, ruled from the city and Sanctuary of Baiseen.

Pandom City—the seat of rule for all of Tangeen, the realm across the sea to the west of Palrio. The rulers are the Magistrate Riveren and the High Savant Havest. This is the home realm of Belair Duquan.

Path—the *path* is the road to An'awntia one walks. No one is fully aware of how far they've come along the path with each new lifetime, or how far they have yet to go. It is believed that the savants are closer to An'awntia—further along the path—but it has never been proven.

Petén Adicio—second son of the Magistrate of Palrio, the non-savant brother of Marcus.

Phantoms—a phantom is energy in the savant's inner being and can rise only when the trained savant drops one or both knees to the ground. At that point, the phantom rushes out of the depths of their core, into the earth and rises, blasting from the ground and taking form. In essence, it is a materialization of the savant's shadowed, subliminal, often unknown side of themselves. It is all that is suppressed, and all that is yet to actualize. All that is potential. The savant must come to terms with their own fears and longings if they are to control their phantom, serve the Sanctuaries and protect the realm.

Phantom Throne—the throne in the Hall of Baiseen. In the time of each magistrate's reign, their phantom is carved into the massive wood of this high-backed seat. Over the centuries, it explodes with dozens of phantoms, Jacas's wolf being the most conspicuous.

Piper—an orange-robe, one of the top healers in the Baiseen Sanctuary who raises a double-headed black serpent *healer*. She's the official healer on Marcus's initiation journey to the Isle of Aku.

Potentials—the children whom the Bone Throwers deem worthy to try to raise a phantom. They are sent to the sanctuaries at eight years of age. The brown-robes receive intensive training to see if they are indeed savant. Most will fail and go back to their families, declared non-savant. Those who do raise their phantom will stay on as blue-robes and train up through the ranks, as far as they can go.

Realms of Amassia—see the map and individual realms for details.

Palrio
Tangeen
Isle of Aku
Nonnova
Sierrak
Gollnar
Northern Aturnia
Southern Aturnia
Avon Eyre

Recorder—a wordsmith or scribe, usually savant, who chronicles the initiation journey and other significant events of the realm.

Retoren—an ancient language Ash tries to translate.

Rhiannon—Baiseen's treasurer's most ambitious daughter, yellow-robe to a meercat *caller* phantom and childhood friend/once love interest of Marcus.

Rigg-tackle-stuggs—a Sierrak football game played with two balls, four teams and four goals, one on each point of the compass.

Rowten—non-savant captain of the Baiseen Palace honor guard.

Rune bands—also known as rune chains—manacles or bracelets made from copper, bone, or sometimes gold. Etched with runes from the ancient sea scrolls, when worn they are said to keep a savant's phantom from rising and cause terrible pain if they try.

Salila—a Mar woman with extreme appetites, intractable will, and no obvious morals. Her only fear is Teern, known to all Mar as Father, and King of the Sea.

Samsen—a yellow-robe savant who raises a part *caller*-part *alter* phantom that is confined to various forms of birds. He accompanies Marcus on his initiation journey as guard.

Sanctuaries—the temple retreats devoted to the training of savants and their phantoms.

Savant—One who can raise their phantom, bringing forth a manifestation of their being that is either *caller*, *ouster*, *alter*, *warrior*, or *healer*, or some combination of two. The ranks are:

Brown-robe—those deemed as potentials by the Bone Throwers who, when eight years old, are brought to the sanctuaries to try to raise their phantom

Blue-robe—successful potentials who have begun their training at the sanctuary

Green-robe—more advanced savants but haven't held their phantom to form

Yellow-robe—savants who have successfully completed their initiation journey

Orange-robe—highly trained savants who have reached master level

Red-robe—the highest-ranking savant in a given sanctuary

Black-robe—one of the Bone Throwers whose phantoms never hold solid form

Sea Eagle—Captain Nadonis's carrack that sails Marcus and his party toward Aku.

Second Sun (also Dark Sun or Twin Sun)—Amassia's binary sun that travels an extremely eccentric orbit. It can be viewed by the naked eye once every twenty-five-million years, when it heralds the next Great Dying.

Sierrak—the realm to the far north, main Sanctuary in Asyleen. Sierrak is the home of the High Savant Tann, and famous for their starwatchers, and finely made distance viewers.

Summits—These are meetings attended by council members, usually yellow-robe and higher, to make policies for the realms. A vote on the Summit carries weight, as even the Magistrate must uphold Summit decisions, agreed with or not.

Talus—a mysterious white-robe savant Ash meets on the Isle of Aku.

Tangeen—the realm to the west of Palrio, whose seat of rule is Pandom

City. Home of Belair Duquan. Also home realm to the most beautiful Sanctuary in all of Amassia, Whitewing.

Tann—a red-robe, High Savant of Lepsea, Sierrak, who raises a reptilian *ouster* phantom.

Taruna—the Ma'ata keeper charged with minding the Mar's underwater tombs off the coast of Kutoon in Gollnar.

Teern—called Father by all Mar, and the King of the Sea, Teern has the responsibility of ensuring the survival of his people. Some say he isn't Mar himself, but the last of the old gods, surviving many cycles of the Great Dying and remaining unchanged.

Tessellated columns—the monoliths that rise when *called* to protect Baiseen. Nearly three stories tall, they are carved from obsidian found in the high ranges of Palrio. Ancient legends say they were set by Mar, back when the southwest of Palrio was under the sea.

Tutapa—the island archipelago realm in the South Seas. Their Sanctuary, La'hanta, is very small and thought not to host an original whistle bone.

Tyche—granddaughter of Yuki, a ten-year-old orange-robe savant who raises a *caller* phantom in the form of an impala.

U'karn—head of the war council of Baiseen.

Warriors—phantoms that train for battle, prepared to guard and protect their realm. Seen more in Sierrak and Aturnia but can be found in any realm, though very rare in Palrio.

Whistle Bones—carved from bone, baleen, shell, or tusk. Only the whistle bones, thrown by the black-robe savants, can predict which child will raise their phantom, which will be non-savant, and which is marred and must be sacrificed to the sea.

Yuki—the High Savant of Aku and Tyche's grandmother.

Zakia—High Savant of Kutoon in Gollnar who raises an *alter* phantom.

Zarah—an orange-robe warrior from Northern Aturnia who teaches on the Isle of Aku, Marcus and Belair's instructor.

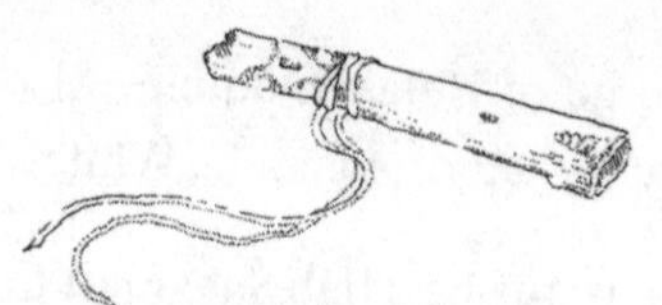

ACKNOWLEDGMENTS

It takes far more than a village to bring a book to life. For everyone who has had a hand in this one, and every single person who reads it, my heart sings out to you.

Special thanks go to Aaron Briggs for the brainstorming, cinematic and gaming vision, eagle-eyed continuity detection and action-packed choreography. Without your collaboration, this book would only be half a world, half a story. And blessings to my invincible agent, Nicole Resciniti, whose inspiring contributions, logic, strength, and faith surpass my wildest dreams. You are the best!

Truckloads of gratitude to my brilliant sister, Shawn Wilder, for her endless reading and feedback of version after version after version and the support from the rest of the Wilder clan, Zac and Grayson. To Stephanie Smith and Natalie Costa Bir who read and offered notes in the very early days before the story took flight overseas, and to all the authors who have read and offered quotes, support, and friendship in tough times! Special shout-out to Greg Briggs and Katherine Petersen who proofed tirelessly right up to the eleventh hour, two people who know the difference between fletches and fetches, boson and bosun, among other things!

Gratitude goes to everyone at Entangled Publishing—Liz Pelletier, Heather Howland, Stacy Abrams, and Nancy Cantor for the fantastic structural, line, and copyediting as well as everything else that happens behind the scenes. And to Tera Cuskaden who championed the story right from the start. Deep appreciation as well goes to Heather Riccio, who always makes me smile no matter how stressful things get, Jessica Lemmon, Curtis Svehlak, Bree Archer, and Jessica Turner. You all are champions!

Finally, a special thanks to those who have stood by me in so many ways over decades of writing: Jeannette, Adriene, Jodi, Jean, Ly, Anna, Victoria, Jacque, Greg, Sara, Candy, Jimmy, Helen, Merrie, Traci, and my deep inner circle who cheer me on every day: Aaron, Ochre, Kayla, Kinayda, Son, EJ, and the wildest members of the team, Sin and Ra. I hope you all love this book as much as I do!

Keep reading to sink your teeth into the smash-hit series from *New York Times* bestselling author Tracy Wolff.

crave

NEW YORK TIMES BESTSELLING AUTHOR

TRACY WOLFF

Just Because You Live in a Tower Doesn't Make You a Prince

I can't see clearly—distance, darkness, and the distorted glass of the windows cover up a lot—but I get the impression of a strong jaw, shaggy dark hair, a red jacket against a background of light.

It's not much, and there's no reason for it to have caught my attention—certainly no reason for it to have *held* my attention—and yet I find myself staring up at the window so long that Macy has all three of my suitcases at the top of the stairs before I even realize it.

"Ready to try again?" she calls down from her spot near the front doors.

"Oh, yeah. Of course." I start up the last thirty or so steps, ignoring the way my head is spinning. Altitude sickness—one more thing I never had to worry about in San Diego.

Fantastic.

I glance up at the window one last time, not surprised at all to find that whoever was looking down at me is long gone. Still, an inexplicable shiver of disappointment works its way through me. It makes no sense, though, so I shrug it off. I have bigger things to worry about right now.

"This place is unbelievable," I tell my cousin as she pushes open one of the doors and we walk inside.

And holy crap—I thought the whole castle thing with its pointed archways and elaborate stonework was imposing from the outside. Now that I've seen the inside… Now that I've seen the inside, I'm pretty sure I should be curtsying right about now. Or at least bowing and scraping. I mean, wow. Just…wow.

I don't know where to look first—at the high ceiling with its elaborate black crystal chandelier or the roaring fireplace that dominates the whole right wall of the foyer.

In the end I go with the fireplace, because *heat.* And because it's freaking gorgeous, the mantel around it an intricate pattern of stone and stained glass that reflects the light of the flames through the whole room.

"Pretty cool, huh?" Macy says with a grin as she comes up behind me.

"Totally cool," I agree. "This place is…"

"Magic. I know." She wiggles her brows at me. "Want to see some more?"

I really do. I'm still far from sold on the Alaskan boarding school thing, but that doesn't mean I don't want to check out the castle. I mean, it's a *castle*, complete with stone walls and elaborate tapestries I can't help but want to stop and look at as we make our way through the entryway into some kind of common room.

The only problem is that the deeper we move into the school, the more students we come across. Some are standing around in scattered clumps, talking and laughing, while others are seated at several of the room's scarred wooden tables, leaning over books or phones or laptop screens. In the back corner of one room, sprawled out on several antique-looking couches in varying hues of red and gold, is a group of six guys playing Xbox on a huge TV, while a few other students crowd around to watch.

Only, as we get closer, I realize they aren't watching the video game. Or their books. Or even their phones. Instead, they're all looking at *me* as Macy leads—and by leads, I mean parades—me through the center of the room.

My stomach clenches, and I duck my head to hide my very obvious discomfort. I get that everyone wants to check out the new girl—especially when she's the headmaster's niece—but understanding doesn't make it any easier to bear the scrutiny from a bunch of strangers. Especially since I'm pretty sure I have the worst case of helmet hair ever recorded.

I'm too busy avoiding eye contact and regulating my breathing to talk as we make our way through the room, but as we exit into a long, winding hallway, I finally tell Macy, "I can't believe you go to school here."

"We *both* go to school here," she reminds me with a quick grin.

"Yeah, but…" I just got here. And I've never felt more out of place in my life.

"But?" she repeats, eyebrows arched.

"It's a lot." I eye the gorgeous stained glass windows that run along the exterior wall and the elaborate carved molding that decorates the arched ceiling.

"It is." She slows down until I catch up. "But it's home."

"Your home," I whisper, doing my best not to think of the house I left behind, where my mother's front porch wind chimes and whirligigs were the most wild-and-crazy thing about it.

"*Our* home," she answers as she pulls out her phone and sends a quick text. "You'll see. Speaking of which, my dad wants me to give you a choice about what kind of room situation you want."

"Room situation?" I repeat, glancing around the castle while images of ghosts and animated suits of armor slide through my head.

"Well, all the single rooms have been assigned for this term. Dad told me we could move some people around to get you one, but I really hoped you might want to room with me instead." She smiles hopefully for a second, but it quickly fades as she continues. "I mean, I totally get that you might need some space to yourself right now after…"

And there's that fade-out again. It gets to me, just like it does every time. Usually, I ignore it, but this time I can't stop myself from asking, "After what?"

Just this once, I want someone else to say it. Maybe then it will feel more real and less like a nightmare.

Except as Macy gasps and turns the color of the snow outside, I realize it's not going to be her. And that it's unfair of me to expect it to be.

"I'm sorry," she whispers, and now it almost looks like she's going to cry, which, no. Just no. We're not going to go there. Not when the only thing currently holding me together is a snarky attitude and my ability to compartmentalize.

No way am I going to risk losing my grip on either. Not here, in front of my cousin and anybody else who might happen to pass by. And not now, when it's obvious from all the stares that I'm totally the newest attraction at the zoo.

So instead of melting into Macy for the hug I so desperately need, instead of letting myself think about how much I miss home and my parents and my *life*, I pull back and give her the best smile I can manage. "Why don't you show me to *our* room?"

The concern in her eyes doesn't diminish, but the sunshine definitely makes another appearance. "*Our* room? Really?"

I sigh deep inside and kiss my dream of a little peaceful solitude goodbye. It's not as hard as it should be, but then I've lost a lot more in the last month than my own space. "Really. Rooming with you sounds perfect."

I've already upset her once, which is so not my style. Neither is getting neone kicked out of their room. Besides being rude and smacking of nepotism, it also seems like a surefire way to piss people off—something that is definitely not on my to-do list right now.

"Awesome!" Macy grins and throws her arms around me for a fast but powerful hug. Then she glances at her phone with a roll of her eyes. "Dad still hasn't answered my text—he's the worst about checking his phone. Why don't you hang out here, and I'll go get him? I know he wanted to see you as soon as we arrived."

"I can come with you—"

"Please just sit, Grace." She points at the ornate French-provincial-style chairs that flank a small chess table in an alcove to the right of the staircase. "I'm sure you're exhausted and I've got this, honest. Relax a minute while I get Dad."

Because she's right—my head is aching and my chest still feels tight—I just nod and plop down in the closest chair. I'm beyond tired and want nothing more than to lean my head back against the chair and close my eyes for a minute. But I'm afraid I'll fall asleep if I do. And no way am I running the risk of being the girl caught drooling all over herself in the hallway on her very first day...or ever, for that matter.

More to keep myself from drifting off than out of actual interest, I pick up one of the chess pieces in front of me. It's made of intricately carved stone, and my eyes widen as I realize what I'm looking at. A perfect rendition of a vampire, right down to the black cape, frightening snarl, and bared fangs. It matches the Gothic castle vibe so well that I can't help being amused. Plus, it's gorgeously crafted.

Intrigued now, I reach for a piece from the other side. And nearly laugh out loud when I realize it's a dragon—fierce, regal, with giant wings. It's absolutely beautiful.

The whole set is.

I put the piece down only to pick up another dragon. This one is less fierce, but with its sleepy eyes and folded wings, it's even more intricate. I look it over carefully, fascinated with the level of detail in the piece—everything from the perfect points on the wings to the careful curl of each talon reflects just how much care the artist put into the piece. I've never been a chess girl, but this set just might change my mind about the game.

When I put down this dragon piece, I go to the other side of the board and pick up the vampire queen. She's beautiful, with long, flowing hair and an elaborately decorated cape.

"I'd be careful with that one if I were you. She's got a nasty bite." The words are low and rumbly and so close that I nearly fall out of my chair. Instead, I jump up, plopping the chess piece down with a clatter, then whirl around—heart pounding—only to find myself face-to-face with the most intimidating guy I've ever seen. And not just because he's hot…although he's definitely that.

Still, there's something more to him, something different and powerful and overwhelming, though I don't have a clue what it is. I mean, sure. He has the kind of face nineteenth-century poets loved to write about—too intense to be beautiful and too striking to be anything else.

Skyscraper cheekbones.

Full red lips.

A jaw so sharp it could cut stone.

Smooth, alabaster skin.

And his eyes…a bottomless obsidian that see everything and show nothing, surrounded by the longest, most obscene lashes I've ever seen.

And even worse, those all-knowing eyes are laser-focused on me right now, and I'm suddenly terrified that he can see all the things I've worked so hard and so long to hide. I try to duck my head, try to yank my gaze from his, but I can't. I'm trapped by his stare, hypnotized by the sheer magnetism rolling off him in waves.

I swallow hard to catch my breath.

It doesn't work.

And now he's grinning, one corner of his mouth turning up in a crooked little smile that I feel in every single cell. Which only makes it worse, because that smirk says he knows exactly what kind of effect he's having on me. And, worse, that he's enjoying it.

Annoyance flashes through me at the realization, melting the numbness that's surrounded me since my parents' deaths. Waking me from the stupor that's the only thing that's kept me from screaming all day, every day, at the unfairness of it all. At the pain and horror and helplessness that have taken over my whole life.

It's not a good feeling. And the fact that it's this guy—with the smirk and the face and the cold eyes that refuse to relinquish their hold on me even as they demand that I don't look too closely—just pisses me off more.

It's that anger that finally gives me the strength to break free of his gaze. I rip my eyes away, then search desperately for something else—anything else—to focus on.

Unfortunately, he's standing right in front of me, so close that he's blocking my view of anything else.

Determined to avoid his eyes, I look anywhere but. And land instead on his long, lean body. Then really wish I hadn't, because the black jeans and T-shirt he's wearing only emphasize his flat stomach and hard, well-defined biceps. Not to mention the double-wide shoulders that are absolutely responsible for blocking my view in the first place.

Add in the thick, dark hair that's worn a little too long, so that it falls forward into his face and skims low across his insane cheekbones, and there's nothing to do but give in. Nothing to do but admit that—obnoxious smirk or not—this boy is sexy as hell.

A little wicked, a lot wild, and *all* dangerous.

What little oxygen I've been able to pull into my lungs in this high altitude completely disappears with the realization. Which only makes me madder. Because, seriously. When exactly did I become the heroine in some YA romance? The new girl swooning over the hottest, most unattainable boy in school?

Gross. And so not happening.

Determined to nip whatever this is in the bud, I force myself to look at his face again. This time, as our gazes meet and clash, I realize that it doesn't matter if I'm acting like some giant romantic cliché.

Because he isn't.

One glance and I know that this dark boy with the closed-off eyes and the fuck-you attitude isn't the hero of anyone's story. Least of all mine.

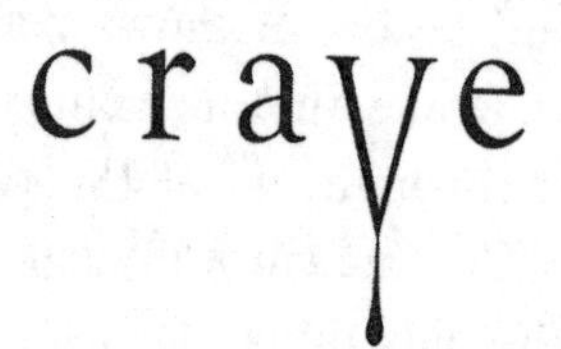

NEW YORK TIMES BESTSELLING AUTHOR

TRACY WOLFF

AVAILABLE NOW!

Let's be friends!

@EntangledTeen

@EntangledTeen

@EntangledTeen

bit.ly/TeenNewsletter

entangled teen
an imprint of Entangled Publishing LLC